BLOOD, SWEAT, & TEARS

D1319849

BLOOD, SWEAT, & TEARS

BUBBA THE MONSTER HUNTER SEASON FIVE

JOHN G. HARTNESS

Charlotte, NC

FALSTAFF
BOOKS

WWW.FALSTAFFBOOKS.COM

I

BORN TO BE WILD

1

I looked down at the little bandy-legged fellow with the curly blond mullet, brown calf-high moccasins, and cut-off jean shorts. "Now, Jimmy Lee, you know how this is gonna end if you swing at me," I said, trying my best not to have to whoop anybody's ass before ten o'clock on a Thursday night.

Jimmy Lee apparently missed the memo that I didn't feel like fighting until at least the house band's second set at the Don't Drop Inn because he curled up his lip in a sneer and said, "What's a matter, fatass, you scared of a little tussle?"

"Boy, you throw that punch, and it ain't gone be a little tussle. It's gone be me opening up a whole can of whoop-ass on you, and don't neither one of us want that."

"What if I do?" His porn 'stache was quivering in righteous fury, even though I had no damn idea what Jimmy Lee was so pissed off about.

"Well, if you want some, come get some, son." I unfolded my arms and pushed my back off the wall where I'd been leaning next to the door. When I stood up to my full six-and-a-half-foot height, Jimmy Lee actually had to back up a step to look at my face. That didn't cow him even a little bit because he threw a punch at my belly that actually had a little bit of mustard on it.

Of course, the last person I got in a fight with was the leader of the damn Wild Hunt, so I wasn't sweating a gut punch from a mortal, especially not a half-pint, half-drunk mortal redneck with more piss and vinegar than sense. Jimmy Lee took his shot, and I looked down at him with a grin twitching the corner of my mouth. "That tickled," I said.

Then I swatted him upside the head. I didn't slap him, exactly, just laid a big open hand against the side of his jaw and ear and rang his bell. I liked Jimmy Lee, so I didn't want to hurt him. I just needed him to calm down a little bit. If we got the fights started too early, the Drop was going to be hip deep in assholes by last call and I was going to have to get serious about my bouncer duties. I didn't like having to get serious.

Jimmy Lee went down to one knee, shaking his head from the ringing swat I laid on him, but he was right back up a second later and threw a kick at my knee. I lifted my leg to catch the kick on the side of my calf, instead of the surgically repaired knee, and scowled at the man. "That wasn't nice, Jimmy Lee. You know I hurt that knee playing football. Now are we gonna play, or is this gonna turn into a real fight?"

"Oh, it's real, Bubba. I'm tired of you walking around this bar like you're the King Shit of Turd Mountain, so I reckon it's time for some-body to take your crown." Then he charged me with his head down and slammed his shoulder into my gut.

I love rednecks. I mean, I am one, so it makes sense, but some-times, like now, I *really* love rednecks. Only a full-on Hank Jr. singing, Bud drinking, pickup driving, shotgun shooting, Skynyrd-loving redneck is going to say crap like, "I'm gonna take your crown and be the new King Shit of Turd Mountain," then try to tackle a man twice his damn size. I couldn't help myself, I laughed. Of course, that made Jimmy Lee madder than a hornet, and he backed up and slammed into me again. I might have moved about an inch, but then I was backed up against the wall again, and there wasn't anywhere for me to go, even if Jimmy Lee was big enough to move me.

I shook my head, reached down, and grabbed a fistful of blond mullet curls. I twined my fingers tight into Jimmy Lee's pride and joy, and I jerked him straight up by his hair. His eyes popped open wide from the skin on his face being pulled backward, and I leaned down 'til I was right in his face. "Now I told you this wasn't going to end well. So don't blame me if you wake up in the parking lot again."

"I ain't waking up nowhere, you asshole," Jimmy Lee snarled at me, and I caught a glint of light out of the corner of my eye.

Shit. This just got real. I planted my right hand in Jimmy Lee's chest and shoved, letting go of his mullet as I did. I slid sideways to my right and pivoted off the wall, giving myself room to maneuver and trying to get a better look at whatever weapon my idiot opponent just brought into play. It was the old Buck hunting knife he carried on his belt everywhere, and its scarred blade gleamed bright in the neon bar signs.

"Jimmy Lee, calm down," I said. "I don't want anybody to get hurt."

"Oh, it ain't so damn funny now, is it, fat man?" Jimmy Lee's face split with a cruel grin, and I remembered what a dick he was back in high school. "You all big and funny 'til shit gets real, ain't you?"

"Nah," I said. "I'm still pretty funny when shit gets real." I reached around to the small of my back and drew my Judge revolver. I leveled the pistol at Jimmy Lee's crotch and pulled the hammer back. "This is a four-ten shotgun shell full of birdshot, son. It probably won't blow your dick off, but I reckon you don't want to have some nurse in the emergency room pulling pellets out of your pecker all night. So why don't you drop the knife, and I don't have to shoot you in the junk?"

Jimmy Lee's tanned face went ghost-pale, and he put both hands in the air like we were on an episode of *Cops* or something. "Shit man, I was just messing around. I didn't mean no harm."

"Drop. The. Knife. Right damn now, or we're going to see how much damage birdshot does to your little bird balls."

The knife hit the wood floor with a clatter, and I nodded. "Good." I de-cocked the pistol and slipped it back into the holster behind my back. "Now go home. You're out of here for a week. Seven days, Jimmy Lee. If I see you back in here before next Thursday, I'm not gonna give you a warning, I'm just gonna break your damn nose and throw you out the door. We clear?"

He nodded and scurried for the door. I leaned over, picked up the knife, and threw it in a box by the door marked "Lost & Found." It currently held three knives, one sawed-off shotgun, a derringer, a quarter bag of weed, and an old Betsy Wetsy doll. That last one confused me, too, especially when I found it in the men's bathroom, but I put it in the box with all the other confiscated and abandoned shit the Drop collected in the course of a week. Every Saturday night at last call, we auctioned off anything left in the box, and whatever didn't sell, we gave to the Goodwill on Sunday.

I looked around the bar, but most of the clientele seemed to have completely ignored my disagreement with Jimmy Lee. That's how I liked to keep it—subtle and low key. God knows there hadn't been a whole lot of that in my life lately. The only people paying me any attention were Skeeter's uncle Rufus, who owned the bar and was pouring drinks, and my girlfriend Amy, the Drop's newest, prettiest, and most dangerous waitress.

Amy filled out Rufus's "uniform," which consisted of whatever flavor short shorts the girls wanted to wear paired with a Don't Drop Inn t-shirt tied up to expose her midriff, better than anyone in the room and somehow managed to put up with a lot less uninvited petting and grabbing. Might have had something to do with the Sig Sauer forty-caliber pistol she carried on her right hip. The gun was a compromise she made with Rufus to convince patrons to be less handsy after she sent three good ol' boys to the hospital with dislocated fingers in one night. The clip in the gun was empty, but the two riding on her left hip weren't. So far, she hadn't needed to draw down on any drunken idiots, and the number of problems the other girls were having had dropped to almost zero, too.

Normally, or at least normally until four months ago, the only way we'd be working in a dive bar in Georgia was if we needed to smoke out some kind of supernatural threat posing as a dishwasher. The dishwasher at the Drop wasn't the least bit supernatural. He was Rufus Jr., Skeeter's cousin. He was a moron, but that's not really out of the ordinary for backwoods Georgia.

Unfortunately, when we got back into this dimension from Fairyland, me, Amy, Skeeter, and Uncle Father Joe had all been fired for going MIA for a year and a half. The U.S. Government and the Holy Roman Catholic Church both take a dim view of their field agents, Templar Knights, and contract Monster Hunters vanishing for an extended period of time. They take an even dimmer view, if that's possible, of finding out that aforementioned Monster Hunter is half-faerie and the grandson of two of the monarchs of the Summer and Winter Courts. So they both blacklisted me, and in a show of solidarity, Amy and Joe quit. Which meant that three of the four of us needed jobs.

Skeeter was fine, of course. The little computer genius just threw out some feelers online and got more freelance gigs in half a day than he could finish in half a year, plus he had a bunch of cash tucked away from when we were getting paid by both the Church and DEMON. I didn't have any kind of nest egg like that. I pretty much spent all my money on beer and ammunition.

So me and Amy went to work for Uncle Rufus, and Joe went to Florida to see if there was any spark left with an old flame of his down there. Rufus didn't pay me for shit, but Amy made great tips, so we were okay moneywise. Plus, I owned my house and the land it sat on, so that helped, too.

It was quite the adjustment, not carrying around Bertha, my Desert Eagle pistol, every day, and not looking for bogeymen around every corner. Our little corner of the northwest Georgia hills wasn't exactly known for supernatural activity, at least not since I killed my psychotic werewolf brother. That's why it came as quite the surprise when I noticed the vampire sitting in the corner booth.

He didn't look like a TV vampire. He wasn't all that pretty and didn't look like he used much hair product at all. If he had a long black coat, it must have been folded up on the seat next to him, and he wasn't drinking wine. He did have a bottle of Sweetwater 420 sitting on the table in front of him, which was about as high-tone as beer got in the Drop, so he was at least working toward some level of refinement. Or maybe he just didn't like the taste of the horse piss the rest of our clientele drank by the gallon. I couldn't really blame him on that one.

Either way, he was just sitting in the booth, watching everything that went on over the lip of his pint glass. I reached behind me to the Judge and, by years of practice and the benefit of having truly gigantic hands, was able to rotate the barrel twice without bringing the gun around. Then I walked over to where the vampire sat, slid into the booth opposite him, and brought the gun around in front of me under the table.

"I've got a shotgun shell loaded with holy water and silver shot pointed at you under the table. I'm going to ask you some questions, and if I don't like the answers, you're going off like a Roman Candle, and cleanup be damned. Do you understand me?"

He nodded and leaned forward. "I can rip your throat out before you can even think about squeezing that trigger, Robert Brabham, but I'm not here to kill you or your girlfriend. I'm here because I need your help."

Shit, he knows my name. Double shit, he knows who Amy is. "What do you want?" I asked.

"Somebody's hunting me, and I need you to help keep me alive."

I leaned back in the booth and laid the gun on the table. I looked at the vampire, and from what I could tell, he was as sincere as could be. He looked nervous, and it didn't have a damn thing to do with me or the pistol in front of him. The way his eyes flicked to the door every time the bell over it rang, the way he drew in on himself whenever somebody walked past—this dude was on the run.

"Well, shit," I said, slipping the Judge back into the holster at my back. "This oughta be interesting, if nothing else."

"So who do you think is hunting you, what do they want to do with you if they catch you, and what do you want us to do about it?" Amy asked the jumpy vampire.

"And can you pay us to keep you alive? Undead. Whatever. You know what I mean," I added.

The vamp straightened up a little and got an expression on his face that was almost offended. "I thought you helped people. Word on the street is that's kind of your thing. I didn't know I'd get a bill for my rescue."

"You ride in an ambulance, you get a bill. You pay taxes for fire-fighters. Everybody's gotta get paid, buddy. It's an ugly old world, but them's the breaks." I hated bringing up money to somebody who needed our help, but I hated bouncing at shithole bars and watching old rednecks slap my fiancée on the ass more.

The Drop was closed, and me, Amy, and the vampire were the only people left. Rufus just told us to push the red button to turn the alarm on and go out the back door when we left. It'd lock behind us. Amy and the vamp sat across from each other in the booth, and I had a chair pulled up to the end of the table. Booths ain't exactly built for men my size. We've got a little more padding through the middle than fits between the seat and the edge of the table comfortably.

"What Bubba's trying to say is that since our recent trip to Faerie, we find ourselves running a little shorter on cash than in previous years, so we are forced to fund our operation through contributions from those seeking our aid," Amy said. She had a much nicer way of saying "pay me, asshole" than I did.

"Oh. I thought you were a federal agent?"

"And she just likes waiting tables at dive bars and getting her ass pinched so she slings Bud here for fun?" I asked.

"Good point. Well, I do have money, so I can certainly pay something for your assistance."

"Sounds good," I said. "We can figure out how much once we're done."

"No, I think I'd prefer to settle on an amount up front. That way there will be no disagreements once the job is completed. How about five hundred per day, plus expenses?"

I nodded. "That sounds fine. We'll want the first two days paid up front, plus two hundred for expenses. That should be enough to get us going."

"Not a problem." He reached into his pocket and peeled twelve hundred-dollar bills off a roll and passed them to me. That's when I realized he meant five hundred *each* per day. All of a sudden, I was real interested in keeping this bloodsucker alive for a very long time. As long as he was paying me more than double what the Church did, I was more than willing to watch his back.

I managed not to choke as I pocketed the cash and kept my foot planted very firmly on Amy's toes. This was not the time for her to get a bad case of morality, not with my truck payment late and us low on ammunition. I forgot how expensive full-sized pickups were when DEMON and the Catholic Church were taking turns replacing the ones I destroyed. And target practice was a lot less fun when you paid attention to the fact that bullets for Bertha were almost a buck apiece.

"Okay, let's get some details and start building a suspect list," I said, patting my pockets for something to write on, giving up, and nodding when Amy pulled out her phone to take notes. My first chance to put all those holiday weekends spent bingeing *SVU* and *The Closer* to use and I don't have a notebook or a pen. I felt like a total rookie. Somewhere Ice-T was looking on and shaking his head in disappointment.

"Who holds a serious enough grudge to want you dead, Mr....um... what was your name again?" Amy asked.

He smiled, and a little hint of fang showed in the corner of his mouth. "I wondered if you were ever going to ask. My name is Caufield Evers Oglethorpe IV, Terror of the Highlands, Horror of the Moors, Scourge of the Southlands. I am the monster under the bed and the stuff of children's nightmares. I am the thing that keeps grown men up at night trembling in fear. I am the Vampire of the Mountain!"

"I bet that's a lot more impressive with the right lighting," I said.

"And a cape," Amy added. "I bet a cape would add a lot."

"Maybe some smoke."

"A strobe? Or would a strobe be too much?" Amy asked.

"Yeah, that's a little over the top. It's not 1984 anymore."

"Bubba, I was a toddler in 1984."

"So you're saying you remember it fondly?"

"I'm saying I don't remember it at all." Our little comic routine ran out of steam, and Amy turned back to the chagrined vampire. I bet he would have even blushed if he had enough blood in his system. "So, Mr. Oglethorpe. Or would you prefer Mr. Of the Mountain?"

"Just Caufield is fine. Sorry for the theatrics. It becomes habit after a couple of centuries, you know."

"About that list of people who want you dead?" I prodded.

"I guess we should stick to the ones on this continent, shouldn't we?" Caufield asked.

"Yeah, and maybe the ones that have enough power to actually kill you. How have they been trying to accomplish this, anyway? I've fought a few vampires in my time, and the list of ways to kill you guys is pretty short," I said.

"There have been attacks on my home and on my person. There was an attempt on my life just as I was walking into this bar tonight. A wild-eyed scrawny old man accosted me with a Bible just as I reached the front steps. He pressed the book into my chest as though it would set me ablaze. Those things don't really work, but he was obviously deluded enough to think that his silly holy book would have an effect."

"Well…not really," I said.

"What do you mean?"

"That was Holy Rollin' Herb. He stands out in front of the Drop most nights exhorting about the evils of sin and iniquity, telling everybody who walks in how much danger their immortal soul is in just by being on the premises. He rails on and on about Whores of Babylon, sodomites, moneychangers, and all the other evils that go on inside the Drop," I explained. "Herb was home-schooled. His exposure to the world was little…limited in his formative years. Not to mention his mama was batshit crazy."

Caufield looked confused. "I was here for several hours and saw no prostitutes, very few gay men or women, and…what was the other thing? Moneychangers? In a country bar?"

"Nobody ever said Herb was smart, just enthusiastic," Amy said. "And yeah, none of the things Herb preaches about actually ever happen in here—"

"Except maybe sodomy, but whatever two grown-ass people want to do at home is their business. Long as I don't have to clean it up out of the bathrooms, I don't care," I said.

Amy gave me another long-suffering sigh. I was pretty happy to be getting my average number of those down to around five or six per day, but I wasn't sure if this counted as a new day or not. It was after midnight, so Shakespeare would say we were up early, but we hadn't been to bed, so I wasn't sure. She gave me a *shut up* look and tried to bring the conversation back to the vampire at hand. "So it's unlikely that Herb was trying to actually destroy you with the Bible. He was just trying to save your soul."

The vampire looked really uncomfortable all of a sudden and looked at his intertwined fingers on the tabletop. "Oh."

"Dammit. You didn't eat Herb, did you?" I asked.

"Not much. I just took a little nibble to top off the tank, so to speak. And I may have laid a compulsion on him to violate the nearest cow that he could find. Spiteful, I admit, but I didn't kill him."

"You sent him to go screw a cow?" Amy asked, holding back a grin.

"Hell, that's not a big deal," I said. "Catching Herb banging cattle is practically a weekly event at the Dalton PD. You didn't make him do anything he wouldn't do on his own. If I know Herb, and I hate to admit that I do, he probably already had his eye on a new heifer. Now back to the matter at hand. Who hates you enough to want you dead?"

"Or who would gain enough money or power by your death to want to make that happen?" Amy added.

"I'll tackle the second part first because it's the easiest. No one. I don't dabble in vampire politics, and everyone who does knows that. Killing me doesn't gain anyone territory, vassals, or even a significant amount of money. I'm well-off, but not filthy rich, and everything I have except for some cash that I keep lying around is tied up in trusts and investments, things that are easily transferable on paper if I need to appear to die and return a few days later as my own long-lost cousin."

"Is there anyone set up to inherit in the case of your actual demise?" Amy asked.

"A couple million to my current Renfield, and the rest to various charities, all in the form of stocks and mutual funds. And no, Jorgé isn't likely to kill me for the money. He stands to make far more by keeping me happy and staying by my side than if he kills me."

"So we move on to people who don't like you. I'm guessing that list is a lot longer," I said.

"You live long enough, you piss some people off," Caufield replied.

"In some cases, you don't even have to live that long," Amy said with a pointed look at me. I put on a fake affronted look, and she laughed.

"How wide a net should we cast?" Oglethorpe asked.

"Let's stick to people you've pissed off in the last century and have the resources to come after you," Amy said. "If we need to broaden the search, we can do that after we check out the most likely suspects."

The vampire leaned forward and put his elbows on the table,

steeling his fingers. I took a good look at him while he thought. He was a decent-looking guy. Not Skaarsgard-level vampire hot, but decent. A little under six feet, and lean, with long brown hair tied back in a ponytail. I didn't know enough about vampire hair to know if that's how long it was when he died, or if vampire hair kept growing. It wasn't on the list of things I'd ever wondered about. Usually I was just wondering where the best place to shove the stake was.

"Well, there's a father in Greenville who was pissed off when I turned his daughter," he said after a few minutes. "That was the most recent one I turned, so he's probably still alive."

"Isn't the *Twilight* thing cliché?" Amy asked.

"Ew." Caufield wrinkled his nose. "It was nothing like that. The girl is in her twenties and was doing promising research into Alzheimer's when she ironically was diagnosed with an aggressive brain tumor. I turned her so that she could continue her research."

I was a little stunned, to be honest. "That's...altruistic."

"My last Renfield died of dementia. It was horrible to watch. He was a good man, and I did not enjoy watching him suffer. I would prefer no one have to go through that."

I needed to get this guy safe and out of my hair before he went and changed all my preconceived notions about vampires.

"Okay, who else?" I asked after taking a few seconds to process the magnanimous vampire.

"Well, there's a necromancer in Atlanta with an office over The Vortex. He and I have had a few less than pleasant interactions."

"That seems like a strong lead," Amy said. "But I'm guessing he's not the only option, or you would have just killed him yourself."

"Oh, there are plenty more." He held up a hand as if to tick off suspects on his fingers, but just as he opened his mouth to speak, the front door of the bar exploded inward in a shower of smoke and splinters.

3

I was out of the booth in a flash with my pistol in my hand. I flipped the nearest table on its side for cover and leaned my arm on it, barrel pointed toward the door. I felt more than saw Amy sprint behind me and vault over the bar. I expected her to come back up with Rufus's twelve-gauge pointed at the door.

"Get down!" I yelled to Caufield.

"Sod off," he growled. "This bastard has finally come after me face to face, and I'm not going to miss the opportunity to end this once and for all." I never saw him move, but the vampire was kneeling behind the table next to me.

"Drop your weapon!" Amy roared from the bar. I stood up, planning to take advantage of whoever was after us turning to her and most likely blowing them to Kingdom Come.

Of course, all that came screeching to a halt when I realized that it was Skeeter standing in the doorway holding his Mossberg pistol-grip shotgun and looking way more butch than normal. I put out a hand to the vampire and said, "Don't kill him. He's one of the good guys."

I put my pistol away and righted the table. "Skeeter, what the holy hell are you doing? How did you even do that to the door?"

My best friend and tech guru looked thoroughly confused as he swept the barrel of the shotgun across the empty bar. "Where's the vampire?"

Caufield stood up next to me and raised his hand. "So you are looking for me? Good, now I can kill you."

I reached out and grabbed his belt before he ran across the room at Skeeter. "Hold on there, Speed Racer. Let's try a little more asking questions and a little less shooting first. God, I can't believe I actually said that. Who even am I? Whatever. Skeeter, I'm gonna repeat this. What the holy hell are doing busting in here like that? You know Rufus is going to beat your ass when he sees what you did to his door."

Skeeter looked around at the splinters spread across the ten feet nearest the entry to the bar. "Um...I'm rescuing you from a vampire attack?"

I shook my head and pointed to the undead menace standing calmly beside me, arms folded over his chest as he watched me and Skeeter try to figure out if we were going to wind our asses or scratch our watches. "Skeeter, meet Caufield Evers Oglethorpe IV. He's our new client. Our exceptionally good-paying client, I should add. He's not attacking us, he doesn't have us under some kind of mental thrall, and he has no plans to do us harm. At least not until we figure out who's trying to kill him and deal with that threat. How did you know we were here talking with a vampire in the first place?" Skeeter had a bad habit of bugging me and/or tapping into security feeds of places he wasn't supposed be tapping into when he was bored, and I wanted to know if he'd hacked the microphone on my phone. Again.

"Oh, yeah. Rufus called on his way home and told me he left y'all here talking to some vampire in one of the corner booths."

"Rufus knew Caufield was a vampire? They weren't within ten yards of each other all night," Amy said.

"Uncle Rufe has seen some shit," Skeeter said. "So if he ain't here to eat you, why is he here?"

"Someone is trying to kill me. I have retained your friends, and apparently by extension, you, to ensure that doesn't happen."

"Who wants to kill you?" Skeeter asked.

"Hold up." Amy held up a hand. "We need to back up to the part where you blew the door off its hinges. How exactly did you do that?"

Skeeter walked down the steps from the doorway and sat down at the table I'd flipped over. "Detcord," he said, still giving Oglethorpe the hairy eyeball. I don't know if he was trying to be intimidating or not, but it came off more funny than scary. Of course, it's been a long time since anyone my size was scared of somebody Skeeter's size just from them talking. Except Jet Li. He's a badass.

Amy grabbed a chair and turned it to face my little buddy, who was really determined not to look her in the eye. "What the hell are you doing with detcord and where did you learn how to use it? That stuff is extremely dangerous, Skeeter!"

"Not really. It's pretty stable until you put a charge to it," Skeeter said.

"And at what point did anyone decide that you were somebody who should have access to high explosives? Detcord is not something that you just grab off the shelf at Lowe's," Amy said.

"I might have ordered a bunch of different stuff when we were still in tight with DEMON," Skeeter said. "Seemed like the best way to get in here in a hurry, since the door was locked."

"You couldn't just ask Rufus for a key?" I asked. "Or knock?"

"If you were in trouble, you wouldn't answer the door. And if it was dangerous, I'd rather come in with a boom than just walk in all casual."

"Plus, this way you got to blow stuff up," I said.

"You ain't the only one that was raised in Georgia," he said. "You give a redneck a chance to blow something up, something's getting blown up."

"Well, aside from how pissed off Rufus is going to be, there's another big reason you should have tried the key, Skeeter," Amy said, getting to her feet and hauling ass back over to the bar.

"What's that?"

Amy pointed the shotgun at the front doors. "Because if you'd used the key, the zombies wouldn't be able to just walk right in."

I looked past Skeeter, and sure enough, there were four zombies shambling through the now wide-open portal where there used to be a pair of sturdy double doors. "Skeeter, did you see anything on the news about a weird disease outbreak or a zombie apocalypse today?"

"No, but there sure seems to be one in the Drop."

"Yeah, but if there's nothing online about it, then it's probably targeted at Oglethorpe, which means they're magic zombies and not infectious zombies."

"What's the difference?" Caufield asked. "Zombies are zombies."

"Big words from a guy who can't catch diseases. If they're magic zombies, I can just wade right in kicking ass. If I have to worry about getting bit, this is gonna take a little more finesse." I wasn't just standing around debating the rules of the zombie apocalypse in the middle of a zombie apocalypse. No, while I yammered with the vampire and Skeeter about what kind of zombies we were facing, I also ran over to the back area of the bar, where Rufus had two pool tables set up. I grabbed the half dozen warped pool cues from the rack on the wall and carried them back over to where everybody was clustered behind a wall of hastily overturned tables.

I snapped some of the pool cues in half and kept one for each hand, then passed the rest around. Caufield waved me off, which made sense because he was the one most likely to rip a zombie's head from its shoulders and squish it like a grape. Skeeter kept his cue long and swung it like a baseball bat, while Amy broke a little off the end of hers and shoved one end through her belt.

"Nothing online about zombies, apocalypse, or mysterious disease outbreaks," Skeeter said. "Far as I can tell, those are the only zombies in the United States right now." He pointed toward the door, where two more zombies had shuffled in. At least these were slow zombies. I'd never dealt with fast zombies, but they scared the crap out of me in the movies.

"Okay, me and Amy will deal with these assholes. Skeeter, you stay here and keep Oglethorpe covered. Do not point that shotgun anywhere near me or my fiancée, or I will take it away from you and beat your ass with it. Do I make myself clear?"

"I'm getting better," Skeeter protested, but he pointed the barrel of the gun away from me. He was right, his shooting had improved, but only to the point where he could hit the broad side of a barn on most Tuesdays now. My brother from another mother was never going to get into sniper school, and we all knew it.

I nodded to Amy, and we charged around the barricade from opposite sides, converging on the mini-horde in a blur of whirling sticks and rotted gray matter. Let's be clear: there is nothing about fighting zombies that is not butt-nasty. They started off dead before they came after you, and these weren't even *The Walking Dead* zombies that had been laying around. These people had been dead and buried, embalmed and entombed, then dug up or released from their coffins some other way to wreak havoc on the Don't Drop Inn.

So we faced half a dozen dead hillbillies in their Sunday finest, and you could tell right away who had closed caskets and who didn't, and whose casket was open halfway. Like the fat dude with a jacket, tie, and dress shirt on, but his zombie willie flapping in the breeze, because who dresses the bottom half of a corpse if nobody's gonna see it? I cracked him over the head with the butt of a pool cue and dropped him like a side of beef. That's kinda what it sounded like when he fell, too—like if you drop a raw steak on linoleum.

Amy tussled briefly with a woman in a long, flowered dress that had rotted half away before she shoved the narrow end of the cue through the zombie's eye. That's the only good thing about zombies— the lore is pretty much right. Every zombie I've ever fought, and that is a pretty damn high number, goes for the long sleep when you smash or pierce the brain.

I stepped in between two zombies, crushing one with an overhand blow of my stick and shooting the other in the ear with the Judge. The little pistol was loud as hell inside the Drop, and every zombie in the place froze for a second, then turned on me. And there were a lot more zombies than there should have been, since we killed four in the first minute. I looked up at the door, and there was a steady stream of undead shambling into the bar and down the front steps.

"Goddammit, Skeeter, there's more of them!" I hollered, but the only answer I got was the boom of a twelve-gauge. I hazarded a glance over my shoulder and saw the back door laying on the floor with another river of zombies pouring in. "Shit," I muttered. "Amy, help Skeeter!"

"On it," she yelled, dropping another zombie with a pool cue to the eye and letting go of her weapon as she turned to run back to the barricade. She took over shooting zombies from Skeeter, who built up the pile of tables and chairs until it looked like a miniature *Les Misérables* set in the corner of the bar. I half expected to see Caufield grab a red flag and start a rousing chorus of "Do You Hear the People Sing?"

Satisfied that my best friend, fiancée, and meal ticket were safe(ish) for the moment, I spun around and started wailing on zombie skulls like John Bonham on a set of floor toms. The zombies were slow, weak, and prone to fall apart, but there were a bunch of them. It felt like the cemetery of every Baptist church in three counties had emptied out and they were all expressing their dislike of demon liquor on my ass at the same time.

I garnered a few scratches, and even fell down a time or two, but for the most part it was just crush skull, shove to ground, repeat. I fought until my arms got tired, then I fought some more. I fought until there was a pile of zombies stacked around me like sandbags against a flood, but they kept coming.

"I can't do this much longer," I heard Amy yell from behind me. It had been a while since the last time I heard the shotgun, and when I looked back at her, I saw her swinging the shotgun like a baseball bat with a zombie going down every time she stepped up to the plate. Skeeter and Caufield had table legs in their hands and were bashing skulls as fast as they could, which after half an hour of constant zombie-killing, wasn't very fast.

"Yeah, I don't have a whole lot left in me, either," I hollered back.

"I've got an idea!" Skeeter yelled.

"Better or worse than blowing the front door off this place?" I asked.

"Depends on who you ask," he said, then vaulted the barricade. He sprinted across the bar, ducking and weaving like we were back in high school and the whole varsity baseball team was chasing him to whoop his ass. Again. He leapt over the bar and came up a few seconds later with two handles of Bacardi 151 in his hands and no shirt on. "Come on, we're blowing this pop stand!"

Then he ran out the front door. I looked at Amy, who shrugged and grabbed Caufield's arm. They scooted around the wall of furniture and out the front door, dodging and smashing zombies along the way. I dropped a few more undead, who had thankfully stopped pouring in the front door, and ran for the hills myself. I didn't know what Skeeter had planned for the three dozen zombies still inside the bar, but at least the parking lot was pretty clear.

"Gimme your shirt, Bubba," Skeeter said, holding out his hand.

"What for?"

"We ain't got time to explain, just strip!"

I did as I was told and winced as he ripped my vintage 5XL Ric Flair t-shirt into long strips and poured high-octane rum all over it. Then he shoved a scrap of shirt into each jug of liquor and passed them to me.

"When I light this, you better fling it," he said. Then he pulled out the old Zippo Rufus kept behind the bar and set my t-shirt on fire. I got the idea and flung the Rumotov cocktails back at the entrance to the Drop, where the first zombie was just shambling out. The bottles smashed on the wood, and fire shot across the floor, catching the door frame and porch on fire.

"What happened to your shirt, Skeeter?" Amy asked.

"I needed another fuse," he said. "Remember that stash of shine Uncle Rufe kept under the bar?"

Before Amy could answer, a mighty *BOOM* came from inside the bar, and a pillar of fire thirty feet high leapt into the night sky. Skeeter's makeshift incendiary bomb took the roof off the place and turned it into an amazing conflagration of zombie parts, wood, and cheap liquor. Even the hardiest of zombies were instantly burned to nothingness in the booze firestorm Skeeter created.

I looked at the burning pyre of undead and alcohol and turned to Skeeter. "Your uncle is gonna be *pissed.*"

4

Three hours later, we left the Drop parking lot after answering a lot of uncomfortable questions from the fire department, having an even more uncomfortable conversation with Uncle Rufus, which included a lot of words like "idiot" and "fired," and walked into my house smelling like smoke, zombie brains, and cheap liquor. So, in other words, smelling completely normal.

"Do I still have a change of clothes in the dresser in the back room?" Skeeter asked.

"I haven't thrown anything out, so probably," Amy replied.

"Then I'm gonna take a shower."

"Me too. I smell amazing, and not in a good way," Amy said.

"Need me to wash your back?" I asked.

"No, I need you to bring in a couple of plastic chairs off the porch and set them up in the den. Then I need you to close the blackout shades and keep Caufield company while I get cleaned up."

"Why don't we just hang out on the porch until y'all get done?" I asked.

"You could do that, but I thought the limit was still one fire per night," she replied, pointing toward the east-facing porch and the lightening horizon.

"Good point," I said as Amy headed into the master bedroom and toward the attached bathroom for her shower. Vampires and sunrise don't make for great bedfellows. Unless you like ashes in your bed. "Come on, buddy. Let's get some furniture in here before you're trapped inside all day."

"What's wrong with the furniture you have?" he asked as he followed me out and picked up a plastic patio chair.

"There's nothing wrong with the furniture," I replied. "But you and me are covered in soot and zombie drippings, and Amy doesn't want to have to get the living room furniture reupholstered. Again."

"Oh." He looked down at the smears of nasty all over his shirt and pants. "That makes sense. But what about your truck?"

"I got the interior Scotch-Garded all to hell. I can just drag the water hose over to the driver's side door and spray the insides down. Long as I don't short out anything, I'm good."

"Smart."

"This ain't the first time I've gotten covered in monster guts and had to drive home."

"No, I expect it isn't."

"Say, I got a question," I said as I started lowering the blackout shades over the living room windows. I laughed when Skeeter had those things installed, but this wasn't the first time they'd come in handy. They made it way better having movie night in the daytime, too.

"Go ahead."

"How did you find me? I mean, I'm not surprised that the monster community knows there's a Hunter in this part of the world, but I thought I'd been pretty good about keeping my home address off the radar. Except for Barry and the other Sasquatch."

"First, we don't like the term monster. We prefer to be called by our name, our species name, or 'supernatural creature.' Second, I have a friend in the government who is familiar with the issues of the paranormal, and I asked him if there was anyone within two hundred miles of my home who might be able to find who wants me dead and remove the threat. He pointed me in your direct. He also mentioned that you recently lost your position with DEMON and would probably be looking for work."

"Does this friend of yours have a name?"

"Yes."

After a long pause, I asked, "Would you like to tell me that name? I might want to send him a thank you card."

"No, I don't think I would. He could get into a great deal of trouble for simply speaking with me, and if I got my source in trouble, I wouldn't have that source very long."

I couldn't argue with that. The windows covered, the only light leaks in the room were around the edges of the doors, so as long as Oglethorpe wasn't a complete idiot, he oughta be able to move around without getting crisped. "You want a beer?"

"It's six a.m."

"I'm out of OJ, so mimosas are off the menu, sorry. You want a beer or a Coke?"

"Coffee?"

"For a dude who wants my help, you're a demanding little shit, aren't you?"

"For someone making a thousand dollars a day, you're a petulant bastard, aren't you?"

I took a deep breath, remembering that the vampire probably wasn't as tired as I was from fighting zombies, and could probably rip my arms off and beat me with them. "I'll see if we've got anything."

"There's coffee pods in the drawer to the left of the sink," Skeeter said, walking out of the guest room wearing a pair of beat-up blue jeans, no shoes, and a worn Dalton High School Water Polo Team t-shirt. Our high school never had a water polo team, but Skeeter made the shirts for our fifteenth high school reunion a couple years ago. It showed a dude on a horse with a polo hammer wearing scuba gear. I had to admit, it was a pretty funny shirt.

"Hey, Caufield," Skeeter said. "There's some of Uncle Joe's spare clothes in the guest room dresser. Y'all are about the same size, so you can grab a shower while Bubba gets the coffee going."

"A splendid idea," he said, rising from the patio chair and walking to the guest room.

"Good thing we put in that tankless water heater back when I was still employed," I grumbled. "You want coffee?"

"Yeah, that'd be good," Skeeter said.

"Good. Get over here and make it. You're the only one who drinks the stuff. I don't even know how to run this damn Keurig thingy." I grabbed a beer out of the fridge and carried it over to the couch. I caught myself just before I sat down and put myself in the doghouse for a month of Sundays, looked at the patio furniture, then at my belly, then back at the plastic chair, and decided I could drink standing up.

"You just put the pod in, put the water in, and push the red button," Amy said, coming out of our room with a towel wrapped around her head.

"Or I get Skeeter to make his own damn coffee," I said, walking past her to the shower.

"You taking your beer to the shower with you?" she asked.

I looked at her like she was crazy, turned up the bottle, and drained the rest of the beer in two big gulps. "Nah. What do you think I am, a Neanderthal?"

Twenty minutes later, we were all clean and sitting around the kitchen table with plates full of eggs and bacon. Well, except for the vampire. I didn't keep bags of blood around, but he assured me he didn't have to drink blood every day to stay alive. Good thing. Letting him starve to death would put a serious crimp in our working relationship.

"Alright, so whoever wants to kill you definitely has some necromancy," Skeeter said, pointing his fork at Caufield with a sausage link skewered on the end of it.

"That seems to be the case from last night's encounter."

"And you said there was a necromancer in Atlanta that had beef with you," I said.

"Yes. His name is Lester, and he has a lair above The Vortex restaurant in Little Five Points."

"What can you tell me about this Lester?"

"He is a pompous ass with little regard for the rules of discretion that have kept the paranormal world hidden for centuries. He advertises in the Yellow Pages. He has a website. He has a *Facebook page*." His lips curled up, and I could see a hint of fang. This dude really did not like Facebook. I couldn't blame him on that one.

"Okay, he goes to the top of the suspect list," Amy said. "Who else?"

"There is Frederick, the Alpha of the North Georgia werewolves."

"There's werewolves in North Georgia?" Skeeter asked.

"Why wouldn't there be?" I asked. "It ain't like they're particularly citified creatures."

"Yes, there are werewolves in North Georgia, and their leader doesn't like me very much. They operate out of a strip club in Blairsville."

"I didn't know there were any strip clubs in Blairsville," I said.

"That's shocking," Skeeter said. "I thought for sure you knew about every topless joint and nudie bar on the eastern seaboard."

"Yeah, me too," I said. "That's why I'm surprised." I could almost feel Amy glaring at me, but I decided this wasn't the time to get into a discussion about my long-term support of single mothers all over the Southeast. I swear two dozen strippers across Georgia, South Carolina, and Tennessee saw a dip in their 401(k) when we started dating.

"It's not actually ever open for business," Caufield said. "It operates purely as a front for the werewolves."

"Oh, that makes more sense, then. What's the Alpha's problem with you?" I asked.

"I bit his niece."

"That'll do it," Skeeter said. "People get all kinds of touchy about you making undead out of their relatives. Especially nieces. Folks are touchy about nieces and sisters, man."

"I didn't turn her," Caufield said. "I just drank from her. Not enough to kill her. Not even enough for her to notice. If she hadn't gone to visit her uncle a few hours later still smelling like a vampire, there would have been no problem. And I didn't know she was his niece."

"Did you try explaining that to the Alpha?" Amy asked.

"I don't explain myself to dogs. He sent two of his men to attack me, so I sent them home with broken arms. I'm sure they healed, I did nothing to permanently damage them, but the message was clear."

"Yeah," I said. "Better put him on the list. Who else?"

"There's a Faerie who runs an herb shop in Marietta that I've had some arguments over recipes with."

"Faeries are easy," I said. "I can use the grandson of Mab thing to get her to lay off."

"She is an unlikely suspect, but possible," Caufield said. He thought for a few minutes. "That's all I can think of. At least in Georgia. There are a few from my time living in New Jersey, but most of those are organized crime bosses, not necromancers. They'd send men to shoot me, but their world is very mundane. They don't know that I'm a vampire, so they wouldn't know how to actually do me harm."

"Well, whoever sent a pack of zombies after you still wasn't doing a very good job at killing you," I said. "They were annoying, but I don't know if a brainless zombie *could* kill a vampire."

"Pretty sure you eat a big enough chunk out of anybody's brain, they're going to die," Skeeter said.

"He is correct," Caufield said. "Complete destruction of the body, including heart and brain, will kill us, even without a stake or sunlight. Had the zombies succeeded in ripping me limb from limb and consuming my flesh, I would have died."

"Good to know. And yuck," I said. "So where do we start?"

"Well, I've always like Vortex food," Amy said. "We could get a couple hours sleep and get there for a late lunch."

"Sounds like a plan," I said with a yawn. I looked over at Caufield. "Don't open the door for strangers, and everybody's a stranger. There's no password on the laptop, but if you surf porn, clean up your browser history when you're done. I don't want no freaky vampire porn popups on my computer."

"I might," Skeeter said. "Lemme get you my iPad."

"I am not interested in internet pornography," Caufield protested.

"Yeah, sure, whatever," I said. "I'm gonna get some sleep. You stay out of the really freaky shit. Or don't. You're a grown-ass vampire. You be you." Leaving the vampire protesting his moral superiority to porn in my living room, I shuffled off to catch a few hours shut-eye before going to interview a necromancer over a restaurant built in the shade of a giant human skull.

5

The Vortex is an Atlanta landmark. The entrance is shaped like a giant skull, and the interior looks like a punk rock club threw up all over the walls. The food is fantastic, the menu is hilarious, and the wait staff take no shit. It's very much my kind of place. I'd been there several times and never knew anything about a necromancer working out of the upper floor of the restaurant. And let's be real; somebody doing death magic within fifty feet of my fries is the kinda thing I want to know about.

Me and Amy walked in, took a table in the corner, and ordered a couple of burgers with onion rings. I got the Hell's Fury burger, and Amy got a fried chicken sandwich with pepper jack and bacon. When our waitress, a woman with almost as many visible piercings as I had visible tattoos, brought our drinks, I leaned forward.

"I hear there's a wizard upstairs," I said, keeping my voice down in case they didn't want the entire neighborhood to know somebody was slinging black magic in the building. When I thought about it, I remembered I was in Little Five and probably half the stores around me had some kind of witch or wizard working out of a back room.

"You mean Lester? Yeah, he's upstairs. Probably not awake yet, though. He was up late last night 'performing dark rituals.'" She made air quotes with her fingers on the last bit.

"So he wasn't performing dark rituals?" Amy asked.

"Not unless you perform dark rituals with half a dozen grad school dropouts and a shitload of dice. Nah, last night was his weekly D&D game, so there's no way he's awake yet. I'll call up, and by the time y'all are done eating, he'll have time to shit, shower, and shave. And trust me, you want him to have a shower."

I was starting to question how powerful this necromancer was, but since I'm also the guy who once got trapped in a graveyard full of zombies by a guy I didn't think could raise a fuss, much less a horde of undead, I tried hard to withhold judgement until I met the guy.

Half an hour later, I paid the check, wiped the sweat off my face, and tried to ignore the chuckles from my waitress. They weren't kidding about the name of my burger—that shit set me on fire. "Can we go up and see Lester?" I asked between big gulps of water.

"Yeah, he's waiting for you. Stairs are over there." She pointed to a dark corner of the restaurant where I could just make out a narrow stairwell. I wondered for a minute how I was going to fit when the waitress said, "Walk sideways. That's what Lester's gamer buddies have to do. They're pretty healthy, too."

"That's not a word I'd use to describe Bubba," Amy said, with a pointed look at my belly. "And trust me, I've used a *lot* of words to describe him."

I ignored the jab at my weight, which admittedly had crept up a few digits since our return from Fairyland. Eating a lot more fried food and walking a lot less had stretched the boundaries of my jeans, so I was secretly glad to have a case that might require me to move a little, instead of just stand by the door at the Drop and glare at teenagers with fake IDs.

Amy followed me to the stairs, and I did have to turn sideways to fit, but so did she, because no normal human being could walk up those narrow-ass steps without it. This was obviously a modification that had been done well after any building inspectors had set foot in the joint. I decided against drawing my pistol, since barging into a wizard's lair with a gun drawn usually didn't work out well for me. Amy, however, had her gun out, since no one would be able to see her behind me, and she could assess the situation before she came in.

The narrow wooden door had a pink neon "OPEN" sign next to it, and the jovial glow bathed my face as I knocked. "Enter!" a voice boomed from within. It was a good voice, a commanding voice, the kind of voice that makes people want to sit up and take notice. It was a Gandalf-level voice, which made the image that met me when I opened the door all the more disappointing.

I stepped into a small room that barely met the qualifications to be called an apartment, much less an office. It looked like the common room of a dorm, or a really low-rent studio apartment. There was black carpet with thick pile and enough pizza boxes scattered around to make me really glad the carpet was dark. There was a couch, a couple of armchairs, and one of those round wicker chairs that you see in most college apartments but nobody ever remembers buying. A round wooden table that had seen better days commanded the center of the room, covered in grid paper, hardback *Dungeons & Dragons* books, and hand-painted miniatures. There were also two or three ashtrays with tiny little roaches nestling in the cigarette rests. This dude took his dope-smoking at least as seriously as he took his role-playing. I could admire his dedication.

Lester, at least I assumed it was Lester since he was the only person in the room, sat perched on a backless bar stool with his feet tucked into the legs like a gargoyle with long hair and a particularly big nose. He wore a big floppy brown hat, purple pajama pants, no shirt, and no shoes. He had just the barest hint of a goatee and a nice spray of acne scattered across his nose and cheeks. He had a music stand in front of him, with KSU stenciled on the back, presumably from the university music department he stole it from. On the makeshift podium was a thick book, reminiscent of a big old family Bible, but I had a pretty good idea this wasn't anything close to the word of God.

Every inch of wall was covered with posters and fan art of Tolkien, D&D, Pathfinder, video games, or comic books, with a smattering of massively endowed anime girls scattered throughout. The scent of weed was so thick I could barely see, and old Skinny Puppy pounded a low rhythm through the room. The whole room was dim, lit by a couple of floor lamps with bandanas over the shades, casting weird shadows all around and generally making the place look and feel like a nerdy opium den.

"You must be Lester," I said, stepping into the room fully and letting Amy slide around behind me. I heard the *click* of the button on her holster close as she put her weapon away. This was not a dude that needed to be shot. Held down and scrubbed, maybe, but not shot.

"When conducting mystical business, I prefer to be addressed by my name in the wizarding world, Darian the Dark," Lester said, tilting his head back so he could look up at me while still looking down his nose. A pretty good trick.

"I don't give a shit what they call you at Hogwarts, pal. I've got some questions." I pulled a chair out from the table and sat across from him. "Talk to me about Caufield Evers Oglethorpe IV."

Well, that did it. Lester sprang off his stool like his ass was spring-loaded, planting one foot in the center of the table and leaping right over me on his way to the door. He probably would have made it, too, since there wasn't enough room for me to turn around with any speed.

Except for my badass fiancée. Amy took one step to the right so the skinny bastard didn't barrel into her, hooked an arm around Lester's waist, and yanked him back into the room like somebody was standing behind him pulling a rope. He stumbled backward a couple of steps, planted his heel on a pizza box, and went down flat on his back.

He was resilient for a skinny bastard, I had to give him that, because he didn't lay there long. Almost as soon as he landed, he rolled over, scrambled to his feet, and bolted for the lone window in the apartment. I hadn't even noticed it until he threw the curtains back, since it was completely blacked out with fabric. Lester raised the window and slid half his body out before I got to him and jerked him back inside. I held the flailing wizard up with one hand while I closed the window with my other, then dropped Lester to his stomach on the carpet.

"What the hell, Dorkian?" I asked. Lester tried to rise, but I put one foot between his shoulder blades and pressed him back to the floor. I didn't put much weight on him, just enough to hold him down. As skinny as he was, I didn't want to break a rib or worse.

"Please don't kill me! I'm too young to die! I've never known the touch of a woman! I've never known the touch of a man! I've never known the touch of—"

"You can stop the list right there," I said. "We get it, you're a walking stereotype: a *D&D* player that's never managed to get laid. You live on pizza and Mountain Dew and smoke more weed than Jerry Garcia."

"Who?" the scrawny bastard under my foot asked, prompting me to press down a little harder on his ribcage. No self-respecting stoner doesn't know the Dead.

"Whatever, shithead. Wake up. It's the twenty-first century. Geeks are cool. *The Big Bang Theory* has been on TV long enough to get boring. Thor movies make money. You could probably get laid if you ever came down that narrow-ass staircase."

"But that's not why we're here," Amy cut in, bringing me back on track and reminding me that one nerd's virginity was not the mission. My wallet was.

"Right," I said. I reached down and pulled Lester to his feet, then shoved him toward the couch. He crashed into it and an avalanche of pizza boxes and a puff of dust. I turned my metal folding chair to face him, leaving Amy standing between the nimble necromancer and the exits in case he tried to rabbit again. "Now, why are you trying to kill Oglethorpe?"

Lester's eyes bugged out and he swallowed huge. "What?!? I'm not trying to kill him! I thought he sent you here to kill me!"

"Kill you? Why would he want to do that?" Amy asked.

"Why would he bother?" I asked at the same time.

Lester looked to me first. "Ouch, dude. That's kinda harsh."

"You live like a college freshman, smell like a Bob Marley concert, and you don't know who Jerry Garcia was. Add in the pompous necromancer gimmick, and I'm all out of need to make you like me, shithead."

"Bubba, don't be mean," Amy said.

"Yeah, *Bubba*," Lester said, curling up one corner of his mouth at me. "Fat old rednecks who answer to Bubba don't get to give other people shit about their life choices."

I reached around behind my back and pulled the Judge from its holster. I laid the pistol down on the table and grinned at the now-silent Lester. "When I'm the one with the gun, I get to talk all the shit I want. Now tell us why Oglethorpe would want to kill you."

"Well...that's kind of a long, embarrassing story."

I sat back in my chair, pistol still very close to my elbow, and folded my arms across my chest. "That's my very favorite kind."

6

"It was about five years ago," Lester said as he packed a bowl and settled into his papasan chair. I watched Amy's face out of the corner of my eye as he took a huge drag off his pipe and offered it across the table to her.

"I'm good, thanks."

He held the swirled glass pipe out to me, but I shook my head. "I try not to smoke when I'm armed."

"Oh. Good call, man." He leaned back in the bowl-shaped chair and started his story, his eyes half-lidded in the universal look of stoners everywhere.

"So about five years ago, this gamer dude rented out The Masquerade, this big three-story dance club in town, and held a huge LARP."

"A lark?" Amy asked.

"Wow, dude, your nerd street cred just took a big hit, lady," Lester said, coughing and chuckling around his pot.

"I'm okay with that," Amy said. "Now what's a lark?"

"LARP," he corrected. "It's a live-action roleplaying game, kinda like improv meets D&D."

"I think I saw a movie about that, with the guy from *Game of Thrones*."

"Yeah! *Knights of Badassdom*, with Peter Dinklage! That flick was awesome, dude. So yeah, this was kinda like that, except we weren't playing a medieval setting, we were playing *Bloodsuckers*."

"I'm guessing this means something more specific than you were dressing up and pretending to be vampires," Amy said.

"Oh, yeah. Sorry, sometimes I forget what it's like to talk to people who aren't gamers."

I almost burst out laughing because he made *not* being a huge nerd sound as bad as the jocks back in school made *being* a huge nerd sound back in the day. Times sure have changed.

"Sorry my nerd-fu isn't as strong. But you were going to explain about your game?" Amy steered Lester back on track. It was almost like she had a lot of experience in conversation with the really drunk or spectacularly high. I wondered where she got that from, then decided it was probably best not to poke that one too much.

"Yeah, well *Bloodsuckers* is a live-action role-playing game where people get together and portray different characters that they either bring with them or are assigned by the GM. Do you know what a GM is?"

"Yes," Amy said. "I played a little *D&D* in college."

"I'm good," I said. Amy gave me a surprised look, and I shrugged. "Skeeter's my best friend. I've got mad nerd skills."

"Okay, so this particular LARP was built around several different themes, one of which was that there was a vampire hunter in the building trying to infiltrate the undead society and destroy us from within. Then there's the normal vampire politics, like people trying to overthrow their coven leaders and rival covens making moves against each other, and shit like that. Then there's the people who just like to dress up in black leather pants and go to these things to get laid."

"Now you're talking my language," I said, grinning.

"Dude, I don't think they could make leather pants for you if they used three cows," Lester said with a loopy grin.

"Still armed," I growled. "How does Caufield figure into any of this?"

"Oh, yeah. Well, I'd been there for an hour or so, gotten my coven assignment and been given my objectives, and I was working on my second glass of wine when I spotted him. I thought I wasn't seeing straight at first, on account of the molly, but—"

"Wait a minute," I stopped him. "You went to a vampire role-play while you were rolling?"

"Dude, that's the best way to go. Everything just *feels* better. The colors are a little brighter, everybody's a lot prettier, and *way* more interesting. I won't do a LARP unless I know at least two of my dealers are going to be there."

"Two?" Amy asked.

"Yeah, you want competition. Keeps prices stable. If there's only one dude holding at a party, they can get a little greedy, especially if there's a bunch of tourists there because they don't know any better."

"I was more referring to the fact that you have multiple drug dealers."

"Oh, yeah. You've got to, on account of everybody's a specialist nowadays. My weed guy only does weed. Well, and CBD oil, but that's kinda the same thing. My molly guys only do synthetics, but they'll do all kinds of stuff, from molly to bath salts to acid. I only meet them at parties and places where there's a bunch of people around. Some of their customers are kinda sketch. Then there's my organic guy. He only does shrooms, but he's got some different strains of fungus that will make you think you can see God. Then there's the guys that sling the hard stuff, but I don't really mess with that. I'm all about expanding my mind and making the experience better, you dig?"

"We dig," I said, holding up a hand to Amy before we got any more education on Lester's philosophy on psychedelics. "So you saw Caufield, but you thought you might be hallucinating because you were high as a kite?"

"Yeah, pretty much. I was dancing and talking to this one couple about maybe hooking up after the game was over, and my weed buzz was wearing off, but the molly and the wine were really kicking in, so I was feeling righteous. A little sweaty, but that comes with the territory, you know. That's when I saw him."

"Caufield?" I asked.

"Yeah. It was like he glowed, man. It was like the dark wrapped him in its embrace, and he just radiated blackness. He was a walking aura of evil and bloodlust and power, and I wanted a piece of that. He was pretty hot, too, so that didn't hurt. So I walked up to him and asked if I could buy him a drink. You know what he said? Do you know what this dude's first words to me were?"

"I can only imagine," Amy said.

"He looked at me with those dark, brooding pools of evil he calls eyes, and he said, 'I do not drink...wine.' I shit you not! He dropped a Bela Lugosi line on me the first thing he ever said to me! I almost creamed my pants, but I tried to be cool. I mean, he had me frozen with his gaze. I was mesmerized, just like in the books."

"You were too high to move," I said.

Lester shook his head. "Nah, dude. I mean, yeah, I was high as shit, but this guy had some magic to him. So I bought him a drink and chatted him up in-game, trying to get information for my coven, you know? We hung out for a little while, and then we were walking upstairs when it happened."

"What happened?" Amy asked.

"We walked past a big antique mirror hanging on the wall, and when I looked over his shoulder, it was like he *wasn't there*. He didn't have a reflection. I totally dropped my wineglass, and he caught it before it spilled a drop. That sealed it right there. This dude was a legit vampire."

"Did that make you want to sleep with him more or less?" I asked. I was more curious than anything, but I figured since the opportunity was there, I'd ask.

"A little more, actually. I've had a lot of sex. And I mean a *lot* of sex, but I've never slept with anybody that was dead. Or anybody who could kill me with one finger. It was kinda hot."

I looked around the room and reserved comment on the possibility of this dude having a lot of sex. After all, everybody deserves love, even people with questionable shower habits with mold-encrusted pizza boxes stacked halfway to the ceiling in their living room. Plus, drugs can make anybody sexy. That's why I try to keep

Amy on a steady dose of hallucinogens at all times. It's the only way I can score a chick that far out of my league.

"So how did we get from you two wanting to bone to him sending assassins after you? Or you sending a horde of zombies after him?" Amy asked, trying to steer the conversation back onto some semblance of a track.

"I told you, I didn't...did you say zombies?"

"Yep, zombies," I said. "Couple dozen of them. They came after Caufield last night in Dalton. I had to burn down a bar to get rid of them."

"I didn't think that would work," Lester said. "I always figured if you set a zombie on fire, you just get a flaming zombie."

"That's true, but you put enough alcohol in one place, with enough fire, and you get a big boom. They're going to be picking zombie parts out of the trees for miles around."

"Oh. That had to be pretty cool." He chuckled and leaned forward, stretching his fist out toward me. We bumped knuckles, and he leaned back. "But I didn't send any zombies after Caufield. I didn't send any zombies anywhere. Hell, I don't even know how to do something like that."

"I thought you were some kind of big necromancer?" Amy asked. "Are you saying you're a fake?"

"Oh, total fake. I've got about as much magical juice as this table. I couldn't raise a dead hamster, much less a zombie. It's just a gig, man. I do some Tarot, get clients a little high, and let them talk to their dead relatives. Sometimes I'll go out to the graveyard with them and do some made-up ritual to help their loved ones rest. It's just a way to make people feel better and keep me in pizza and beer. And weed. I read my dealer's cards once a week in exchange for a quarter. He thinks I steer him away from the cops, but really I just tell him not to sell dope to school kids and the cops won't give him any shit."

"So you're not a necromancer," I said. This had been a waste of a trip. At least lunch was good. And I was getting a little bit of a contact high off Lester's pipe, so that kept me mellow.

"Nah, dude. I'm a gamer who likes to make people feel better about their dead relatives. Until I met Caufield, I didn't think any of that supernatural stuff was even real. Hell, that's how I got in trouble with him in the first place. That's why I thought y'all were here to off me."

"Yeah, we never got that part of the story." Amy folded her arms across her chest.

"It's not as interesting as you think," Lester said. "Once I realized Caufield was really a vampire, I had all these questions for him. He answered some of them and showed me the answers to some others. We talked for hours, man. But when we were done, he swore me to secrecy. He told me that if I ever told *anybody* about him, or what I knew about vampires, that he'd kill me. He wasn't playing, either. I could tell by the look in his eyes that he meant every word."

"So you blabbed, and thought he sent us to kill you for it," I said.

"Worse. I…kinda blackmailed him first. I told him I'd been recording our whole conversation, and if he didn't pay me, I'd send the file out to everybody in my contacts list. It was total bullshit, of course. I hadn't recorded anything, but he couldn't figure out enough on my phone to tell that. He's a little out of touch with technology, you know."

"Being several centuries old will do that to you," Amy said.

"Yeah, so I blackmailed him. And he paid me like ten grand."

"And that's why you thought he sent us," I said.

Lester looked down at his lap. "Well, not exactly."

"Oh, Jesus. What did you do?" I asked.

"Well, I've got this blog…"

"Oh, hell."

"Yeah. I was still pretty high when I got home, and I wanted to write stuff down, so I didn't forget how cool all the stuff he told me about being a vampire was, and I couldn't find a pen, so I just popped open the laptop and wrote a blog post. But then I forgot to set it as private, and I went to sleep."

"And published the blog," Amy said.

Lester still didn't meet our eyes. "Yeah. That happened. I didn't think it was going to be a big deal, because I've only got like ten followers on my blog, but one of them reblogged it, and then somebody else reblogged it, and by the time I woke up, that shit was viral, man. I took it down, but you know the internet. Once it was out there, it was out there. There was no putting that genie back in the bottle."

"So you thought Caufield sent us here to kill you for outing him, even after he paid you a bunch of cash," Amy said.

"Pretty much. It was a pretty big hassle for him, at least going on the pissed-off calls I got from him. He had to move, change his name, do the whole thing where he invents a new identity. The last time he called, he said if he ever saw me again, he was going to rip my heart out and eat it while I watched. That's when I left my mom's place and moved in here. I thought it would be safer."

I looked at Amy, who shrugged. This wasn't our guy. Not only could he not raise zombies, he was also a huge chickenshit. "Do you know anybody else in Atlanta that might want Caufield dead?"

Lester laughed. "Dude, he's already dead. Or did you miss the whole vampire thing?"

"How about you not give me any more reasons to want to punch you in the face and just answer the question?" I cracked my knuckles as I spoke. Weed made me a little mellow, but not so much that I thought Lester was witty.

He gulped and sat up a little straighter. "Nah, man. We just hung out that one night. I don't even know anybody else who knows vampires are real. Except for Big Tony."

"Who's Big Tony?" Amy asked.

"He's the vampire who ran the LARP. He claims to be one of the boss vampires in Atlanta. I always thought that was fake, but after meeting Caufield, maybe he really is some kind of alpha vamp. If anybody would know, I guess it would be Tony."

I looked at Amy, who nodded. I turned back to Lester. "So where could we find your pal Big Tony?"

7

Big Tony's office was in the back of a CrossFit gym out near the airport, which seemed really strange to me until I stepped inside and realized that the entrance was actually a light-tight vestibule with three doors to get through before you made it inside the main room, and every single door was reinforced steel set into steel frames. It not only kept the sunlight out, but also created a choke point for defense and gave an added layer of warning for any unpleasant visitors that might happen by.

The gym didn't look like anything out of the ordinary at first glance. Nobody was pushing any obscene amounts of weight, at least not that I could see from a distance. Then I got closer to the first guy and noticed that the weights on his bar didn't look like the normal forty-five-pound plates I was used to seeing. The color was a little off, and instead of "45" on the side, "100" was stenciled on the plate.

"Tungsten," said the spotter.

I looked up, and the guy who'd spoken grinned at me. "I saw you looking. The plates are made of tungsten instead of iron. About two and a half times the weight, with the same form factor so we don't have to buy different racks. We do have to use tungsten bars, though, to handle the weight."

"So that dude is benching..." I did a quick count of the number of plates. "Eight hundred pounds."

"Nine," he corrected me. "The bar is heavier, too. But we've got some human weights, too, if you're looking for a workout." The way he looked at my beer gut, the "you need it, fatass" was pretty well implied.

"Nah, I'm good," I said. "We need to talk to Big Tony."

The guy reached down and helped the behemoth on the bench rack his weights, then pointed across the room at a door marked "OFFICE." I nodded to the weightlifters and headed across the room.

"That looked really heavy," Amy said.

"Yeah," I replied. "The current world record on the bench press is around eleven hundred pounds, and that guy was pressing nine hundred like it was nothing."

"How much can you press?"

"My top end now is probably around three hundred. More when I'm lifting on a regular basis, but that's been a long time now. I think the most I ever pressed one time was four twenty-five, but that was back at the height of my football days."

"And you're pretty strong."

"Yeah, I'm no slouch. But I'm also human, and I don't hit the gym every day. These guys are in another class entirely, in a lot of ways."

By now we were at the door to the office, and when I knocked, a loud voice called out, "Come in!"

I pushed open the door and gazed upon the largest vampire I had ever seen. Most of the time when somebody has a nickname that includes an adjective, it's ironic. Like guys who are called "Tiny" are always huge, and you expect the dude called Big Tony to be short and scrawny.

This Big Tony was the exception that proved the rule. He was a big mother, and not big in the way that I'm big, which is the kind of corn-fed big country boy with a lot more beer and fried food piled on his plate than he oughta have but can still go when the shit hits the fan. No, this Big Tony was at least as tall as me, which put him north of six and a half feet tall, and looked like he bench-pressed Volkswagen

Beetles for a warm-up. His muscles had muscles, and they were pretty much always flexed.

His nickname wasn't ironic; it was just truth in advertising. He stood up from behind the cheap desk and held out a hand the size of a dinner plate. "Big Tony," he said.

I shook his hand and said, "Bubba Brabham."

Amy stared at the massive appendage and shook it. Her hand disappeared in his. "Amy Hall." She looked the giant up and down, then shook her head in disbelief. "They named you right, didn't they?"

"Pretty much. I was a powerlifter before I got turned. Now that I can push a lot more weight, I like to stay around other people that like to lift heavy things." He gestured to a couple of chairs in front of the desk, and we all sat.

"But it's not like you can see any gains, right?" I asked. "I thought vampires were magically strong and kinda stuck in the bodies you had when you were turned."

"Yeah, I don't get any stronger, but it's still fun to slam big stacks of weight around, and it's fun to help some of the weres and Fae get stronger. You haven't seen hilarious until you've watched a female were-squirrel squat seven-fifty." He chuckled, and I joined him.

Amy looked a little confused. "I guess that's a lot?"

"My personal record squat when I played football was five hundred fifty pounds, and that was one time," I said.

"And this were-squirrel was five-two and weighed a buck ten. But you aren't here to learn about the fitness habits of the Georgia super-natural community."

"No, we aren't," I agreed. "We've got some questions about Caufield Evers Oglethorpe IV."

"That douche? He left town. He's somebody else's problem now."

"Yeah, mine," I said. "Somebody's trying to kill him."

"Not surprised. I did mention he's a douche, right?"

"Yeah. So do you know anyone in particular that took exception to his douchiness?" Amy asked.

"Not enough to kill him. I don't know if you noticed, but a lot of my people are kind of assholes. I don't know if it comes with immortality, or with being really strong, or what, but most vampires are dicks. So Oglethorpe didn't really stand out, you feel me?"

"Yeah," I said. "Do you think anybody out there would know anything?"

"Probably not. Gerald, if anybody. He's the were-panther leading the tai chi class over against the far wall." He pointed to the big LCD TV mounted on the wall, its screen divided into a dozen or so security camera feeds. I saw the guy he was talking about, a bald black guy in a gi with about half a dozen people echoing his movements in two lines of graceful kata.

"I'll ask him," I said, standing up. "Thanks for your time." I held out my hand.

Big Tony stood up and clasped my hand in his. It felt like I was shaking an iron glove. "No problem. If you ever want to come in and lift, the first week is free."

"Thanks, but I'm not local. And you guys push a little more weight than I ever worked with."

"We have some human clients. You wouldn't be the only one working with the little stacks."

For once, I didn't let my ego speak for me, and I just shook his hand. Amy did the same, and we headed out into the main room to speak with Gerald. Of course, it wasn't going to be that easy, because nothing can ever be easy. As soon as we stepped out of the office, there were half a dozen hairy guys with muscles in places I didn't even know were places standing in a semicircle glaring at me.

"It's okay, guys. We won't be here long. We've just got a few questions for Gerald, and then I'll get my unsightly BMI out of your gym," I said, stepping forward.

The muscle heads crowded together, blocking my path. I heard Amy unsnap her holster behind me, and out of the corner of my eye, I saw the door to Big Tony's office was still open. Good. If things went really sideways, Amy could get to cover while I got my ass beat. Not what I'd call an optimal plan, but at least it was a plan.

"You killed Jason," growled a stocky guy with a ponytail and Hugh

Jackman sideburns. I was willing to bet he was a were-badger because he looked like he just didn't give a *single* fuck.

"Jason was our leader," a lean were with a goatee and a shaved head said, scowling at me. I pegged him for a were-tiger or some other kind of big cat. He had that feline, sinuous look about him.

"You killed the Messiah. Now we're going to kill you." Now this guy. This guy had to be a were-douche. He had blond hair styled to within an inch of its life to look like it wasn't styled at all, no shirt, purple compression tights with black lightning bolts running down his legs, and a puca shell necklace. I was pretty sure I hadn't seen anyone wear a puca shell necklace since *Baywatch* went off the air. Were-douche (in my head, I named him Brad) held a twenty-pound dumbbell in one hand, definitely enough to crush my skull if he hit me with it.

"Nah," I said, pulling the Judge from behind my back and shooting Brad square in the chest. The little .410 shotgun shell was deafening in the enclosed space of the gym, and even worse if you had a were's heightened senses. Brad dropped like a sack of potatoes, and the rest of the goons turned away or dropped to one knee with their hands clapped to their ears.

I moved right to the were-badger, who was one of the ones on his knees. I slammed my own knee into his nose, shattering it, and he fell flat on his back, out of the fight for the moment. I reversed my grip on the Judge and slammed the butt of the revolver into the temple of a bulky were next to me, dropping half of the assholes blocking my path in the first few seconds of the fight. Good thing, too, since that's about when things went to shit.

"Bubba, look out!" Amy called from the door, and you've gotta know that by the time you hear and process somebody telling you to look out, it's already way too late to look out. I turned to look at her and caught the end of one of those special tungsten weight bars right in the gut. I doubled over, and the trim were I'd pegged for some type of cat swung the bar up and met the side of my face on the way down. The bar kept going up, and I kept going down, this time with far less control.

I hit the deck and rolled over, raising my pistol and squeezing off another shotgun round. This load of birdshot went right into Hello Were-Kitty's crotch, and the bar he was beating me with clattered to the ground as he went down screaming.

"That's silver shot, asshole. You're not going to be able to heal until you dig every pellet out of your nuts," I hissed at him as I struggled to my feet.

I heard the flat crack of Amy's pistol, then a thud as another were went down. Amy's voice cut through the air with the kind of authority that comes from years of carrying a badge and a gun for a living. "That was the last warning shot, assholes." I looked up in time to see her swap out magazines and run the slide on her pistol. "This new clip is all silver, so the next one of you that so much as looks at us funny gets a lobotomy. Are we clear?"

The weres on the floor all nodded, except for were-kitty, who was just clutching his jewels and moaning a lot. Amy went on. "Yeah, Bubba killed Jason. Because Jason wanted to kill him. They were brothers, and you all understand how complicated family stuff gets." There were a lot of nods all around. "So you don't get to kill him for killing his shithead brother. Jason was his brother to kill, and trust me, he's done enough soul-searching and suffering on account of it. Now we've got a couple of questions to ask Gerald over there, and then we'll be on our way. Does anybody have a problem with that?"

None of the assembled weres volunteered to argue with the lady holding the gun loaded with silver bullets, much to no one's surprise. Amy helped me up, and as we turned to walk over to Gerald, Big Tony called out to us from the doorway.

"You can go. You don't need to talk to Gerald."

"Why not?" Amy asked. "You said he would know if anyone wanted Caufield killed."

"Yeah, about that." Big Tony at least had the good grace to look a little embarrassed. "I lied. I knew the boys were going to try to ambush you—I could see it in one of my other monitors. I wanted to know if you were as badass as I heard, so I made sure you wouldn't expect it."

"You asshole," I muttered, straightening up. I wasn't in what I would call top vampire-fighting form after getting a hundred-pound bar of metal slammed into my face, but I was willing to give it the old college try.

Amy yanked on my arm. "I have twelve rounds of silver ammunition, and you have three left. We cannot shoot our way out of this, and you can't kick his ass in the shape you're in. Better to live to fight another day."

"Listen to the lady, Bubba. Right now, you've proven all the hype about you is at least close to true. Take the win, and your human, and get the hell out of my gym. Nobody here knows shit about Caufield, and nobody cares."

Amy and I walked to the front door, her helping me weave around the weight benches and equipment and dodge the stars and birdies flickering in my vision. We got to the door, and I turned back to look at Big Tony standing in the door of his office. "You were right about one thing," I said.

"What's that?" the muscle-bound vampire asked.

"Vampires are dicks." Then I turned and limped out the door, battered, bruised, and without a single idea where to proceed. I walked out, got in the truck, and saw five missed calls from Skeeter.

I pressed the redial button on my phone and cranked the truck. Skeeter's voice came over the Bluetooth connection in the truck's radio. "Bubba, where the hell are you?"

"I'm down in Atlanta trying to figure out who wants to kill Caufield. What's up?"

"Well, you better get your ass back up here because there's some crazy bitch on my porch with a gun and a grenade, and she says if I don't open the door, she's going to blow it off the hinges!"

"I'm on my way." I put the truck in gear and looked over at Amy. "Well, I reckon we figured out who wants to kill him."

"You mean who wants to kill him today. Seems like there might be a waiting list."

8

There was indeed a woman sitting on Skeeter's porch when we pulled up in his driveway. She wasn't beating on his door, but she was sitting on the front steps with an AR-15 across her lap and what did look to be a grenade lying on the porch next to her.

I stepped out of the truck and raised my hands. "Hey there," I called to her.

"Hello." She didn't raise the gun, but her hands were in the right position to bring it up and draw a bead on me pretty quick. Quicker than I could draw and fire the Judge from behind my back, at any rate. She was too far away for me to be accurate with any speed anyway. I'm good for about ten yards with the little pistol, but she was on the far edge of that, and I put my chances of dropping her before she filled me, Amy, or my truck full of holes at less than forty percent.

"Want to tell me what you're doing on my buddy's porch? You got him mighty nervous in there."

"He call you for help?"

"Half a dozen times."

"Too bad. You aren't going to be much help."

"Why's that?"

"Because there's a vampire in there, and I'm going to kill him. Then I'm going to turn his head over to Director Shaw and collect the bounty."

"Director Shaw? Who's that?"

"He runs DEMON, the Department of—"

"Yeah, I know what DEMON is. I used to work for them."

Her eyes went a little wide. "Are you Bubba?"

"Yeah, that's me."

She hopped up to her feet, bouncing on the balls of her feet like she was either real excited or really had to pee. Or both. "Holy shit, man! You're a legend! People say you beat the shit out a Sasquatch butt-naked on top of a fire ant hill!"

"Well…" I wasn't naked. The Sasquatch was naked, but I had my pants and shoes on. And I don't remember anything about fire ants. And if we're being honest, I cheated like hell. But I did fight a naked Sasquatch. "It wasn't quite like that."

"And you fought an honest-to-God bridge troll!"

"Okay, that I did." Got my ass kicked, too, but I didn't need to relive every single bruise I picked up working for the government.

"And that thing with the elf a couple of Christmases ago? Man, that was legendary!"

I felt myself grin a little. This little run of hero worship was nice, if a little over the top. A fellow could get used to this. I was kinda wondering where this chick found a copy of *Bubba the Monster Hunter's Greatest Hits*, but the adulation felt so good I shoved any worries about it aside.

Her eyes went cold, and I almost stepped back at the intensity. "But then you went off to Faerie and turned traitor. Why'd you do that? Get all cozy with the monsters? And now you're harboring a bloodsucker? That's not what we do. We're *Hunters*, man! We kill the bad guys. We don't make them cookies."

"Are there cookies? Because it's been a little while since lunch, and I'm getting a little peckish."

"Focus, babe. Keep your eye on the prize. Like she forgot to do."

Amy stepped up behind the girl and pressed her pistol to her head. "Surprise."

Amy slapped a pair of plastic cuffs on the Junior Hunter, and while she relieved the girl of her rifle, the pistol on her hip, the knife in her boot, the knife in her other boot, and the two grenades on her belt, I took a minute to really look at the girl. She was *young*. Maybe twenty. Younger than I was when I started, and I came from a family of Hunters. Hell, a girl her age shouldn't even be able to buy most of the ordinance she was packing.

I walked up onto Skeeter's porch and pressed the intercom button above the doorbell. Skeeter's face popped up on the screen. "Did you shoot her?"

"Skeeter, I do not shoot everybody I have a disagreement with. If I did, you'd have more holes in you than your granny's colander."

"You punched her, then."

"I don't hit every stranger I meet, either. I'll have you know I almost made it through the whole trip to Atlanta without hitting anybody."

"Bubba, you literally knocked the shit out of the second person we spoke to in Atlanta. There was the waitress, then Lester. And you smacked the hell out of Lester."

"Well, I didn't hit the waitress. And I didn't hit Big Tony. That's got to be some kind of achievement."

"We went two places. You got in a fight in both of them." She had a point. Trouble did have a way of finding me. Of course, I made for a pretty big target, so I was easy to find.

"Whatever. Let's take this party indoors before the neighbors call the police. Open up, Skeeter." I heard a buzz as Skeeter disengaged the electromagnetic lock on his front door. I didn't want to disappoint Exploding Grenade Skipper, but she didn't have enough artillery to get into Skeeter's house. I've broken into magical castles that were less fortified.

I walked the kid into Skeeter's living room and plopped her down on the couch. She fell over sideways, and I watched her struggle with her hands tied behind her back for a minute or two before Amy walked over and pushed her upright.

The mini-Hunter glared at me. "Dick."

"Fair assessment."

There was a loud *hisssss* as the seal on Skeeter's panic room opened and he came through the vault door hidden behind one of his bookcases. "Shit. You really didn't shoot her."

"I told you I didn't shoot her. Damn, does everybody believe I'm all ultra-violent?"

"It's kinda your brand, Bubba," Skeeter said. He came into the room and sat down in an armchair facing the couch. "Why did you bring her in here? And don't give me that shit about neighbors or the cops. You know there ain't another soul for two miles, and that my cousin is the sheriff."

"Oh, that? Yeah, there's no beer on your porch." I walked over to his fridge and opened the door. "What the hell? There's no beer in here, either!" I turned back to Skeeter, who at least had the good grace to look embarrassed.

"Sorry. I haven't been to the store since the last time you were over and drank all my beer. And by the way, you owe me a case of beer."

"Skeeter, I'm literally the only person that comes over here that drinks beer."

"And I'm getting tired of paying for your alcohol."

"You're the one that still has a job. How am I supposed to buy beer and ammunition?"

"We all have sacrifices to make, Bubba."

"I don't know that beer is a sacrifice I'm willing to make."

"Hey! Are y'all gonna interrogate me or just whine a lot?" the kid on the couch asked.

"Well, I reckon so." I grabbed a Coke out of the fridge and walked back over to the den. I plopped down in the recliner by the end of the couch, leaned forward, and looked the kid straight in the eye. She didn't look scared at all, more annoyed than anything.

"Why are you here?"

"I told you. There's a vampire. I'm here to kill it."

"Yeah, yeah. And this Director Shaw put a bounty on Caufield's head?" I asked.

"Nah. He's got a bounty on all supernatural creatures. They each come with different payouts. Vampires are the best return because they cost as much as werewolves, but they sleep all day, so they're easier to bag."

Me, Amy, and Skeeter exchanged a look. DEMON was putting bounties on *all* supernatural creatures? This wasn't just a change in policy, this was a huge problem. Now every jackass in the country was going to be wandering around in the woods trying to bag a Sasquatch. I needed to let Barry know what was going on and pass the word along to the other Hunters I knew. Mason would want to know for sure. That soft-hearted bastard pretty much adopted half the cryptos he met.

"You thought you could come in here, stake Caufield while he slept in Skeeter's guest room, and take him back to DEMON for a quick hundred bucks or something?" Amy asked.

"More like a quick ten grand, blondie."

Holy. Shit. "So what were you going to do about Skeeter?" I asked. I wanted to know if she was nuts or a total psychopath before I figured out what to do with her.

"I was going to start by offering him a cut. If that didn't work, I figured I'd knock him out, tie him up, and cut him loose when I left. I don't hurt humans."

"I don't have the same compunctions," Caufield said from the door to the safe room. "Especially not against humans who try to murder me in my sleep. Which I'm not, by the way. Asleep, that is."

"That all sounded better in your head, didn't it?" I asked.

"Much. I think I was taller there, too." He walked over and sat down next to the Hunter on the couch. "Now, where were we? Oh yes, you were going to murder me in my sleep. That seems rude, don't you think? What should I do about that?" He leaned in close and sniffed the girl's neck. "Ah, the sweet smell of fear. Do you smell it, Bubba? That stink of cold sweat and the hint of a bladder almost to the point of release."

"If you make her pee on my couch, I'll stake you myself," Skeeter said, breaking the moment completely.

"Yeah, and that whole neck-sniffing thing? That's just creepy, dude."

Caufield sat back on the couch and crossed his arms over his chest. "You guys are no fun. You're not even going to let me eat her, are you?"

"We didn't let her kill you in your sleep, so we shouldn't let you eat her," Amy said.

"Spoilsports," the pouting vampire said. "And I wasn't asleep. That's a myth. We don't sleep all day. We sleep when we need to, which might be only every three or four days. So you were going to come in here with mortal weapons against a fully-awake vampire. How do you think that was going to turn out?"

The girl didn't speak for a long moment, then she looked around at us. "What? Oh, that wasn't rhetorical? I thought you were still being all dramatic."

Caufield looked disappointed. "Well, I was, but you were still supposed to answer. Whatever, the moment's gone now." He looked at me and Amy. "What are you going to do with her? And what did you find out about Lester?"

"Lester is not trying to kill you. He's scared shitless that you're trying to kill him."

"The thought had crossed my mind," Caufield admitted. "Now what are you going to do with her?"

"Well, I reckon we oughta at least ask her name," Amy said, looking at the girl. "Okay, sunshine. Who are you?"

"You mean you haven't recognized me yet?" the girl asked.

"No. Should I have?"

"Not you." She jerked her chin at me. "Him. Look closer, Bubba, you rat bastard." There was a fire in her eyes that wasn't there before, and I started to think there was more to her being here than just hunting Caufield.

"Sorry, kid. I don't know you." But I did. Or at least, I felt like I knew somebody that looked like her.

"I wasn't even ten years old the last time I saw you, and you could still play football."

Skeeter's eyes went wide. "No."

"Keep your mouth shut. I want him to figure it out." Somehow this girl, hands tied behind her with zip cuffs, was in total control all of a sudden.

"Sorry, kid. I got nothing. But I drink a lot, so maybe—"

"I'm wearing her shoes."

"Huh?" I looked down at her feet, and my stomach dropped down to my toes. Red and white canvas sneakers. Generic as hell, nothing out of the ordinary except they looked a little dated. And there was a spot of brown on the toe... "Britt?"

"Geri," she corrected. "Brittany was my sister. Your girlfriend. And you got her killed, you half-human son of a bitch. You got my sister killed, and now I'm here to kill you."

I looked in her blazing eyes, and it was clear as day. Britt's baby sister, maybe six years old when I last saw her, but she grew up to have her sister's mouth, her sister's nose, and a cold look in her eyes that told me she remembered exactly who was to blame for her sister's death.

"Well, fuck."

9

The girl on the couch now looked familiar. Too familiar. "Geri, I…" I sat there with my mouth hanging open. I didn't know what to say. What the hell could I say? She blamed me for her sister's death, and she was right. My father killed her sister. Murdered her right in front of my eyes because my kid brother was a murderous psychopath who wanted nothing more than to make me suffer. Well, eventually he wanted to destroy most of humanity and turn the world into a playground for supernatural monsters and burn our mother at the stake. But in the beginning, he just wanted to hurt me, and he killed Brittany to do it.

"Where's your smart remarks now? Or did you actually think that I was excited to meet you because you got lucky and took down a few cryptids? You seemed a lot smarter when I was seven." The sneer she aimed at me made me feel bad for her parents through her teen years. The Geri I remembered was a bright, sunny child with pigtails and training wheels on her bike.

But that was before I got her sister killed. Before I was responsible for her world exploding. Before I left her and her family to pick up the pieces with no better explanation than "a bear attack" because that was the best thing I could think of between my grandfather dying on my watch, my girlfriend dying in my arms, and me shooting my were-wolf father full of silver buckshot in a creek behind my house. To say I wasn't at my best was putting things mildly.

I felt bad that I never spoke to Brittany's family again after she died. I couldn't stand to look in her mama's eyes. Every time I did, I saw nothing but my failure there. She didn't know what really happened, but she knew the truth of it: I failed to protect her daughter. I got Brittany killed. Now, fifteen years later, it looked like the last loose threads of that day were tying themselves around my neck, in the form of a furious twenty-something brunette sitting in my best friend's living room.

I took a deep breath and convinced myself that I was a better man now than I was when Britt died. "I'm sorry."

Geri just looked at me, hatred in her eyes. "Sorry for what, asshole?"

"I got Britt killed. It was my fault."

"Yeah, I figured. When I got to UGA, I read up on you in old college papers. Then I went online and read more. The stuff I found after college was a lot more interesting. When I found the bit about your father turning werewolf around the same time a bear killed my sister, I put two and two together. When Director Shaw recruited me, he gave me DEMON's file on you, and I got the whole story. You're kind of a fuckup, you know that?"

I looked over at Amy. "DEMON's file?"

My fiancée held up her hands. "Sorry. You were part of the job for a long time, babe. I took a lot of notes."

"Including what happened to Britt." I wasn't pissed. She was right; it was her job. We were just barely together when I told her about that, and she couldn't know this would come out of it. I never told her Brittany had a sister. Hell, I'd pretty much forgotten myself.

I turned back to Geri. "Then you know I killed my father."

"Not before he ripped my sister's heart out." That one hit me like a hammer to the gut. When she said it, I remembered what she looked like, laying in the creek with her blood turning the water red as it eddied around the rocks and sand.

57

"No," I said. "Not before he killed Brittany. I thought he was dead, but I was wrong. And me being wrong cost Britt her life. That's something I've had to live with for the last fifteen years, and I'm—"

"If you say you're sorry one more time, I swear to God I will snap these cuffs and rip your goddamn eyes out," she spat.

"What do you want me to say, Geri?"

"I don't want you to say anything. I want to kill your fat ass!"

"And I want a pony for Christmas, so I reckon we're both going to be disappointed," I said. "Because I don't have anywhere to put a pony, and I sure as hell ain't going to just let you kill me."

"Why?" she asked.

"Why what?" I was pretty sure she wasn't asking why I wasn't going to let her kill me, because that would be a stupid question, and she was a smart kid, even when she was seven.

"Why did he kill her?" This was what she wanted. She wanted, no, needed to understand why Brittany died.

"You read the file, right?" She nodded. "Then you know there was a lot more to it than just my daddy turning wolf and going nuts." Another nod. "My brother had some problems. One of those problems was he felt like he was always overlooked because I was older, and better at football, and better looking—"

"Nah, that was never it," Skeeter cut in. "Jason hated you for a lot of reasons, but even before he got turned, he had the looks in the family."

"Skeeter, would you pretty please piss off?" I asked. "Anyway, Jason had this crazy idea that he was going to unite all the monsters and take over the world. Keep humans as a food source and slaves and wipe out most of the rest of us."

"Your little brother was the Messiah?" Caufield asked. Hell, I'd almost forgot he was there, I was so focused on Geri. "That guy was crazy. I remember hearing about him and his plan to take over the world, or destroy the world, or something. He was nuts."

"Yeah, he was," I said, my voice flat.

"Whatever happened to him?"

"He got dead."

"Oh."

I turned my attention back to Geri. "So now you know. Jason had my father kill Britt, then I killed my father, then I killed Jason. There's a whole lot of dead people, and we're still alive. So what are we going to do about it?"

"I'm going to add one more to the list of dead people," Geri said, then she came off the couch at me, her cuffs gone and a short-bladed knife in her hand.

I wasn't nearly as surprised as she probably wanted to be, since this was exactly what I expected her to do. There was no way she came in here without at least one blade I didn't find, and she was way too compliant sitting on the couch to not be up to something. I knew she was probably going to get loose, and almost certainly come at me, so when she did, I just stood up and pushed her to my left as gently as I could. I didn't want to hurt her, I'd done enough of that, but I wasn't going to just let her stab me, either.

She was nimble, I had to give her that. She didn't hit the floor when I changed her flight path, just kinda rolled and spun and sprang at me again like one of the guys on those parkour videos. I've fought a lot of monsters that are faster than me, and with my bulk and bad knee, just about everything in the world is more agile than me, but I've got something very few humans have going for them—I'm built like a brick wall. A brick wall with more than a few extra fries and beers, sure, but there's a *lot* of me, and when I reached a hand out to stop a hundred-twenty-pound girl in midair, she damn well stops.

Geri ran into my outstretched palm with a *whoof* as the air rushed out of her lungs. I reached over and plucked the small knife out of her right hand and tossed it over to Caufield. "Hold that." He looked startled but caught it, which was better than me putting a hole in Skeeter's drywall with it. Then I shoved Geri straight back, and she fell down flat on her butt. "Sit still," I said. "I don't want to hurt you."

"Too bad," she wheezed. "Because I damn sure want to hurt you." She pulled up her pants leg and snatched loose another knife from a sheath on her leg. Dammit, this chick carried more armament than I did. How the hell did I miss that one? Must have been distracted by the other knife in the same boot.

She came up off the floor at me, waving the knife around like she knew how to use it, and I didn't know what to do. I could take the knife away from her, sure. But I didn't know if I could do that without hurting her, and that was the last thing I wanted to do. Okay, die was the last thing I wanted to do, but hurting Britt's baby sister was pretty low on my list, too. "Back off, kid. If you keep waving that thing around, somebody's going to get hurt."

"That's the point, asshole." She lunged at me, and I danced back. There wasn't a whole lot of room in Skeeter's den with me, Geri, Skeeter, Caufield, and Amy all in there, plus furniture, so this needed to end fast, or one of us was going to end up bloody.

I took another step back and almost went over backward when my heel caught on Skeeter's coffee table. I managed to hang onto my feet and dodge the knife slashing at my guts, but it was a near thing.

"Oh, for Christ's sake," Amy said. "Get out of the way." She pushed past me and stared down the furious girl. "Calm your tits, kid, or I'm going to knock the shit out of you."

"Get out of the way, lady. I don't want to hurt anybody but Bubba."

"Too bad. You threaten my fiancé, I get protective. Now put the knife down before I put you down."

"Okay, your funeral." Geri reversed grip on the knife and rushed Amy. Bad idea. My badass fiancée, who a few months ago battled a literal dragon in Fairyland, was not worried about a pissed-off millennial with a boot knife. She stepped into Geri's charge, dropped her shoulder into the girl's stomach, and wrapped her right arm around her attacker's leg. Amy straightened up, hoisting Geri up onto her shoulders, and before the kid could react, just fell backward onto the coffee table in a picture-perfect Samoan Drop.

Geri landed hard, and the coffee table exploded into a shower of Swedish splinters as Skeeter's IKEA furniture met up with two angry American women. Amy rolled to her knees, then stood up, snatching up the knife and tossing it to the side. She reached down and pulled the groggy girl to her feet by her collar. Dragging Geri up to her face, she looked the dazed would-be avenging angel in the eye and said, "Calm. The Hell. Down."

Geri took a second to focus her eyes, then gave Amy a snarky grin and spit a gobbet of bloody phlegm right in her face. "Screw. You."

"Okay, kid. Your call." Amy let go of the girl's collar, took one step back, and laid a right hook on the side of Geri's face that spun her around twice before she dropped to the floor, out before her head hit the carpet. Amy turned to the rest of us and said, "Sorry about your table, Skeeter. Bubba, stop being such a little bitch. That girl came here to kill you. You want to win her heart and mind, fine. But try that *after* you make sure she can't murder your big dumb ass."

"Yes, ma'am," I said. I try not to disagree too much with women that just put serious pro wrestling moves on somebody in my best friend's living room.

"Good. Now what are we going to do with her?" Amy asked.

"Before you worry about that question, perhaps you should determine what you're going to do about that." I turned my attention to Caufield, who stood beside the front door pointing out one of the side windows.

"What is it?" I asked, moving his way.

"If I didn't know better, I'd say that a giant pile of very angry rocks is walking toward the house."

Well, shit.

10

S ure enough, it looked for all the world like Skeeter's front yard was all pissed off and walking toward the house. I mean, I assumed it was pissed off because every supernatural creature I ever ran into was pissed off about something, usually me. "What the ever-loving hell is that?" I asked.

"Another golem?" Skeeter stepped up to the window and scooted around to look through one of the lower panes. I figured we resembled nothing more than an episode of *Scooby-Doo*, but that kinda fit with us. The thing cast long shadows across my truck as it moved forward, lit up by the floodlights Skeeter mounted to the corners of his roof. Despite it being full dark, there was no problem with visibility.

"That, gentlemen, is an earth elemental," Amy said from the other side of the door. "Or at least a reasonable facsimile. It's an animated and sentient creature made from the soil and minerals of a certain area. They occur naturally but are exceedingly rare in the eastern portion of the United States. They're much more common out west, where the population is sparser and the land has room to exist with less interference from men and their technology."

I stared at my fiancée, who suddenly sounded like an encyclopedia entry on a creature I only knew from a Kevin Hearne novel thirty seconds ago.

"What? I do some research. What's the point of working for a shadowy government agency if you don't study?"

"You've just never done anything like that before," I said.

"You've already known about everything else we've run into, or there wasn't anything in the files, so I didn't know anything, either. But I read a lot about elementals. At least it isn't fire or air. Those are really hard to deal with."

"And that thing isn't?" Right now, it looked like the only thing we had going for us was that it was slow as hell. It hadn't even gotten all the way up Skeeter's driveway yet, much less across his front yard. But once it got to the porch, I had my doubts about whether or not the reinforced door frame, or the wall it was set into, could stop that thing.

"Oh, it's hard as hell to take out, but it's not living flame, so it won't be able to burn you to a crisp from fifty feet away or suck all the oxygen from your lungs without laying a finger on you."

"Yeah, that's worse," I agreed. "Skeeter, load up your Mossberg with slugs and cover me." I pulled open the door, but Amy reached over with one hand and slammed it shut.

"Do you have a plan?" she asked, her blue eyes boring holes into me. Ever since we got engaged, she was a whole lot less willing to let me run face-first into danger like an idiot. I wasn't sure if she was practicing for a lifetime of keeping me from killing myself, or if she didn't want me doing anything to screw up her wedding plans.

"Of course I have a plan," I said, stepping back from the door to let Skeeter go get his shotgun and start loading it up with silver slugs. "I always have a plan."

"Is it stupid?"

Okay, she had me there. While I always *had* a plan, I didn't often have a *good* plan. Most of the time my plans consist of shooting or punching things until they stopped moving. Since the thing in Skeeter's yard was made of nothing but animated red Georgia clay, I didn't think there was a whole lot of chance of me getting anywhere with my fists. So I was pretty much down to Plan A. "I'm gonna go out there and introduce that muddy-livered bastard to Bertha. A lot."

"You think you can kill an earth elemental by shooting it with a pistol?" Amy didn't look like it was the craziest thing that had ever come out of my mouth, but let's face it, that's a pretty high bar. And we just spent a year and a half running around every corner of Fairyland, so her tolerance for crazy was pretty high. But she did look like I'd made the Top Ten with a bullet.

"It's a really *big* pistol," I said. I even pulled Bertha out of my holster to show her. She knew, of course. She knew exactly how big Bertha was, and exactly the kind of damage that fifty-caliber bullets did to most things, supernatural or otherwise.

"That is an almost obscenely large pistol. If I were more Freudian, I would say you must be compensating for something," Caufield observed drily from the doorway of the safe room. "I am going back in the vault. Anyone who would like to join me, the door will remain unlocked for two minutes. After that, I am engaging the interior locks."

"You should go with him," I said to Amy. "I'll take care of Rocky out there and let you know when it's all clear."

"Rocky?"

"What else would you call him?"

"You're impossible."

"That's why you love me. You like a challenge. Now grab Sleeping Badass over there and get to safety. I'll let you know when it's clear." I pointed to the unconscious Geri.

"We'll know everything that's going on," Skeeter said, bringing me the shotgun. I holstered Bertha and slung the twelve-gauge over one shoulder. "I've got security cameras mounted to the roof that cover the whole yard. But turn your earwig on."

I fished it out of my pocket, blew the lint off, twisted it on, and stuck it down in my left ear canal. Now Skeeter could talk to me. I wasn't a hundred percent sure if that was a good thing. "I better go. Y'all get into the safe room. I'll be back when I blow Rocky all to hell."

Amy gave me a quick kiss and went over to haul Geri into the vault, and I walked to the front door. "Lock it behind me, Skeet."

"Don't get dead, brother."

We bumped fists, and I stepped out onto the porch, unslinging the shotgun from my shoulder and checking the chamber. Loaded. Good. The elemental looked even bigger from out here, but it was a lot closer, too. It was now even with my truck, and I really wanted to move the conflict away from my wheels, but there wasn't enough room between where it stood and the porch for me to do anything but what I do best—charge right in.

"Hey, Rocky! Watch me pull a shotgun out of a hat!" I yelled, then leapt off the porch and dropped to one knee. I blasted the pile of rock and mud with a twelve-gauge slug from ten yards out, and its head exploded. "Hell yeah!" I hollered. "I got it, Skeeter!"

"You got it, but it didn't fall down. Or stop. Or really seem to give a shit," Skeeter said in my ear. I'd forgotten exactly how much I didn't like having him riding along with me everywhere like a gay Jiminy Cricket, which might be redundant. I've never thought about Jiminy Cricket's sexual orientation before.

But Skeeter was right. I blew the elemental's head right off, but it didn't miss a step. It just grew another head right out of its torso, just sprouted a new glob of red clay and granite right on top of the other globs of red clay and granite. "Well, shit."

I ran at the thing, firing the shotgun as I went. Every blast hit, and every blast blew off chunks of mudman, but it never slowed. It didn't even lose mass because after the third time I shot off a chunk of its torso, it just stopped for a second, then sank into the ground a little. When it stepped out of the hole, I realized that the damn thing had just absorbed more soil and rocks into itself to replace the missing bits. "Double shit."

I stood still and fired the last couple of slugs at the thing, this time aiming at its knees. That, at least, knocked it over and slowed its progress, but just long enough for it to suck up more of Skeeter's front yard to replace its pieces.

"You can't kill that thing, Bubba. You can't do enough damage to it," Amy said in my ear.

"I noticed," I replied. "Any bright ideas? How do you make one of these things? Is it like a golem, where there's a scroll in its mouth?"

"No," she said. Which was kinda good, since I'd blown the thing's head off three times, and I knew whatever was important wasn't there, and I really didn't want to think where else I was going to have to stick my hand.

I froze as an idea hit me. It was kind of an awful one, but as long as I made myself keep saying, "It's only dirt," I might be able to manage it. "You said I couldn't do enough damage. What did you mean?" I asked. The elemental was starting to rise, having grown its legs back, so I drew Bertha and shot off its brand-new legs. A fifty-caliber bullet isn't as big as a slug from a shotgun, but the results are pretty close to the same thing.

"The only ways to destroy an elemental are by exposure to its opposite element, in this case air, or to damage its body enough that the component parts forget that they're supposed to be together. Then the... I don't know, the soul of the elemental just returns to the earth until the next time it's roused."

"What's the opposite element of earth?" I asked.

"Air."

"Well, that don't make no sense. It's exposed to a shitload of air right now, and it ain't hurting it none!"

"If you can pull a tornado out of your ass, that would probably do the trick."

"I can't, but I might be able to do the exact opposite," I said. I shot off the thing's regrown legs again, and the elemental flopped face-down on the dirt. If I had enough ammunition, I could just stand there and shoot it until it got bored, but I had the sneaking suspicion that wasn't going to be anytime soon.

With it crippled from being shot in the kneecaps again, the monster was just lying on its front in the yard sucking up dirt and rocks to put itself back to together. I had probably twenty seconds before it got back to its feet and I had to either shoot its legs off again or come up with a new plan. So I walked around behind the thing, shook my head at the thought of what I was about to do, and pulled one of the grenades I took off Geri out of a side pocket of my pants.

"You know, at this point in my career, I ain't even embarrassed about this," I said, looking straight at the camera mounted under the eave of Skeeter's porch. Then I bent over, whispered "I'm sorry about this" to the elemental, and shoved the grenade up its ass until the pineapple-shaped explosive was in there up to my elbow. I yanked my hand out, bringing the pin and the lever out with me. I felt the warm embrace of the red mud of the creature all the way in and out, and when my arm came out, there was a wet squelching noise.

I didn't take time to think about what I'd done; I just hauled ass away from the elemental and ducked down behind Skeeter's car. I hit my knees just as a muffled *whomp* came from the grass, then rocks and mud and dirt cascaded down all over the yard like it was a damn rainstorm. I stood up and looked around, and there wasn't a chunk of animated earth bigger than a dinner plate left intact anywhere. "I got it," I said.

"Did you just shove a grenade up an earth elemental's ass?" Skeeter asked over the comm.

"Yup."

"That might be the most disturbing thing you've done since you grabbed Bigfoot's wiener."

"Yup."

"You seem remarkably calm about this."

"Thing's dead, right?"

"Yeah."

"We're not dead, right?"

"Yeah."

"If it keeps me and mine alive, I'll shove grenades up as many asses as it takes, Skeeter."

"That's a sound philosophy, Bubba."

"I thought so. But I think I've got a weird ringing in my ears. More like a rumbling."

"That's not your ears. You really hear a rumble. About a dozen motorcycles just turned off the main road and are rolling up my driveway. We've got company."

"Did you make a bunch of new friends in the Hell's Angels you ain't told me about, Skeeter?"

"Nope."

"Then this is gonna suck."

11

I didn't even bother going back in the house. I just sat down on the porch and waited. I had Bertha, one extra magazine of regular ammunition, one magazine of silver bullets, and half a mag of cold iron rounds. The Mossberg was pretty much just an over-priced baseball bat, but the Judge was packing three shells of silver shot and two .45 long rounds. Besides that, the knife on my belt and one grenade was what I had to work with. And my wit and charm, of course.

I was probably going to need more bullets. Inspiration struck just as the first bike cleared the top of the driveway, and I went over to the truck, flipped up the back seat, and grabbed a box of ammo for Bertha. Then I went back to the porch and sat there reloading the magazine while company came up into the yard.

One or two of the guys on motorcycles looked vaguely familiar, but it wasn't until the last guy rolled up on a metallic purple trike wearing an open-faced helmet and a grinning skull facemask that I had any idea who they were.

But when Big Tony stepped off his trike onto Skeeter's driveway, there was no mistaking him, mask or no mask. He wore a leather vest instead of the tank top he sported when we were in his gym, but those arms were pretty unmistakable. I don't meet too many dudes with biceps the size of my quads, and when I see them twice in one day, well, night by this point, they tend to stick out. Once I recognized Tony, the rest of the group all clicked into place. They were the weres that had been lifting at Tony's gym.

"It's a long ride from Atlanta, Tony, and it ain't been dark that long. Did you stop somewhere to peel off the sun-proofed bodysuit?" I figured he was here to try and kill me, so there was nothing to lose by needling him a little.

"I have a van," the musclebound vampire said. "Soon as I could get some wind on my face, I did." He peeled off the helmet and mask, then hung his safety glasses on the handlebars, showing that he had, in matter of fact, not let any wind touch his face at all, but I didn't think that one was worth commenting on.

"What can I do for you, Tony? Did you suddenly remember who wanted to kill Caufield and couldn't just look up my email on MonsterHuntin.com, so you had to haul ass up here and tell me in person?"

"Why did you send 'em, you son of a bitch? We weren't bothering nobody. We just wanted to pump a little iron, chill out, and be left the hell alone. So what the hell did you send them after us for?"

Now, I've spent a lot of time in my life confused about all kinds of things. I mean, we live in a world where Clemson wins national championships, and when an ACC school that ain't FSU wins football games, you know there's some weird shit going on. But I had rarely heard anything as absolutely indecipherable as what came out of Big Tony's mouth. I was so confused all I could do was look up from my seat on the porch steps and say, "Huh?"

"Don't you 'huh' me, asshole! I know you sent 'em because you were the only stranger to come to the gym this whole week. So it ain't no coincidence that not an hour after you left, two van loads of DEMON agents pulled up in our parking lot and tried to haul everybody off to some kind of cryptid concentration camp. So quit acting innocent and stand up so I can whoop your ass like a man!"

I stood up, slammed the magazine into Bertha, and chambered a round. Then I slowly de-cocked the hammer and holstered my girl. I stepped forward, not far enough to be within arm's reach, but close enough to show I wasn't intimidated by the musclebound vampire. And I wasn't, if we're being honest. A scrawny wuss-looking vampire or a short fat one is likely to be just as strong as Meathead here, and if I wasn't scared of Poindexter vamp, I sure wasn't going to be worried about Hulkamania vamp.

"I'm standing," I said, holding my hands out at my sides. "But I didn't send no agents to your place. I ain't exactly DEMON's favorite person these days, on account of being half-Fae myself."

"You're a half-Faerie?" Tony asked, looking me up and down.

"I'd show you my pointy ears, but apparently that only happens in video games. But yeah, my mama is Fae. Daughter of Mab and Oberon, as a matter of fact, so I reckon I'm like a better-looking Jon Snow."

Tony laughed. "You know nothing, Bubba Snow. That's some rich shit. But we didn't come here to listen to you spout some bullshit about being innocent. We came here to beat your ass." As much as he said he wanted to kick my ass, his eyes kept scanning Skeeter's house like he was looking for something else.

"Well, I hope you packed a lunch, son." I drew Bertha and took two steps back so I stood on the porch instead of in front of it. This gave me the slight defense of Skeeter's porch railing to funnel them to me and make it harder for me to get flanked. I hoped.

"Guns? I thought you were a real man. Asshole." Tony spat on the ground next to me, and I decided it was time to cut the bullshit and get things rolling. So I shot him in the leg.

The giant vampire dropped like a stone, his leg half blown off from the big bullet, and I heard the door of Skeeter's cabin click open.

"Straight back, Bubba," Amy said, and I moved backward as fast as my legs would carry me. The weres around Tony stood frozen at the sight of their leader screaming on the ground with blood spouting from his leg, but the wound was already starting to heal. I didn't really want to kill anybody over a misunderstanding, so I didn't use silver. He'd heal, but that was going to hurt like hell while he did.

I made it through the door and heard the reassuring *thunk* as Skeeter engaged the locks. "That won't hold them long, but it'll give us a few minutes," he said.

I looked around the den, and it looked like everybody but Caufield was out of the panic room. Even Geri was there and didn't look like she wanted to murder me right that second. "Good news," I said. "We know how to fight weres and vampires. Bad news, there's a bunch of damn weres out there."

"How did they find us?" Skeeter asked. "I keep this place pretty off the map."

"He said DEMON agents came to his gym, right?" Geri asked.

I looked at her, and she didn't have the look of somebody who was trying to get me killed, so I just answered her. "Yeah."

"Then he probably grabbed a tracker from one of their team and traced you that way," she said.

"What tracker?" I asked.

"The tracker DEMON puts in all their agents." She held up her arm, palm toward her body, and pointed to her forearm. "You can feel the little lump right above your wrist. That's where they usually put it. If your arms are skinny, they might put it in your thigh." She directed this at Skeeter, but I held my spaghetti arms comments for the time being.

"I didn't sign up to have no damn tracker put in my arm," I said.

"I did, though," Amy said. "I'm sorry. I just forgot about it. I figured they stopped tracking me when they fired me, so I never imagined they'd come after us or anybody around us."

"They must have kept track of your movements today and pegged the gym as a place with a significant cluster of paranormals. Then they sent in a team. Those guys are lucky. Usually those teams don't leave survivors."

"Did you see the arms on that guy? The team will be lucky if they aren't bent into pretzels," I said. As if to prove my point, a thunderous *BOOM* came from the front door. I looked to the TV over the fireplace, where Skeeter had rerouted his security cameras. That boom? That was just Big Tony's fist.

"Get your ass out here, Bubba!" he yelled through the door. "You come out here, take your ass-kicking, and nobody has to die."

"I thought we were gonna kill him, Tony," one of the beefier, but apparently not brighter, weres said from beside the musclebound vampire.

"We don't want to tell him that, moron. We want him to come out here and think it's just going to be a fight, not a slaughter."

"Oh, sorry." The guy turned to the door. "We totally aren't going to murder you! Just beat you up a little. It's going to be a fight, no slaughter at all!" He looked at Big Tony, who just shook his head and punched the door again.

"How long do you think that door will hold, Skeet?" I asked.

"The door? Forever. The rest of the building? About thirty seconds after they realized not every wall is as reinforced as that one."

"Shit. I need a plan." I looked around the room for inspiration, but nothing was coming.

"You might need two," Geri said. Every head in the room whipped around to her. "Well, you need a plan to deal with the weres, but you're gonna need a plan to deal with DEMON, too."

"How do you mean?" Amy asked.

"If DEMON is tracking y'all and taking out people you visit, that means they've decided that you're not any more use to them as assets. So you're disposable."

"And you think they're on their way here to do that disposing," I said.

Geri pointed to Amy's arm. "That little beacon right there is going to lead them right to you, too. So if you need me, I'll be back in the safe room." She turned and walked into the panic room, Caufield at her heels.

"Hey!" I protested. "Where are you going? You're the strongest one here."

"I'm a lover, not a fighter," Caufield replied. "Keep me alive, and I'll pay you double."

73

"Triple," Skeeter said. "Retroactive."

"Done." Then the vampire and my dead girlfriend's kid sister went into the bank vault-like safe room in my best friend's house and pulled the door shut.

Amy looked between me and Skeeter. "Now what?" she asked.

"I've got a plan," I said. I pulled out my pocketknife. "Skeeter, get the vodka."

"Your plan involves your pocketknife and vodka?" Amy said. "This I gotta see."

"No, sweetheart, this you gotta be a part of." I dragged her over to the kitchen table, sat down, and took the bottle of vodka from Skeeter. I stretched Amy's forearm out over the table, poured a healthy splash of vodka over it, and then poured some more over the blade of my pocketknife.

"What the hell are you doing?" Amy asked, trying to yank her arm back.

"Hold still," I said. "Skeeter, rub her arm until you find the tracker."

His eyes got big as he figured out at least part of what I intended. "Is there any way this turns out to be a good idea?" he asked.

"You hear that pounding on your front door?"

"Yeah."

"You hear the slightly less terrifying pounding on your back door?"

"Yeah."

"You got a better idea?"

"No."

"Then show me where that tracker is." He pointed to a spot on Amy's arm, and I looked my fiancée in the eye. "Remember. You love me," I said, then sliced open her forearm. That part was bad, but it wasn't the worst part. The worst part was when I reached into her arm, when I parted the skin with my fingers, and pulled out the little Tic-Tac-sized tracking device.

"Got it," I said. "Skeeter, get that arm bandaged up." While he took a heavily cursing Amy over to the sink and started cleaning her arm, I washed the tracker off with more vodka, put it in my mouth, and swallowed it.

"There we go," I said. "The tracker is taken care of. At least for a couple days."

"Did you smash it?" Amy asked.

"Nope. If it went offline, DEMON would just trace it to the last location. This way, they've got something to follow."

"Follow where?" she asked.

"I need to get somewhere with more guns," I said. "And if I end up having to fight somebody for real, I want my sword and my gauntlets." The gauntlets in question were a pair of *caestae* that Amy got me for Christmas a couple years ago. They came with a set of silver spikes, pretty damn good for werewolf punching.

"You're going to your house?" she asked. "Bubba, that's ten miles."

"Not as the crow flies," I said. "If I go through the woods and the hollers, it ain't but about two. I can run it in twenty minutes or so, and the weres will follow me. Then the DEMON agents will track me, and they'll show up at the house. The two groups will fight each other, and I'll sit on the porch and drink beer."

"That's a terrible idea," Skeeter said.

"Yeah, but it's the one we've got. You take care of her," I said. Then I walked down the hall to Skeeter's back door and yanked it open, much to the shock of the were-bear standing there beating on it. I assume he was a were-bear, given his height, bulk, and impressive amount of body hair. But maybe a were-gorilla. I can't tell the difference in their human form. I didn't bother to ask. I just shot him in the right shoulder with Bertha, punching a hole the size of a dinner plate in his back as the bullet went through. Regular bullet, though. I still didn't want to kill these guys if I could help it.

He dropped like a stone; I stepped through the door and pulled it closed after me. Then I shot the two weres on the back porch and hopped down to Skeeter's back yard. I jogged over to the fence and spun around to face the back of the house.

"Hey, assholes!" I yelled. "Back here!" Then I fired Bertha twice more, this time straight up, hopped the fence, and started the run from Skeeter's house to mine. A few seconds later, I heard the sound of a dozen or so weres crashing through the underbrush in hot pursuit.

So I was running through the woods in the middle of the night, a hundred pounds overweight, with bad knees and a lifetime of injuries from sports and monster hunting. I was being chased by a pissed-off vampire and a passel of bloodthirsty shapeshifters. I really, *really* wanted to go back to just being the bouncer at the Don't Drop Inn.

12

It's not easy running through the woods with a pack of werewolves on your tail at night. It's even harder when you're reloading your pistol while running. I wish this was the first time I had cause to learn that. The good part was that I had a full moon to give me some light, so I wasn't trying to navigate by the light of my cell phone light while giving my pursuers essentially a neon arrow over my head giving away my location. Not that there was any secret as to where the hell I was. Dudes my size do not move through the woods without breaking a few branches, or in my case, saplings.

The other good part was that I knew the woods between Skeeter's house and mine like the back of my hand. It was basically down a deep holler, up the other side, over one hill, up that gulley to my place. I'd walked it a thousand times or more. Usually in the daytime, but not always, and not always this sober, either. The bad part was the full moon that gave me all that light? Yeah, it also supercharged the passel of weres on my tail.

Now weres, be they wolf or what have you, can transform whenever they feel like it. And they aren't forced into the change every night of the full moon. It's a lot easier that time of the month, and most of them usually *want* to shift then, because they're stronger, faster, and all their senses are heightened. All the things that I really didn't need from a bunch of monsters that happened to be pursuing me through the woods.

The first one to catch up to me was a half-shifted fox. She was a little thing, but she was *fierce*. She came flying at me out from behind a big old oak and slammed me right into a pine tree, almost knocking the poor evergreen clear to the ground. In her half-shifted state, she was about four feet tall, with sleek red hair all over her body, and small razor-sharp claws tipping her fingers. She came at me with those claws flashing, and I dropped to one knee and punched her right in the guts.

I'm usually pretty averse to punching a woman, but this was a choice between punching her and shooting her in the face, so I thought hitting her was the more chivalrous option. I also didn't want to kill any of these folks over a misunderstanding. I might be the type to shove a grenade up an elemental's ass without so much as a "Hey, please stop trying to kill me," but if I've got the chance to talk things out, I usually will. Unless it's just a bar fight. Sometimes you need to blow off a little steam, so you break a few tables. That's just good, clean fun.

She doubled over when I hit her, but it wasn't because I knocked the wind out of her. Nope, she just bent at the middle to bite a chunk out of my ear with her needle-sharp little fox teeth. "Ow, goddammit! Cut that shit out!" I yelled, standing up. I swatted her off the side of my head, but she launched herself at me again, reaching for my eyes with all ten claws. I decided enough was damn enough, and with blood streaming down the side of my neck and profanity flowing like water, I snatched her out of the air and slammed her headfirst into the trunk of a nearby tree. Her eyes rolled back in her head, and she shifted back to her very muscular, very naked, human form as she slumped to the ground, out cold.

I couldn't just leave her there like that, it wouldn't be right. I knew that weres have different views on nudity than I do, but I was raised to try and respect women, and I couldn't just leave her laying out there all naked. So I stripped out of my long-sleeve overshirt, laid it over her, and took off running for Skeeter's again. I figured that not only had any lead I once had evaporated while I danced with Foxy Loxy, but now I was leaving a blood trail to go with the swatch of fast destruction I was carving out of the wilderness. If I had any chance of getting away from these folks, it was long gone.

I kept on running, though. I couldn't turn around, and stopping would just leave me surrounded, so I pushed on, even when I started to catch glimpses of half-stooped forms out of the corner of my eye. I kept running, and I regretted every single morning that I laid in bed watching Amy's ass while she did her morning yoga instead of getting up and exercising with her. I didn't regret watching her ass—it was truly spectacular, a damn natural wonder—but I did regret not working on my cardio.

Finally, I staggered out of the woods behind my house, panting for breath and sweating buckets. Half a dozen weres of various breeds stood in a semicircle, some leaning against the house, some just standing with their arms folded waiting for me. None of them looked like they even broke a sweat. Foxy had shifted back to her half-vulpine form, but she did have the good grace to bring my shirt with her. It was folded up on the back steps of the house. I'd probably have to wash it if I didn't die. Wouldn't do to have Amy finding a strange fox's hairs on my collar.

"Okay," I panted. I looked around at the assembled shifters and raised my fists. "Who wants some first?" The answer wasn't me, but I didn't think I had a choice in the matter.

"Do you need some water, dude? You look like you're about to fall over," a young were-tiger said, his voice low and gravelly around the fangs.

"I'll be fine. Y'all just figure out who I shoot first." I reached under my left arm and unsnapped Bertha from her holster. "My sweetie here is loaded with silver now, so I'm done screwing around. If y'all feel froggy, jump on."

"I find that phrase offensive," a little human-looking dude with kinda bugged-out eyes said.

"Are you a were-frog?" I asked.

"Well, no. I'm a were-lemur."

"Then shut the hell up."

"Dude, that is exactly what we keep trying to tell him." This was the stocky dude I remembered from the gym. Judging by his half-shifted form, I was right when I pegged him as a were-badger. Not only did the coloring and stripes seem to match, he just carried himself like he didn't give a shit. "He's a monk from the Temple of the Perpetually Offended or something. But look, we came all the way here, and it wasn't for tea and friggin' cookies. We're probably gonna kill you, we just wanna know why first."

"Why what?" I asked. Walking toward my back door, I stopped and stared at the guy sitting on my steps in human form. "You wanna get the hell outta my way, or do you want to get shot in the face?"

He didn't answer, just slunk away. Not making any challenges for Alpha anytime this century, that guy. I sat down on the steps and looked at Were-Badger. "Like I told Tony back at Skeeter's place, I didn't send no DEMON agents to y'all's gym. Hell, even if I did call them, I doubt they'd listen to a tip from me anyhow. They were probably tracking Amy from some damn chip they implanted in her arm back when she worked for 'em."

"You expect us to believe that the government microchipped its employees like a Labrador?" asked a dude covered in sleek black fur. I was guessing were-panther.

"What? You think the federal government suddenly developed a conscience?" I shot back. I looked back to Badger. "How did y'all find us? I didn't exactly leave Big Tony an address so he could come tip back a few cold ones."

"We took a GPS tracker off one of the...shit."

"I'm guessing the rest of that sentence went something like you took a tracker off one of the DEMON agents and it led you right to the cabin?"

"Yeah, pretty much."

"So now you believe me?"

"Hell no. You're still in the government's pocket! Let's kill him!" I don't know what this dude was half-shifted to, but whatever it was, it was ugly as sin, covered in short, bristly hair, and had the beginnings of a pair of tusks growing out of the corner of his mouth. He stepped closer, trying to loom over me.

Bad idea. I loom better than just about anybody, and I sure as shit don't appreciate people trying to do it to me. When Tusk-Boy came in close, I stood up, fast. As I did, I brought Bertha up under his jaw, snapping his head back and leaving his throat exposed. I put my fist right on his Adam's apple, and he crumpled like generic tin foil. I whirled around, yanked open the back door of my house, and darted inside.

I slammed the door behind me, knowing full well that wasn't going to hold for more than a few seconds. I didn't need it to. I just needed time to get to the den, snatch my gauntlets and sword off the mantle, and haul ass to the front yard where there was more room to maneuver.

I blew through the front door about the same time I heard the back door disintegrate behind me. I shoved Bertha into her holster, slung the sword across my back, and snugged up the *caestae* on my fists. The left glove had cold iron studs screwed in at the knuckles, a remnant from our recent trip to Fairyland, but I'd swapped out the right-hand studs with silver last week when I was polishing them. I thought having the one fist shiny and the other fist dark looked cool on the mantle, but right about then, I really wished I was into more bling so I'd have two fists wrapped in were-beating metal.

I got myself out into the yard with a good twenty feet of clear space around me by the time the weres came around, through, and *over* my house. Yeah, a pair of them, apparently were-chimps, came over the rooftop and screeched down at me. I flipped them off.

Badger came through the house and never stopped moving. He ran straight at me like I was between him and his favorite dessert, head down and arms pumping. He was solid, but he still gave up nine inches and at least a hundred pounds, so I just braced myself and slammed my right fist into his forehead right before he could reach me with his curved claws. He stood straight up on impact, his eyes crossed, and he collapsed to his back, out cold. That was how all my fights should start—taking out one of the baddest dudes in the bunch with one shot.

That was not how this fight would continue, of course. There were too many of them, and I was just one (mostly) human against almost a dozen weres of various species. I scrapped pretty hard, but I knew I was fighting a losing battle. I just hoped my hunch was right and the cavalry was about to come rolling up the hill.

I slammed an elbow into the back of Mr. Were-Panther's head as he tackled me, knocking him loopy and giving myself some separation from the pack. No cavalry. I ducked under the leaping were-chimps and backhanded one of them across the yard. No cavalry. I wrestled the were-bear until I had to cheat and knee him in the balls to get out from under his smelly ass, but still no damn cavalry. I was starting to think my hunch wasn't worth a shit when Big Tony stepped out of the woods.

"Stop playing around," he said. "Grab his arms." The heretofore inept weres latched onto my forearms, jerked them out straight from my body, and stripped my gauntlets off me in two seconds flat. Then the nearest were-chimp twisted my arms around behind me, held my wrists together, and secured my hands with oversized zip ties. I tried very hard not to wonder where he carried zip ties when all the shifters were naked as jaybirds. I tried even harder not to wonder why the zip ties were so warm.

"Now, I've got some questions, Bubba. And the answers to these questions will determine if we beat the shit out of you or if we rip your throat out and leave you to drown in your own blood. Do you understand me? And know that if you give me a smartass response, I will knock the ever-loving shit out of you."

"What about a dumbass response? Because that's what Amy and Skeeter say I give to most questions." He was true to his word. He laid his open palm across my cheek and slapped the piss out of me. I went over like a sack of smashed potatoes, and the were-chimp had to pull me back up to my knees.

"Now, do you understand me?"

"I understand you alright. I just don't give a shit." Sometimes I get myself in troubling situations, and I ask myself "What Would Jesus Do?" Big Tony didn't make me wonder. He didn't even make me do what Jesus would have done. He turned the other cheek for me and slapped the hell out of the other side of my face. This time I had a mouthful of dirt and grass to spit out when the were yanked me up.

But this time I didn't stop when he pulled me to my knees. I got my feet under me and pushed myself off the ground, stepping forward until my face was barely an inch from Big Tony's. "You think that intimidates me? You think I'm scared now because you slapped the hell out of me? You don't know where I've been, son. I've seen the inside of Fairyland dungeons, been tortured for hours, then healed up so I could be tortured again, fought a damn *dragon*, and had to share a bathroom with Skeeter. There ain't shit on this world can scare me, son. So go ahead. Beat my ass. Rip my damn throat out. Do what you're gonna do. I double-damn dare you."

He drew a breath to speak, but I cut him off. "But before you raise your hand to me again, know this—I had nothing to do with DEMON coming after you in Atlanta. I didn't know they had a tracker in Amy, and them coming down on your gym had not a damn thing to do with me. You have my word on that shit."

That's when I heard it. All my running, all my scuffling, all my bluster, and all my stalling had finally been enough. I heard the sound of tires on gravel, and a pair of headlights crested the rise of my drive-way, followed by three more as four matte-black Suburbans rolled up into my front yard and disgorged a score of DEMON agents in full tactical gear.

I grinned at Big Tony as he turned from the men with submachine guns to gape at me. "This right here? These assholes rolling up in my driveway and drawing down on us? Yeah, that one's all me."

1 3

A tall, almost skeletally thin black man with a trim goatee and salt-and-pepper hair stepped out of the passenger seat of the lead SUV. Unlike all the tactical troops around him, this man wore a suit, dress shoes, and a long black wool coat. He had gold wire-rimmed glasses and no tie, his once concession to informality. He held up a hand, and the DEMON assault team pointed their guns to the sky. "We don't shoot first, gentlemen. That's not how civilized beings behave. Is it, Mr. Brabham?"

"I wouldn't know," I said, thickening my already-heavy Southern accent. "I ain't never been called civilized much."

"You can play the uncultured hick as much as you like, Mr. Brabham, but I assure you that I have read your file and know exactly how intelligent you are." The reflection off my security lights obscured his eyes and made him look somehow unearthly, even though everything I'd heard about this dude said he was nothing but pure human through and through.

"Please allow me to introduce myself." He stepped forward but froze at a growl from Honey Badger.

"Let me guess," I said. "You're a man of wealth and taste?" He looked puzzled, so I decided he wasn't a Stones fan and just motioned for him to go on.

"My name is Director Sebastian Shaw, and I am the new Director of Cryptid Affairs for DEMON. I have been tasked with evaluating, and if necessary eliminating, the supernatural population of the entire United States."

I couldn't help it. I knew I was going to regret it the second I opened my mouth, but I couldn't stop myself. Sometimes I'm like a spectator to the train wreck that is my life, and this was absolutely one of those times. "Was your dad a huge comic book nerd, or did your mom have an affair with Chris Claremont?" Two or three of the weres laughed out loud, and I saw a couple of the agents snicker.

Shaw, of course, just looked confused. Naturally, a dude who wouldn't realize he was quoting Mick Jagger didn't know he had the same name as a comic book villain. "I'm sorry?"

"Yeah, me too," I said. I shook my head. "No, really. I'm sorry. I'm being childish. It's just that you have the same name as a bad guy from the *X-Men* comics, and I found it funny. Please go on. You were standing in front of a dozen werewolves, were-badgers, were-panthers, and other lycanthropes telling the heavily armed half-Fae man how you were going to bring the monsters and the freaks under control." That time I didn't bother trying to sound polite. If this asshole was going to come up in my yard and threaten me, I saw no need to pretend to be nice about it.

"There is no need for bile, Mr. Brabham. I—"

"Bubba," I corrected.

"Excuse me?"

"My name is Bubba. You keep calling me Mr. Brabham, and I wonder if my Pop is around somewhere. And that would be kinda weird since I killed my werewolf father about a half mile back in the woods behind my house. So if he is here, we've got bigger problems than fleas and a bunch of toy soldiers."

"Okay…Bubba it is. I don't need to be an adversary. I can help you. I can help you and your kind acclimate, move somewhere safe where you will be well cared for and allowed to live out your days among your own kind. We don't need to fight."

I leaned against one of the posts on my porch. "Damn, that's impressive."

"How's that?"

"I ain't never heard somebody get 'you peopled' in his own front yard and then get offered a place on the reservation in the next breath. You are an impressive son of a bitch, Director Shaw, I will give you that."

"You peopled?" He looked a little confused.

"Come on, dude. You're a black guy standing on a mountain in Georgia. Don't tell me you don't understand what it's like to have somebody look at you and talk about 'you people.' Judging from your suit, it's been a while since it's happened to you, but I know you know what I mean."

In the dark it was hard to see, but I'm pretty sure I detected a slight flush to his dark cheeks. "That's not what I—"

"Meant?" I cut him off. "Let me guess. Some of your best friends are monsters. There's this one dude you play golf with that's something like one-sixteenth Faerie, and you don't treat him any different." I straightened up and stepped down off the porch. "Let's be real damn clear here, Director. You didn't come here to send me and this bunch of shifters on some modern-day Trail of Tears. You rolled up here heavy as hell, guns out even though the sun ain't out, ready to open up a can of whoop-ass on whatever you found. Only problem is, you didn't bring but twenty dudes. And you know as well as I do twenty dudes can't take down a dozen pissed off weres, and when you figure in Big Tony and me, the odds get even worse. So you decided to talk your way out of this mess."

The whole time I'd been talking, I'd been walking forward real slow. Big Tony and the weres (which sounds like a badass cover band) caught on to what I was doing and advanced on the soldiers, making a semicircle stretching out to either side of me. By the time I finished, I was about six feet from Director Shaw, and I could see the lone bead of sweat break free and run from his temple down the side of his face, curling around the hinge of his jaw before it disappeared under his collar.

"There's just one problem, Director." I took another tiny step forward. "The problem is…you don't talk for shit." Another tiny step and I was almost right up on him. "You're probably real good in a board room, where you're surrounded by yes-men and sycophants, but out here?" Step. I was looking over him now, close enough I could smell the sweat biting the shit out of this morning's antiperspirant. "Out here, where the rubber meets the road? Out here where the fangs aren't in pictures and the claws aren't just pixels on a screen? Out here where if you say the wrong thing, somebody's going to get hurt, maybe killed? Out here, you're just another chickenshit paper-pusher working his way up the ranks without ever getting his hands dirty hiding behind the brave men and women whose asses have to cash the checks your mouth writes."

"Well now, Director Shaw, shit is about to get real, and you're right in the middle of it." I raised my right fist and drew back to punch this prissy bureaucrat right in the nose.

"You don't know how right you are, you half-breed piece of shit," Shaw said, his face twisting into an ugly snarl. "Shit is about to get real, because I didn't bring twenty agents. I brought fifty. And I brought this, too." Then he yanked a stun gun out of his pocket and jammed a million volts of electricity into my nuts. That's when my night really started to suck.

I dropped like a rock. A very large, very pissed-off rock, but a rock nonetheless. I had just about enough control of my muscles to see another shitload of DEMON agents come out of the tree line, guns drawn. They didn't give Tony's guys the first second of warning; they just opened fire. The chatter of MP-5s set for three-round bursts filled the night air. Half the weres went down in the first volley, but Big Tony didn't get hit, and the other half of the motley pack shifted into either their full of half-shifted forms and took the fight right to the agents.

Honey Badger barreled into four agents, and they all went down in a tangle of black tactical gear and lycanthrope fury. Big Tony was an almost literal bur of motion as he leapt from agent to agent, snatching guns away and punching people out right and left. None of the weres killed anybody, not that I could see. They could. It wouldn't take anything for a half-shifted wolf to rip an agent's throat out. Hell, it would probably be easier than keeping their opponents alive. But despite the fact that the government assholes were pumping out nine-millimeter rounds faster than a Kardashian takes selfies, the weres worked really hard to subdue, but not kill.

The DEMON agents were under no such orders, but strangely enough, for a bunch that should know everything there is to know about cryptids, they seemed to be firing regular bullets. There was plenty of lead flying, but that was just the problem. With the exception of me and the agents, there was nobody in the fight that could be killed by a lead bullet.

"Skeeter," I whispered into my comm. "Something weird is going on over here."

"It sounds like damn World War Three *and* Four is going on over there, Bubba." Skeeter's voice gets even more high-pitched and nasally when he's excited, which is just about any time he's on comm with me. That might be partly my fault.

"There's fifty DEMON agents shooting the shit out of my front yard and a bunch of werewolves beating the hell out of them, but nobody's trying to kill anybody."

"That don't make no sense," Skeeter said.

"I know," I whispered. "The feds are using regular bullets, and the weres are pulling their punches. I don't know what's going on."

"I believe I may," Caufield said, and for the first time, I realized they must all be listening to me on the system in the safe room. I'd thought me and Skeeter were having a phone call, and it turned out he had me on speakerphone. Good thing I didn't say anything too embarrassing.

"You want to clue me in?" I asked.

"This Director Shaw, is he a thin black man of about fifty years, or at least that's what he appears to be?"

"Yeah," I said.

"That's not what Director Shaw looks like. He's black, but he's barely thirty and looks like Carlton on *The Fresh Prince of Bel Air*," Amy said.

"I should be able to explain everything in a matter of moments," Caufield said. "Mr. Jones, please open the door."

The comm clicked off, and I looked up to see Shaw staring down at me with a smile on his face. His stun gun gone, he now held a Beretta pistol aimed down at my face. "I wondered how long it would take for you to make the call. Now that it's done, we can end this farce."

He raised his other hand, and a brilliant flash of amber light came from it. The gunfire stopped like somebody flipped a switch, and as soon as the weres saw nobody was shooting at them anymore, they stopped beating the shit out of the feds. Except Honey Badger, who looked around, grinned, and knocked out one last DEMON agent before shifting back to human and walking over to where Big Tony stood by the SUV.

I managed to pull myself up into a sitting position, not putting my hands anywhere close to either of my guns on account of the man with the gun aimed at my face. I watched in growing confusion as Big Tony, the pack, and the agents all gathered around the back of two Suburbans and started passing out beer and bandages. The weres took turns picking lead out of each other's hard to reach places, and they all generally behaved like a bunch of guys who just finished the eleventh inning of a marathon church softball game.

"Would somebody like to tell me just what the shit is going on here?" I asked. "I thought y'all were trying to kill each other. Now you're best buds? Did I miss a memo?"

"No, Bubba." Caufield's voice came from the corner of my house. He stepped into the clearing, his clothes a little worn from his sprint through the woods. "They were never here to kill each other, or you. They're all here to kill me."

1 4

I sat on the ground leaning against the SUV, looking from Caufield to Shaw to Big Tony and back again in a dizzying triangle of assholes and confusion. "Would somebody tell me exactly what the ever-loving shit is going on here?"

Shaw pointed to Caufield. "I believe you've figured it out, haven't you? Would you like to dazzle your fat friend with your intellect?"

"Right here," I said. "And I'm big boned."

He looked down at me, his lip curled up in a sneer that made me want to punch his face in. Unfortunately, I was still at the "trying to control my bladder" phase of recovering from being tased. "There are no bones in a beer gut. You're just fat."

I wasn't strong enough to punch him, but my middle finger had regained all mobility. I demonstrated that flexibility to him.

"This was all about getting to me," Caufield said. "And it was all him." He pointed to Big Tony, who shrugged and gave a little grin.

"Yeah, it was me. Took you long enough to figure it out."

"Your pet wizard has gotten stronger," Caufield said.

"There was a big kerfuffle downtown by the Ferris Wheel a couple years ago, and Sebastian picked up a new grimoire. He learned all sorts of things from it, including how to raise zombies. That was pretty cool, huh?" The big lummox seemed disproportionately happy with himself. Of course, he wasn't the one getting chased by the zombies and having to burn down his place of employment to get rid of them.

"Still waiting on somebody to tell me what the hell is going on?" I asked from the ground. I was also waiting on enough mobility to come back into my arms to draw my gun and shoot this asshole wizard, but I thought telling them that might be giving away the farm.

"Tony wants my hunting territory in Atlanta. I'm older, so I have a more affluent hunting zone. The only way to get a better place to hunt is to convince the vampire that holds the territory to give it to you. Usually that convincing involves killing the vampire. But Tony didn't want to face me like a real vampire, so he had his pet wizard come up with underhanded tactics to destroy me."

"I prefer to think of it as a more modern approach to problem-solving," Tony said. "But that's the gist of it. Caufield's been hunting Buckhead for fifty years, and I'm stuck out by the airport. I wanted some upscale cuisine, and he didn't want to share. He's a couple centuries older than me, so I didn't have a whole lot of shot in a fair fight. The whole system is tilted in favor of the wealthy and the estab-lishment, so I needed a new path to success. Enter Sebastian."

"How did you know where to send the zombies?" I asked.

Shaw looked down at me. "Tracking spell. I had a tiny amount of Caufield's hair from his Atlanta residence, and I used that to cast a tracking spell and send the zombies after him using that. Unfortu-nately, the spell only lasts for eight hours, so when you destroyed my zombies, I had no way of finding him again."

"Until I showed up at the gym," I said, glaring at Tony. I had feeling back in most of my body but still wasn't sure I had complete control of my extremities. I didn't want to try to throw a punch and look like Plastic Man flailing around.

"Exactly. That was expensive, by the way. I had to bribe every dark mage in Atlanta to have them funnel you to me. I couldn't know you'd find Lester first. You cost me a great deal of money, Bubba."

"I plan on costing you a lot of blood before I'm done," I growled from the ground.

"Bold words from a man who can't stand. When you came into the gym, I sent Ethan outside with an iPhone. He taped it inside the back bumper of your truck, I turned on the phone tracker app, and voila, instant tracker."

I had to give him props for that one. "Probably cheaper and more effective than most, too."

"Yep. So then we knew where to send the elemental. But given your effectiveness in dealing with the zombies, we figured we'd better follow up with a personal visit."

"So who the hell are those guys?" I asked, pointing at the DEMON agents, who now looked a lot like just an average bunch of mostly fit dudes hanging around a tailgate party.

"Oh, them? They're actors. Terry knew them from back when he was alive. I told him to come up with a distraction so we could draw Caufield out when we got here. I think he overdid it a little."

"I can't help it," said Honey Badger. "I did a lot of community theatre before I got bit. I couldn't resist the chance to stage one more big production number. I called up a bunch of guys I know who did stunt work on the last *Avengers* movie and told them we'd pay a couple hundred bucks plus catering, but they might really get punched a little. Then I told all our guys to pull their punches and try not to hurt anybody."

"What about him?" I pointed to the guy Honey Badger, now Terry I reckon, decked right at the end of the fight.

"Oh, that's Brad. He's a dick, but he's George's brother, and I wanted George to drive one of the SUVs, so I had to hire Brad. I'll pay him extra, but it's worth it for getting to lay his ass out."

"So this whole thing was a damn show? None of these are DEMON agents? Y'all weren't trying to kill anybody?"

"You're lucky he didn't add in a musical number," Tony said. "I'm serious. He was looking into speakers for the Suburbans when I told him we had to go."

"So all that bit about agents showing up at the gym?" I asked. I thought I knew the deal, but I just wanted to lock it in.

"Total bullshit."

"So Geri? Was she part of this mess? You sent her to plant the idea of DEMON tracking us and get me to cut the bug out of my fiancée's arm?"

"Who's Geri? And DEMON really did put trackers in y'all? That's messed up, man." Big Tony had proven that he was a good liar already, but I believed he didn't know anything about Britt's kid sister. She probably really was there to kill me.

"So now what?" I asked. "You didn't kill Caufield with magic. You didn't even kill me, so Caufield still has some protection. What are you going to do next?"

"I reckon now I'm just going to do this the old-fashioned way," Tony said. "I'm going to kill Caufield, and you're going to stay the hell out of it. If you don't, a shitload of lycanthropes are going to forget they ever swore not to eat long pig, and they're gonna feast on your fat ass."

I stood up. I was a little unsteady, but I drew myself up to my full height and said, "I'm getting about damn tired of people making disparaging comments about my weight."

"What the hell do you think you're going to do about it?" the skinny wizard said. He had to look up at me now, but I didn't like the way his hands glowed when he talked.

"I'm gonna start with this," I said. Then I reached out and covered the entire side of his head with my hand and slammed his face into the hood of the Suburban behind me. I bounced his head off the SUV twice, then added one more for good measure and let his limp body fall to the ground. "I feel better now. Anybody else got a comment about how damn fat I am?"

I looked around at the extras and the weres, but nobody looked real interested in arguing with three hundred fifty pounds of irritated redneck. "Good."

I stepped up to Big Tony and said, "Your little magician buddy caused me to burn down my place of employment, then you lied to me, chased me through the woods, and had a bunch of fake government agents shoot up the front of my house. That ain't even talking about the damage you did to Skeeter's door, and that thing was expensive."

"You want me to pay for all that shit? Kiss my ass."

"I don't want you to pay for all that. I want you to give me access to all your bank accounts, pack up your shit, get the hell out of Georgia, and never look sideways at me, Caufield, or any of my people ever again."

"And if I don't?"

I pulled Bertha from her shoulder holster, ejected the magazine full of regular bullets, and slammed home a clip of silver ammo. "If you don't, I'm going to kill you and take all your shit, just like you're a boss fight in a video game. You came to my house with this territory bullshit, shot up my front yard, and had your little asshole wizard tase me in the nutsack. I've staked vamps for looking at me wrong, so don't think I'm all cute and cuddly just because I've got a lot of body hair. I might not be able to bench press a Buick, but I got no qualms about shooting you again."

Tony reached out and slapped Bertha out of my hand, sending the big pistol flying to land in the grass twenty feet away. He got just a few inches away from my face and snarled at me. "What are you going to do now, human? Your gun is way over there, and you couldn't beat me in a fair fight when I was alive. Now you stand your fat ass down before I end you, and if you behave, I'll leave you breathing after I take out Caufield and add his territory to my own."

"I said I was getting tired of people calling me fat," I said, then I shot Tony in the gut with my Judge. It was awkward as shit drawing the little pistol with my left hand and getting it around without anybody noticing, but with Tony right up on me, I couldn't miss even with my off hand.

His eyes got big, and he took one staggering step backward, both hands clutching the hole in his stomach. Then he stopped and grinned at me. "Bullets don't hurt vampires, moron. What else you got?"

I switched the pistol to my right hand, pointed it at his face, and pulled the trigger. A shotgun shell full of silver pellets at five feet is a bad day for anybody, especially parasitic undead assholes allergic to silver. He slapped both hands to his face, screaming, and dropped to his knees. I kicked him in the side of the head and straddled his writhing body. I looked down at the shrieking vampire, shook my head, and shot him through the heart with a silver .45 long round.

"I told you to leave, asshole." I looked around the assembled weres and actors. "Who's the Alpha dog?"

Terry the Honey Badger stepped up. He looked from Big Tony to me and back, obviously trying to decide whether he wanted to fight me or not. "I'm the pack leader."

"I've got two chambers in this pistol still loaded. Both are shotgun shells packed full of silver. You want to dance, or you want to go home?"

"Tony wasn't a member of my pack."

"Tony was an asshole," I said. "Tony wanted to take something that didn't belong to him and was going to murder somebody to do it. Now Tony's going to lay out in my front yard until the sun comes up and burns him to ash. I don't want to fight a pack of weres, and I sure don't want to mess with a bunch of heavily armed thespians. So if y'all want to go home, you can load up Sir Douche-A-Lot and trot your happy asses back down to Atlanta. But if you want to dance, strike up the band."

"But he don't dance alone." Amy's voice came from the front porch, and I turned to see her, Skeeter, and much to my surprise, Geri, standing there armed to the gills. "Every gun we've got is loaded with silver, and unlike your featured extras over there, I really was trained to kill monsters by the federal government."

Terry held up his hands. "We've got no fight with any of y'all. We just came up here because Tony said he'd pay the talent three hundred bucks for a day and promised all of us a free month's membership at the gym. He was a workout buddy, but not worth dying for. Even Sebastian didn't like him that much."

"Nope," came the groggy comment from the wizard, who leaned against the side of the Suburban. His eyes didn't quite focus just yet, but he seemed to know most of what was going on. "I'm just his business manager. You want to run his shit, go for it."

"Run his shit?" I asked.

"The gym and pizza parlor. And he owned the building the gym is in. You killed him, so I guess that shit's yours now, right? Like a boss in a video game?"

I looked over at Caufield, who shrugged. "I don't want it. I have enough work for a property manager already."

Honey Badger said, "I ain't gonna fight you for it."

I looked at Sebastian. "You promise not to steal from me?"

"Not more than five percent."

"That sounds fair. Get the books in order. I'll come to Atlanta next week and we'll get everything figured out about the pizza joint. Terry, you wanna job?"

"Doing what?"

"Somebody's gotta manage the gym." I didn't want a day job, and I sure as hell didn't want to move to Atlanta. The traffic alone would turn me homicidal.

"I reckon I could do that."

"Okay." I handed both of them one of the business cards Skeeter made for me. They were a little sweat-stained and crumpled from riding around in my back pocket, but my phone number and email were clear enough. "Get back to Atlanta and get all the paperwork ready for transfer. I'll come down in a couple days and we'll settle all the details."

"What about them?" Skeeter asked. He'd come off the porch when it became apparent there wasn't going to be a fight. Now he pointed at the fifty actors standing around a pile of empty pizza boxes and staring at the dead vampire in the grass.

I looked over at Terry. "Pay 'em double." I raised my voice. "How many of y'all believed in vampires and werewolves before lunchtime today?"

Not a single hand went up in the air. "How many of y'all believe now?"

Everybody raised their hand. "How many of y'all think you'll get locked in a padded room if you go back to Atlanta and tell everybody I killed a vampire in my front yard?"

All the hands just stayed up. I turned to Skeeter. "I think we're good."

I shook Terry's hand. "I'll talk to you in a couple days."

I looked at Sebastian. "Sorry about your concussion."

"Sorry about your balls."

"We good?"

"I don't feel the need to send an elemental to kill you in your sleep, if that's what you mean."

"Close enough. Whatever Tony was paying you, give yourself a twenty percent raise. Maybe that'll keep us from trying to kill each other for a couple months."

"Oughta work," he said, then opened the passenger door to the SUV. "Load up. It's a long drive home, and I've got one mother of a headache."

Terry turned to the rest of the shifters. "Anybody got a problem with this?"

The tai chi-teaching were-panther stepped forward. "Do we still get a free month?"

Terry didn't even look back at me. "Yep."

"Then there's no problem."

"Okay, then. Let's get over to the little dude's house and get our bikes." He turned to me and held out his hand. "See you in a couple days, boss. For the record, I'm glad we didn't have to kill each other."

"Me too," I said. "That's just a hell of a way to start a business relationship." And two minutes later, the weres, the wizard, and the actors were on their way back to Atlanta, and I was sitting on Skeeter's porch steps wondering how the hell my life got so weird.

"Well, Mr. Brabham," Caufield said. "I must say this was not how I expected this situation to be resolved, but it certainly seems to have worked out. I believe we are still within the two days I initially paid you for, so would you agree that no additional recompense is required?"

It took me a couple seconds to realize he was saying he didn't think he needed to pay me any more money, but I just nodded. "Yeah, that's about right. We're square."

"In that case, I shall take my leave." He walked to his car, a Mercedes sedan that had been sitting in my yard since we came over from the Drop last night. Man, that was just twenty-four hours ago. Seconds later, with a nod and a wave, Caufield was gone. I felt like I was going to see him again but wasn't sure that was a good thing.

I looked over at Geri. "You still want to kill me? I'm tired as shit, but if we gotta throw down, let's get it over with."

"I don't think I want to kill you. I'm not a hundred percent sure, but I think you're a decent guy. Stupid, hot-tempered, and with a bad habit of letting your mouth write checks your ass can't cash, but you're not evil."

"Damn, Bubba," Amy said, and I could hear her barely holding back the laughter. "She just met you tonight, and she's got you pegged."

I ignored my fiancée and focused on Geri. "So what are you going to do?"

"I don't know. All I've wanted to do since I got out of college is to hunt monsters and shoot you. Now…DEMON is looking like it might not be right about all supernatural creatures being evil, and I don't want to shoot you, so my world's kinda upside down."

I sat there for a long second, looking at this confused kid with my first love's eyes and a lifetime of pain on her face. I opened my mouth to say something, but Amy beat me to it.

"We've got a guest room. You're welcome to stay here until you figure it out." She said pretty much exactly what I was going to, only there was no chance it would sound creepy coming from her.

Geri looked back and forth between Amy and me. "Are you sure?"

"You promise not to try and kill me in my sleep?" I asked.

She crossed her heart with her finger. "I promise if I decide to kill you, I'll do it to your face."

"That's a better deal than most of your friends give you, Bubba," Skeeter said. "Welcome to the team, kid." He handed Geri a beer and perched on the porch railing.

I sat on the steps of my porch listening to the cicadas roar and looked at my oldest friend, my truest love, and my newest frenemy. All in all, it felt like a decent crew to roll with and a pretty good beginning. Of what, I had no damn idea, but I was damn sure it was going to be interesting.

THE END

II

SWAMP MUSIC

1

"I ever tell you I hate Florida, Skeeter?" I said as the tires on my F-250 hummed down I-95, the sun hammering off the dark blue hood.

"Only every hundred miles." Skeeter's voice came from the truck's speakers instead of my phone, thanks to the dash mount and Bluetooth thingy he rigged up for me. He wasn't any less irritating coming through the seven speakers in my radio, but he wasn't quite as squeaky sounding. "How much longer you got?"

"That's supposed to be my line, Skeeter," I replied. I looked at the GPS built into my dash. "According to this, I oughta pull up to Uncle Joe's place in about forty-five minutes. You heard anything from him today?"

"Nothing." I could tell by his voice that Skeeter was worried. Joe called last night close to midnight telling us he needed my help down in Florida ASAP, but he couldn't talk much about it on the phone. I packed all my gear and hit the road soon as I was sober enough to drive, but Skeeter had to stay behind with Amy. There was some weird shit going on back home that he had to keep poking around in, and some news coming out of Pennsylvania and from the other regional Hunters that I wanted to make sure he kept an eye on. He wasn't happy about it, what with Joe being his actual uncle and all, but he also knew he wasn't a whole lot of good in a fight, either.

Amy had to stay behind to keep working on figuring out what the hell was going on inside DEMON, the government agency that she worked for up until recently, when they decided they took exception to their agents fraternizing with non-humans.

"Non-humans." That's me, apparently. It's a hell of a thing finding out after almost forty years of living that your mama's a legit fairy princess, your grandparents are Queen Mab and Oberon, and you're basically made of magic. Wish I'd known that shit twenty years ago. I coulda used some magic in the game where I blew out my knee back in college. Either way, when DEMON found out about my heritage, they severed their relationship with me as a consultant and fired Amy.

But lately we'd been hearing a lot of rumblings from all over about DEMON and other alphabet soup agencies doing more than studying cryptids, so Amy stayed back in Atlanta to dig up some old contacts and see what she could find. She hinted that there might be some magical dude up in Charlotte she was thinking about calling on, but apparently he was a bit of an asshole. We kept him for a last resort.

And that's how I ended up rolling south to answer Uncle Joe's distress call without either of my top two choices for backup. But I wasn't alone. Oh no, that would have made life way too easy. No, curled up on the passenger seat of my truck, snoring a little and getting drool on the window, was Geri, the now-grown baby sister of my college girlfriend, who died at my father's hands. Brittany, my girlfriend, was the first victim of the war between me and my kid brother Jason that ended up running for more than ten years and came within an inch of unleashing a horde of monsters on the earth like nothing that had ever been seen. Geri blamed me for her sister's death, and I was only about thirty percent sure she was done trying to kill me. But she was a good shot, and she hated monsters more than anybody I'd ever seen, so I brought her along with me.

That and I figured if I left her alone with Amy, one of them would be dead and my house would be burned to the ground ten minutes after I left. They'd brokered about the most uneasy truce I'd ever seen once Geri decided she only stuck me with half the blame for her sister's death, but I still didn't want to test it. Besides, the girl could shoot the nuts off a buzzard at a hundred yards and carried more knives than a Bud K catalog.

I ended the call with Skeeter and tapped the screen on my phone again. I hit the "Joe" button in my contacts list, and the phone rang a few times before a familiar voice came on the line. "This is Joe."

"This is your favorite nephew's favorite person," I replied.

"Denzel? How did you get this number?"

"Funny, Uncle Joe. We're less than an hour out from Orlando. We meeting you at your place still?"

"No," he replied. "Meet us at the museum. Becca had to go in to work. You remember how to get there?"

I'd first met Rebecca Knowles, Joe's once and current girlfriend, when we'd been called in to investigate some weird happenings at an exhibit in the museum where she worked a couple years ago. It turned out to be one of her co-workers messing around with demons and other magic he oughtn't have been messing with, but we took care of it. And I didn't even break too much priceless crap, which I counted as a double win.

"Yeah, I think. It's right there on International, ain't it?"

"That's it. In a wing of the old convention center."

"Okay. We should be there in about forty minutes."

"We?" Joe asked. "Did Amy decide to come after all?"

"No," I said. "Her name's Geri. She's...it's complicated. I'll explain it when I see you."

"I'm his dead girlfriend's sister who has reluctantly agreed not to kill him until we get more pressing shit sorted out, then we'll revisit whether or not I murder his fat ass," Geri said.

"Okay," I said. "Maybe it ain't all that complicated. Either way, I'll see you in a little bit." I clicked off the call before Joe could hit me with any questions I didn't feel like answering.

I looked over at Geri, who sat in the passenger seat grinning like a cat whose chin was covered in canary feathers. "You're a little bit of an asshole, ain't you?"

She just smiled at me. "I'm not trying to kill you. Take the little victories."

O rlando traffic is stupid at the best of times, and I've never found the best of times, so it was downright ludicrous getting to the Museum of Antiquities, nestled in part of the old convention center, a sprawling monstrosity eclipsed by the sprawling monstrosity that is the new Orange County Convention Center across the street. I've never been much of a convention kinda guy, more a knife and gun show fella myself, so I can't imagine what in the hell they need so much space to show off. Roller coasters and airplanes, I reckon. Either way, I pulled around the end of the old convention center and parked near the employee entrance to the Museum of Antiquities.

I got out of the truck and opened the back door. I lifted the back seat and popped the lid on the top drawer to start gearing up. I noticed the opposite door open and looked up to see Geri staring at me.

"What?" I asked.

"How much hardware do you carry?" she asked, her tone almost reverent. "There's enough shit in here to take over a country."

"Maybe a real small one, like Belize or Lichtenstein," I replied. "And who wants to run Lichtenstein?" I pulled on the shoulder holster for Bertha, my Desert Eagle, and made sure I had a spare magazine of silver and one of cold iron in the slots on the opposite side. I put a spare regular magazine in my right back pocket, and one with alternating silver and white phosphorus rounds in the left. Then I slipped my Judge revolver in a paddle holster in the small of my back and tossed an obnoxious purple and blue Hawaiian shirt on to mask the armament. I strapped on a knife belt with a Buck hunting knife on my right hip and a silver-edged kukri on my left. There was nothing I could do to hide that, so I just closed the gear locker and reached for the door.

"Hey, what about me?" Geri asked.

"What about you?"

"You got anything in there in a more human size?" I thought about it for a moment, then nodded. She hadn't tried to shiv me in the eight-hour drive, hadn't garroted me at a rest stop, and hadn't even tried to grab the wheel and run us into oncoming traffic. I guess our truce was holding and she was serious about abandoning her quest to murder me because I got her sister killed. I still wasn't a hundred percent sure I wanted her walking around behind me with a pistol, but on the other hand, if I took her into danger unarmed, I could end up being responsible for the death of her entire generation. After a moment's thought, I lifted the lid again.

I pressed my thumb to a touchpad on the side of the locker, and a drawer popped out about an inch. "You oughta find something in there more your size. That's where I keep the guns Amy and Joe use."

"What about Skeeter?" she asked.

"Skeeter ain't allowed to use anything but a shotgun, on account of him not being able to hit the broad side of a barn, and that's a little conspicuous even for Florida."

"Good point," she agreed. "We ain't in Texas, after all." She ran her fingers over the pistols lined up in the drawer, all tucked in their nice little foam cutouts, then pulled out a pair and set them aside. "These oughta work."

"Good choices," I said, looking at the guns she picked. A Sig Sauer P226 in a shoulder holster with a P365 strapped around her ankle for a backup.

"I like the way the Sig feels in my hand," she said. "It's small enough for me to carry, with enough rounds in the magazine for me to handle most anything."

I raised an eyebrow, and she laughed. "I've seen some shit, Bubba. You aren't the first monster I've hunted, just the ugliest."

Ouch. "I reckon I deserved that," I said. I mean, I did get her sister killed.

She glared at me. "No, you didn't. I was screwing with you. You're going to have to get over yourself if we're going to work together. Yeah, you got Britt killed. Yeah, a part of me is always gonna hate you for that. But I know it wasn't your fault, and if you'd ever get your head out of your own ass, you'd see that, too. Now let's get in there so I can see for myself if this Uncle Joe character is as pretty as your girlfriend says he is."

With that, Geri slid the P365 into her backup holster, rolled her jeans down, and slammed the back door of the truck. I stood there for a second trying to process everything she'd just laid on me before I realized she was almost at the door to the museum and if I didn't haul ass, I was going to have to explain her to Joe *after* she had a chance to speak. And nothing good came out of letting that chick talk unsupervised, that was for damn sure.

2

B ecca, Joe's...I reckon she was his girlfriend, although it was pretty hard for me to wrap my head around *that* particular change in circumstances, stood in the entryway waiting for us. Her auburn hair was longer than last time I saw her, and pulled back in a ponytail, but she had the same spray of freckles across her nose and cheeks, and the same no-nonsense walk. She was in a denim long-sleeve shirt over a white t-shirt tucked into her jeans, with a pair of sturdy hiking boots on her feet. I wondered a little bit about her outfit for somebody who worked in a museum all the time, but it wasn't my place to judge if she wanted to dress like a modern-day female Indiana Jones.

"Bubba," she said, stepping forward and holding out her hand. "Good to see you again. I hope this trip will be less...eventful than your last visit."

I shook her hand. "Thanks, Doc. I mean, Becca." She'd explain on our last visit that pretty much everybody in the building except me was a doctor of something, so I should use her first name to keep things from getting all confusing. My life was confusing enough without any help, so I did as she asked.

"This isn't...Amy, is it?" she asked, giving Geri a sideways look.

"Oh, *hell no!*" Geri and I said at the same time, both jerking back and looking at her like she'd just poured scalding water on us.

"I'm Geri," the younger woman said, stepping forward and holding out her hand. "I just started working with Bubba and his team."

"Oh, good," Becca said. "No offense." She directed that at me. "But she looks a little young for you."

"Yeah, a little bit," I said. "And no offense taken. Where's Joe? He in your office?"

"No," Becca said, turning to grab our visitor badges from the guard at the desk and lead us through the double doors into the back of the museum. "We're going to chat in the conference room. We need a few more chairs than my office can hold."

"Frankly, I reckon I probably take up more space than an office in a museum's gonna have," I said.

Becca laughed, and I could see some of what Joe saw in her. She had an easy laugh to her, and that was something a person needed when they dealt with some of the shit we saw on the daily. "You're right there, Bubba. But there are also a couple of people you need to meet, and we're going to need the big monitor in the conference room to show you the location we'll be hunting."

She pushed open a door, and I stepped through to see Uncle Joe sitting on the near side of the conference table across from two of the oldest women I had ever seen in real life. They were straight out of a horror movie where the idiot college kids run into an old woman who warns them about a curse in the woods. You know, the warning the kids promptly ignore when they perform their "joke" ritual that ends up bringing a demon or something to eat them all alive?

Yeah, these two looked like they competed for all those creepy old woman roles. One of them was a big woman. Tall, thick through the arms and the middle, looked like she could wrestle a gator for an hour to a draw and still chop up a cord of firewood before she skinned a deer for supper. I put her at maybe her mid-eighties, with deep scowl lines running down her face and long black hair streaked through with silver and pulled back to hang down past her shoulders. She wore a flannel shirt with the sleeves rolled halfway up her forearms, and I was torn between thinking they were prison tats peeking out at me, or maybe Russian mafia ink.

But it was the other one that was scary. She was ancient, a hundred years old if she was a day. Withered up and shriveled like an apple left out in the sun too long, she wore a Florida Gators hooded sweatshirt that I think started life as blue but was faded almost to white. Her long, crooked nose poked out of it, and I could see the glint of her eyes, but that was about it. I couldn't tell if she looked more like a Jawa or the evil witch from *Snow White*. Either way, I took one look at the gnarled and knobby fingers she had clasped across her chest and could easily see her sending some Emperor Palpatine lightning bolts out to fry my nuts if I pissed her off.

"Granny, Aunt Ethel, this is the Hunter I told you I was bringing in. He's a friend of Joe's. He's gonna help us find Terrell." Becca stepped to the head of the table and pulled out a chair. I felt a sharp poke in one kidney and realized I was still standing in the door staring at the women. *Did she just call the old one Granny?* I thought as I took the seat closest to Joe.

"Hey, Bubba," Joe said, studiously not turning to look at me.

"Joe," I said, in a tone that was intended to convey that we had a lot to talk about, and that talking would require him to buy me a *lot* of liquor when we got out of this room.

"Who's your friend?" Joe asked.

"That's Geri," I said. "She's…well, one thing at a time. I reckon we both gonna have a few things to explain when we get to the bar after this one."

"Oh, you ain't even begun to know the questions you gonna have for me," Joe said. "But I promise you this—they're all good people, and they need our help."

"That's enough for me," I said. I meant it, too. Me and Joe had been through it all, from regular old monsters to interdimensional fairies, and he'd always had my back. If he said these were good people, I believed him. Didn't mean I wasn't still gonna make him buy me a bunch of drinks, just meant I might not make him buy me more than two rounds of the good stuff.

I walked around the table, making sure I kept as much surface between the weird old women and me as possible, and I sat down in the biggest chair they had. It creaked under me, stopping just short of screaming for mercy, but it held. I reckon most museums don't have anybody my size on the payroll. "What's the deal, Joe? I reckon y'all didn't call me down here for a family reunion."

"No, but my family is the reason you're here, Bubba." Becca moved to the end of the table, with Creepy Granny on her right side and Uncle Joe on her left. "I need to tell you something that I don't usually let strangers know about me, but we need your help, so you deserve to know exactly what you're getting into."

I looked at her for a long moment, wondering what the hell she was talking about, then she spoke, and whatever I was expecting, this wasn't it.

Becca looked at me and Geri and said, "Me and my family are were-gators."

I looked over at Creepy Granny, and damned if she didn't do that freaky eye thing alligators do where they blink the milky membrane across their eye. I scooted my chair back a little bit as her skin took on a yellowish-green hue and her pupils turned into vertical slits. "Well, that's...unexpected, to say the damn least."

I looked at Joe. "Did you call me down here just to tell me your girlfriend's a were? What's the deal, did you pop the question and wanted to make sure I wasn't going to shoot up the wedding reception?"

"No!" Joe and Becca both said at the same time, then they looked at each other and laughed.

"I mean, that's not something we've really..." Joe trailed off, trying not to look completely flustered and failing miserably.

I waved a hand at him. "I'm joking. Mostly. I promise not to shoot your girlfriend or her kin. As long as they don't try to eat me."

"Eat either of us," Geri muttered from beside me.

I paused for long enough to let her know I was giving it some real thought, then said, "As long as they don't try to eat either of us."

"We don't eat humans," Creepy Granny said, and her voice

sounded just like I expected it to, kinda like a cross between finger-nails on a chalkboard and a cat that just got its tail stepped on. There was a hint of sibilance to it, like her mouth wasn't completely shifted back to human, but I wasn't interested enough in that to look at her real close. Even with her eyes back to normal, she creeped me out.

"Okay," I said, turning my attention back to Becca, who stood at the front of the room waiting for the discussion to calm down. "So, you're a were-gator. What's the big deal? Some of my best friends… well, that ain't true, but I reckon I've met one or two weres that I didn't need to shoot, and I know a fellow up in Pennsylvania that uses a werewolf as a guard dog. Why call me down here and out yourselves?"

"Because my boy's done gone missing, and we need somebody to go find 'im." This was Ugly Auntie instead of Creepy Granny, but she was no less disturbing now that I knew some of her strange demeanor came from not wearing human skin all the time. Her voice was low, like a perpetual growl, and had the same sibilance that Granny's had.

"You need me to hunt down missing were-gators in a Florida swamp?" I asked, giving Joe my very best "you're an asshole" look. He was unfazed. I think I need to work on a new glare. The ones I've got now just don't get the job done anymore.

"Yes," Becca said. "Joe says you're the best, and from your perfor-mance here in the museum a few years ago, I can't argue with the effectiveness of your methods. You may not be as familiar with the swamp as my family, but you know more about other monsters than we do, and you can apply that knowledge to the hunt, while utilizing our people as guides."

"We ain't used to nothin' huntin' us," Auntie said. "We usually the ones that does the huntin'." She grinned, and there was a flash of yellow in her eyes.

"Are you sure the missing…person didn't just decide to leave?" Geri asked, leaning forward in her chair. She had her phone out and was making notes in an app like she was actually going to be my assistant instead of just running along with me making smartassed comments. I could get used to this kind of thing if I wasn't careful.

"Terrell, that's my cousin, he just got engaged to a girl in Kissim-mee," Becca said. "He's a junior at UCF majoring in forestry and plan-ning to go to work for the parks service when he graduates. He's a good, stable kid, with no reason to leave on his own. And he certainly wouldn't leave without telling the only girl he's ever kissed."

"Okay, that's one," I said. "Are there more of your people missing? And if so, is it just gators, or are there shifters of different types that have gone missing in the area?"

Becca looked surprised. "I never thought about that."

"Never cared, neither," Auntie said.

"Well, we better care," I shot back. "Because if there's somebody or something out there big enough and bad enough to hunt a were-gator, it's gonna take everything we got to fight it and get your people back."

"Does that mean you'll help?" Becca asked.

I looked at Joe, saw the hope on his face. There was no way I'd leave him in the lurch, even if I wasn't curious to find out what could hunt a were-gator. He'd been by my side on too many hunts, too many tough fights, for me to leave him high and dry now.

"Yeah," I said, nodding. "I'm in."

"*We're* in," Geri corrected.

Joe reached over and shook my hand. "We're in."

3

I didn't know what I was getting myself in for when I agreed to help y'all." I had to yell to be heard over the airboat's engine. Wind whipped through my hair and blew my beard sideways as we roared through the swamp. Becca was behind us in the driver's seat, with me and Joe on the bench in front of her. I've got better than a hundred pounds on Joe's narrow ass, so the boat had a decided lean to it as we cruised through the swamp.

I didn't have a long gun. That's never really been my thing. I'm more of a get in the middle of things and tear shit up kind of guy, so I had the spiked caestae that Amy gave me for Christmas a few years ago on my fists. I switched out the knuckle spikes to alternate between silver and cold iron, since I wasn't sure what I was hunting. If it was fae, the iron would get the job done. If it was another lycanthrope hunting Becca's family, the silver would be what I needed. And it if was neither of those, it probably still wouldn't like a giant redneck punching it in the face with inch-long metal spikes. I'd traded my Hawaiian shirt in for a long-sleeve overshirt and stuffed the pockets with extra ammunition, just in case.

Becca was unarmed, insisting that once we got to a good hunting ground, she'd be in better shape to fight anything in the swamp than any of us. I didn't ask any questions. I'd never fought a were-gator before, but I'd wrestled a normal alligator once on a bet, and I knew they had thick hide and teeth that could tear flesh like paper, with jaws strong enough to snap bone. They could also take a hell of a punch and didn't enjoy being wrestled by overweight hillbillies with more tequila than sense. I did not learn that last bit watching Animal Planet.

Becca's family stayed behind at their cabin on the edge of the swamp where we left my truck and Becca's car. Creepy Granny even smiled at me as we were leaving, or maybe that was her making a sign against the evil eye. I couldn't quite be sure. It took a fair bit of persuading, but after I mentioned the number of different kinds of snake that lived in the swamp, I convinced Geri to stay behind with Granny and the rest of the family for backup in case we sent up a flare. I didn't take a flare gun, but I didn't bother to tell her that. I was not getting her killed in a swamp in God's Own Butthole, Florida.

"How much further?" I yelled over my shoulder, hoping Becca could hear me over the giant fan behind her.

"About another fifty yards," she called back. Becca guided the airboat over to a grassy outgrowth and cut the motor. "This is where we found Terrell's cell phone," she said, jumping over onto the small island. "There was nothing to indicate a struggle, just his phone lying out here in the middle of nowhere."

"Okay, then. Let's see what our tech support can find out for us," I said. "Skeeter, did you get that?" I said, tapping the Bluetooth earpiece.

"Yeah, I got it. I have y'all on GPS, and I've overlaid that with Google Maps imagery of the swamp. But it shows you as standing in the middle of water," Skeeter replied.

"These little islands of grass don't stay in one place very long," Becca said. "Might not have been solid ground here when those pictures were taken."

"Skeeter, can you get us any more current satellite images?" I asked.

"You mean, can I get you the kind of stuff we used to have when Amy still worked for DEMON and Uncle Joe had a direct line to the

Vatican, and our biggest problem was keeping the Archbishop from finding out exactly how much of our expense report was your beer tab?"

"Yeah, that's pretty much exactly what I mean," I replied.

"No," Skeeter said. "Sorry, but we're stuck with the same shit everybody with an internet connection has. That's why we've got to talk over cell phones instead of the embedded comms we had been using. All that crap got turned off when the feds decided you weren't human enough for them."

"Racists," I grumbled. Just because I turned out to be the half-fae grandson of two of the rulers of Fairyland, they got all uptight about me not being human. Hell, I didn't have wings or pointy ears or any of the cool shit you'd think I'd get from being part fairy. And I had to deal with job discrimination too? I tell you, nothing in my nearly forty years of being a straight white dude prepared me for that. "Alright, what can you tell us, Skeeter? Is there anything nearby?"

"Well, the detailed images of the swamp suck, and the cell coverage goes from spotty to shitty in about a hundred yards, so you're probably one clue away from being out of contact. But there's what looks like a structure about half a mile northwest of where you're standing. I can't tell if it's on the same little island you're on, because according to my imagery—"

"We're in the middle of water right now," Joe finished his sentence. "How big is this building, Skeeter? Big enough to hide a couple of alligators, or a few people?"

"Yeah, it looks like it's probably twenty feet on a side. Single story, cinderblock, can't see if there are any windows or doors, but if I zoom in as far as I can, I see a trail leading from your direction to the building, and another trail leading away on the opposite side."

"Are there—" I started, then stopped myself. "You're not looking at anything live, are you?"

"Nope," came the answer.

"That answers that, then," I said. "You can't know if there's anybody around. Okay, we'll go check it out."

"Sounds good," Skeeter replied. "If we lose contact, how long should I wait before I send in backup?"

The way Skeeter sounded, it was almost like he expected me to end up in over my head. I wasn't sure if that was on account of us being rogue operators after having all the backup of the Church and the government for the last few years, or if he just had a bad feeling about what we were getting into. Either way, he was worried. And Skeeter being worried made me worried.

I looked up into the bright blue Florida sky. It was already afternoon, and I didn't know how fast it got dark out here in the swamp. I didn't want to cut our searching too short, though. "How about midnight?" I asked. "If we lose contact, which we probably will, and you don't hear anything out of us by midnight, start calling in reinforcements."

"Sounds like a plan." I turned to Becca. "You want to get changed into your gator suit?"

"Sure," she said, unbuttoning her shirt as she kicked out of her hiking boots. I turned around quickly, feeling the red start to creep up my neck. Shapeshifters are a lot more casual about being naked than I am, and I woulda felt all kinds of uncomfortable seeing Uncle Joe's girlfriend in her altogether. After about a minute of popping, cracking, squelching, and generally disgusting noises from behind me, I felt a heavy hand on my shoulder.

I turned around and almost peed my pants at what stood there. What had been a highly educated museum curator a minute before was now a seven-foot-tall half alligator monstrosity that I was pretty sure was grinning at me, but it might have been sizing me up as an appetizer.

Becca's half-shifted form was something seriously terrifying, and I've fought a dragon and grabbed a Sasquatch's wiener, so I am not normally someone to be considered faint of heart. She was covered in thick, rubbery-looking green skin, and looked just like you'd expect an alligator to look standing on two feet, except her arms and legs were still mostly human, and her head was only about half-shifted. Her face had elongated into a snout full of razor-sharp teeth, and her eyes had moved to either side of her head, so she could only look at me with one eye or the other. She was massively muscled, with biceps bigger around than my thighs, and I am a girthsome fellow, to say the least. Her tail stretched out a good three feet behind her and had a double ridge of thick spines down the length of it. It was about a foot in diameter tapering to a point and looked like it would solid lay you out if she swung it at you.

"Well hey, Becca," I said, taking one giant step back. "Remember when I said I ain't never seen a were-gator before?"

She nodded, her new face obviously not being built for speech.

"Yeah," I said. "Now I have. And I gotta say, you are without a doubt the no shit scariest shifter I have ever been around, and I've seen everything from werewolves to lamias. But you take the cake, lady."

She nodded at me, then raised her arms before bringing them down in an exaggerated bodybuilder pose. Yep, a half-shifted were-gator just flexed on me in the middle of a Florida swamp. My life was totally keeping to its normal quotient of weird.

"You gonna gawk at my girlfriend, or we gonna hunt?" Joe asked, stepping up beside me.

"I reckon this ain't your first time seeing her like this?" I asked.

"No," he replied. "It gets easier to wrap your head around after a while."

"I'll take your word for it." I turned in the direction Skeeter said there was a building. "Let's go see if there's anything interesting in the abandoned building in the middle of the creepy swamp where the alligator shifter got kidnapped."

"Yeah, that sounds like the best idea, said literally nobody ever." Joe muttered as we followed his half-shifted were-gator girlfriend into the swamp.

4

The building was right where Skeeter said it would be, and cell signal was just as shitty. I lost him the second we caught sight of the squat cinderblock structure, so I took the Bluetooth thingy out of my ear and shoved it in a pocket of my jeans. I was bad about losing the stupid things, and we had a budget to pay attention to nowadays. Well, more like we *didn't* have any budget, but you get the point.

The path through the swamp ended in a clearing about fifty feet from what I reckoned was the back of the building. I couldn't really tell, but there was a plain steel door set into the block wall, and no markings of any kind. No windows, either, which should have made our approach easier, but Joe grabbed me by the belt just as I was about to step out of the trees.

"Cameras," he said, pointing to a corner of the building. Sure enough, there were cylindrical little security cameras poking out of the eaves, and they looked to cover the area around the building pretty tightly. I wondered what in the world anybody was trying to protect all the way out here in the middle of nowhere. There was one big exhaust fan sticking up from the roof, so meth lab wasn't out of the question, but most of the time you can smell the cat piss stench of them places from a hundred yards, and there was none of that. It was too small to be a drying shed for weed, and not accessible enough to be a whorehouse.

The place was bigger than Skeeter said, though. It was at least sixty feet square, a single story of unpainted cinderblocks. The roof was just tin sheeting, but it looked to be in good repair, and the grass was short. All the weeds and brush was cut back about twenty yards from the building, and I could just make out the other path cutting through the swamp on the other side.

There was another thing that stood out about the place, other than being a building all the way out here in the middle of a swamp with no cell service, no apparent power, and no people. Planted all around the building, in a carefully tended bed about three feet wide, were beautifully landscaped bushes and flowers. I recognized Black-eyed Susans, daylilies, mums, and even a few lilac bushes and some type of hibiscus. I'd learned way more about flowers than I ever wanted to since Amy and me both got fired and she decided to decorate around the cabin. The splashes of color stood out in a sharp contrast to the drab gray block construction.

"Do we want to try and slip around to the other side through the woods?" I asked Becca.

The were-gator shook her head, then pointed off to the right. The underbrush was thick, with cypress roots sticking up out of the ground all over the place and vines hanging down. Between the undergrowth and the vines, there was no way we were getting through that mess without making at least as much noise as if we just walked up and knocked on the door.

And that's exactly what I did. I looked at Joe and said, "Cover me." I looked at Becca, but I was not about to tell the were-gator how to do anything in her own damn swamp, so I just drew Bertha from her shoulder holster, made sure there was one in the chamber, and walked out into the clearing, fully expecting the door to slam open and men in black suits to rush out and arrest me, or worse, make me do paperwork.

That didn't happen. In fact, nothing at all happened. Nobody came out the door, nobody shot at me, nobody rappelled down out of a silent black helicopter. I was almost disappointed, but then I remembered that I kinda liked not getting shot at. As I got closer to the building, I looked up at the camera, fully intending to do the mature thing and give whoever was watching the finger. Except the cameras weren't on. I could see the LED indicator that was supposed to show me that Big Brother was watching, but it was completely dark.

I stepped up next to the door, keeping my body tucked in behind the walls instead of the door in case something came running out, and knocked three times. I pressed my ear to the wall but heard nothing through the thick cinderblock. I don't know what I would have done if I did. I mean, Bertha can punch through a cinderblock, but I try real hard not to shoot at things I can't see. Especially when whatever is on the other side of the wall might not be something that a bullet can stop.

I waited about thirty seconds, then banged on the door, hearing the empty boom echo through the room on the other side. Still nothing. This is the time on the tv shows where I would yank the door open, throw in a flash-bang, and rush in to overpower the stunned bad guys. There were two problems with that scene. First, I didn't have any flash-bangs. Second, I'm not so much with the rushing since my knee got wrecked playing football. My rush is more like a wobbly amble, kinda like a bear walking on two legs. It happens, but you're watching just wondering when everything is gonna come crashing down.

I sighed, wondering why my family business couldn't have been something safe, like underwater demolitions or cobra milking, and yanked the door open, planning to rush inside and beat the hell out of any bad guys on the other side.

Except the door was locked, so I just stood there like a dumbass twisting the knob. Joe and Becca walked up behind me, having finally decided that they could either watch me live out a really bad *Call of Duty* session or they could actually get something accomplished.

"Didn't check the door, huh?" Joe asked. He'd been in this situation with me more than once in our years of working together.

"The door ain't never locked on TV," I griped. I took a step back and aimed Bertha at the knob. "Don't worry, I brought a key."

Becca put a scaly hand on my shoulder, and I looked over at her. She shook her head and stepped up to the door. This was when I learned exactly how strong were-gators are. She grabbed that steel doorknob in one big mitt and gave it a light twist. Nothing happened. She let out a low growl, and I saw the muscles in her arm bulge a little. The knob surrendered with a squeal of tortured metal, and half a second later, Becca turned around and handed me the twisted hunk of steel that used to be a doorknob.

"Was that supposed to be quieter than Bertha?" I asked. "Because I'm pretty sure anything on the other side of that door knows we're here now."

"You just knocked on the door like the world's most pissed off pizza delivery guy. Pretty sure the subtlety ship has sailed. Now are we going to stand out here waiting on whoever's inside to get *more* ready to kill us, or are we just gonna...oh, screw it." Joe shouldered past me and Becca and pulled the door open, a task made somewhat more difficult by the lack of knob, but he managed to get his index finger in the hole and yank it open.

He stepped into darkness, and I saw him peel off to the left. I followed, moving right to clear the entry for Becca, who was absolutely going to be the one of us going straight up the gut on this play. It was darker than the inside of an elephant's butthole in there, and I felt around on the wall behind me, found the switch, and flipped the lights on.

Fluorescents buzzed to life, and we all froze, stunned by what we saw, and at the same time, the smell of blood and death hit me like a hammer. I wasn't sure what we'd walked into, but it was *way* not good. In front of me, along the right-hand side of the building, were cheap interior walls that looked like they'd been thrown up by the lowest bidder. The room nearest me in the back corner looked the biggest, just guessing off door placement, with a couple of small rooms in the middle of the wall and a bigger room in the front corner.

But it was the rest of the room that was the most disturbing. The place was full of cages, different sizes and materials set up in rows like some kind of sick warehouse. There were a couple of big cages in front of us, maybe twenty by twenty and made of heavy steel bars with solid diamond-plate steel roofs on top of them. Whatever they were keeping in there, they did not want them getting out. There was straw on the floor and a bucket in each cage, but no animals.

There were no animals anywhere, but the smell of them was almost overpowering. The whole place reeked of animal funk, and animal waste, but under all of that was the coppery smell of blood. Lots of blood. And burnt hair and flesh. A lot of animals had died in this place, and not that long ago.

Next to the row of big cages was a row of what looked more like cells than cages. There were built out of steel, too, but there was also Plexiglas lining the three small rooms. The doors to all the cages hung open, and from where I stood, I couldn't see anything in any of them. The cages got smaller as we moved across the room, with five-by-five cages in a single freestanding row, then a wall lined with small cages stacked almost to the ceiling. That far wall looked kinda like a pet shop, if the owners hated animals and never cleaned a cage, ever.

"What the hell is this place?" Joe asked.

"Nothing good," I said. "But if we're going to find out, the answers are gonna be in one of these rooms." I pointed along the wall of closed doors. "We can see from here there ain't nothing in any of those cages, and…what is that? Some kind of lab?"

Sure enough, in the far-left corner of the building was a glassed-in laboratory, with tables and counters and cabinets with their doors hanging open. A splash of brown dried blood across one window told me that maybe the evacuation of this place hadn't been exactly peaceful.

"It looks like they held cryptids here," Becca said, back in her human form. I turned to her, then averted my eyes as I saw she was standing there butt-naked. "Oh, get over it, Bubba. They're boobs. You've seen them before."

"Not very often for free," Joe said, smirking at my discomfort.

"You can give me a dollar if it'll make you feel better," Becca said.

"Hand me your backpack, baby." Joe passed his bag over to her, and she got dressed quickly in a t-shirt, jeans, and sneakers. She pulled a pistol in a holster out of the bottom of the bag and clipped it to the waistband of her pants. After checking the chamber, she fished a couple of spare magazines out of the bag, slipped them in her back pockets, and put the backpack across her shoulders.

"Better?" she asked, giving me a raised eyebrow.

"Well, your odds of distracting any bad guys we run into dropped a whole bunch, but I think that 1911 on your hip will make up for it," I replied.

"Okay, if we're checking rooms, where do we start?" Joe asked. "Right here?" He walked over to the door of the nearest room and pulled it open, then fell back on his ass as a six-foot-tall lizard flew through the door at him and bowled him over.

I guess not everything escaped before we got there.

5

I couldn't get a clear shot at the lizard, on account of it rolling around on the floor with a couple hundred pounds of defrocked priest, so I stood back and waited for an opening. I rolled my head from side to side and slipped the caestae on my fists.

The lizard was friggin' huge, at least as long as Joe was tall, and I swear it looked just like the cheeky little bastard on the GEICO commercials, except it had darker skin, claws at the end of its fingers and toes, and a shitload of razor-sharp teeth in its mouth. It also wasn't saying anything clever or drinking coffee, so I reckon it wasn't anything like the little dude on the commercials.

No, what it was doing right now was grappling with Joe and apparently trying to rip his guts out onto the concrete floor. It had him down, and Joe managed to grab hold of both the lizard's front claws at the wrist, for lack of a better term. The critter's back feet were on the ground on either side of Joe's waist, and it was snapping at his face with its jaws and slamming its tail into his legs. Joe was struggling to roll the thing over, or at least off of him, and I saw a glimmer of an idea materialize.

"Try to shove him straight up!" I hollered as I stepped forward. Joe did, managing to get the lizard's middle to hunch up in the air just enough, and I punted the scaly bastard right in the ribs. It let out a screech like Wolverine going at a chalkboard, but it rolled off Joe and scrambled up onto two feet, using its tail for balance behind it.

"Get out of the way, Joe," I hollered. "I got this." I couldn't draw and fire Bertha with the gauntlets on, so I just waded in, figuring after all the things I've fought, how hard could fighting one lizard be?

The answer is hard as shit, frankly. I tried to bull-rush the thing, but it sidestepped me like the Carradine dude in *Kung Fu* reruns and slashed down my back with its claws. I felt three lines of fire open up down my right side as it scored the flesh there, and I spun around with a backhand, hoping to catch it sleeping on my speed. There wasn't much speed to sleep on, since I missed the lizard by a country mile. It squared up on me again, and I would almost swear I saw it *smirking*. Then it reached out with its long, bright blue forked tongue and licked my blood off its fingers, and I knew it was screwing with me.

I let out a bellow and charged straight at it again, but this time, just as I got close enough for it to dive sideways and peel another couple strips off my back, I stopped in my tracks and kicked the son of a bitch right in the crotch. Its eyes went wide, and it let out a very small *squeeeeek*, and staggered back.

But this is where my complete and utter ignorance of lizard genitalia came back to bite me in the ass. Because, as I learned from researching exactly what in the absolute hell happened to me later, lizards don't have external genitals. That meant that when I tried my damnedest to kick the lizard in the balls, I kicked it in something called a cloaca, which is a pouch up inside its body where it keeps its twig and berries stored until they're needed. When I kicked it in the cloaca, the toe of my boot, all the way up to the damn instep, went up *inside* said cloaca, causing the lizard extreme pain and discomfort.

And lodging my foot up in the lizard's nutsack tighter than a golf ball going through a garden hose. There I was, standing on one foot, with my other boot jammed in a giant lizard's reproductive organs, trying to figure out what the hell to do next. The lizard, for its part, was writhing around and bouncing from one foot to the other and screeching in pain while it tried like hell to cut my leg off with its claws.

I couldn't reach the lizard with my fists, I couldn't draw Bertha with the damn gauntlets on, and I had my foot stuck in a lizard's ball pouch. So I did the only thing I could think of, knowing it was gonna hurt like a son of a bitch but also knowing I didn't have another option. I pushed off the ground with my left foot as hard as I could, spun my body to the right, and extended my left leg as I went up. This is a move you see about nine millions times on every wrestling show in the world nowadays. It's called an enzuigiri, and it usually ends up with the dude doing the kick slapping his thigh to make a loud sound while it looks like his foot smacks the other dude in the side of the head.

I didn't slap my thigh. I also didn't make it look nearly as cool as any of the guys from New Japan Pro Wrestling. What I did was manage to get my gargantuan ass up off the floor enough to kick the lizard in the side of the head as I twisted around in midair. The impact forcibly removed my foot from the lizard's cloaca, then my body kept rolling, so I crashed to the concrete floor on my front, breaking my fall a little bit with my hands, and a lot with my gut.

"Shoot it," I gasped from the floor. Every single part of my body hurt except maybe one toe and my left ear. The rest was beat to absolute shit. I heard five quick reports from over my head, then a wet slapping *thud* as the body of the lizard fell backward to the floor.

I lay still for a few seconds, trying to make sure I hadn't broken anything, then I very slowly pushed myself up to my hands and knees, then struggled to my feet. My back and side burned where the lizard clawed me, and my right shin looked like it had been attacked by a weed whacker. My knees hurt from landing on concrete, as did pretty much every other part of me, and when I looked down at my right boot, it was covered in a viscous red and yellow sludge that I didn't even want to think about trying to clean off the leather. This gig was definitely going to cost me a new pair of boots. And a hip replacement if I had to do another move like that.

"I didn't know you could move like that, Bubba," Joe said, walking over to me. He looked like a double helping of refried dog crap, too. His shirt was shredded, and the flesh underneath was covered in long, deep scratches. His arms were similarly tore up, and he was favoring his right leg where the lizard took him down. If this was how beat up we were after the first damn thing we ran into, we might not make it out of this swamp at all.

"I can't move like that, Joe," I said. "But desperate times call for desperate measures, and I ain't been in many more desperate times than hopping around on one leg with my foot stuck in a lizard's crotchal region."

Becca laughed and walked up to me. "You don't know much about reptiles, do you, Bubba?"

"I know a lot more now than I ever wanted to. Nice shooting."

"Thanks. You grow up in the swamp, you gonna grow up shooting at things you'd better not miss with the first shot. 'Cause you ain't gonna get a second one." She ejected the spent magazine from her pistol and slapped a fresh one home. "Now then. Let's go see what this fella was protecting so hard."

We let her lead the way to the door the lizard burst out of, mostly because me and Joe are hell-bent on equality, but also because neither one of us could really walk worth a shit. The door was standing wide open, and as we looked into the room, I felt the hairs stand up on my arms.

"Is this what I think it is?" I asked as I followed Becca inside. It was about twenty by ten, with a concrete floor, sloped a little to a drain roughly in the center of the room. There was a metal rack about waist high with a conveyor belt running along it that led to a big black cast-iron furnace. There was a door set into the wall of the furnace at the end of the conveyor, and a big red button set into one of the far walls.

"It's a crematorium," Joe said, his voice quiet. "And it looks big enough to accommodate humans."

"Or giant lizards," I said, thinking about the dead beastie on the floor outside.

"Or were-gators," Becca murmured. I looked over and saw Joe standing beside her with a hand on her shoulder.

"We don't know anything," Joe said. "We shouldn't jump to conclusions."

"Then let's see what we can find out," I said. I walked over to the furnace and knelt down beside the conveyor. I opened a square door set into the metal face and peeked inside. This was obviously an ash collection port, with a shovel leaning against the wall right next to it. I grabbed the shovel and raked it through the inside of the incinerator. It scraped against the metal, and in a few seconds, I had a foot-high pile of ash on the floor in front of me.

I sifted through it with my fingers, finding an odd chip or bone here and there, but most of whatever had been put through this place had been completely destroyed. There was nothing identifiable left at first, but after a couple of passes through the pile, my fingers hit on something rounded and solid. I grabbed it and pulled it out, shaking the dust off as I did.

I had what looked like a spike a few inches long with a light curve to it and a half-sphere on the end. I turned around and held it up to Joe and Becca. "Why does this look familiar?" I asked.

"Because you saw the x-rays when my aunt Eulah Mae had her hip replacement four years ago. That's an artificial hip joint, Bubba. Out of a human."

"Or a dead lycanthrope," Becca added. "Granny's got a metal rod in her leg from a four-wheeler accident about ten years ago. I don't understand how it works, but it's still there whenever she shifts, and her legs ain't long enough in gator form to have no rod in it. If a were had a hip replacement and died, they'd shift back to human form with the hardware intact. Don't make no sense to me, but that's magic for you."

"Darling, we literally went to Fairyland and fought a dragon. Who turned into a crotchety old man. It's gonna take more than disappearing medical implants to throw me at this point," I said. "But this means whoever was running this place was up to some nasty shit."

"It also means we can identify at least one of the victims," Joe said, reaching out to me. I gave him the joint, and he turned it over in his hands. "I can't see it, but I know all these kinds of things have serial numbers on them. If we turn it in to the proper authorities, they can notify the victim's relatives. Give them some closure at least."

"That's good of you, Joe, but I got a pretty bad feeling the 'proper authorities' might be the ones heading up some of this crap." I gave them a brief rundown on our run-in with DEMON a few weeks back. "I heard about some really nasty shit they had going on up in Pennsylvania, too. We might want to hold off notifying anyone from the government until we know we can trust them."

Becca snorted at that. I looked over at her, and she shrugged. "What? You trust the government?"

"Hell no," I said. "I used to work for them. I know they're all screwed in the head. Let's see if we can find any records anywhere else in this place that might lead us to your cousin."

"If we ain't already found him," she replied, looking at the furnace.

"Well, then maybe we'll find records of that," I said. "Knowing would be better than not knowing."

"Would it?" Becca asked.

"I don't know," I said. "I can't think of a time I've learned something awful that I woulda rather not known it. But the knowing of it was still terrible."

"Whatever we find, I'm here," Joe said.

"Me too," I agreed. "Unless we find another giant lizard. If I have to jam my foot in anything that nasty again, I'm outta here." We all laughed at my stupid joke, and with the tension broken, we went out to explore the rest of the chamber of horrors.

W e walked out of the crematorium and turned our attention to the rest of the building's interior. The next room was a break room that wouldn't have looked out of place in an episode of *The Office*. It had cheap tile flooring, a drop ceiling, a battered fridge, sink, and a microwave on a scuffed counter. A pair of doors with male and female silhouettes on them sat against the exterior wall, and both restrooms were empty, except for a copy of the *Sports Illustrated* Swimsuit Issue in the men's crapper.

"It looks so...normal," Becca said, staring at a lame motivational poster with a picture of a whale's tail on one wall.

"The real monsters always do," Joe said, putting an arm around her. I thought about the folks we met on our sojourn through Fairyland and decided he was right. Granny Mab and Granddaddy Oberon let an innocent girl die just to try to get the upper hand on one another, and they both were gorgeous. Most of the real gruesome critters I'd had to put down over the years couldn't hold a candle to the nasty shit cooked up by humans and fairies.

With nothing to learn in the break room, I stepped back out into the warehouse. The next room was storage, with shelves of toilet paper, copy paper, cleaning supplies, and the like. I poked through a few boxes, but everything was exactly what it said it was. There were a few boxes of things like latex gloves and respirator cartridges, but most of it was the same kind of crap you'd find in a place that wasn't disgusting and evil.

The next door was locked, but it was a cheap hollow core wooden door with a lock from Home Depot on it. It barely held against me jiggling the knob and flew to splinters when I kicked the door in. "Now we might have something," I said, looking back over my shoulder as I stepped into a small office.

It looked like a basic middle manager's office, with a couple of filing cabinets, a desk with a chair that leaned a little to one side, threadbare carpet, a whiteboard with the ghost of notes barely visible, and a pair of guest chairs in front of the desk. And on the desk, the one thing I hoped more than any other we'd find—a big computer monitor. I walked around the desk and pulled the chair out but froze as Joe called to me from the door.

"Freeze, Bubba."

I froze. After going toe-to-toe with a six-foot lizard, I wasn't taking any chances with whatever Joe was seeing. "What is it?"

"Let Becca deal with the computer. You'll just break it," he said, stepping in and walking over to one of the file cabinets.

"That's cold, man." I stepped around the desk and gestured to the chair. "But you're right. Go for it, Becca."

She nodded and slipped between me and the desk. She sat down and jiggled the mouse, but the screen stayed dark. "That's odd," she said, bending over to look under the desk. "Bubba, where did you see the CPU?"

"The what?" I asked.

"The part that does all the computing?"

"Oh. I don't know. I just saw the screen and thought it was one of them all-in-ones like Skeeter's got."

"Nope. This is an all-in-nothing. The CPU is gone. Nothing here."

"Here either," Joe said, closing the bottom file drawer. "Both cabinets are empty."

"Well, shit. There ain't even a phone in here, either," I said, thinking if we at least had that, we could call Skeeter and see if he could dig up anything about this place.

"Well, there's just one place left to look," I said, heading out the door. I'd put off checking out the room in the front of the building as long as I could, because after going through the crematorium, I wasn't sure I wanted to look in there, but we didn't have a choice anymore. As I stepped out of the office, I looked at the big room that took up almost a quarter of the building. It had windows running floor to ceiling, showing anyone who cared to look exactly what was going on in that room.

And judging from the lab equipment and the metal tables in the middle of the room, nothing good went on in that room.

The smell of bleach almost knocked me down as I opened the door to the lab, but even through the acrid smell, the coppery smell of blood lingered. This was a room where bad things happened—a lot of them. It was a twenty by forty rectangle, with a row of cabinets along the far wall, and half a dozen workstations with smashed computers along the exterior long wall. Both interior walls were completely glass, but when I rapped on one, it *thunked* like Plexi instead. The fluorescents were augmented by high-powered work lights over four metal tables on wheels in the middle of the room, and there was a drain in the floor. No tools or scientific apparatus remained, just a bunch of broken glass and trashed computers.

"Guess they couldn't carry everything with them when they bailed on this place," Joe said, looking around.

"Probably stored all their research on portable drives or in the cloud. That way they could access it from any workstation," Becca said.

"What the hell were they doing here?" I asked, kneeling by the drain and picking at a clump of hair with my pocketknife. It came loose of the drain and a claw fell out, but not a claw from any animal I'd ever seen. It was long, needlelike, and seemed almost to be made of bone instead of nail.

"I'd guess they were experimenting on cryptids," Joe said. "Between the giant lizard, the cages, and that claw, they weren't testing eyeliner on bunnies in here."

"People do that?" I asked. Joe and Becca both stared at me, and I just shrugged. "I don't know shit about eyeliner."

"Yes, people do that, Bubba," Joe said. "But without any tech left behind, I can't see any way for us to find out if your cousin was here, and if he escaped, was released, or..."

"If he's dead," Becca said.

"I don't reckon gators got some kind of super sense of smell, like bloodhounds?" I asked Becca.

"Actually, we do. But I have to be fully in gator form to use it. That's a harder shift than my hybrid form, and it takes a lot more out of me. If I go full gator, I won't be able to shift back for several hours."

"That's gonna make communication difficult," Joe said.

"Nah," I said. "We can do signals. You bite Joe one time on the right butt cheek for 'Yes,' and one time on the left cheek for 'No.'"

"What if I don't know the answer to your question?" Becca asked. "Do I bite you?"

"Oh, hell no! You're banging him, he's the one gets bit. If you don't know the answer, just thwack him with your tail."

Joe and Becca exchanged a look. "Makes as much sense as anything," she said, then reached down to peel off her t-shirt again. I resolutely turned my back. "You literally just saw my boobs five minutes ago, Bubba," Becca said.

"Don't matter. You're Joe's girlfriend, so I don't need to be looking at you naked. Unless you're a stripper. Then it's a professional thing."

I heard her take a deep breath, like she was going to say something profound, then she just let it out, and the only thing I heard was the squelching and cracking sounds that accompanied a hundred-eighty-pound woman transforming into a quarter-ton reptile. I ain't never been close enough friends with a shifter to ask where the extra mass comes from. I always just figured it was magic, and I didn't ask too many questions. I mean, who am I to question the physics of some-body turning into an alligator? Once I accepted that as reasonable, everything else just kinda fell into place.

"Okay, Bubba, you can look now," Joe said.

As alligators go, Becca was an impressive example. She was at least ten or twelve feet long, with dark green skin. She saw me looking her over and lifted her head, opening her mouth in a broad grin that showed off the truly stupendous number of teeth she was rocking. I wondered at the sanity of anyone who would think they could cage one of these beasties.

"Do you smell your cousin?" I asked.

Gator Becca lifted her snout and nodded, then waddled over to the door leading out of the lab. I looked at Joe. "I'll admit I'm disappointed she didn't want to go with the butt cheek biting method of communication."

"I'm not," he replied, following his girlfriend out the open door of the lab. "Let's go."

Becca stood at the front door of the building, facing us and swishing her tail back and forth. "Oh, sorry," Joe said, stepping over her. "I forgot you can't open doors in that form."

She snapped at his butt as he walked by, and when she looked back at me, I'd swear I saw that gator smiling. Becca led us out the front door of the lab and made a beeline for the swamp. There was a pretty obvious trail, wide enough for one vehicle, and we stuck to it, with Becca in the lead, me in the middle, and Joe bringing up the rear. We'd been walking for about twenty minutes when Becca froze, holding her tail up in the air. I froze and put a fist up. Joe bumped into me about half a second later.

"Sorry," he whispered. "I was looking behind us." I couldn't give him too much shit. It's not like any of us were Navy SEALs or anything.

I pointed off to the right of the trail, and Joe slipped through the trees with barely a sound. I did the same thing to the left, as Becca crept down the trail toward the voices we could all now hear. I should say, I tried to slip through the trees without a sound. In reality, I managed to go ten feet without breaking more than half a dozen branches, and I didn't fall down. I also didn't want to think about what all was getting into the cuts on mine and Joe's legs. We were gonna have to get some serious shots when we got out of this swamp.

As the three of us crept forward, the trail opened up into a clearing about fifty feet wide, about twenty yards from a rickety pier that jutted out over the swamp. Three airboats were tied up to the pier, and about ten men were milling around the clearing. They were obviously waiting for someone or something. After a few minutes of watching, I figured out that one of the guys, a tall balding dude in a white lab coat, was trying to make a phone call. He had a satellite phone and was walking around holding it up like a bad Verizon commercial. There were half a dozen four-wheelers with trailers parked around the clearing, and each trailer had one or more cages on it.

The cages all held cryptids of some kind, from a pair of what looked like oversized housecats, except for the six legs, to a couple of humans, or maybe fairies or lycanthropes or something else that *looked* human, to one large cage with a very cramped alligator folded almost in half. All the beasties were obviously drugged, and the gator wasn't moving at all.

From what I could tell, these were the creatures they decided to keep when they bailed on their lab. What I couldn't figure out from the scene in front of me was why they ditched the lab in the first place, or what they were trying to do there. That was going to be something I brought up with the man holding the satellite phone. I found myself really hoping he didn't want to tell me.

I was trying to form a plan that was better than "walk into the clearing and shoot everybody" when I heard a familiar sound getting louder by the second. An airboat, or more than one from the sound of it, was approaching. If we were gonna save Becca's cousin, we had to move *now*.

7

I charged out of the brush, jamming the gauntlets onto my fists as I went. These guys all looked like humans, so I was pretty sure I didn't want to kill any of them. I wasn't a hundred percent sure that slamming a steel-clad fist with spike sticking out of it into the side of somebody's head wouldn't kill them but knew for damn sure shooting them with a fifty-caliber round from a giant pistol would. I hauled ass, and I could hear Joe charging in from the other side of the road, but we were way behind Becca.

I had forgotten one thing in planning this assault. Alligators are *fast*. Even on land, they haul a whole lot of scaly ass. And giant alligators motivated by abject fury of seeing their family locked in cages move even faster than normal. Becca was nothing but a grayish-green streak across the ground, outdistancing us easily, and drawing the first fire from the men we were attacking. A pair of the men raised shotguns, but Sat Phone Guy yelled something at them, and they slung the guns over their shoulders and drew Tasers instead. They fired at Becca, but the prongs couldn't penetrate her thick hide.

Then she was on them. She leapt, way higher than I expected those stumpy little legs to be able to propel her, and knocked one dude flat on his ass. I heard ribs crack all the way across the clearing, and I winced in sympathy. I've had a lot of broken ribs in my life, and they all suck. But I've never had as many at one time as this dude had. He was not going to be blowing up any balloons for a long time.

Becca lashed out with her tail, sweeping the other dude's legs out from under him, then she slammed her tail down on the back of his head, either stunning him or knocking him out cold. Then she charged farther into the mass of men, trying to drive them away from the four-wheelers, each of which had a hunting rifle strapped across the handlebars.

By the time I got to the nearest dude on the left side of the crowd, he'd realized I was coming and was trying to yank his Taser free of the holster. But he forgot the strap across the back of the handle, and all he was doing was yanking the holster up his leg real hard. I saw where the leg strap was going and figured he was gonna have a seriously swollen ballsack to go with the headache he was gonna wake up with, then I swung my fist around in a big, clubbing blow, turning my hand so I didn't bury a spike in his skull. He dropped like a sack of potatoes. It don't matter if I pull my punch or not, when a giant hillbilly with a fist wrapped in steel hits you, odds are you're hitting the ground.

I turned and strode across the clearing, making a beeline for Sat Phone Guy. He saw me coming, tossed the phone to the side, and adopted a martial arts stance. I hate martial artists. I'm a big dude, and running straight at something and knocking it down is kinda my default maneuver in any fight. Martial artists screw up that plan by using my size and momentum against me because of physics or some other kind of black magic. Any time I've ever squared off against a real martial artist, it hasn't ended well for me.

Unless I cheat. Amy's been teaching me some of her better moves since she got fired from DEMON, and now that I own a CrossFit gym, I've ridden into Atlanta a few times and trained with our instructors there. One of them's a badass were-panther who fights with a blend of *capoeira* and kickass that beats anything I've ever seen. Beats me, too. Like every time we spar, he beats me black and blue. But one thing I've learned from him is how to cheat when I face a better fighter than me.

Sat Phone was in his stance and he was ready to go. He was ready for any punch, any kick, any charge. But he wasn't ready for me yanking a knife off my belt and randomly flinging it at his face. It wasn't any kind of real throw, and I didn't figure I had a snowball's chance of doing any damage with it, but when something comes flying at your face, it takes your full attention until it's not flying at your face anymore. I took advantage of that distraction to pour on an extra burst of speed and dive at Sat Phone's middle like I was back running between the hedges at UGA.

Sat Phone Guy weighed about a buck-seventy, maybe one-eighty. I've been on a diet and exercise program that's got me down to a lean three-ten. So I didn't slam into his gut with twice his body weight, but I still nailed him with a whole lot of Bubba. I heard the air rush out of his lungs, then I heard a strange *hurk* kinda sound and drove him into the dirt like a fence post. I pulled up off him a little, and he rolled over, bent double, and I realized that noise was him trying to puke up everything he'd eaten for a week.

With him out of the fight, I looked over to see how everybody else was doing. Becca had another guy down and was chasing one around the clearing, playing with her food more than anything. Joe stood toe-to-toe with a dude holding a knife, and there was a long, bloody slash in his side. Two guys were down on the ground beside him, and he waved me off when I started in his direction, so I shifted my attention to the last two guys. One was standing on the end of the pier jumping up and down and waving at a bunch of airboats that were getting closer by the second, and the last had freed a hunting rifle from one of the four-wheelers and was lining up a shot on Becca as she chased his buddy.

I couldn't get to him quick enough, and I only had the one knife to throw. I didn't have any choice, so no matter how much I hated shooting humans, I flung the caestus off my right hand and drew my Judge pistol. I dropped to one knee to get a steadier aim, and I fired off a four-ten shotgun shell of silver buckshot, catching the rifleman in the leg and taking him down. The gunshot echoed loud in the clearing, which had been relatively quiet except for the sounds of punching and cussing. But now I'd added guns to the equation, and everything was different.

The shooter went down, and his buddy that Becca was chasing stopped in his tracks and stared at me. Becca took the opportunity to sweep his feet out from under him and club him unconscious with her tail, and Joe stepped forward and decked his knife-wielding opponent while he was distracted. I ran over to the bleeding man, who lay screaming on the ground. I rolled him over and looked at the wound. I got him in the meat of his thigh, just where I'd aimed, and he wasn't bleeding like I'd hit an artery. His leg was messed up something fierce, and he'd need a hospital soon, but he wasn't going to bleed out in the middle of the swamp as long as he got bandaged up pretty quick.

"Is that all of them?" Joe asked, jogging over to me and kneeling by the man I shot. "Hold still, and I'll bandage this up," he said to the man.

"Screw you, monster-lover," the dude said, then spit in Joe's face. Joe jerked back, stunned, and I punched the dude in the side of the head. His eyes rolled back, and he went limp. It'd be much easier to treat his gunshot wound now.

"There's one more, plus whoever's coming in on..." My words trailed off as I looked toward the dock and saw two dozen heavily armed men coming off the airboats. "Those boats I heard."

"You two back the hell up and get your hands in the air," yelled a giant man in an alligator-skin vest, cut-off jeans, and neon pink Chuck Taylor high-top sneakers. The insanity didn't end with his clothes, though. He wore his hair in a short mohawk dyed bright pink, and he wore a goatee dyed to match that hung at least six inches off the bottom of his chin. He sported mirrored aviator sunglasses and had flames tattooed up both arms. Full sleeves of fire. I looked down at my own inked-up arms, a mixture of designs and symbols representing people I'd known and places I'd seen and thought that while it lacked something in overall design aesthetic, the consistency of matching full sleeves did have some benefits.

Then my attention snapped back to what G.I. Mohawk was saying, and the AR-15-looking rifle he was carrying with what appeared to be a grenade launcher attached underneath it. I was pretty sure he didn't pick that up at Cabela's. "All y'all back up off them boys, now. I done told your asses once, and if I have to say it again, I ain't gone be so polite!"

I did as he directed, and he walked up to the first unconscious man and nudged him in the side with his foot. "Government pussies. I told y'all you shoulda hired my boys." He turned to look over his shoulder at his men, who were all dressed in some version of work shirt and jeans, every one of whom held a nasty-looking rifle. Except one short dude with the biggest pompadour I'd ever seen. He had two pearl-handled 1911s out, one aimed at me and one aimed at Joe. I wondered for about half a second how he got that hair to stay in that shape on an airboat, then turned my attention to more pressing matters. Like not getting shot.

"You, fat boy. Drop that pistol," Mohawk said.

I looked him up and down, wordlessly comparing our very similar waistlines, but it was one of them things where King Kong Bundy looks at The Big Show and they just decided to let it go and not bring up the obvious. I tossed the Judge to the ground a few feet off to my right, in a patch of grass just tall enough to make it a pain in the ass for them to find if they wanted to steal it.

"Now the hand cannon." He gestured at me again, and I drew Bertha from her holster with two fingers and pitched her into the same clump of weeds. "You packing anything else?"

"Your mom was impressed with what I was packing last night," I said before my brain could rein in my big mouth.

Mohawk crossed the distance between us in four quick steps and buried the butt of his rifle in my gut. I didn't tense up or try to prove anything, I just took the shot and dropped to my knees like he wanted. I'd already made one bad decision in the last five seconds; I figured another one might end up with me dead.

"You got any more guns, smartass?" he hissed down at me.

"No," I wheezed.

"Alright, here's what's gonna happen." He was staring at me, but he was speaking loud enough for Joe to hear, too. I suddenly realized Becca was nowhere to be seen. She must have slipped back into the swamp as they approached. Good thing, too. A pair of armed assholes trying to rip off their boss was one thing, but a pair of armed assholes with a were-gator was another thing entirely. The kind of thing that led to people shooting people I really didn't want to get shot. Like me.

"We're gonna load up the cargo on our skiffs. Then we're gonna load up these government pussies, and we're leaving. We're taking your rifle, but we don't want your pistols. They ain't good for much of shit out here but killing snakes, and Irene does that just fine." With that, he raised the barrel of his AR to his lips and kissed it.

Yep, he kissed his gun. Now, I love Bertha. We've been together a long time, and she's gotten me through a lot of tough spots. But I ain't kissing my gun. That's just one rung too high on the ladder of batshit crazy for me.

"You need to kill them," Sat Phone Guy said. I looked past Mohawk and saw that Sat Phone was sitting up and not puking anymore, but he looked like the only reason for that was the tank was empty.

"You didn't pay for that. You got more cash?" Mohawk asked.

"We can get you the money."

"This ain't exactly a credit operation, Director Shaw," Mohawk said.

"Don't use my name, you moron!" Sat Phone tried to jump up to his feet, but he got reacquainted with just how hard I'd hit him, and he stopped at being up on one knee.

Mohawk turned the rifle on Sat Phone, and I thought for a brief second that some of our problems were about to solve themselves right in front of my eyes, but he showed amazing restraint for a man with that kind of fashion sense, and just snarled at Sat Phone. "You think he whooped your ass, you snotty little prick? You call me a moron one more time, and I'll learn you what an ass-whooping looks like. Now you paid us to pick up you, your men, and your cargo, take you to our place, and keep y'all safe until your people get down here to pick you up. We're gonna honor our end of that bargain. You want to amend our arrangement, we going to have to go back to the negotiating table, and I have to say, I ain't liking your offer so far."

"I'll give you fifty thousand dollars to shoot them both right now," Sat Phone said, finally getting to his feet.

"Okay," Mohawk said. I looked at the clump of weeds where my guns were, wondering if I could get to them and get more than one shot off before I got too shot up. "You hand over fifty large, and I'll put holes in 'em right now."

"I don't have it with me," Sat Phone said, to my eternal gratitude.

"I might have mentioned this ain't a business that runs on credit. No cash, no killing. Let's go, boys. Load up them cages, then put the sleeping dumbasses on top of 'em. Director Shaw can ride with me."

Sat Phone sputtered a little, but in less than two minutes, Mohawk's boys had the air boats loaded with snoozing men, little rafts they were towing along behind the airboats loaded with cages and were all headed back toward the swamp. Mohawk walked over to where I knelt. I hadn't bothered to get back up after he hit me in the gut. I figured might as well keep to as small a target as I could make. "Now this would be the part where I said don't follow us, but since we're taking the boats, and the four-wheelers are out of commission, I ain't worried about it."

I must have looked confused because he chuckled and said, "Oh yeah! I knew there was something I was forgetting." Then he turned and shot out two tires on each ATV, one right after the other. He never needed a second shot, and he never took more than half a second to aim. This was a dude who knew how to shoot. In less than ten seconds, every four-wheeler was disabled.

"Now, as I was saying, there ain't no point in you trying to follow us. So don't. Go home. I don't know what your beef is with Shaw and his DEMON dudes, and I don't care. If I see you again, I'm not gonna be nearly as nice."

With that, he turned and walked back to the lead airboat, leaving me on my knees in shock at the last thing he'd said. After the airboats were gone, I stood up, got my guns, and walked over to where Joe was wiping down the cut in his side with a strip torn off his undershirt.

"Did he say those guys were from DEMON?" Joe asked.

"Yeah," I replied. "And he called the dude with the satellite phone Director Shaw."

"What's that mean?"

"Director Shaw is the new head of cryptids at DEMON."

"Is he the one who fired you?"

"I think so. Except I've heard of Director Shaw before. And he's black."

"That dude was so white I think this was the first time he's seen the sun in a year."

"Yeah, I noticed." I shook my head, trying to figure out what the hell DEMON was doing with cryptids in the Florida swamp and what was going on with everybody and their damn brother apparently being named Director Shaw all of a sudden.

Just then Becca stepped out of the woods. She was back in human form, back in her clothes, and had a grim look on her face.

"I'm sorry, babe," Joe said. "We had them, but then those other guys showed up."

"Yeah, I know. Sorry I bailed, but there was too many of them, and I figured if they knew I was a shifter, they'd throw me in a cage sure enough."

"Yeah, probably so," I said. "I don't know how the hell we're gonna track them now. We'll have to go all the way back to our airboat and hope Skeeter can come up with some kind of tech magic, I reckon."

"We ain't gotta track 'em," Becca said.

Joe and I both looked at her, and after a second, I said, "Okay, I'll play. Why don't we have to track them?"

"Because that asshole with the mohawk? His name is Gator Clyde, and he runs an exotic alligator show about twenty miles from here. He wrestles alligators for a living, and my family has been trying to prove he's also poaching gators for years. We don't have to track him. I know where the son of a bitch lives."

8

Half an hour later, we were back at our airboat with Becca weaving us through the swamp at speeds that made me unsure if she was running a rescue operation or trying out for NASCAR. We bounded over clumps of grass that I woulda swore were way too big for the boat to clear, swung around others that I thought should be no problem, and navigated the channels of water, land, and whatever was between like a really noisy rocket.

Right about the time I started wondering if I was gonna have to revisit everything I'd eaten for the past week, she cut the motor and we glided up to bump against a finger of verdant land jutting out at the beginning of a large patch of what looked like solid land. In front of us was mostly normal wetland forest, thick foliage and under-growth, but the ground looked solid. I could hear the hum of cars coming from not too far away and gave Becca a quizzical look.

"We're coming up on the back side of GatorLand," she said by way of explanation. I kept looking at her long enough that she got the picture that I didn't have no damn idea what GatorLand was, and she chuckled and nodded. "Sorry. That's where Clyde does his shows. He's got this big-ass chunk of property right on the edge of the swamp. His granddaddy was on the county zoning committee back in the forties and found out early where they were gonna put in the road through the swamp, so he bought up two or three thousand acres right here at the mouth of the swamp, knowing the value would go through the roof once the road got built. Clyde inherited what was left of it, about three hundred acres, and turned the front-facing half of it into a gator park and zoo."

"You figure that's where he took the cryptids and the DEMON agents?" I asked.

"It's the only place that makes sense. He's got plenty of room to store the creatures in those cages without anybody being able to see them, and there's access for big trucks to come in and transport them out of here. Which I reckon is probably going to happen tonight."

"Yeah," I agreed. "If DEMON wasn't planning on hitting the road as fast as they could, us showing up and screwing up their escape plan woulda accelerated the timeline."

"But they were moving out before they knew were here," Joe said. "Why? They had a secluded spot to do whatever they were doing, and I doubt more than a handful of people even knew they were in the state. Why burn it all down now?"

"No telling," I said. "Could be something happened that ain't got anything to do with us. Could be their budget got cut, and this is what happens when they downsize."

"Cremation is kind of a shitty severance package," Becca said.

"Alright, Becca," I said. "This is your territory, which means it's your show. What's the plan? We go buy tickets and gawk at the gators, then jump the rail at the finale and stage a jailbreak?"

"I thought we might try to be a little more subtle than that," she replied, and I saw a little grin poke through the grim cloud that had hung over her since Clyde and the cryptids got away from us.

"Oh well," I said, mock-disappointed. "I reckon subtle is probably the way to go. After all, I forgot my grenade launcher when we were loading up for this rescue."

"Well, now, that's just sloppy," Joe said. "Obviously things are falling apart without me there to watch over y'all."

"You ain't far from wrong," I agreed. "Okay, lady. You're driving. Where we headed?"

"We're on the southwest corner of the GatorLand property. He's got a basic chain link fence that goes around most of the perimeter starting about ten yards in. See it?" She pointed through the trees, and I could see a fence about ten feet tall topped with concertina wire. "It's tall, and it's reinforced every six feet instead of eight to make it sturdier."

"Why so strong?" Joe asked. "Or tall, for that matter."

"Panthers," Becca said. "That's the reason for the height, anyway. He had the fence at eight feet originally, without the razor wire on top, but a panther jumped clean over it one night and ate up all his flamingos. That's when he went higher and added the top wires. The reinforcement? That's probably me and my folks' doing. We might have broke in once or twice and set a bunch of his gators loose."

"Might have?" I asked.

"I ain't confessing nothing, Bubba. You never know who might be listening." Given that just a few months ago I'd dug a tracker out of my fiancée's arm that her last employer planted there so they could keep tabs on her, I couldn't argue.

"Okay, then since you might have broke in once or twice, you might have an idea of how the place is laid out," I said.

"I might," she replied with a grin. "The first fence ain't the problem. It's what he's got set up after you get through the first fence. There's a second fence, just as high, and this one's got enough current running through it that I can't stand to touch it even in full gator form. Not that I can shift again this soon anyway. Like I told you, going from hybrid to human and back and forth, then full gator to human took a lot out of me. I gotta recharge my mojo, so to speak."

"Alright," I said. "So, we got an easy fence, and we got a hard fence. Any ideas on how to get through the hard fence?"

"Yes, but you're not going to like it," Joe said.

He was right. I didn't like it. I even said as much, more than once, as we waited in line to buy our tickets to get into Clyde's Colossal Reptile Extravaganza and Alligator Emporium. We stood out a little, given the amount of mud on our clothes, but not too much. More than one person in line with us looked like they had just slithered out of the swamp on their bellies, and ours wasn't the only airboat tied up to the dock.

"This is a terrible idea," I muttered.

"You got a better one?" Joe said, his voice just above a growl.

"No."

"Then shut up and buy the tickets."

I did as I was told, showing my AAA card to get five percent off admission and still feeling my eyes bug out a little at the ticket price. We paid for the Park Pass, which gave us all day admission to wander around the gator farm and bought the cheap seats to the last Extravaganza of the day. I figured if we were stuck in this redneck hell, we might as well get a show out of it. Maybe I'd get lucky and Clyde would feed a DEMON agent to a gator.

Becca stayed behind, waiting outside the electrified fence at a spot Joe marked on his cell phone's GPS. She figured that there had been enough bad blood between her family and Gator Clyde that her picture was probably number one on his Do Not Fly list at the front gate. Me and Joe walked in without incident, and I had to give them props for the way they shuffled us from the ticket counter through a pavilion dedicated to educational displays about alligators, snakes, and other swamp-dwelling creatures like herons and snapping turtles.

Right by the exit of the education pavilion was a big rack of cheap digital cameras, disposable cameras, binoculars, colorful maps, and glossy guidebooks of the park, all for sale at prices that made me choke a little. I thought about buying a bottle of water, then I saw the price on those and decided if I couldn't find a water fountain, I'd sooner drink out of a mud puddle than pay that much money. Wouldn't be the first time I've drank questionable things off the ground.

It was late in the afternoon, with only about forty-five minutes before the final show of the day, so all the foot traffic was moving at a pretty good clip around the loop the whole park was built in. It was built in such a way as you couldn't go straight to the big plaza where they held the shows, you had to walk through the whole park to get there, which would send you past a couple of kiosks with sunglasses, more maps, and more cameras, plus a couple of small full-service restaurants set in the far back of the park, right about the midpoint of the long loop through.

The displays and habitats actually were pretty good, especially for a private zoo. The areas where the animals lived were expansive and seemed clean, with good signage around the guardrails telling what was in each wide pen. The animals were sectioned off from each other, but there were no cages in sight, just landscaped chunks of swamp divided by fake stone walls and iron bars, with deep ditches to keep stupid humans from going into the habitat, either on purpose or accidentally.

That didn't stop a pair of dumbass teens from climbing up onto a guardrail and posing there while their friend stepped back right into my chest trying to get a better shot on his cell phone camera.

"Hey, fatass, get outta the way. I'm trying to take a picture here," the kid who bumped into me snarled.

I looked down at him, all hundred-twenty pounds of acne and attitude, and contemplated just chucking him into the pen to see if the gators inside were hungry, but after a second's thought, I decided that would be cruel to the reptiles. I just stepped out of the way, wishing I wasn't trying to be all covert so I could turn him upside down and pound him into the mud like a tent stake.

I bent down to Joe and said, "Let's get out of here before I kill somebody. There's way too much gawking, and it'd probably be better if we didn't end up in anybody's selfies."

"Good point," he said with a nod, and we pushed on, sweeping quickly through the rest of the park. The rendezvous point with Becca was behind the restaurant at the very back of the park because we all figured it wouldn't be too out of the ordinary for a couple of folks out of uniform to wander around back there looking for a crapper. I figured that excuse was at least good enough to buy us time while I knocked anybody who found us unconscious.

We grabbed a couple of seats way back on the aluminum benches that passed for seating in Gator Clyde's Reptile Pavilion, waving off the two teenaged girls in purple t-shirts and khaki shorts marking them as park employees who tried to sell us programs for twenty bucks. Somehow I managed to hold out even against the temptation of them letting me pet the snake hanging around their necks.

When we got to our seats, I leaned over to Joe and whispered, "I thought boa constrictors were from South America."

"There are some in Florida, too," Joe replied. "I don't know if they started off as pets that got set loose, or what, but the climate agrees with them, so you can find them living wild in the swamps. Usually a little farther south of here, but they are a native species now."

"You've learned a lot about Florida reptiles since you came down here," I said.

"Date somebody who spends part of her time as one and you develop a lot more interest in reptiles than you ever had before," he replied. "I think they're starting."

Sure enough, the lights on the stage had come on, and the strains of AC/DC's "Thunderstruck" were coming out of the PA system. Spotlights ballyhooed all over the arena, and colored lights flashed on an arch made of aluminum truss at the back of the stage. The stage was a raised area about three feet off the ground in front of a wide dirt floor some sixty feet wide by twenty feet deep. A pair of ramps led off either side of the stage to the floor, and a curtain of shiny silver slit fabric hung in the arch. It reminded me uncomfortably of most strip clubs I'd been to, and I really hoped there weren't going to be naked women with alligators at any point in the show. That's a kind of mixing business and pleasure I wasn't interested in.

The music grew louder, the lights flashed faster, and the spotlights swept around one last time and locked in on the arch just as the song reached a crescendo. The shiny curtain yanked back, and through the arch, standing on the back of a pair of alligators and riding them like living skateboards, one under each foot, was a grown man that looked like the love child of David Bowie and Macho Man Randy Savage got caught in a craft store explosion.

If his earlier outfit had seemed flashy, it was now obvious that he was being subtle in the swamp. Now he wore hot pink metallic platform boots with lime green spandex pants tucked into them. He still had on the gator-skin vest, but this one was the same shade of pink as his boots, and underneath it was a lime green lamé long-sleeved shirt. He wore huge sunglasses on his face, and I could count at least half a dozen hoops hanging from his ears. The whole look was topped off not just by his hot pink mohawk, but somehow he had taped LED light strips to his scalp on either side of his 'do and his head changed colors along with the music.

The gators moved forward, carrying the man on their backs like some kind of modern-day twisted Cleopatra surfing on giant lizards. The music got louder and louder, and the lights on his head flashed brighter and brighter until he threw up his hands, letting loose of the leashes he was using to guide the gators, and in a flash of fireworks shooting up from the dirt and a curtain of sparks shooting down from the ceiling, Gator Clyde had arrived.

9

After all the effort put into the entrance, the show was a lot less impressive. Clyde stepped down off his gator-skis, who made no attempts to chew his feet off, disappointing me and I'm sure about half the people in the stands. Then he had his lovely assistants, a quartet of, shall we say, *enhanced* young women, walk around for the better part of an hour holding snakes, lizards, and baby gators while Clyde paced the stage with a microphone in his hand. It was kinda like a really boring nature documentary, where nothing gets eaten for the whole damn hour.

Then, at about the fifty-minute mark, the girls cleared out of the dirt ring in front of the stage, and Clyde walked down one of the ramps, talking as he went. "Now, ladies and gentlemen, and the rest of y'all too." He paused here for a laugh that the crowd obligingly gave him. I reckon when you pay nearly two hundred bucks per ticket, you're gonna be determined to have a good time. Me, I was just hoping that I could go through Clyde's wallet after I beat his ass. Otherwise, I was gonna have a tough time affording gas to get home when we were done with this trip.

"It's now time for the main event, the part of the show you've all been waiting for. Now is the time when I will take my own life in my hands, trusting only on the body the Good Lord above has given me, my wits, and the good karma of all you people to help me in this challenge. It's time for me to wrestle the biggest, the meanest, the most homicidal alligator I've seen in my thirty years working around reptiles. Ladies and gentlemen, I'm gonna wrestle The Leviathan!"

With that, he made a grand sweep of his arm toward the stage, and a door under the center of the platform slid open. We all stared into the blackness for a long heartbeat, then another, then, just as I was about to yell out something at least I would have found funny, the biggest damn gator I've ever seen strolled out from under the stage like it owned the whole arena. Which, at that moment, it did.

This monster was close to twenty feet long, with a wide head and thick legs longer than any I'd ever seen on an alligator. I leaned over to Joe and whispered, "Is that some kind of super-gator I ain't never heard of, or did they just import the son of a bitch from Chernobyl?"

"It's a were-gator," Joe replied, keeping his voice to a whisper. "Look at his eyes."

I did as he said, and sure enough, there was an intelligence there I wasn't used to seeing in the reptiles we'd been surrounded by on our walk through the park. This gator was watching the crowd, looking for the quiet sections and turning its massive snout toward those people, all the while keeping a close watch on Clyde for signals.

"Are weres always bigger than normal gators?"

"It depends on whether or not they're big people, Bubba. Becca isn't any larger than a typical female alligator, and her granny is downright small. She told me she's got cousins that don't come out of the swamp very often that are better than twelve feet long, but I'd lay good money this guy's a behemoth in all his forms."

"You're saying he's probably strong as shit either in this form or his hybrid form?" I asked.

"You saw how strong Becca is when half-shifted. This guy would be probably twice as powerful. Why?"

"Well, since he's obviously in on the show with Clyde, I bet he's got something to do with the cryptid smuggling, too. And that means at some point before we get out of here, I'm probably gonna end up fighting him. I'm just trying to figure out exactly how much he's gonna kick my ass before it happens, so I can know how much ibuprofen to stock up on for the drive home."

"I'd say a lot."

"Yeah, I'm thinking the same thing." I turned my attention back to the dirt floor, where Clyde and Leviathan, or Levi for short, were stalking each other in a circle, eyeballing each other like boxers feeling each other out. That works a little different for alligators, since their eyes are on the side of their heads, so Levi kept swinging his head from side to side to keep Clyde in his field of vision. I've done a little gator wrestling in my time, but I figured this was likely to be a lot different from those times. For one thing, there were no coeds in bikinis, no mud, and I wasn't drunk as a skunk, mired in deep depression and half-suicidal with guilt over getting my girlfriend killed by my werewolf father.

My twenties were a difficult time.

The trick to gator wrestling, as I was told back nearly twenty years ago, was to jump on the alligator from above and behind, where it couldn't see you. Then you wanted to flip it over onto its back and immobilize its jaw as fast as possible, preferably without getting your hand in its mouth. That was a good way to end up with the world's best Captain Hook cosplay. I don't remember a whole lot about my match against the gator, on account of most of a handle of Captain Morgan being in my belly before I dove into the mud on top of the beast, but what I did remember went contrary to everything Clyde was doing, giving even more credence to my theory that this was all choreographed.

Suddenly, with a blur of dark green and yellow, Levi streaked across the dirt toward Clyde, who dove out of the way at the last second, somehow in his complete surprise still managing to dodge the attack in a perfect forward roll that had him bouncing to his feet almost before the crowd was done gasping in fear for his life. Then

Levi charged again, not giving Clyde a chance to catch his breath. This time the brave crocodile wrestler leapt high into the air, letting Levi run right under him. Clyde hit the ground, spun around, and sprang for the gator's back, just like I remembered doing so many years ago.

Except there wasn't a gator there when he landed, and Clyde slammed to the dirt spread-eagled. The whole audience, me included, winced at the massive *thud* and the cloud of dust he made when he landed, then everyone held their breath as Levi barreled in toward the defenseless Clyde from his right side. With a thousand pounds of gator bearing down on him, Clyde barely managed to scramble to his feet and start running around the floor, Levi in lukewarm pursuit.

We'd seen a few hours ago exactly how fast an alligator can move when it's motivated, and this alligator was totally unmotivated to catch up to its prey. It waddled along, letting Clyde grow the distance between them until he lured the alligator back to the center of the ring. Then Clyde leapt up onto the stage, sprinted across the elevated platform, and dove onto Leviathan's back. He landed solid on the gator's back and wrapped his arms around the creature's body right behind its head, where a human being's neck would be. Then he grabbed his right elbow with his left hand and curled his right arm over the top of the gator's head, squeezing it tight to him.

I leaned over to Joe. "Did he just put an alligator in a sleeper hold?"

Joe grinned at the spectacle in front of us. "Yep. Looks like it's gonna work, too. If there was a ref, this is where he'd be lifting up ol' Leviathan's arm to see if he was still awake."

There wasn't a ref, so we had to take it on faith that the alligator was unconscious when it flopped on its belly to the dirt, and Clyde carefully disentangled himself from the beast. He reached up to the stage, where one of his lovely assistants appeared out of nowhere to hand him a microphone. He panted a little as he addressed the crowd, his amazing ensemble now covered in dust and scuffed up in more than a few places.

"Leviathan will be out for about two hours, then we'll feed him a couple of guests who wandered off the marked paths earlier today, and he'll be right as rain." Clyde laughed. "Just kidding, folks. We'd never feed you to our alligators. After all, we don't know where you've been. But Leviathan is completely unharmed, just knocked out by my pinching the carotid arteries that carry blood to his brain. He'll sleep for a little while, then wake up feeling as refreshed as if he'd had a nice nap back in his habitat.

"But that's our show for today, folks, and since it is our last show of the day, please go ahead and make your exit through the gift shop, where you can pick up your very own 'I Wrestled Leviathan' t-shirts, plush alligator dolls, and signed eight by tens of me with all four of my lovely assistants, Gracie, Maisie, Daisy, and Lacey. Give them a big round of applause!" He gestured to the four young women standing on the stage, all waving in such a way to make sure their most crucial attributes to Clyde's show bounced around a lot.

"We will also have pledge cards in the gift shop where you can make a monthly donation to keep things going here at GatorLand, Central Florida's home for reptile conservation and education. We are a federally recognized non-profit, so your donations will be tax-deductible! And don't forget to tell all your friends about the great time you had at GatorLand, and we are available for private tours, weddings, birthday parties, bar mitzvahs, and gender reveal celebrations!"

I looked over at Joe, but he just waved a hand at me. "Don't ask. It's some crazy white people thing."

"Joe, we're white people," I reminded him.

"We're not *that* white. What's the plan?"

"We swim upstream and try to work our way back to the restaurant, hide out until the place is empty, then cut power to the fence so Becca can get in. Then we find her cousin, set him loose, and try to do it without the giant were-gator catching us and biting off any parts of me that I'm particularly attached to."

"Are there parts of you that you aren't all that attached to?"

"Not a one. Now let's steer clear of Sleeping Beauty over there if we can. I left Bertha on the other side of the fences with your girlfriend, so all I've got is my Judge, and I don't think that's going to do the job against that dude in any of his forms."

"Probably right. Okay, the crowd seems to be slacking off. Let's try to make our way back to the restaurant." He led the way, and we moved up to the back of the arena and started walking in the opposite direction as everyone else. We got clear of the steady stream of park guests, but hadn't made it much more than another dozen feet when a teenaged boy with a STAFF shirt and a nose that probably came with its own zip code stepped in front of us with a hand out.

"The exit is in the other direction, sirs," the kid said, a gentle "old people are stupid" smile on his face.

"I left my phone in the bathroom at the restaurant," Joe said. "I just noticed when I tried to take a selfie in front of the stage. We're just going to run back real quick and grab it."

I could see the war going on inside the kid. He had his orders to not let anybody go back into the park, especially not without passing through the gift shop, but he understood the symbiotic relationship most people who aren't me have with their cell phones. Dark clouds of indecision flitted across his face.

"Come on, man," Joe said. "I really want to send a selfie back to my daughters. They decided to stay at the hotel and hang out by the pool, and I've got all these pictures on my phone to show them how cool this place is and how much fun they missed. If I don't have those pictures when we get back to the hotel tonight, I'm gonna be just lame dad again."

That pushed the kid over the edge. "Okay," he said, stepping out of the way. "But hurry. And if somebody else stops you, and they probably will, just tell them Tyler with security gave you permission to go back and get your phone."

"Thanks, Tyler," Joe said.

"Oh, I'm not Tyler. That guy's a douche. If anybody's gonna get their ass handed to them for you two goofs wandering the park alone, I'm good to let it be him."

I held up a hand, and the kid gave me a high five. I approve of a little creative misdirection, and I approve of placing blame on assholes whenever possible. This kid was gonna do just fine in life. Joe and I stepped past him, walked down the stairs to the door we'd come in through, and in just a few seconds, we were hauling ass through a deserted reptile farm to cut open the fence and execute our rescue mission. For once, it looked like everything was going according to plan.

I have got to learn to stop thinking stupid shit like that.

10

We hid in a storage shed right beside the employee bathrooms behind the restaurant until everything outside quieted down and we could no longer hear any movement or conversation. Joe's phone told him it was just a few minutes until sunset, so we figured it was as close to safe as it was going to be to go hunting for the switch that would turn off the electric fence. We stepped out of the shed, looked around, and immediately set off in opposite directions.

That could be a metaphor for mine and Joe's entire adult relationship—trying to do the same thing in totally different ways. He was always looking for compromise while I was always kicking down doors. He was going to church while I was going to strip clubs. His way usually ended up with fewer bruises, but mine ended up with better stories to tell around the campfire with a beer in hand. But this time I stopped, turned around, and followed his lead. We were here to save his girlfriend's cousin, so I'd let him run the show.

Turned out to be a good thing, too. It was only about five minutes of weaving through shadowy patches trying to avoid security cameras before we came to a big building that had "Mechanical and Electrical" on a placard beside the door. A couple of truck-sized paths led up to the building, which had a big garage door on the side, and a regular-sized door on the end. It was a single-story block building with a metal roof, kinda like a short aircraft hangar without any door big enough to get an airplane out of. There was a massive transformer sitting on a concrete pad outside, and power coming in off three different electrical poles.

"If we take out that box, I bet we kill all the phone and internet for the whole park," Joe said, pointing to another pole on the opposite side of the building. One slender cable dropped down to a metal box on the side of the shed.

"Probably," I said. "But what does that do to get the power out to the fence?"

"I hope it would buy us a few minutes of confusion before they got out here to see the power had been cut and keep them from calling the local police on us. At least for a few minutes."

"Joe, these dudes are smuggling gators and working with black helicopter-type government agencies. I think Deputy Buford T. Beergut is the least of our worries. But if you want me to kill the data line, I'm your huckleberry." I took one step forward and stopped abruptly as Joe had a hold on my belt. "What?"

"Surveillance cameras," he said, pointing to the red light over the door of the shed.

"If we ain't been seen yet, we ain't gonna get seen. We done walked by about ten cameras getting here, and that's just the ones we've seen and tried to avoid. No telling how many we missed. This dude must be the most paranoid sumbitch in Florida, and that's a pretty high bar. Now are we gonna do this, or not?"

"Okay," Joe said, releasing his hold on my britches. "You take out the phone and internet. I'll deal with the door to the shed. Meet me inside in five minutes."

"No problem," I said, taking off at a brisk walk across the open area between buildings. I felt exposed, like in those dreams where you show up for work and you're naked and everybody else is wearing clothes. Except this time, I didn't think it was funny and twirl my wiener around like a helicopter prop the way I always did in those dreams. This time it was just uncomfortable and itchy between my shoulder blades like somebody was watching me.

I made it to the side of the building with nobody yelling or shooting at me, so that was a win. I stuck close to the side of the shed, and about a third of the way down, I found the electrical box I was looking for. A small padlock hung off it, but since I wasn't looking to do any delicate work, I didn't really care if I could open the lid or not. I reached up to the top of the box, where a pair of thin cables came in, grabbed them in my fist, pressed my other hand against the side of the building, and gave a good yank.

The result was pretty anticlimactic for all the sneaking around we did to get there. I didn't expect a whole lot, but at least a spark woulda been nice, maybe some kind of zappy electrical sound of expensive equipment dying a sudden and painful death. But nope. Nothing like that. The wires ripped out of the top of the box with barely any resistance, and I turned to go meet up with Joe at the front of the building. Maybe whatever he was planning would be more exciting.

I came around the corner and stopped cold, because standing at the front of the building, holding Joe by the front of his shirt and surrounded by three dudes in black t-shirts with SECURITY on the front who looked like they were Mr. June, July, and August of Meth Lab Monthly's annual calendar, was Gator Clyde himself. Clyde had Joe slammed up against the front of the building, and his fist was coming back for another punch to my favorite almost-uncle as I rounded the corner.

"Oh good, I was wondering if you brought your lard-ass friend with you," Clyde said, grinning at me. He and I were going to have a real serious chat about fat-shaming here soon. Probably within the next thirty seconds.

It was a good thing their shirts identified the goons with him as security guards, because the first thing I think of when I see scrawny rednecks with prison tattoos, missing teeth, and stringy, unwashed hair isn't, "Oh good, I must be safe in their hands." It's usually not so much thought as it is my putting one hand on my wallet and the other on my pistol. I didn't want to shoot anybody tonight, though, so I just squared up and waited for Clyde to give the inevitable order. After grinning at me like a chimpanzee for about five seconds, he did. "What are you morons waiting for? Kick his ass!"

Being the biggest dude in almost every fight, you get used to a few things. Fat jokes are one. Jokes about "how's the air up there?" are another. And getting dogpiled by three or four of the littlest assholes in any brawl is another. I don't like any of them, but I think I hate fighting multiple douchebags the most. Or maybe fat jokes. It might be a tossup.

And now I'd had both in one day, so I was in a peach of a mood as the first meth-mouthed inbred swamp rat reached me. I didn't pull my gun, since I try really, *really* hard not to shoot humans. But I did take one big step forward and slam my fist into his nose like I was hitting one of those punching bag games in the back of a bar. I heard multiple things in his face go *crunch*, and his eyes were rolled so far back in his head he could probably see the brain damage close up when he hit the ground.

The other two got to me at about the same time, but it was obvious from their hesitation that they didn't have any practice trying to beat up the same guy at once. On the other hand, I'd been getting double-teamed in every fight and football scrum since middle school, so having two dudes trying to kick my ass at the same time was nothing new to me. The only difference this time was they didn't have knives or broken beer bottles to slice me open with.

After feinting in a couple of times, the one on my left finally decided to go for it, and he dropped his head and tried to grab me around the thighs and take me down. Now I'm a big dude, and I'm kinda top-heavy, but it's gonna take a lot more than a hundred-sixty pounds of skinny asshole to knock me off my feet. I looked down at his back as he squirmed and tried to pick up my legs and topple me and decided this was the perfect time to channel my inner Dusty Rhodes. I reared up on my tiptoes, raised my right arm high above my head, and dropped all my weight down on the skinny guard's ribcage, leading with the point of my elbow. He fell face first to the asphalt and grabbed his back, writhing in pain.

I looked up at the last guard and grinned. He grinned back, then pulled a switchblade out of his back pocket and flicked it open. *Shit.* This was gonna hurt. There's only one thing to know about fighting a dude with a knife: you're going to get cut. The goal is to make sure you don't get cut or stabbed anywhere too important, so you try to control what parts of your body you offer up to the knife. Then you use other parts, like your fists, to beat the shit out of the dude with the knife before he kills you.

I shouldn't have worried. This brain surgeon didn't come at me, didn't try to charge in while I was adjusting to the idea of him having a weapon, didn't do anything that would make me think he'd ever actually been in a fight before right that minute. No, he twirled the knife around between his fingers like he was a majorette leading a parade, grinning at me the whole time.

"What do you think about that, tubby?" he said, that stupid grin stretched from ear to ear.

"I think you're a dumbass," I said, taking one big step forward. I got to about three feet in front of him and kicked him square between the legs like I was the second coming of David friggin' Beckham, only with more hair and no Spice Girl. Meth-head Number Three's eyes bugged out and the knife tumbled from his fingers as he clutched his now-powdered family jewels with both hands. I hit him right below his left ear with a haymaker that spun him around twice and almost did the same to me, and when he hit the dirt, he was in Dreamland with his buddy, and not the killer barbecue place in Alabama, either.

The whole affair took less than ten seconds, and then it was on to the main event. I looked at Clyde, expecting him to be watching the whole scrap, only to see Joe slumped against the wall of the building with his eyes rolled back in his head. I looked around for Clyde, but all I saw of him was a pink mohawk hauling ass away from us on a four-wheeler, yelling into a walkie-talkie about intruders and moving merchandise.

"Well, shit," I said, looking down at Joe, who had the beginning of one hell of a black eye and a busted lip to go with it. "There went the subtle approach. You wait here. I'm gonna go get the damn fence powered down and get Becca in here before the Gator King gets away into the swamp with her cousin and God only knows who else they've got in them cages."

Joe nodded up at me, rubbing the back of his head. I saw his fingers come away red and figured Clyde must have smacked his head into the cinderblock wall a time or two. Seemed like ol' Gator Clyde had a little more power under the hood than a normal human. Good. That way I wouldn't need to feel bad when I beat his ass like a drum.

I kicked the shit out of the door to the shed, which was a lot less effective than you might expect. It's been my experience that kicking down doors works best when they open in. This one didn't, it opened out, and was made of steel. So I fell flat on my ass next to where Joe was sitting, and it was a mark of how bad his head hurt that he didn't say a damn thing about it to me.

"I unlocked it before he jumped me," Joe said with a groan.

I got up, turned the knob, and pulled the door open. With a sigh and a shake of my head, I walked into the electrical shed. It was like most big electrical rooms, full of junk that shouldn't have been in there in the first damn place, so it took me a couple of minutes of pushing through cleaning supplies, wheeled mop buckets missing one wheel, and a couple of random Food Lion shopping carts. I didn't even know they had Food Lion in Florida, but Gator Clyde at least had a couple of half-rusted shopping carts.

I worked my way to the back wall where the biggest breaker panels were, figuring that the fence would take a lot of juice, but the electrical system was as cobbled together as everything else about Clyde's Gator World, or whatever the hell he called this joint. Nothing was labeled, there were panels wired to other panels with orange extension cords just coming out of one, swinging in midair and going into the side of the next one, and a couple of them didn't even have cover, just bare wire and breakers exposed for anybody to jam their finger into. I guess given how slack they were about electrical code, you could consider all the junk blocking the path to the breakers a safety device.

I stared at the mess for a long moment, then muttered, "Screw it," and worked my way back to the main power for the park. Now this I recognized. There was a big panel with a two-thousand-amp main breaker coming in off the power line. I pushed down on that, having to lean on it a little to throw the massive switch, and the whole room plunged into darkness as I shut off every bit of electricity across the entire compound.

"Let's see how you do in the dark, Clyde," I muttered. I pulled my phone out of my pocket and used the flash to light my way back out of the maze of crap, then I turned around and drew the Judge pistol from under the tail of my shirt. Bertha would have been a better choice if I'd had her on me, but judging by the shower of sparks when I emptied the pistol into the front of the cabinet, it was gonna take more than just flipping the switch to get power back to that fence, or anything else in the park for that matter.

I stepped outside into the gathering dusk just as a maintenance guy rolled up in a golf cart. He stepped out and looked at Joe, then looked at me coming out of the shed where all his troubles lived. "Hey! What are you—"

I never slowed down. I just walked right over to him, hit him in the nose one time, really hard, and shoved him flat on his ass. Then I squished myself into the golf cart and called to Joe. "Let's move, Padre! We got gators to save and assholes to hunt!"

Joe got in beside me and hung on for dear life as I tore off toward where we'd left Becca. I figured she would have already ripped through the fence the second the juice went down, but we still needed her to guide us to wherever she thought Clyde would be keeping Cousin Terrell.

I was right, and by the time we made it back to where we'd left

Becca, she was already headed our way. She handed me my shoulder holster and jumped onto the bench at the back of the golf cart, sitting up on her knees so she could see where we were going. "What took y'all so long?"

"Clyde found us. He whopped Joe a good one on the gourd and took off. I beat the shit out of three of his goons, but he's got a big head start on us," I said.

"Plus, we don't have any idea where we're going," Joe said. "We got turned around twice just coming back to you."

"Yeah, I think Clyde laid this place out to be confusing on purpose, so he could get free gator food from people getting lost back here," Becca agreed. "Go that way." She pointed over my shoulder to the right. "That leads to the docks, so the airboats had to land there. The shipping and receiving warehouse for the park is over that way, too. I'd guess that whoever your Men in Black are, they'll be bringing a truck in there."

"How do you know all this?" I asked.

"Look around, Bubba. Do you think there are that many places a were-gator is gonna want more for a summer gig in college than working here? Just about my whole family has worked at Clyde's going back nearly twenty years. Ever since he opened this place, it's been almost a rite of passage to spend a summer or two working at Clyde's. Up until the last few years, that is. Take that path on the left."

"What happened a few years ago?" I asked.

"Clyde went from being a swamp rat with a couple of gator pits and a hundred acres to some kind of circus clown with pink hair and a gator-skin vest. When he started, he actually cared about the animals. The gators that were here were the ones that got hit by cars and couldn't go back out into the wild when they healed up, or they were pets people got on vacation and couldn't take care of once they got big. It was a rescue, a sanctuary, with a real vet on staff and every-thing. Then Clyde started watching this redneck on YouTube with his tiger park and decided to follow his lead.

"Next thing you know, this place goes from donations for people to come see gators in pretty much their natural habitats to a couple hundred dollars a ticket for an 'experience' that comes with a tour, your picture riding on a gator or holding a baby alligator, and that bullshit show he does at the end of every day where he brings in every stripper for fifty miles and parades them around with the gators. I keep waiting for one of those ol' chompers to take a bite out of a boob and pop an implant like a damn water balloon, right there on the stage!"

"He went from a conservationist to a showman," I said.

"Yeah," Becca agreed. "It's like one day he was Marlin Perkins and the next day he's Jerry Springer. My people quit working here after that, and then we started hearing about him hunting gators out of season, raiding nests to take the babies so they would grow up in his show, taking way more alligators than the law allows, all kinds of poaching and stuff. But we never could get Fish and Wildlife to do anything about it. The guys we talked to made it sound like Clyde had somebody up the ladder looking out for him."

"Somebody like a bunch of government agents hunting, trapping, and killing cryptids in the swamp," I said.

"Somebody who doesn't want to be disturbed, so they keep the local gator poacher out of jail, and he keeps everybody away from their lab," Joe agreed.

"You say this all started a couple years ago?" I asked.

"Yeah, two, two and a half, something like that. Turn right and pull off after the turn. We're almost there."

"Just about the time we left for Fairyland," I said. "Dammit."

"We don't know that we could have done anything about it even if we were here," Joe said. "It's not like were high up on DEMON's ladder in the first place."

"No, but if Amy had any idea they were doing this kind of crap..."

"What, Bubba?" Joe asked. "What could you have done? Or Amy? Or me? Could we have taken on an entire government agency on our own? The best we could have done was leak the information to the other hunters, so Mason, and Mark, and Caitlin, and the others would have all known what was going on. We couldn't have stopped this two years ago. Hell, we probably can't stop it now. Not all of it. It's too big.

We're just a couple of regular guys with a few pistols and a bad attitude. And one bitch of a headache," Joe said. He rubbed the back of his noggin' for emphasis.

"Well, let's take those pistols, and that attitude, and go beat Gator Clyde's ass," Becca said. "The docks are right up ahead, and the warehouse where I expect they'll be loading up is just past that. If Cousin Terrell is still here, that's where he'll be."

"He'll be there," I said as we got out of the cart and moved forward on foot. "And we'll get him out. I promise."

She smiled up at me. "I appreciate it, Bubba. But I know the deal. Don't make promises you can't possibly know if you can keep."

Joe let out a sharp bark of a laugh. "Becca, let me introduce you to my friend Bubba. He's a washed-up ex-football player who's never held down a real job, finished college, or to my knowledge filed his taxes on time. But when he makes a promise, he comes through. The last time I saw him promise something, he promised to bring a missing girl home. He literally went to another dimension and broke out of a dungeon to do it. He went back to that dimension a year later and fought a *dragon*. He's not the brightest bulb in the box, and he could really use a shave, a haircut, and a mani-pedi, but there's not a person on this earth that I'd rather have standing beside me when the shit hits the fan. If he says we're getting Terrell back, you can set his place at the dinner table."

I didn't have anything to say to that. To be honest, I didn't think I could have said a word if I'd wanted to. It was pretty much the nicest thing anybody had ever said about me where I could hear it, even the bit about me needing a manicure. I just reached out, patted Joe on the shoulder, and gave him a nod. He nodded back, and without another word, we went to go bring her cousin home.

It took less than two minutes for every little bit of that to go sideways.

1 2

We spent a minute and a half of that two minutes just getting into position, which oughta tell you something about how fast the pooch got screwed. I sent Joe and Becca in through the docks to cut off that avenue of escape, while I looped around between buildings, sticking to the shadows the best I could as I came in from the shipping and receiving road. I jogged in with Bertha drawn, then sprinted from the corner of a big warehouse to the front of the cargo truck sitting there spewing diesel fumes into the twilight.

I could hear Clyde yelling at people to get stuff onto the truck, and it sounded like Sat Phone, aka yet another Director Shaw, was calling out orders, too. I slid past the driver's door, my attention focused on trying to be as stealthy as possible when I heard the creak of a hinge behind me and a voice yell out, "Hey! I got some asshole sneaking around over here."

I spun around to see the truck driver swinging down out of the cab with a baseball bat in one hand. He dropped to the ground with a *thud*, and I almost felt the ground shake under him. He was a short dude, maybe five foot six, but he was about five and half feet in all directions. I swear this dude was a sphere with a scowl and a baseball bat, all stuffed into a pair of blue jeans that looked like sausage casing, a Garth Brooks t-shirt that was stretched about to the absolute limit, and a greasy red Bubba Gump Shrimp Co. trucker hat. I felt like there was something ironic about an actual trucker wearing a trucker hat and wondered if that was meta enough to count as hipster. Then I remembered the bat and focused on the subject at hand.

I looked at Bertha in my hand and silently apologized to her for the indignity I was about to inflict upon her. I couldn't shoot the Oompa-Loompa-looking bastard without killing him, especially at six feet, and I didn't have enough time to holster her and lay him out before I got a face full of ash wood. I took two steps forward and slammed the butt of my pistol right into Cracker Fat Albert's forehead. His eyes crossed, then rolled back in his head, and he fell over backward. Kinda. When you're that fat, you don't hit the ground all at once. He kinda fell back, hit his ass, and then kinda rocked back and forth like a porch chair somebody had just stood up from.

Now a Desert Eagle is about four pounds empty. And I don't carry an empty pistol. Bertha slammed the weight of a bag of sugar into Tubby's forehead in an area smaller than my fist. He was unconscious before the bat fell out of his fingers. But fall it did, clattering to the asphalt like ringing a damn dinner bell.

With stealth completely out the window, I gave a quick look behind me and saw Clyde staring at me and waving off to somebody I couldn't see. I figured I was about to get some company I wouldn't like, so I decided to eliminate one problem, namely these assholes getting away easy if they managed to kick my ass. I took a few steps back from the side of the truck and shot out the driver's side tire, then put a round in the gas tank for good measure. The truck sagged to one side, and the bullet made a smallish hole going into the tank but blew a chunk the size of my fist out of the other side. Gasoline poured out onto the ground, ensuring that Clyde's buddies weren't going anywhere with their load of poached cryptids.

I holstered Bertha, and it was time to kick some ass. Half a dozen scrawny three-toothed security meth heads came around the truck, headed my way at a dead run. A couple of them had hunting knives out, and the first one to reach me had a pair of brass knuckles on his skinny fist. It didn't do him any good because I stepped out of the way of the punch he threw at my face, grabbed him by the belt and the front of his shirt, and spun around in a circle before I flung him at the next two idiots in line. They went down in a tangle of profanity and bad decisions, and I picked up the discarded bat as I walked past them.

The next goon was one of the guys with a knife, which would have worried me a lot more if he'd looked like he had any idea how to use it. I poked him in the gut with the baseball bat, then slammed my fist into the side of his head as he doubled over. He dropped to the pavement, and then there were two. The other moron with the knife was obviously the smartest one on his shift, because he stopped cold, looked at me, then just slid the hunting knife back into the sheath at his belt and raised both hands.

"Hey, Clyde," he called over his shoulder.

"What?"

"I quit." He took off his SECURITY t-shirt right there, threw it to the ground, and walked right past me, muttering, "I don't get paid enough for this shit," as he bailed in the middle of the scrap.

The last guy didn't have any kind of weapon visible, but also wasn't showing any inclination toward running away. "We gonna do this, or you just gonna bask in my glory all damn night?" I asked.

"You should run away now, fat boy," he said, and there was a sibilance to his voice that I didn't like.

"What is it with all the fat cracks?" I asked no one in particular. Not waiting for an answer, I stepped toward the goon and swung the bat at his shin. I thought if I broke his leg, he'd be out of the fight, but I probably wouldn't kill him.

He caught the bat one-handed and snatched it out of my hands like taking a rattle away from an infant. He seemed to be getting taller by the second, and his skin had a distinctly greenish cast to it. I watched as his eyes turned yellow, and his face morphed into a hybrid between a giant lizard and a human, which are not two species that make an attractive mix.

"A were-lizard? Are you friggin' kidding me?"

He wasn't, and the claws now living at the end of his fingers were no joke, either. He sprang toward me, arms extended, obviously expecting me to try to dodge around him. I didn't. I just let him crash into me, and we went down. It hurt, landing sideways on my arm as I tried to draw my Judge, but I managed somehow. I pressed the barrel to the side of the were-lizard's head and squeezed the trigger, not looking forward to picking shards of lizard skull out of my beard.

I heard the dry *click* of an empty pistol and too late remembered emptying the gun into the breaker panel to shut down the gate. I swear the lizard man smiled at me, at least until I reversed grip and knocked him out with the butt of the gun. It wasn't near as big and heavy as Bertha, but with a giant were-lizard about to rip my guts out, I was more motivated than when I knocked out the fat truck driver.

The lizard slumped on top of me, out cold. I wriggled free and got to my feet, stopping cold as I saw six DEMON agents with rifles trained on me. "Don't move," said Sat Phone Guy, who stepped out from behind the truck and walked over to me. He reached out and unsnapped the holster, then drew Bertha and looked at her. "That's a big gun."

"I'm a big dude."

"Compensating for something?" he asked with a sneer.

"I'll be wanting that back," I said.

"People want all sorts of things, Mr. Brabham. I wanted to be a surgeon. Couldn't make it through organic chemistry. But you wouldn't know anything about that, would you?"

"No," I replied. "I didn't have any problems with organic chem."

His head snapped around, then he laughed. "Director Shaw was right; you are a funny man."

"I thought dipshit over there called you Director Shaw." I pointed to Clyde, who took a menacing step forward but somehow managed to restrain himself before he actually got in front of any of the men holding assault rifles.

"Oh, I am Director Shaw. There are a lot of Director Shaws."

"Is this like a Negan thing? Do y'all wear red hankies around your neck and name your toys?"

"We are scientists, Mr. Brabham. We are scientists, and we are guardians. We are patriots, protecting humanity and the American way of life from monsters. There are monsters among us, Mr. Brabham! Sometimes you can't even see them until they let you. Like this piece of swamp trash." He pointed to the unconscious man beside me. He'd reverted to human form when I cold-cocked him, so instead of a giant scary lizard, he looked kinda peaceful. He was even snoring a little, which would have been a lot cuter if there hadn't been a little bubble of snot puffing in and out of his left nostril with every breath.

"You're protecting the world from the monsters. Okay, whatever. That's been the deal all along. Why are y'all all gung ho to kill all the cryptids now?"

"We're under new management," Shaw said with a nasty smile. It stretched across his face like a snake and just sat there, all venom and capped teeth. "And our new boss, well, she's got a whole new vision of the way things need to be done. And you, Mr. Brabham, you and your defrocked friend and his were-alligator girlfriend are screwing up the way things need to be done in Florida. Now we have to load these creatures into a truck and drive through the night to another research facility, all because you and your friends were snooping around."

"You're gonna need to call the rental place, too. I think your truck's leaking a little fuel." I took a deep sniff. "Yep. That's definitely diesel. I bet if you call them right now, they can get you another truck out here by morning."

Shaw lifted Bertha and pointed her up at my face. "Give me one reason I shouldn't just put you down right now, half-breed."

Man, I was getting really tired of being insulted. Half a dozen people had called me fat, and now this skinny prick was giving me shit because my mom's a fairy princess? I was through. I bent at the waist and pressed my forehead to the barrel.

"Do it, asshole," I said. I kept my eyes locked on Shaw's, and I saw his go wide. "Go on, shoot me. See just how damn magic I am. This is when you find out if bullets even hurt a half-fae. Pull the trigger, son. You know you want to!" I knew I didn't want him to, but I also knew I needed every bit of his attention locked onto me at that moment. I stared into his eyes, boring a hole in the back of his skull with my anger. At least, that's what I hoped it looked like. In reality, I was pretty close to pissing my pants because if this didn't work, I was going to end up on that truck next to Becca's cousin, and I did not want to end up in a lab like the one we found back in the swamp.

"Go on, Shaw," I goaded him a little more. "You feel froggy, son? Jump! Go on, jump! You want to do something? Then by God DO IT!" I roared the last bit at the top of my lungs and thanked everything I'd ever worshiped from Jesus to Jack Daniels to Hugh Hefner that Becca and Joe knew when to take a friggin' hint and opened Terrell's cage right on cue.

Because I saw Shaw's finger start to tighten on the trigger just as the roar of a furious alligator split the air. It sounded like exactly what it was—a prehistoric creature out of nightmare turned loose on a modern world, and it was coming for payback.

13

Becca was impressive in her alligator form. And by impressive, I mean scary as hell. She was long, and strong, and looked like something out of a dinosaur movie, only smarter and meaner. Add a couple hundred pounds of muscle, a few feet in length, and a healthy dash of really pissed off, and that's what she let loose when she opened Cousin Terrell's cage. My gambit to buy her and Joe time to free the captives worked, and now Terrell was ready to pay back every indignity that had been done to him, with interest.

He was a monster even as monsters went, better than fifteen feet long and half a ton if he weighed an ounce. And none of it was fat. Not that I'd know where gators get fat in the first place. But he was a lean, mean, ass-kicking machine, and he came out of that cage in fourth gear and picking up speed. There were three DEMON agents within ten feet of the cage, and they hadn't all turned around good before Terrell had bowled one of them over and just run him slap over, then tail-whipped the other pair of them flat on their backs.

Shaw, or whatever his name was, flinched and pulled Bertha's barrel off my forehead, which was the opening I was looking for. I straightened up and snatched my gun back. Then I took my left hand

and slapped that mealy-mouthed government douchebag so hard across the face that my palm hurt.

He gaped at me and reached for the pistol at his side, but that wasn't happening. I switched hands with Bertha and balled up my fist. I threw a right hook that bent Shaw's nose at a sharp angle to the rest of his head, and blood exploded from the center of his face like a watermelon at a Gallagher show. He just sat down, right there on the asphalt, like a toddler losing his balance, flat on his ass looking confused. I holstered my gun, grabbed him by the back of the head, and slammed my knee into his forehead. His eyes crossed, then closed as he slumped to the ground.

I took a look around the shipping yard, and it was chaos like I hadn't seen since that time Skeeter dragged me to Thunder from Down Under in Vegas. Only this had less baby oil and fewer dollar bills. DEMON agents were running around trying to get away from Terrell, who was herding them like a thousand-pound sheepdog made of teeth and retribution. Every once in a while one would stop and take a shot, but the were-gator's hide was too thick for their bullets to penetrate, so they were learning firsthand what the humans felt like in a Godzilla movie.

He wasn't biting anybody, not anywhere that really counted, just a chomp on the ass here and there, but he was definitely distracting the three remaining agents while Becca and Joe opened the rest of the cages. There were a few of Clyde's security goobers getting in the way, but nothing that pair couldn't handle. That left me with the fun stuff.

"Hey Clyde, wanna dance?" I yelled across the asphalt. I held out both hands in a "come at me" gesture and watched the Gator King's mohawk quiver in anticipation. He started walking toward me, not hurrying, just a steady, measured pace. I did the same toward him, figuring we'd get some space around us, I'd beat his ass, and then all the good guys could go home.

Then, as always seems to happen to me, it all went sideways. Because as Clyde walked, he got bigger. And bigger. And hairier. By the time he was halfway to me, Clyde was seven feet tall and must have weighed four-fifty or so. He walked on his hind legs with no trouble, and except for the pink strip dyed in the fur on his skull, he was completely covered in black fur.

Clyde the Gator King was a were-bear. Son of a *bitch*. This was gonna suck. I thought about pulling Bertha and just shooting him right there but couldn't in good conscience just straight murder the dude. "Joe!" I shouted above the fray. "Tell me you brought my gloves!"

"Catch!" he yelled back, flinging a backpack through the air. It fell way short, but at least it was off to the side and not between me and the giant fuzzy asshole lumbering toward me. I poured on the speed and ran for the bag, snatching it off the ground without slowing down. I kept running, knowing there was no way in hell I could outpace a black bear, but willing to give it the old college try. I bowled over a DEMON agent, and we went down in a tangle of arms, legs, and curse words. I ended up on top of the pile with the bag in my hands, so I ripped the top open and yanked out my caestae. The gauntlets weren't going to help with reach or power, but every other spike on the knuckles was clad in silver, so I could at least hurt the bastard.

Said bastard was looming over me as I scrambled to my feet, and I swear I saw his furry face split in a big grin. He reared back with one massive paw, and I did the last thing either one of us expected—I rushed him. I charged across the few feet separating us, getting inside his swing and keeping myself from taking the full force of his blow. He still clipped my shoulder pretty good, which made my left arm go numb all the way to the fingers.

But my right still worked, and it still had a big damn metal glove with silver spikes on it. So I punched the were-bear in the chest as hard as I could. With absolutely no effect. Sure, there was a little singeing of the fur where the silver touched, but my punch didn't do shit. The spikes weren't long enough to get through all the fur and hide, and he was too heavily muscled for my pitiful human strength to do any damage.

The same could not be said for the massive lycanthrope strength of the angry were-gator that snuck up on Clyde while I provided a distraction. Cousin Terrell slammed his tail into Clyde's legs right behind both knees, and the were-bear went down like somebody tipping over a refrigerator. Cousin Terrell backed up, then shifted to his hybrid form faster than I'd ever seen a lycanthrope change form. By the time Clyde was back on his feet, Terrell was upright and charging.

Sometimes, the best offense is a good defense. I should know, since I played on a pretty damn good defense back at UGA. Since college I've learned that sometimes the best defense is getting the hell out of the way, and that's exactly what I did. I didn't need to be anywhere in between that particular Godzilla versus Bearthra face-off, so I looked around to see if Joe or Becca needed my help.

They had everything pretty well in hand, with all the other cages and crates open and several cryptids either gathering around them or hauling ass back into the swamp. There was a skinny woman in her sixties with pointy ears and a pissed off expression, so I assumed she was a fairy. Next to her stood a little sawed-off dude with a pointy red hat, and I *knew* what he was. I'd had to fight a redcap on our trip through Fairyland, and they were mean, nasty, and fast. If I had to go anywhere near that little bastard, Bertha was clearing the way.

A big hairy backside was all I saw of the occupant of one of the cages, but by the fetid odor that wafted over, I assumed he was a skunk ape. I always thought they were taller, but he wasn't much bigger than the redcap. Funkier, though. And there was a slender, green-skinned creature with fins where his ears oughta be leaning heavily on the side of a cage. Joe saw me watching them and waved me over.

"Bubba, help get him into the water," he called. Joe had one of the creature's arms stretched across his shoulders, and I hurried over to him and did the same thing on the other side, shucking off my spiked gloves and tossing them to the ground as I went. The fish-person was built mostly like a human, except for the scales all over their body, the webbed fingers, and the elongated webbed feet. Oh, and the coloring, the fins for ears, the dorsal fin that ran from their forehead all the way down their back, and the smooshed-looking face with no nose.

Okay, the creature was bipedal and about six feet tall, but that's as far as any similarities to a human went. We got to the edge of the dock and slowly lowered the creature into the water. They sank beneath the murky water, then popped back up almost immediately, a smile showing off teeth that were way pointier than I was comfortable with, given how close those teeth had been to my throat thirty seconds before. The fish-person gave us a little wave, a burble of noise that I assumed was Flounder for, "Thanks, dude," and with a flap of their feet, was gone.

"That all of them?" I asked Joe.

"Except the vampire. She hauled ass the second we got her light-tight box open. They aren't nearly as fast as on *True Blood*, but she was *moving*."

"The fae together?"

"No, they seem to hate each other. The girl says she is Summer Court, and the redcap proudly pledged his allegiance to Mab and threatened her vengeance should he have to suffer any more indignities at the hands of stupid mortals."

"Great," I said. "Not only do we have a psychotic knife-wielding fairy, we have a *pompous* psychotic knife-wielding fairy."

"They took his knives, too. That's something else he's bitching about," Joe said.

"Oh, then that makes everything a *lot* easier. I walked over to where Becca stood between the fairy woman and the redcap, who were both yelling obscenities and insults at each other. I stood about three feet away and made a show of drawing Bertha. I ejected the magazine, then cleared the chamber and pushed that round back into the mag. I stuffed the clip into my back pocket and pulled one of my reloads from the shoulder holster. After checking the bottom to see the blue stripe of paint, I slammed the magazine home, chambered a round, and pointed Bertha at the fairy's face.

"Shut up," I said. I didn't raise my voice, didn't try to put any particular menace in it, I just stood there at six and a half feet tall holding a fifty-caliber handgun, and used my most matter-of-fact tone. The fairy shut up. "Thank you. Now hold whatever thought you were about to unleash while I deal with this dude."

I turned to the redcap, who glared at me and immediately started protesting his treatment, demanding his weapons, and threatening to bring down the wrath of my psychotic grandmother Queen Mab on our entire world if he wasn't sent home through the nearest ring of toadstools. I just put my hands on his shoulders and gently spun him around until he was facing the other direction. Then I picked him up by his belt and collar, spun around twice, and released on the third spin. The redcap sailed clear of the docks and hit the swamp with a massive *splash*. It was only about two feet deep right there, so he was able to stand up and have water only up to his armpits.

"Get yourself home," I yelled. "And tell Granny Mab I said hi. But if I ever see you again, I'm going to put a very large bullet made of very cold iron in your face. Is that clear?"

The redcap nodded and turned away, sloshing deeper into the swamp in search of a ring of toadstools. I turned back to the fairy, but I was distracted by a bellow of fury from where I'd left Terrell about to beat the shit out of Clyde the Were-Bear Gator King.

Things hadn't gone as planned in the time since I left Clyde in Terrell's apparently less capable hands than I thought because the bear was standing up over a prone hybrid man-gator, and it looked like he was about to rip Terrell's guts out.

After all the swamp-tromping we'd done to get him back safe, there was no way I was letting Clyde murder Terrell right there in front of me. I shot the pink-haired were-bear right in the chest four times with one of the biggest handguns in the world.

But since it wasn't with silver ammunition, all I did was piss him off.

14

W ell, I did a *little* more than piss him off. I got his attention, and I knocked him back a few steps and made him sit down on his big furry butt looking all confused like a punk-rock Yogi who lost his picnic basket. "Come on, bib boy," I said with a snarl. "You want to mess with the bull? You gonna get the horns!"

Yeah, it didn't make any sense to me, either, but I didn't get into this gig because I'm good at witty repartee. I got into it because I'm good at a couple of things—kicking ass and chewing bubblegum. And guess what I had run slap out of?

Gator Clyde, the were-bear—and take a second to wrap your head around *that* one—didn't stand back up on his hind legs like I expected. No, he just kinda rolled around on his butt, ended up on all fours, and ran at me that way. You know, like a bear usually does. I don't know why I was surprised by this because even in his hybrid form, it was easy to see that he'd be equally comfortable on two legs as on all fours, but it stunned me for about half a second.

But only half a second, because after that I had to go from antago-nizing the redneck lycanthrope amusement park entrepreneur to running like hell from him. I turned on my heels and hauled ass toward the docks, hoping that what I'd heard about bears not liking water was true. I ran right off the end of the wood planks, with a were-bear hot on my heels. I hit the murky green water with a huge splash, one which was eclipsed by the cascade of water Clyde kicked up when he came in after me.

That thing I heard about bears not liking water? Either I heard that way wrong, or whoever I heard it from was the world's biggest dipshit. Clyde hit that swamp like a fat kid cannonballing into the pool at the YMCA—you know a lot of water is about to get displaced, and you're pretty sure he's gonna pee on you at some point. My only saving grace was the fact that we were in a swamp.

Swamps aren't exactly known for their rocky, solid footing under-water. Hell, they ain't known for solid footing on land, either. But the muck I splashed down in was one-hundred percent mud, and I sank down to my ankles. Clyde, being much heavier than me, sank way deeper. And since he hopped right in on all fours, all four feet went down almost to the knee in muck. He was stuck tighter than a golf ball trying to go through a garden hose, and his head wasn't but about an inch above the water's surface. This was my only shot. I hated doing it, because despite the truly astonishing body count I've built up over the years, I don't like killing cryptids. Especially not the ones that are human some of the time.

Then I thought back to Clyde's fashion sense, and "human" stopped being a word I applied to him. I pulled my feet free, curling my toes to keep my boots from pulling off, and when I was able to move, I slowly lurched over to Clyde, my feet coming free of the mud with an audible *sllluuuurrrrppp* every time I lifted my feet. I came around to Clyde's left side as he wriggled and pulled and jerked trying to get loose. If he woulda slowed down a second and focused on getting one leg free, he could have been clear in seconds, and probably gutted me before I ever laid a hand on him.

But Clyde was not, in fact, smarter than your average bear, so he just thrashed around and splashed around and generally did nothing, until finally I was close enough to grab hold of the back of his neck and pull myself up onto his back like Hannibal riding his elephants into battle. Only, not an elephant, and without being a brilliant general. So really nothing like Hannibal and a lot more like a fat redneck riding a were-bear.

But I got up there, and I leaned forward, and I wrapped my arms around his thrashing neck, and I squeezed with all my might. I managed to get my left arm under his chin and pressed my right against the side of his head to control his movements. Then I grabbed my right forearm with my left hand and cranked that sleeper hold tight as I could. I scooched forward so as much of my weight was on his shoulders as possible, and I squeezed his throat and the sides of his neck while using my body weight to press his face down into the water. I have no idea if a bear has a carotid artery, but if they do, I pinched his off. And I choked him out. And I drowned his hairy ass. I kept Clyde all bound up and underwater until he stopped twitching and turned back to his human form.

The sudden shift and reduction in mass was startling, to say the least, and I basically fell off Clyde and ended up face-first in the swamp myself. But since nobody was trying to choke me to death, I just stood up and looked for the next ass to kick.

My eyes lit on the wobbly form of the one person I figured most deserved another bloody nose—Director Shaw, if that was his real name. The skinny prick was back on his feet, and he had his satellite phone in hand. "You think you've won? You think you've accomplished anything, you idiots? I make one phone call and you all end up disappearing! You'll be wiped off the map! No one will even remember you exist!"

He held the sat phone up high over his head with a giant shit-eating grin on his face. A grin that fell like a sparrow, with provenance, as a shot rang out across the swamp and his phone exploded in his hand. Shaw looked like something out of a Tex Avery cartoon with his eyes bulging out of his head as he looked up at the scraps of plastic and wire he held.

A hum like a horde of angry hornets filled the air as nearly a dozen airboats rushed in to the docks, every one of them loaded down with rednecks, and every one of them armed to the teeth. Better armed than that, given the expected number of teeth in any gathering of swamp folk. Creepy Granny piloted the lead boat, and standing in the bow grinning like a Cheshire Cat and holding Joe's rifle, was Geri. I shoulda known she wouldn't be left out.

She was out of the boat as soon as it got within a few feet of the dock, hopping off and fast-walking in our direction, never taking the gun off of Shaw. As she got to me, she reached down with her left hand and took something out of her pocket. I recognized a Bluetooth earbud and put it in.

"You need to answer your damn phone when I call!" Skeeter's voice screeched in my ear. I resisted the urge to pluck the earpiece out and fling it into the swamp, but just barely.

"I'm pretty sure my phone is either crushed, or drowned, or both, Skeeter. And I thought we didn't have reception out here, anyhow?"

"You're at a friggin' amusement park, Bubba." I could almost smell the disdain coming off Skeeter's voice. "You think that dumbass with the mohawk didn't get a cell tower put up? I've been able to track y'all's phones ever since you got there, but not a damn one of you will answer!"

I shook my head. "So you got Geri and the white trash army to come save us?"

"Be careful how you talk," Skeeter said. "Them's Becca's people." I looked around, and sure enough, about half the men and women coming off the boats were holding shotguns (and one flamethrower, which made me really jealous) on Shaw and his men, and the other half were shaking hands with Joe or hugging Becca.

A man who looked to be about sixty walked over to Terrell and knelt next to his head. He had a backpack over one shoulder, and he started pulling out clothes. When there was a whole outfit there, Terrell shifted back to human form and got dressed, then hugged the man like he was a life preserver. When they pulled apart, I could see the resemblance. Terrell had his daddy's nose.

"Are they all were-gators, Skeeter?"

"I don't know, Bubba. You want to ask 'em?"

I decided against it, since we had more important stuff to take care of. Like deciding whether or not to shoot this version of Director Shaw. I stepped over to the terrified little man, who was frantically looking around for a rescue. There was nothing coming. Clyde was dead, Shaw's goons were all either unconscious or beat to shit and disarmed, and the last of the park "security" had gone running off into the night, dropping pieces of his uniform as he went.

"You got some questions to answer, Shaw," I said, looming over him.

"I don't have to answer anything!" he yipped up at me. "I know my rights, and I am a duly authorized agent of the federal—"

I slapped him again, this time with my right hand. I didn't hit him quite as hard this time, not out of any new regard for his comfort, but more because I thought I might need to hit him more than once, and I was saving something for the next smack. "I don't give a flying rat's ass about your rights. I'm not a part of the government anymore, remember? You shitheads fired me. But I am a very large, wet, angry man who is going to slap the taste out of your mouth every time you say something I don't believe, or any time you don't answer one of my questions. Is that clear?"

Shaw just glared at me, a little vein starting to pop out in the center of his forehead. I slapped him again, congratulating myself on the foresight to hold something back for future beating. "I asked you a question, dickweed. Is. That. Clear?"

"Yes." He didn't hesitate this time. He was a prick but a prick who could learn. Good.

"What the hell were y'all doing in that lab?"

He paused, and I raised my hand. I figured I'd backhand him this time, just to mix it up a little, but he held up his hands. "Wait! It's complicated, and I don't understand all of it. I'm not a scientist, just an administrator."

"What were you administrating?" I asked. My voice was low, and I hoped it sounded dangerous, because that's how I felt.

"We were experimenting on cryptids to test their genetic material, to see how many markers they shared with humans."

"For that you had to keep them in cages? Cut them up? Cremate them?" I asked.

"Once we determined which ones had the right number of markers, we needed to harvest enough genetic material for other teams to use in their experiments. If they didn't have enough similarities with humans..." His voice trailed off, and I slapped him. "Hey! I answered. You know what happened to the other ones."

"Yeah, I know. You murdered them and burned the bodies. I just wanted to slap you again. Who's in charge?"

"I was the administrator of this facility, but not of Project Prometheus as a whole. That's run by—" His words cut off suddenly, and his eyes went wide. "Wait!" he yelled. "I wasn't! I wouldn't! I swear—"

Blood started to seep from his nose and the corners of his eyes. First a drop, then a little rivulet of red, then it started to pour from his mouth, his ears, everywhere. I took a couple of big steps back as he collapsed, screaming, to his knees, then fell over in a spreading puddle of blood. He twitched for a few seconds, then burst into blue-green fire. Flames engulfed the howling man, then he fell silent as the fire burned brighter and brighter until finally it flared nova-white, forcing me and everybody else to look away.

When I could see again, I turned back to where he'd been writhing on the ground seconds before, but there was nothing left of him but some melted puddles of fillings and a black scar across the asphalt. Director Shaw had retired. Abruptly. Seconds later, the exact same thing happened to every other DEMON agent we saw. Within a minute, there was nothing left of them but a hint of ash. They were burned far more effectively than the crematorium we'd found.

"What the *fuck* was that?" I asked.

Creepy Granny walked over, dragging her left foot a little. She bent down, ran her finger across the scorched pavement, sniffed the air twice, and said, "Magic."

"Ya think?" Geri asked after a couple of seconds, and the tension was broken.

I looked around the shipping and receiving yard. There was a lot of wrecked stuff, but very little blood, and now no bodies, except for Clyde floating face down in the swamp. "What in the hell are we going to do with *that*?" I asked.

Terrell waded into the water and dragged the dead were-bear back onto land by the collar of his cheesy vest. He walked up to me and kept on walking, back toward the main body of the park.

"Where you going?" I called after him.

Terrell didn't break stride, just kept walking, dragging the corpse with a pink mohawk along the paved trail. "Time to feed the gators."

EPILOGUE

A mohawk?!? Seriously?" I watched Amy reach for the bottle of red wine beside her, look at her glass, then just gently slide the glass aside and drink straight from the bottle. "Good lord, I am never letting you go off without me again. Please tell me there are pictures."

"Well, not of what he looks like now…" I said.

"But his website is still up," Becca said. "And he's got a YouTube channel with something like two hundred videos, most of them railing against some conservationist from New Jersey."

"That's what you got from all that?" I asked, looking around the table at the others. "I kicked a lizard in the taint, wrestled a were-bear at a gator farm, and we uncovered a massive government conspiracy—"

"Plus a weird *Walking Dead* homage," Geri added.

"And all you can marvel at is Gator Clyde?" I asked.

"Well, I, for one, am wondering how in the hell you didn't blow yourself sky high shooting the gas tank of a truck like that," Skeeter said from his half of the screen.

"It's actually a lot harder to blow up a gas tank than it looks like on TV," I said. "And diesel is even harder to blow up than gasoline. I

190

mean, it can be done, and I'll admit I thought the potential for big booms increased a lot when Becca's cousin with the flamethrower showed up."

"Cousin-in-law," Becca called from the couch behind me.

We were sitting in her living room video conferencing with Skeeter and Amy. Becca was drunker than Cooter Brown off a jar of corn liquor Creepy Granny had brought over, and the smell of meat grilling wafted in from her backyard. There was one hell of a home-coming party going on out there for Cousin Terrell, who was getting all kinds of attention from the more available (and more distant) cousins of the "kissing" variety. Me, Geri, Becca, and Joe were all scattered around the den on sofas, chairs, and in Geri's case, an ottoman. Skeeter was in his bunker back in Georgia, and Amy had her tablet set up out on my back deck, making me miss the view and her even more.

"What the hell is DEMON up to?" Geri asked. "They recruited me to kill monsters, they've got some kind of crazy lab going on down here—"

"There's apparently at least one other lab, according to Mark," Amy added. Mark Wojcik, the Hunter from Pennsylvania she'd been talking to, had got in some kind of scrap in an abandoned mental hospital that ended up having something to do with ghosts, Nazis, and government agencies. I didn't understand it all, and I'd only hit Becca's jar of 'shine a couple of times.

"And apparently everybody is named Director Shaw. I can't tell if it's *The Walking Dead* or *The Matrix*," I said. I did my best Hugo Weaving impression, which was admittedly terrible. "Mr. Anderson..."

"I don't get it," Amy said. "None of the people I knew at the home office are there anymore. They either took early retirement, or transferred to other agencies, or they're just plain gone. And nobody will talk about anything. I can't get any information on who these Director Shaws are, or who's really running the store up there now."

That tickled something in the back of my head. "Maybe they *can't* say anything," I said. "Think back to some of the weird shit we saw Mab and Puck do in Fairyland. They could make you think or see just about anything. Who's to say there isn't a spell to make you unable to give up certain information. On penalty of death, I mean. Magic killed this Shaw and all the agents he had with him. Maybe it's something tied to whoever is behind the curtain at DEMON. They even consider telling what they know, they go boom."

"That would be some serious magic," Skeeter said. "I've heard of a few people who can do stuff like that, but to have that spell just sitting there on somebody like a bomb, waiting for them to say the wrong thing? That's complicated stuff, and I don't know who could do it to that many people and keep it active."

"That's a question that's going to have to wait for another day," Amy said. "Because I am out of wine, so this meeting needs to be over."

"And I've got about fifty cousins out in my back yard that want to meet my boyfriend," Becca said, standing up from where she was sitting on the couch with Joe's arm over her shoulders, then holding out both arms for balance. "Whoa. Cousin Hiram didn't cut that batch as much as he usually does."

I laughed as she led Joe out into the back yard, then turned back to the screen. "We'll crash here for the night, then hit the road first thing in the morning. Oughta be home a little after lunch." I paused for a second, then said, "This doesn't feel like it's over, does it?"

"Bubba," Skeeter said. "I don't think it's even really begun."

"Something's coming," Geri said. "I don't know what, but something big is happening with DEMON and all these labs, and there's no way it's good."

"I wish I thought you were wrong, kid," I said. "But I don't. There's a dark cloud on the horizon, and I just hope we can all weather the storm."

III

HOUSES OF THE HOLY

1

The events in this book happen concurrently with Conspiracy Theory.

I woke up tied to a wooden chair, one of the big sturdy ones with armrests and thick legs. It was a heavy sumbitch, resisting all my rocking side to side and back to front trying to get it to tip over. I'm not exactly sure what I woulda done if I had managed to tip the chair over, especially backward. Probably given myself another concussion, which is pretty low on the "shit I need in my life" list. After about two minutes of pulling against the zip ties I could feel around my wrists, biceps, and ankles, I gave up and sat still, trying to sit quietly and just take in my surroundings. This might possibly be one of the rare times in my life when brute force couldn't get me out of whatever mess I'd landed myself in.

I doubted it, but stranger things have happened. I couldn't see anything. Like, not a goddamn thing. I could feel the blindfold wrapped around my head, but there was more to it than that. I'd been blindfolded a bunch, for both pleasant and nefarious purposes, but this wasn't just that. I could also feel the weight of the bag over my head, coming all the way down to my shoulders. They'd taken precautions against me managing to slip the blindfold. Or maybe wherever I was could be recognized by even the slivers of vision that usually get past one layer, so they double-bagged me.

I was gagged, too, and while this again wasn't my first rodeo, it was the first time I'd ever had a ball gag stuffed in my mouth and then had something tied around my face to hold *that* in place. I was blindfolded, gagged, gagged *again*, and had a bag thrown over my head. Shit, next thing you know I'd have special headphones jammed in my ears blasting white noise so I didn't pick up any auditory clues. This was starting to feel less like a monster hunt and more like a Liam Neeson movie. And while I had a very particular set of skills, none of them really applied here.

I could hear a little, but I couldn't really smell anything past the scent of WD-40 clinging to the bag. They must have used ether to knock me out, or at least to keep me out while they tied me up. Who "they" were was still undetermined. I assumed DEMON, since they were the assholes du jour, but there were still a few other groups that wouldn't mind tying me up and carving off pieces like I was their very own Thanksgiving Day turkey.

"He's awake," said a voice from just behind my right elbow.

"Are you sure?" someone said from my left side.

"Yeah," Righty said. "He flexed his fingers and feet. He's trying to see if he can get loose."

"No fucking chance of that," Lefty replied. "Those zip ties have a cold iron thread running through them. Freaks like him don't have any of their powers with those things touching their flesh."

So these assholes knew I was part faerie. Joke was on them, though. I didn't have any powers even without their stupid iron zip ties. Talking to my mom, who was a real faerie, I'd spent too much time in this world and none in Fairyland as a kid, so that part of me never developed. Probably for the best. I'm way too big for the whole "gossamer wings" shtick.

In a normal abduction, I'd be making smart comments at this point. It says a lot about my life that I have standards for a normal abduction, but I'm not your average hillbilly. Unfortunately being double-gagged kinda put the kibosh on my sparkling wit. At least until I could figure out how to either chew through these things or free at least one hand. I had no idea how long that first idea would take, this being my first time with a ball gag and all, so I focused my efforts on yanking my right hand free. A few experimental tugs told me that there was no way the zip tie was going to break, which meant my best option was the arm of the chair giving out. I yanked straight up. Nothing. I tried again. Nothing. On the third try, I felt two things: the arm of the chair started to separate from the body a little, and a bolt of frigging lightning shot through my leg, sending off sparks of white light and pain behind my eyeballs and locking up my every muscle tighter than Fort Knox.

"Stop that shit," Righty said. "My stun stick has plenty of charges, and you don't want me to see how many you can take before you piss yourself." Like I cared about that. I went to the University of Georgia —getting so drunk I pissed myself was an average Thursday night, not something to be all worried about.

He had a point, though. They had all the cards, and the goddamn Tasers. My best move was gonna be to sit tight and wait for my friends to come rescue me, and maybe gather some intel while I tried to survive whatever torture they had planned for me. I only hoped they didn't think I was all faerie, because if they started stabbing me with regular knives thinking I couldn't die to anything except cold iron, we were all going to be real disappointed.

I sat there still for a few minutes, trying to listen for clues from my guards. They gave nothing away, though. Seemed these guys weren't hired for their conversational skills. After a while—I had no real idea how long because of the whole blindfolded and gagged thing—I heard a door open and close, then footsteps approaching.

A new voice spoke, this one from directly in front of me. It sounded like it was maybe ten feet away. "Take off the hood."

The world around me lightened a tiny bit as Lefty yanked the bag off my head. "Now the gags." I felt more than saw or heard Righty move around behind me and untie the fabric gag. He leaned down toward my ear. "I'm going to take the ball gag out. If you try to bite me, I'm going to cut off your ear and shove it up your ass. Nod if you understand me."

I nodded. I was less concerned about where he was going to put it than the idea of him slicing my ear off in the first place. I like my ears. They're not too big, not too small, and do a good job holding up my sunglasses. I figured I'd miss one if he cut it off, and I definitely believed he'd do it. A pair of thick fingers reached into my mouth and plucked the ball gag free, and I worked my jaw to loosen it up.

"Gross. He slobbered all over it," Righty said. I heard a little *splat* as he dropped the ball gag to the floor.

"The fuck you expect? You had it shoved almost down his throat," Lefty said.

"Silence," said New Guy. I smelled hair gel and shaving lotion as he leaned forward. "We have questions for you, Mr. Brabham. You can either give us the answers the easy way, or we can extract those answers from you. I promise there will be nothing easy about that method. Which would you prefer?"

I licked my lips, feeling the cracks in the corner of my mouth from the gags. Working my jaw a little more, I finally said, "Let's start with easy. If I don't enjoy it, we can upgrade to the go fuck yourself package later."

New Guy laughed and leaned back. "I heard you were a funny guy. That's good. I like funny guys. Now, Funny Guy, why don't you tell us where it is?"

Why do bad guys always have to repeat themselves all the time? The whole "funny guy" shtick wasn't intimidating, and he knew my name, why not use it? I thought about telling him this, then remembered that I was still tied to a chair and blindfolded in a room with at least three guys, none of whom minded the thought of causing me a lot of pain. So I just licked my lips again and said, "Could you maybe tell me exactly what 'it' is? There's a lot of 'its' in the world, and I wanna make sure I'm telling you where to find the right one."

The blindfold kept me from seeing the slap coming, so it rocked my head to the side as New Guy laid one across my mouth like an absolute champ. "That wasn't funny, Funny Guy."

"I wasn't joking, Slappy Guy," I spat back. "What the hell are you talking about?"

"The gem, asshole!" I felt his breath on my face as he leaned down again. "Where is the Star of the World?" He was close enough to head-butt, and if I could see, I probably would have slammed my forehead into his face and broken his nose, but I didn't know where Righty and Lefty were, so I couldn't take the chance. There was also the whole thing about still being tied to a chair, which sucked for me, *and* kept me from squishing New Guy's nose like an overripe tomato.

"Oh that," I said. "I think I sold it on eBay. Or maybe Craigslist. Either way, I don't have it." The last part was true, mostly because I had no friggin' idea what the Star of the World was. I kinda assumed it was the second artifact I'd been sent to Charlotte to protect, but it seemed like maybe not telling me anything about it was a good move, given the sparkling success our trip was turning out to be.

"You think you're funny?" New Guy asked. He yanked my blind-fold off, and I kinda wished he hadn't because now I got a good look at him. His face was getting red, with a vein starting to pop out in the middle of his forehead. I really hoped he wouldn't blow a gasket before I either figured out how to get loose or I got rescued, because I wanted to beat the shit out of somebody, and I draw the line at punching people who are in the middle of having a stroke. For this dick, I might make an exception.

"I think I'm hilarious. I also think you've got bad breath," I replied.

"Where is the stone?" he yelled from what must have been just inches away from my nose, which did nothing to change my opinion on his breath. I was pretty sure there were anchovies involved in his last meal, and maybe pineapple. If anybody ever found out I got kidnapped by some assclown who ate pizza with pineapple on it, I'd never live that shit down.

"I'll tell you what," I said. "You turn me loose and I'll take you to it. I can't tell you where it is, since I ain't from around here. But I can navigate. You'll have to untie me first, though."

"Do you think I'm stupid?" he asked.

I mighta given away my answer by the length of the pause, but I was trying to figure out if I'd get tased again for being honest. I decided to try it. "Yeah, I do. I think you're a giant dumbass."

"I'm a dumbass?" he asked. New Guy straightened up, or at least I assumed he did, since his voice came from a little bit farther away when he next spoke. "*I'm* a dumbass? You're sitting here blindfolded, tied to a chair, all alone with no backup, and *I'm* a dumbass?"

"Yep," I replied, my voice calm.

"Why am I a dumbass?"

"Probably genetics. That kinda thing tends to run in families. Oh, did you mean how do I *know* you're a dumbass? That's simple." I flexed my biceps, hoping with all my might that I'd really felt the chair give as much as I thought it had. I had. The arms of the chair ripped free with a mighty *crack*, and I grinned at my captor, who stood in front of me with all the blood rapidly draining from his face.

"You're a dumbass because you didn't kill me when you had the chance." That's when shit got real.

2

Four Days Earlier

I looked up from the TV, where Keanu Reeves was beating the shit out of about seventeen dudes with one pistol and a stony expression, and saw Amy walking in from the back deck. "Hey, Sensuous?" I called to her.

She stopped and cocked her head to one side, looking at me like a dog watching Pilates—like she knew something weird was going on, but she couldn't quite put her finger on what. "Yeah, Bubba?" she asked, her tone wary. Like I am the type of person who would randomly call my fiancée "sensuous" from across the living room as a joke.

"Since you was already up, you wanna grab me another beer?" I asked, grinning like a fool, because I am *exactly* the kind of person who makes puns like that at my fiancée's expense. She rolled her eyes at me, but she went to the fridge and got me a beer.

She came back to the couch and held out the bottle. "Trade ya," she said. "Give me the remote for a second."

I took the briefest of moments to ponder the ramifications of this request. She did bring me alcohol, which usually obligates me to heed her every request, at least until I finish that drink. But she was also asking for the remote control, which is more sacred to a man than, well, his manhood. Way more sacred, given that a large percentage of the population has part of theirs cut off, but that happens to us when we're newborns, so we don't remember it. But our bond with the remote control is precious, inviolable, sacrosanct, and probably a bunch of other words that I didn't know what meant.

But she did bring me a beer, so I gave her the remote. She muted Keanu and stood right in front of my face, effectively forcing me to pay attention to her. She didn't need to worry. It was just a movie. Not like it was college football season, or something important like that.

"What's up, babe?" I asked, craning my neck to make it very clear that I was looking up at her eyes. Not her boobs, and definitely not watching the fight scene around her. God bless big-ass TVs.

"I just got a call that was kind of confusing," she replied.

"I told you, we don't need an extended warranty on either vehicle. Besides, the kind of shit that happens to my truck isn't going to be covered, no matter who underwrites that shit."

"That's not what I mean. This was from the Department of Homeland Security."

"Goddammit." I patted my pockets, looking for my phone. Nothing. I glanced over to the side table. Nothing there except four empty beer bottles, a bottle of ketchup that needed to go back in the fridge, and the remnants of the Five Guys I'd just finished wolfing down. "I told Skeeter he was going to get us sent to Gitmo one of these days. If that little—"

"They weren't looking to arrest us," Amy said, and I stopped.

"They weren't?"

"No. They wanted to hire us. Well, more like they needed us to contract for a specific assignment. Apparently this woman, Pravesh, the Regional Director for our area, heard we weren't working with DEMON anymore, knew about some of the shady shit they'd been doing since firing us, and wanted to throw some work our way."

I was suspicious. Going all the way back to Great-Grandpappy Beauregard, anytime someone from the government promised they were going to help out folks who lived in the mountains like my people did, it really meant they were going to screw us and not even buy us dinner first. "How did she know all that?" I asked.

"She didn't say. She didn't say much, honestly. Only that there were some missing artifacts and spell components she needed help gathering, and that she would pay handsomely for our assistance. Her exact words. She's…a little precise, it seems."

"You're saying she's a stick in the mud," I replied. I shoved my hand down in the crack of the couch cushions and pulled out my phone. "Ha! Got you, you squirrelly little bastard."

I swiped my finger across the screen. Nothing happened. I rubbed the screen on the leg of my blue jeans for a couple seconds to clean the salt and grease off it, then tried again. This time the screen came to life and I was able to dial up Skeeter.

My best friend and technological guru answered on the second ring. "What do you want, Bubba?" he asked.

"Well, ain't you a grumpy Gus today?" I replied.

"I just woke up, I'm hung over as a dog, I need to pee so bad my eyes are yellow, and the very pretty man that was in my bed when I went to sleep last night isn't there now, so yeah, I'm a little pissy." Skeeter was currently in his first serious relationship in years, with a bartender ten years younger than him, and the late hours were starting to show on my little buddy.

"Getting old sucks," I said. "Course, I reckon it beats the shit out of the alternative. I need everything you can find on Homeland Security Regional Director…?" I looked to Amy.

"Pravesh. Keya Pravesh," she said. I repeated the name into the phone.

"Why you looking up a DHS Director on a Sunday, Bubba? Is she a cryptid in disguise, infiltrating the highest levels of government for her own nefarious ends?" Skeeter asked.

"Don't be stupid," I said. "I want you to look her up because she wants to hire us for a job, and I don't want to go in blind. Been there, done that, bought the t-shirt."

"If you're talking about the GatorLand shirt, you didn't buy it. You stole it out of the gift shop after we shot up the park."

"Whatever," I said. "Just find out what you can about her."

"Alright. I'll hit you back in an hour or so."

"An hour? What the hell, Skeet? Grandma's slow, but she's old! What's your excuse?"

"All our grandmothers are dead, Bubba. That joke's not really funny anymore. And I done told you my excuse. *Excuses*, that is. I'm hung over, need to pee, and I need to find out where my boyfriend went... Oh, never mind. I figured out the last one. I smell bacon, which means there is a delicious man making me delicious breakfast in the other room. Make that two hours!" He hung up without waiting for me to say goodbye, payback for one of the five thousand times I'd done the same thing to him.

I turned to Amy. "He's on it."

"Sounds like that's not all he's on." She grinned.

"Yeah, well. It's about time. Ain't like there's a thriving gay community in Dalton frigging Georgia. I'm just glad he found somebody. And I like Billy. He seems like a good dude."

"He'd better be," Amy said. "Because I'd hate to have to hurt him."

Three hours later, the unlikeliest gathering of monster hunters sat on my back deck, beers in hand, listening as Skeeter told us what he found out about Director Keya Pravesh of Homeland Security. "She seems legit, Bubba. She does a lot of work with that Harker dude from Charlotte—"

"Not a vote of confidence," Joe cut in. "That guy willingly associates with demons, has killed more people than cholera, and was directly responsible for the deaths of close to two thousand people in Memphis last summer. In one weekend. He wreaks more havoc than you, Bubba, and that's a high bar." Joe might have lost some of his contacts when he got defrocked for hanging out with monsters (me) and running off to Fairyland with said monster (also my fault), but he still had a couple nuns and a cardinal or two who would take his phone calls, so he'd been on the phone all morning, too.

Amy hadn't bothered trying to look up Pravesh on her computer or call anyone on her phone, assuming that both would be tapped. I figured Joe was probably under all kinds of surveillance, too, although I thought it unlikely that any of his priestly connections would be saying anything that would get us renditioned. And Skeeter...well, if they were brave enough to try to snoop on Skeeter, bless their hapless hearts.

The last guy that tried to hack into Skeeter's network found that for the next month, no matter what he typed in the search bar or what website he tried to visit on his laptop, desktop, tablet, or phone, the only site he could reach was a custom web page full of dick pics that said, "This what you were looking for, asshole?" across the top. I think he told me that he even rerouted his Netflix connection to only watch Pornhub, too. So I wasn't too worried about Skeeter's network security.

"Yeah, Harker's bad news, but he's also saved the world a couple times," Amy said. "He was at the top of our 'don't screw with these people' list when I was at DEMON, but who knows if that order is still in effect now."

"Oh, it's not," said the newest member of our little band, Geri, the younger sister of the woman I fell in love with in college. She showed up on Skeeter's porch one day with an AR-15, a grenade, and a revenge fantasy that involved my ass, that grenade, and little Bubba bits spraying all across the Georgia countryside. I convinced her not to kill me, and she stuck around. I was at least sixty percent sure that she wasn't just waiting for a good chance to shove explosives in my bunghole, and I've always been a fan of that old saying about keeping enemies closer, so I let her stick around. "When I joined up with DEMON, he was their Public Enemy Number One. I don't know who in the upper echelons has it in for him, but somebody at the top of the food chain over there has a serious hate on for Quincy Harker."

"That makes sense," Amy said. "According to Director Pravesh, she needs us to interfere with some plan one of the DEMON directors has going. A Director…wait for it…Shaw."

"Of course it's Director Shaw," I said. "Which one?" In the past six months, we had encountered two different men claiming to be Director Shaw, and Geri was recruited by a third guy laying claim to that moniker. I was starting to think they were like Hugo Weaving in *The Matrix* and was waiting for one of them to call me Mr. Anderson. Except I'm no Keanu Reeves and I'm way too fat and slow to be dodging bullets.

"This one is a woman, and she seems to be operating out of Charlotte. So that's where we're headed," Amy said.

"Ooooh." I winced a little. "That…might be tough."

Amy gave me one of those looks that women reserve for their men when they are particularly prone to doing stupid shit that gets them banned from entire cities (and states) for life. "What did you do, Bubba?"

"The last time I was in Charlotte, I might have killed an entire nest of vampires in the performing arts center. And on the street out front. The police chief told me that if I ever set foot within the city limits again, he'd bury me under the jail," I said.

"That was you, too?" Geri asked. "Damn, is there a gigantic shit-show in the southeastern United States over the last decade that you weren't responsible for?"

I thought about it for a moment, then shook my head. "About the only two things you can't blame me for is the second half of the Falcons-Patriots Super Bowl, and anything that happened while we were in Fairyland. Otherwise, if it had a monster in it, and it wasn't a demon, it was probably my fault. If it was a demon, it's Harker's. I try to stay away from those things."

"Well, good news. Harker is dating a Charlotte cop, and Homeland Security is the ones hiring us, so I think we're safe from you getting thrown in the pokey the second we get there," Amy said.

"I give it eight hours," Skeeter muttered to Joe, keeping his voice nowhere near soft enough for me not to hear him.

"I'll take the under," Joe replied, and they bumped fists. I shook my head. My friends are assholes. I love them, but they're assholes.

"Okay, we can go to Charlotte and probably not get shot on sight," I said. "What are we doing when we get there?"

"Hunting a pair of relics that this version of Director Shaw needs to cast some kind of spell to end the world or something," Amy said. "We'll meet up with Pravesh at her office and she'll give us what details she has."

I thought about it for a second, then let out a sigh. Why bother thinking it through? I was gonna do it. I knew it, Amy knew it, everybody in the room knew it. I didn't like the fact that we were basically the Larry the Cable Guy version of The Avengers, but that's what we were.

"Alright," I said. "Everybody get your shit and let's roll on up the highway. But just for the record, I'd rather go back to Florida and wrestle were-gators."

3

T hank you for coming," Director Pravesh said as we settled into a conference room at her office in Charlotte. She was a well-dressed woman, with brown skin, brown eyes, and dark brown hair. She contrasted that with a bright red jacket over a purple shirt, paired with black pants. I couldn't see a bulge for a pistol, so either her jacket was tailored to hide it, or she didn't go strapped in the office. As someone who is almost never more than ten feet away from a handgun, I couldn't comprehend not being armed at work, but I've never had what most people consider a "normal" job. She was pretty, with a strong jawline and high, sharp cheekbones, but something about her, maybe the way she looked at everyone in the room like they might be prey of some sort, made me not want to let her out of my sight until I could get to know her a little better.

"I am Keya Pravesh, Southern Regional Director for the Department of Homeland Security. I've asked you here to assist me in securing several items that could be used in a very specific ritual that would possibly mean the extermination of all supernatural creatures."

"Damn," I said. "Kill all the cryptids in Charlotte? That must be one serious spell."

Pravesh looked me right in the eye, unsmiling so there was no chance I thought she might be joking, and said, "Not just here in Charlotte. If cast correctly, this spell could eliminate all supernatural beings. Period. Everywhere. On Earth, at least. We do not know if purely mystical beings, such as angels, demons, and faeries would be affected."

I sat back, hearing the chair creak alarmingly as I did, letting the full weight of her words sink in. "Let me get this straight. You've got a spell that can destroy every cryptid *everywhere*?"

Pravesh just looked, at me, her gaze flat. "I'm fairly certain, Mr. Brabham, that I have not developed a stutter or any other impediment to my speech. Yes, we have reason to believe that a spell has been developed that has the potential to eradicate an entire species, as well as any mutations or offshoots from the main species."

"For example, a spell targeting Sasquatch would also take out Yeti," Joe said.

"Exactly, Father MacIntyre," Pravesh said.

"Just Joe, please. I'm no longer a priest."

"Bullshit," Skeeter muttered.

"Skeeter..." Joe didn't look at his nephew, but I knew that tone. I'd heard it enough times when I was about to do or say something stupid. Joe got defrocked when he went with me, Skeeter, and Amy to Fairyland a few months before. Or at least it was a few months to us. To the rest of the world, we were gone nearly two years. Faerie time, or some such weird shit.

"Skeeter nothing," Skeeter grumbled. "Bunch of old white Italian assholes throwing you out because you went above and beyond the call to help somebody. Ain't that the whole parable about going out after a lost sheep? I mean, shit, I don't know nobody more lost than Bubba, so what kind of priest would you be if you just let him go off on some kind of interdimensional faerie hunt by himself?"

I looked at Pravesh, who didn't seem surprised by anything that was being said. Then again, given what I'd heard about the folks she usually runs with, Fairyland was a pretty tame trip. Either way, this wasn't the time or place for Joe and Skeeter to sort out whatever unresolved family shit they needed to deal with. Southern families are no more or less complicated than families anywhere; there just tends to be more moonshine and fewer teeth by the time their problems are all figured out.

"What do you want us to do?" I asked Pravesh. "Amy said something about you needing us to keep spell thingies out of the hands of some psycho demon chick?"

"Director Adrienne MacDonald Shaw," Pravesh replied, a tiny smile twitching up one corner of her mouth when she saw our reactions to the name Shaw. "I see you've either met her or one of her minions, all named, at least for the time being, Shaw."

"Yeah," I said. "I've run into a couple of them. The last one exploded while I was in the middle of beating information out of him. Ruined a perfectly good ass-whoopin'."

"You understand that you don't have to play the role of the ignorant redneck with me, don't you, Mr. Brabham? I know all about your history, your father, your brother, even your sister. So no matter how thick your accent, I understand the intellect behind it."

I gave the government agent a flat stare of my own, perfected in years of underground poker games with men who carry guns even bigger than mine, and are better shots than me to boot. "I hate to be the bearer of bad news, Director Pravesh, but I am every bit as big a redneck as I seem to be. I check all the boxes. I own more guns than neckties, drive a big-ass Ford pickup truck, own every Sturgill Simpson album, can tell you the difference between Chris Stapleton and Jamey Johnson just by looking at them, and have a tattoo of Waylon Jenning's flying 'W' on my right butt cheek. So don't go thinking any of this is fake." I gestured to myself. "Because what you see in front of you is one hundred percent North Georgia living, moonshine drinking, deer hunting, bass fishing, monster killing redneck. Now if you wanted some kind of Ron Rash mountain man literati, I'm sorry to disappoint, but if you want somebody who only does two things—kick monster ass and chew bubble gum—I'm your man."

I paused for a count of three in my head. "And I just remembered, I ain't got no more bubble gum."

Pravesh laughed, and suddenly all my concerns about her were gone. At least gone enough for me to not think she was going to shoot me the first time I turned my back on her. Given my recent interactions with government officials, that was a pretty solid endorsement. "I had heard you were funny, Mr. Brabham, but I was not informed just how witty you truly are."

"Usually when we're talking about Bubba and wit, the word 'half' gets tossed in there somewhere, too," Skeeter said. I showed him the hangnail I had on the middle finger of my right hand, and then tried to straighten up and act right since Amy was kicking the hell out of my ankle under the table.

"And you are Mr. Jones, technical savant, internet crusader for freedom of information, and white hat hacker of at least seven supposedly secure government servers," Pravesh said.

"Eleven, but who's counting?" Skeeter replied.

"We get it," Geri said. "You know who we are. Obviously, or you wouldn't have called us in. Now, what are we doing and how much are we getting paid?"

"You'll have to forgive Geri," I said. "She's a little mercenary. Scratch that, she's a lot mercenary."

"Five thousand dollars per day plus expenses, with a hard cap of ten days. Plus the satisfaction of knowing that you'll be alive to spend your share of it," Pravesh said, her calm expression not wavering a bit at Geri doing the incredibly un-Southern thing of actually talking about money in a business meeting. Usually there's at least half an hour's worth of "how's your people?" and "yeah, the Braves are gonna suck again this year" before we get down to brass tacks. Geri's got more brass than most. Or maybe she's just more tacky than most. Either way, she didn't give a rat's ass about polite, and that got us to Pravesh's dollar figure a lot faster than letting me or Joe handle negotiations would have.

That was a bunch of money, and cash flow had been pretty shitty since we all got fired for jumping off to Fairyland without notice. I technically owned a shifter CrossFit gym in Atlanta, thanks to our first case back in this dimension, but after I paid the staff and all the other expenses, it brought in just about enough to cover my utilities. I know Joe had been feeling the pinch, too, even though he'd spent most of the time since we got back down in Florida with his girlfriend Becca. It took a lot for me to get used to saying that Joe had a girlfriend. He'd been a Catholic priest since me and Skeeter were in tenth grade, so we'd never been adults in a world where Uncle Father Joe wasn't a father, or could become one in the other sense of the word. And Amy had lost her government job, benefits, security clearance, pension, and everything else just because she was with me.

All that meant that a grand a day was a pretty good deal to my little band of misfits, especially since our expenses were on Uncle Sam's company card. One thing bothered me, though. "Why us?" I asked, putting voice to the question we'd all been asking, either ourselves or each other, the whole drive up here.

"Are you not capable?" Pravesh asked, doing that irritating thing where people answer a question with a question. I hate that shit. Makes me feel like I asked another stupid question in algebra class.

"We're plenty capable, but from what I heard, you've got a pretty damn capable crew up here already, complete with your own pet magician," I said.

Pravesh chuckled again. "It's probably better for all of us if Quincy Harker doesn't hear you refer to him as either my pet or a magician," she said. "I think either or both of those things may offend the poor child. In short, Mr. Harker and his group are otherwise occupied at the moment and I saw fit to call in reinforcements. You."

I wondered for a second what in the literal hell could be so important that it kept her A-Team from dealing with a witch trying to cast a spell to wipe out every cryptid in the world. Then I realized that for five grand a day, I didn't really give a shit. Skeeter chimed in, and I remembered the thirteenth reason I keep the scrawny bastard around —he reads dozens of newspapers and news sites every day, including every major paper from a big city within four hours of our home.

"This have anything to do with the riot downtown a couple days ago? Or the bunch of cops that got chopped up at an Applebee's last week?" he asked.

"It was The Cheesecake Factory, but yes. Harker is, as usual, right in the middle of the biggest helping of bloodshed and mayhem within a hundred miles, so you're here to pick up the slack, as it were."

"Lady, for five g's a day, I'll help carry any slack you got," Geri said, echoing my sentiments exactly.

"Good," Pravesh said, a very slight smile cracking her stern face. It did absolutely nothing to make her appear even the tiniest bit warmer. If anything, seeing her smile made me even more cautious around her. Something was very not right with this woman, and I wasn't at all sure I wanted to find out what. "Then let's get to work," she said.

And that's how the single strangest week of my life started, and I've been to Fairyland. Twice.

4

"I still think we shoulda split up and gone after both artifacts at the same time," I grumbled into the air.

"Bubba, the day we let you decide tactics is the day we stop being even the least bit afraid of dying. I've got Geri and Amy here with me, ready to roll on your location in a moment's notice. If I sent them after the other thingydoodle, we wouldn't have anybody left for backup," Skeeter said in my ear. Pravesh had hooked us up with a pretty nice communications rig, complete with those little earwig thingies that look like a hearing aid but are really high-powered transceivers. They weren't quite as spanky as the ones we used to have from DEMON, but the more I found out about the secret arm of the government we used to work for, the less I liked it.

"Even if they're with you, it ain't like they can get here fast enough to do anything. I don't know how much good having our backup blocks away in some skyscraper is going to do for me."

"They aren't really here to pull your ass out of the fire, Bubba," Skeeter said. "They're here to chase after the sword if you get your ass kicked. Anything that takes you and Joe out is probably not gonna have a whole lot of trouble taking out four of you, so this leaves us with somebody to send after it if you shit the bed."

"I don't like planning for failure, Skeeter. It goes against the sunny optimism I carry through life like an umbrella," I grumbled. I was sitting in my truck outside of a nice little red brick church in downtown Charlotte, which they called uptown for some reason. It was where all the tall buildings were, which made it downtown to me. Not like I'm an expert or anything. My "downtown" was the flashing caution light at the wide spot in the road where the Baptist church sat across the highway from the beer joint.

Joe was next to me, looking uncomfortable as hell in what I always thought of as his "dress blues." Except in his case, it was dress blacks, of course. He wouldn't wear the collar, but he had on his black dress shirt and black dress pants, and if you didn't look too close, you couldn't tell that his shoes were really black combat boots. His black jacket was cut a little loose under the arms to hide the shoulder holster, but if he kept fidgeting like he was, we were gonna be made before we got to the door.

"Sit still, Joe," I grumbled. "You're wiggling around like a hoppy toad on a skillet."

He looked at me. "When have you ever seen a toad on a skillet?"

"Never, but if I had, I bet they'd look like you. What's the matter with you? Too much starch in your underpants? Or did you forget underpants? That happens to everybody now and then. Just don't get anything important caught in your zipper."

"Not only did I not forget underpants, I'm pretty sure that's *not* something that happens to everyone. It doesn't feel right, going in there dressed like this. I feel like I'm misrepresenting myself."

"Are you wearing the collar?" I asked, completely ignoring the fact that I'd spent ten minutes trying to persuade him to wear the collar and only gave up when he threatened to not come with me at all. I'm a moderately religious man, but I'm not the least bit Catholic, and I was nervous enough going in there with Joe beside me. There was no way I'd go in alone. I wouldn't know if I was supposed to confess, genuflect, or kiss somebody's ring. Or do all three.

"No, I'm not wearing the collar," Joe replied.

"Then just pretend it's Johnny Cash cosplay and let's go. We need to see a Father...Croft. He's supposed to be the expert on all things old and weird around here." I got out of the truck and grabbed a faded army green duffel bag out of the back seat. It was heavier than I remembered, which meant either Skeeter had snuck extra grenades into my "oh shit" bag again, or I needed to hit the gym more and the buffet table less. Probably that second thing.

"What's that?" Joe asked as I joined him at the rear of the church.

"Party favors," I said, then moved past him and walked up the narrow back steps to the church. Pravesh had set up the meeting and told us that Father Croft would meet us in the sanctuary. We stepped through a narrow hallway into the warm sanctuary, lit with golden lights highlighting all the rich golden wood used throughout the room.

Father Croft sat on one of the front pews reading, and as he heard my footsteps thunder through the room, he looked up and smiled. "Welcome to St. Peter's. I'm Jonathan Croft." He stood up and met us in front of the platform, holding out his hand. I shook it, being careful not to break the priest. He wasn't a big guy, maybe five-nine and a buck-fifty, with salt-and-pepper hair and tan skin. He was dressed almost identically to Joe, except he wore the collar. He also didn't have on a jacket to hide a gun, and I assumed, but didn't know for certain, that he didn't have a backup piece in a paddle holster at the small of his back. I mean, I figure most priests aren't packing at the pulpit, but we were still in the South, so anything could happen.

"Good to meet you, Father," I said. "I'm Robert Brabham, and this is Joe MacIntyre. We're here to evaluate the security for the sword. There's been some chatter that it may be the target of extremists looking to steal it to undermine people's faith in the Church." Our cover, thin as it might be, was that we were working for Homeland Security, which was technically true, and that we had received a credible threat that someone was going to try to steal the sword while it was in Charlotte. Which was also true, if incomplete. It's not just TV shows where you can scowl menacingly, throw around the words "chatter" and "extremists," and get people to pretty much do anything you wanted them to. Still, it had been a while since I'd legitimately worked for the government, and all that honesty felt a little uncomfortable, like when that spot on your ass itches and you can't decide if you'll be able to reach it better going around your back or trying to reach it from up under your nuts.

None of this addressed the fact that I looked more like a Hell's Angel than a federal agent, and they don't even make those shitty fed off-the-rack suits in my size, but Father Croft didn't bat an eye when he looked me over. Either he really was an unflappable guy, or giant biker-looking rednecks just randomly wander into his sanctuary all the time claiming to be from the government and there to help. I was hoping for unflappable. If shit went sideways, and it's been my experience that shit *always* goes sideways, the less Father Croft could be flapped, the safer he'd be.

"Yes," he replied. "Since the unfortunate destruction of the Ben Long fresco that used to grace the back wall of our sanctuary, St. Peter's has been working with the Vatican to bring relics through our church for visits. To remind the faithful that even though our beautiful fresco was destroyed, there are still wonders in the world."

Joe nodded like he had some idea what the hell the priest was talking about. I had no clue. I wasn't even really sure what a fresco was. Some kind of mural thing, I think. "We heard you have the Sword of Pontius Pilate on loan currently," I said. We needed to get this show on the road if we were going to keep this pigsticker safe from DEMON and their asshole troops. "Can we see it?"

"Certainly," Croft replied with a smile. He led us over to a glass display case sitting off to the right side of the pulpit area. It was on a raised platform like a little table, with a placard identifying it as the sword that pierced Jesus's side, right in front of a small offering box.

"That seems a little mercenary, don't ya think?" I asked, gesturing at the cash box.

"Not if you knew what the insurance premiums on that relic cost us," the priest replied. He didn't seem pissed at my little jab, so I gave him credit for having a thick skin. Or for knowing exactly how money-grubbing it looked having a box with a dollar bill slot cut in the top next to a holy antique.

"What about security?" I asked, looking around. The church was pretty but didn't look all that modern. There were no cameras that I could see, and the door we'd come through had a deadbolt, but it was still just a heavy wooden door in a wood frame. Nothing that would keep out anybody determined to get in.

"They don't have much of a security system, Bubba. I'm not finding any camera feeds, no motion sensors, just alarms on the doors. I don't even think the windows are wired," Skeeter said in my ear.

"We put our faith in God, Mr. Brabham," Croft said.

"Yeah, that reminds me of the old story about the dude in the flood," I said, still looking around to see if there was any way we could defend this room. My gut was telling me that was a big fat nope.

"You mean Noah?" Father Croft asked.

"Nah," I replied. "There was this dude, see. He lived…let's say he lived down in Charleston, or Wilmington, to make it relatable. And this was a church-going old guy, about seventy. Still pretty spry, but no spring chicken anymore. Well, the old dude gets word that a hurricane is coming, and an evacuation order goes out. The cops come by and tell him to evacuate, and he says, 'the Lord will provide.' The hurricane gets there, and it's raining like a sumbitch and the water's rising in the streets, and the rescue squad comes by in a big pickup truck to get him out. He just looks at them and says, 'the Lord will provide.' Well, the water keeps rising, and pretty soon he's gotta go up to the second floor of his house. Then a rescue boat comes by to get him, and he just tells them, 'the Lord will provide.' Finally he's stuck on the roof of his house and the friggin' Coast Guard drops a basket from a helicopter to pull him off that roof, but he just sits there saying, 'the Lord will provide.'

"The old man drowns when his house is completely submerged by the floodwaters, and when he gets up to the pearly gates, he asks Saint Peter, 'Why didn't the Lord provide for me?'

"Saint Peter looks at the dead old man and says, 'You stupid prick, I sent you a cop, a rescue squad, a boat, and a helicopter. What the hell else did you want?'"

Father Croft looked grumpy for a second, thinking I was being insulting I guess, then he chuckled. "Perhaps you are right. Our security is mostly predicated on our faith in the goodness of our fellow man. Do you have any ideas for how we could make the room safer? You...look like someone who is familiar with such things."

"That's a real nice way of saying I look like a dude who goes places he ain't supposed to on the regular," I replied with a grin. "I don't think we can keep anybody from getting into the building, not without some major renovation. Maybe an armed guard or two to watch over your sword might be a good idea."

The small man looked a little embarrassed. "I'm afraid we don't have the funds for that. It's...been a tough year, as I'm sure you know."

"All too well, padre," I said. "Don't worry, though. I know where you can find two pretty damn capable armed guards who won't cost you a cent." With that, I opened up my jacket and let the priest get a glimpse of Bertha tucked under my arm in a shoulder holster. Joe, likewise, swept his jacket back and revealed the butt of his pistol. "It's important to DHS that this relic not fall into the wrong hands. The last thing we need is some bunch of crazies beheading hostages with a holy weapon, or some psychotic backwoods preacher rallying a bunch of white supremacist assholes to his banner claiming to have some mandate from on high just because he's got an ancient sword. If you'll let us set up in here until the sword leaves, we can do a pretty good job of making sure nobody runs off with your holy turkey carver."

He stuck out his hand, a big grin splitting his face. "Well, Mr. Brabham," he said, "I hate to put the lie to your story, but in our case, the Lord certainly did provide. I'll show you to the office behind the pulpit. You can stow any gear you need in there."

He turned and walked off as I looked at Joe. "The Lord provided him with us, huh?"

"Yeah," Joe said. "Miracles have really gone to shit since they fired me."

5

I reckon we'd been waiting in the church for about five hours before anything interesting happened. I'm not saying watching people go in and out of the confessional isn't interesting, but really I am. There's only so much a body can sit and wonder about what somebody is confessing without trying to snoop, and Joe put the kibosh on that real quick. He wouldn't even let me get close enough to the booth to hear any of the penance, much less the good stuff. I tried to remind him that since I ain't Catholic, it ain't sinning, but he was of a mind that it didn't work that way.

Father Croft left about half past five and locked the doors to the church when he did. That wouldn't stop anybody that me and Joe were interested in, but the padre didn't need to know that. I heard something rattle the lock on the front door and went out to the vestibule to see what was up. It was kind of a pain in the ass being without a peephole or any windows next to the door, but Skeeter had repurposed the front door security camera from the Bechtler Museum across the street and was keeping an eye out. And by "repurposed," I mean hacked. It was the tiniest bit less illegal this time, since we were doing it for the government. That's what I planned to tell myself all the way to the big house if we got caught.

"What we got, Skeeter?" I asked, keeping my voice low. I had Bertha out of her holster and held with the barrel pointed at the floor. The last thing I wanted to do was blow a fifty-caliber hole in some poor parishioner who didn't know what time Father Croft went home in the summer.

"Looks like a homeless dude. Maybe the church feeds them or something," Skeeter said over our comm link.

"The priest didn't say nothing about that," I replied. "Does he walk like a homeless guy?"

"I don't know, Bubba. What does a homeless guy walk like?" Skeeter asked.

"Usually kinda beat down by life, shambling along like the weight of the world is on their shoulders. Like they don't really have anywhere to go, but they think if they keep moving, maybe they'll eventually get somewhere better."

"Shit, Bubba." Skeeter sounded impressed. "That was downright philosophical."

"Don't tell nobody," I replied. "I got a reputation to maintain."

"Don't worry. Nobody would believe it anyway. And no."

"No what?"

"No, he doesn't walk like a homeless guy. He moves like he's got someplace to be and something to do when he gets there. His head is on a swivel, like he expects an attack could come from anywhere. He's leaving the front door and hopping over the fence. I think he's headed to the back door."

"That's gonna be our guy. Keep an eye out, and if any more of them come, call for backup."

"You don't want me to get Amy and Geri rolling now?"

"Nah," I said. "Right now it's one asshole. If me and Joe can't deal with one dude, we've got real problems. We don't need to really worry until there's four or five of them, but I don't want the womenfolk to feel left out if we do all the ass-whooping without them."

"Mighty charitable of you, Bubba."

"I'm a saint, Skeeter. Just ask me." I stepped back into the sanctuary and motioned for Joe to take up a position to the right of the door leading through the back wall of the stage to the offices. He drew his pistol and moved to where he was between the door and the case holding the sword, on a diagonal with anybody who'd be coming through.

I went to the left side and pressed my back up against the wall right beside the door. I holstered Bertha, since at that range, I wouldn't be hurting any human I shot, I'd be disassembling them. Besides, if I could just punch him a little, I could probably find out where the real Director Shaw was, give Pravesh that information, and go home early. The money was good on this gig, but sitting on my back deck drinking beer and not getting shot at was better than cash.

It was just about a minute before I heard the back door creak open, and a voice called out from the office. "Hello," the guy said. "Father Croft? Anybody? The back door was open, so I just came in. I hope that's okay. I need to make a confession."

I bet you do, asshole, I thought. I knew damn well that door wasn't unlocked, because I checked it after Father Croft left, which just proved this guy wasn't here to confess jack shit.

"The father isn't here right now. You'll have to come back tomorrow," I said as I stepped into the doorway.

"Who are you?" The guy's voice lost any semblance of civility, and most of its humanity, and when he threw back the hood of the tattered green sweatshirt he wore, I saw red eyes glowing from the deep-set sockets.

"I'm Bubba. I hunt monsters. And occasionally defend rare artifacts from assholes. Guess which one I'm doing tonight?" I drew Bertha, but kept the barrel pointed at the floor. He didn't *seem* human, but I couldn't rule out possession or some kind of mind control. I didn't want to start blowing really big holes in him until I knew there was no chance he was just some rando that got sucked into a bad situation by accident.

The dude smiled at me, a slow grin that started out normal, then stretched into menacing, then spread further and further across his face until the skin at the sides of his mouth split open. He reached up and grabbed his jaw with one hand and the upper half of his mouth with the other, and my stomach started doing cartwheels as he pulled his face apart. The flesh made awful tearing sounds, and the *pop pop pop* of separating bone and snapping cartilage sounded like someone tap-dancing on a bubble wrap floor.

I took a couple of steps back and watched in horror as he kept pulling, and pulling, until he'd basically ripped off a suit of human skin and meat, dropping it to the floor with a wet *shlap* sound. Then he rolled the skin down his arms and dropped those flesh sleeves on top of the rest of his human suit with a sickening squelchy *plop*. He rolled his neck and shoulders, like he was stretching out after being trapped in uncomfortable clothes, and I got my first good look at what I was really up against.

The thing was about seven feet tall and butt-naked, with dark red skin dripping with fat and blood. Its head was slightly elongated, with pointy ears and a narrow chin, and when it grinned at me again, I saw multiple rows of needle-like teeth. It had yellow eyes, a gaunt frame, and each of its three fingers was tipped in an inch-long hooked claw. Its knees bent backward, giving it an almost comical gait, and its long legs ended in cloven hoofs. Its tail, because of course it had a friggin' tail, swished through the air behind it, making a really threatening *whooshing* noise.

"Joe," I called without taking my eyes off the thing. "What the ever-loving fuck is that?"

"I'm pretty sure that's a Reaver demon, Bubba. They're lower-level Pit demons, not all that powerful or smart as demons go, but as vicious and bloodthirsty as anything to ever sully God's creation."

"What ever happened to demons not being able to set foot on hallowed ground?" I asked. The demon laced its fingers together and stretched its arms forward, popping its knuckles with a sound like twenty-two caliber rounds.

"I think that might just be something popular culture made up, like vampires turning into bats," Skeeter said in my ear.

"Mighta been nice to know that before I came in here and set myself up to guard the holy relic," I muttered.

"Would it have mattered?" Skeeter asked.

"Probably not," I admitted. I looked back at the demon, who stood in the center of the small room next to a discarded pile of flesh. "If you leave now, I won't kill you," I said, trying like hell to put enough bullshit in my voice to make anybody, including me, think I had a snowball's chance of even bruising this thing.

"Such a generous offer, human," the demon replied, its Gene Simmons-long tongue flicking out to lick a tiny chunk of flesh off its chin. "Too bad for you I can't truly die on this plane. All you can do is send me home, and I promise you, that isn't going to happen."

Then it leapt at me, and it's not fair when the magical beasties are big, terrifying, *and* fast. Which they almost all are. Even the little ones can check off the terrifying and fast boxes a lot of the time. This thing sprang at me like a damn jackrabbit, showing me the benefit of having legs jointed the wrong way, and I barely managed to dive forward and escape its outstretched claws.

This left me sprawled on my belly in the back office of a Catholic church with my face dangerously near a demon's discarded meat suit and not nearly enough backup for the problem at hand. "Hey Skeeter?" I called out.

"Yeah?"

"This would be the time to call in the cavalry," I said as I scrambled to my feet and charged out of the office after the demon. I had at least a little bit of more-than-human speed and strength, thanks to my mom being a faerie, but Joe was one hundred percent red-blooded American human being, and that meant I had about two and a half seconds before that demon ripped him open from his nuts to his nose, and I really didn't want to explain to Skeeter how I let his favorite uncle get eviscerated right in front of me.

Joe had cut off the demon's approach to the sword by the time I got to the stage, and it loomed over him like this giant inexorable tide of death and destruction and teeth and stank. I skidded to a halt and emptied Bertha's magazine into the thing's back, hoping that seven rounds of silver-tipped fifty-caliber fun would at least get the critter's attention. Something I learned fighting assholes in Fairyland—even if the thing you're shooting can't be killed by whatever you're shooting it with, getting hit with a bullet hurts like a son of a bitch, and getting hit with a giant bullet fired from a gun made by, as Ray Wylie Hubbard said, "badass Hebrews," hurts a *lot*. So when I emptied my magazine into the demon's back, I didn't expect it to die, but I did expect the thing to at least fall down. Maybe even wince a little.

I was disappointed. Not only did the bullets just smack into the demon's back and fall to the floor, the bastard didn't so much as stumble. It did turn around, though. It stopped advancing on Joe and turned to look at me, at which point I decided that I liked things a lot better when it was looking somewhere else.

"Fine," it said, and its voice sounded like Freddy Krueger jerking off a robot, all screeching metal and agony. "You get to die first."

Well, shit.

6

I've fought a lot of bad things in my life. From racist middle school pricks who were beating the shit out of Skeeter, to trolls, to golems, to an Elvis doppelgänger, to an entire guard squadron of faeries (which are a lot tougher than you might expect) and a couple of actual demons, but staring down something that was literally named a Reaver was an unsettling experience for me. Fortunately, I didn't have a lot of time to ruminate on my situation, since it was going downhill rapidly as the demon stalked across the wooden floor toward me.

Its feet singed the floor everywhere it touched, leaving black hoof-prints scarred into the wood and raising a stench of burnt polyurethane in the air. The demon swished its claws through the air, making a nasty whispery-slicey sound and making me not the least bit curious as to what those claws could do to my flesh. I stood my ground, mostly because I figured I couldn't outrun it, and ejected the spent magazine from Bertha. I grabbed one from my left back pocket and slammed it home, racking the slide to chamber a round just as the demon got almost within striking distance.

"You saw how well that worked last time, human. What makes you think your bullets can hurt me now?"

"Not a damn thing, asshole," I replied. "I'm just hoping the holy water in the tips might sting a little." I leveled the pistol at the creature's chest and squeezed off seven rounds as fast as I could pull the heavy trigger back. These weren't ordinary bullets; these were my special vamp-killer rounds. They were your basic hollow point AE round, but I'd added a few drops of holy water into the divot at the bullet's tip and sealed it in with a thin layer of wax. The heat of the barrel melted the wax, so by the time the bullet exited the pistol, it was a holy water-coated ball of (hopefully) demon-killing badassery.

These worked a lot better than the silver bullets. Instead of just slapping into the monster's body and falling to the ground, these things opened up some massive entry wounds in the demon's chest and slammed into it with enough force to drive it back a few steps.

A very few. It didn't go down, it didn't fly into pieces or melt into slag, and it sure as shit didn't stop coming for me. If anything, it moved faster and growled louder as it came. I shoved Bertha back into her holster with one hand as I backpedaled and pawed at the knife on my right hip with the other. I managed to duck under the demon's first slash of its claws at my face and draw my kukri with my left hand just in time to get the blade in front of the other fistful of razor-sharp claws streaking for my eyeballs.

It felt like I'd swung a baseball bat into a light pole. The Reaver's hand slammed into the silvered blade of the kukri and stopped dead, transferring all its force and momentum through the knife to vibrate down my hand, wrist, and arm. I couldn't hold onto the blade, and it clattered to the floor as the demon drew back both hands for another strike. This was ugly, and not getting any prettier. I pulled the other kukri free from my left hip and took up a defensive stance, hoping I could block one slash and then maybe step inside the other before I got my insides turned into my outsides.

Then something weird happened. Weird even for me, which is a pretty high bar. Just as the demon drew back with both hands in a slash that would almost certainly open me up like I had a zipper running from my bellybutton to my chin, glass shattered from behind me and a noise like the peal of a gong rang through the sanctuary. It was a deep, almost deafening sound, and it was accompanied by a light brighter than a flash bang in a bathroom stall. The demon staggered back from me, its eyes going wide and what might have been mistaken for a look of fear coming across its hideous face.

"How? NO!" it screamed, and charged past me, brushing me aside like an NFL running back tearing through a high school junior varsity team. I sprawled across the wooden floor, rolling over to see what the hell had just happened behind me.

What I saw was Joe standing at the edge of the stage with a confused look on his face and the Sword of Pontius Pilate in his right hand. The blade shone with a brilliant white light that grew to encompass Joe's entire form, filling the sanctuary. The demon ran at him, screeching in either rage or terror, I couldn't tell which. Joe stepped to the right, bringing the blade down across the creature's back, slicing a deep furrow down one side. The demon spun around, whipping its claws at Joe's face, but he brought the glowing sword up to block, with a *lot* greater effect than I managed with my knife.

The demon's arm passed right through as if there was nothing there, only the hand didn't go with it. The blade severed the demon's arm at the wrist, and the hand just flopped to the wooden floor, where it started to smoke. Joe gaped at the severed hand for a second, then remembered there was a giant friggin' demon standing right in front of him, and swung the sword around, cutting the creature's head from its shoulders like a hot knife through butter. Or maybe like a holy blade through demon flesh. It fell to the floor in two pieces, and seconds later dissolved into nothing more than a pile of ashes that reeked of sulfur and left scorch marks on the hardwoods that I knew they were never getting out.

He looked over at me, then at the sword, then back at me. "Well, *that* was unexpected."

"Yeah, no shit." I tapped the earwig to make sure it was on. "Skeeter, can you hear me?"

"Well, I could, before it sounded like somebody smacked the transceiver with a hammer. What the hell, Bubba?"

"Sorry. I think we can cancel the reinforcements. Joe just chopped a demon's head off with Pontius Pilate's sword, and…he's kinda glowing right now." Joe looked down at his hands, then back at me, eyes big as saucers. I wasn't making it up, he was really glowing. Like, a lot. It was pretty, honestly, kinda like when Michael Landon used to walk up to Heaven in that old TV show. Not *Little House on the Prairie*, the other one. A soft white light surrounded my friend, and it seemed to be coming not from the sword, but from within him. At least, that's what I took from the fact that his eyes were glowing white, too.

This wasn't the first time something like this had happened. That was in the church down the mountain from my place when there was a psychotic elf bent on ruining Christmas for everybody. Will Ferrell would have been really disappointed. Then it happened again in Fairyland when I was about to get killed by a zombie-raising magical faerie asshole in a village church. Now here we stood, in the sanctuary of a Catholic church, and Joe was so full of the Holy Spirit it was leaking from his eyeballs. I was starting to think there might be something to this religion thing after all.

"Joe, do you feel alright?" I asked.

"Honestly? I'm not sure I've ever felt better," he replied.

"I promise not to tell your girlfriend you said that."

He blushed, and that's how I knew that weird eye mojo or not, it was still Joe, Skeeter's uncle and one of my best friends. As he blushed, the glow faded and his eyes went back to normal, which was a relief. He gestured with the sword awkwardly. "I…I don't know what to do with this thing."

"Yeah," I said. "Not every day you get to slice up a demon with a magic sword."

"Is it the sword?" Joe asked. "Or is it something to do with me? I mean, it's not like this is the first time this has happened."

"No, and all three times we've been in a church or been dealing with a demon. Maybe you get, like, super-holy when you're on hallowed ground or around hell-critters or something?" I held up both hands in a "I dunno" gesture. "I do know this, though. That dude," I gestured to the pile of steaming demon-dust on the floor, "won't be the last thing that comes here after your little pigsticker. So we need to get it somewhere safe, preferably before somebody else shows up and takes an interest in it."

"Good idea," came a woman's voice from behind me, and I spun around, Bertha clearing leather as I turned. I brought the barrel up and locked eyes with a gorgeous blonde in a Sex Pistols t-shirt and ratty blue jeans. She was tall, with long curly hair, and built like the proverbial brick shithouse. I tried my best not to be distracted by her good looks, but let's just say it was really tough to focus on looking at her eyes.

"You can put that away," she said. "I'm one of the good guys."

"You'd say that if you were one of the bad guys, too," I pointed out, lowering Bertha's barrel. I figured I could bring the pistol to bear before she could do anything to hurt either of us. "Who are you, and how did you get in here?"

"I'm Glory, and the door was unlocked."

"You didn't come through the door," Joe said. "I would have seen."

"Probably not," she replied. Then she wasn't standing there anymore. She cleared her throat, and I spun around to see her standing next to Joe. "I'm really fast when I want to be."

I brought Bertha back up, this time cradling her butt with my left hand and aiming down the sights at the knockout's center mass. She hadn't done anything threatening yet, but I was perfectly willing to see how fast she was with half her sternum missing if she tried. "How about you get really fast in explaining exactly who the hell you are and why I shouldn't put half a dozen bullets in you right now?"

She closed her eyes, and the same white glow that had emanated from Joe's eyes moments before enveloped the woman, growing brighter and brighter by the second until she seemed to explode in a blinding flash. I blinked away spots, moving sideways as I did to try and be a little harder to murder, if that was her plan. When I could see again, she floated about five feet off the ground, with a pair of massive white wings stretching out from her shoulders.

"Let's start over, shall we?" she asked. "I'm Glory. I'm a guardian angel. Now will you put the gun away so we can talk like civilized beings, or do I have to take it away from you and shove it sideways up your candy ass?"

There was a beautiful angel floating in the air dressed like a punk rock groupie and quoting The Rock. It was almost enough to make me believe in Heaven.

7

I holstered Bertha. I don't think bullets would do much against an angel anyway, and there was nothing on the hottie's face that made me think she wasn't capable of beating me like a drum. "Okay, I'm all ears," I said.

"No, it looks like you're all tattoos and poor dietary decision-making, but that's neither here nor there," the angel said, floating down to stand on the stage. She looked over at Joe, who still held Pilate's sword, and stuck out a hand, palm up. "Why don't you let me hang on to that for the time being?"

Joe looked at her, and a flicker of doubt crossed his face before his eyes did that thing where they got all serious-looking and he shook his head. "No. I'm sorry, but this was entrusted to our care not only by the woman who hired us, but also by Father Croft. Even though I am not a priest any longer, I still take any duty assigned to me by the Church very seriously."

Blondie gave him a smile, one of those rueful little smiles that says, "You're a dumbass, but you're not hurting anything so I'm just gonna let you keep being a dumbass until it becomes more important." All she said out loud was, "Okay, fine," but the sigh that came along with it said she spent a lot of time dealing with stubborn humans, probably men, and knew when it just wasn't worth trying to convince us not to be morons.

I walked back over to the front pew and sat down, leaning back with my arms across the back of the bench, making a show of stretching my hand as far from Bertha as possible. "Okay, gorgeous, if you're a guardian angel, why weren't you here guarding this thing when we fought off a demon attack? Seems like you fell down on the job a little."

She sat down on the edge of the stage, which was only a couple steps off the main floor, so her feet were flat on the hardwood as she leaned forward with her elbows on her knees. Her wings had vanished as she walked over in my direction, which made her look a lot like a chick from a rock video, and totally out of place in a Catholic church. Of course, I looked pretty damn out of place, too, and I used to work for the Church, so who was I to judge? Joe came over and sat next to me. He put the sword on the pew between us, and I scooted my ass over a little bit. I'd just seen that thing carve through a demon like a hot knife through butter and had no interest in seeing what it would do to me.

"It won't hurt you," Glory said, almost like she could read my mind. "I mean, it's not going to jump out and skewer you. If your friend there decides to bury it in your gut, it's not going to tickle, but I guess if you thought that was likely, you wouldn't be hanging out with him."

"You'd be surprised," I said. "At least one of the people I work with spent years tracking me down so she could kill my ass. But no, Joe isn't going to stab me. He's had plenty of chances over the years, and plenty of times when I deserved it more than I do tonight, so I'm probably safe."

"Safe-ish," Joe corrected. I looked over to him, and he shrugged. "The night's young, Bubba, and you can be very trying. I reserve the right to stab you if I decide that's what needs to happen."

"Let's not stab anyone, okay?" the angel asked. "Now, how much do you know about what DEMON is up to?"

"We know that they're trying to craft a spell that would destroy all the cryptids on Earth, that they have been harvesting genetic material from all types of supernatural beings to do it, and that apparently there are only two more elements they need to make the spell work." He gestured toward the sword on the pew beside him. "One of them is this sword, and we haven't been read in on what the other one is yet."

"Pretty close," Glory said. "And as far as Director Pravesh knows, that might be the whole story. There are more things with enough power and provenance to serve as the divine anchors for the spell, but most of them are inaccessible to Shaw and her goons."

"The divine anchor?" I asked.

"Yes," she said, looking me in the eye. "Do you really care about the magic involved, or can I just tell you yes and move on?"

I thought about it, then shook my head. "Nah, I need to know a little more. We don't usually deal with magic, and demonic and divine stuff is way outside our comfort zone, so the more info we have, the better."

"Okay," she said. "Remember, you asked for it. Most magic is pretty localized. It either affects one person, one being, or a small area. Call up a fireball out of thin air, all you're really doing is exciting the oxygen molecules in the air until they burst into flame, then sending them toward more fuel, often in the form of someone you'd really like to blow up. But all you have to work on is the air in a sphere the size of a basketball or so. Then you toss the sphere, it hits something flammable, and fire does what it does."

"Burn shit up," I said.

"Exactly. Same as when you're casting a spell on someone. Want to make them forget something? You're working on one person's mind. Want to cast a glamour? You're actually creating a cocoon of energy that bends the light around someone or something to look like something else."

"What about teleportation? Isn't that a bigger scale?" Joe asked.

"Not really," she said. "You're still just moving a certain amount of stuff. You don't actually impact the area you're teleporting into, just adding to it. That's why it's bad to teleport into something solid.

Because the thing doesn't move or change, you just try to occupy the same space. It doesn't turn out well."

"Okay, all that makes sense, at least as much as magic ever does," I said. "What does that have to do with Pilate's magical lightsaber?"

"That's normal magic," Glory said. "What Shaw is trying to do is on a much larger scale, affecting thousands of beings, maybe even millions, all over the world, all at once. That can't be done by the forces that work solely on Earth. That takes a boost from outside."

"Like Heaven," Joe said.

"Not just Heaven," Glory replied. "It takes Heaven, Earth, *and* Hell, or at least items anchored to all three planes and drawing power from all of them simultaneously. The sword is the divine anchor. Shaw herself is the demonic anchor, since she's a succubus."

"That figures," I said. Both of them looked at me. "What? Come on, a demon running DEMON? This shit writes itself."

It's funny how I bring out similar reactions in women of all backgrounds. I've seen the same reactions from my Faerie mother, my human Granny, Amy, and now a guardian angel. It must be my superpower—the ability to draw out earth-shattering sighs from the depths of women's souls. And not the good, satisfied sighs that say you did everything just right. Nope, these are the sighs of a woman questioning every choice she has made in her life that led her to putting up with my shit. That's the sigh that Glory uttered as she stared at me.

After taking a moment to compose herself, she took a deep breath and looked at me. "That's not all."

"That seems like plenty," I said.

"It would be, if the idea was just to destroy all cryptids, demons, angels, and anything with even a hint of demonic, divine, or paranormal in its nature. That still leaves out one big class of supernatural creatures, one from a different plane entirely."

"Aw, fuck me," I said as it all came clear.

"And he's got it, ladies and gentlemen!" Glory held up both hands over her head in the universal symbol for "touchdown."

Joe looked at me, confusion written all over his face.

"They need an anchor from Faerie, too," I said.

"Yep."

"That's really why I'm here, isn't it?"

"Yep."

"Because I've got Winter and Summer blood in me, I have a foot in both Courts, plus a foot in this world, or at least I would if I had three feet."

"You don't, but that's the principle," she said. "You are a part of this world and both Courts of Faerie, so you're the other anchor."

"You didn't need me to protect the sword, did you?"

She shook her head. "Sorry for the lying thing. We had Pravesh do it, because, well, government employee and all."

"Yeah, it's kinda their thing."

"We figured you wouldn't have come if we told you that a big part of why we wanted you here was to protect you from a bunch of DEMON agents who want to take you prisoner and use you in a spell."

She was right. I'm not the best at asking for help, and given the number of agents (and the number of Director Shaws) that we'd taken out in the last six months, there's no way I would have come if they told me the truth. "Okay, what's the plan?" I asked. "You gonna babysit me until you hunt down this Shaw chick?"

She raised an eyebrow. "Would you let me?"

"For five grand a day? Probably."

"If I knew all it would take was money, we wouldn't have bothered lying to you about it. Okay, we have the sword, and we have you, so that's secure. We'll send some of your other people to recover the last anchor, and then all we need to do is wait for Q to find Shaw and end her, and we can move on to the next idiot who wants to destroy the world."

"Do your guys usually want to wreck the whole thing?" I asked. "Because I've only dealt with one real world-threatening asshole before, and he wanted to take over, but he didn't want to destroy the world. Seems a little short-sighted, if you ask me."

Glory took a few seconds before answering, like she was waiting for me to drop the punchline, but I was serious. She eventually seemed to realize this and said, "Well, the bunch we fought in the middle of Atlanta didn't really care about taking over the world *or* destroying it. Earth was just going to be collateral damage as Lucifer and his entire host of demons stormed through it on their way to attack Heaven."

"Oh," I said. I was starting to get the impression that these people operated on a very different level than I was accustomed to.

"Then the next one we dealt with was actually Lucifer himself, and he didn't really care what happened to Earth either. He was just trying to get back into Heaven."

"I'm sensing a theme here," I said to Joe.

He shushed me. I let him, because shushing me in church is what Joe's been doing since we were all little kids, and I felt like he needed a dose of stability in his life.

"Then there was the guy who pretty much did want to destroy the world, because he'd been abused as a child or something. I don't really remember. After the first couple of megalomaniacal douchebags, they all start to blend together."

"Your Shaw is a chick, right?" I asked.

"Yeah, she's a succubus. Those demons are always female."

"No boy sex demons? That seems unfair."

"Those are incubi," she replied with a completely straight face.

"Okay, but if she's a succubus, then who's the dude in charge?"

"What dude? Shaw is the boss," Glory said.

"The Shaw that blew up all over me in Florida was freaking out about the boss finding out, but he was totally talking about a guy. Kept saying something about not being able to stop 'him,' whoever he is. So who's the him in question?" I asked.

The angel got a look on her face that I recognized. A look I really, *really* didn't like. When she met my eyes again, Glory was *afraid*. "I have no idea. If there's someone behind Shaw, then we might be well and truly fucked."

"Must be Tuesday," I said.

8

As I sat on the pew with an angel staring at me, and not in a good way, Train's "Hey, Soul Sister" blared out from seemingly nowhere. Glory looked at me, surprised, and pulled a cell phone out of her back pocket.

"Hey, Becks," she said. "What's up?"

I had questions. I was pretty sure I wasn't going to get answers, but I had them anyway. How do you deal with roaming charges on an angel's cell phone plan? Do cell phones even work in other dimensions? Mine certainly shit the bed when I went to Fairyland, but we also spent a lot of time out in the woods, so there might have just been no reception. I never looked at it when we were in Mab's castle, and I spent a lot of my time in Faerie stuck in a dungeon, where I don't expect wireless communications were a big priority in construction. But the biggest question of all, and when I thought about it for a second or two, the thing that really answered any lingering doubts as to Glory's divine nature, was "where did she find women's pants with a big enough pocket to actually hold a cell phone?"

She broke me out of my contemplation of the greater issues of the universe by saying, "Well, shit. Okay, I'm on my way." She looked up at me, apologetic. I didn't know angels got apologetic. I didn't know they dropped f-bombs, either, or had pockets. Or boobs. Shit, this was turning out to be a night full of surprises. "Sorry, I've got to go. Harker has started a giant shitstorm across town, and I've got to go make sure that he doesn't get himself killed, or start an apocalypse, or something worse."

"Bubba, I may never call you the world's greatest troublemaker again," Joe said from the other pew.

"He's decent, but he's not even in the Top Ten," Glory said, standing up and striding up the center aisle toward the back of the church. A few seconds later, the light in the room dimmed as she left. Shit, she literally brightened up the room just by being there. It was like having a nightlight that came to life out of a Whitesnake video or something.

"Not even in the Top Ten?" I mused. "Challenge accepted." I turned to Joe. "So, now what? We've got the magical doohickey, but our angelic escort just bailed on us. Do we stay here and guard the sword, do we take it back to Pravesh for safekeeping, or do we just throw it in the back seat of the truck and go check out this Paper Doll Lounge I've heard about on the south side of town?" I was at least thirty percent joking about that last one. There was no way I was going to convince Joe to go to a strip club with me, defrocked or not. The man, as they said in *Tombstone*, was an oak.

"I think we stay here," Joe said. "If there's something going down with Harker, then Pravesh's attention will be on that, so the best thing we can do is stay out of everybody's hair. Plus, we've already fought off a demon attack tonight. What else could really go wrong?"

I buried my face in my hands and groaned, with an echoing sound of despair coming from my earbud. "Why?" Skeeter wailed across the comms. "Why is everyone I deal with either insane or an idiot?"

"Hey!" Amy's voice came in muted, since she wasn't directly on the mic, but she was in the room with Skeeter, so we could still kinda hear her.

"Baby doll, you're engaged to be married to a giant redneck half-fairy who hunts monsters for a living. If that ain't the textbook definition of nuts, I don't know what is."

He had a point. My fiancée is a lot of things, but ever since beginning to associate with me and mine, insane might be the trait best associated with her. I stood up and started looking around the room, trying to figure out how to best fortify the sanctuary. We'd fought off one demon, but now that Joe had decided to tempt fate, I didn't have a whole lot of faith in our ability to do it twice in one night. "You might want to get Amy and Geri headed over here. I know they're supposed to be on chase duty instead of keep Bubba alive duty, but this feels like time for a change of plans."

"Why's that, Bubba? I'm not getting anything on the security cameras outside," Skeeter replied.

"That's exactly why," I said. "Everything's quiet here. A little too quiet, if you ask me."

"What is this, Cliché Night at the O.K. Corral?" Skeeter asked.

"Okay, more like I heard a Humvee engine pull up across the street and figure this time of night it's more likely to be assholes coming for the sword than it is morons heading out to a bar," I said.

"Especially since there aren't any bars on that end of the street," Skeeter said. "How the hell did you hear that? I found it, but it's almost a block away."

"I'm a redneck, Skeeter," I replied. "You think I can't pick up the sound of a Hummer engine from half a mile away in the middle of a thunderstorm? The day I can't do that is the day I burn my University of Georgia bedroom slippers. You know, the ones that look like bulldog heads?"

"We're on our way, Bubba." Amy's voice was clearer now, coming through her own mic. "We'll be there in less than five minutes. Try not to get dead between now and then."

"Top of my priority list, babe," I replied. "Are they human, Skeeter?"

"Looks like," he said. "I've got them on streetlight cams. Two teams of four. One coming to the front door, the other heading around the building. They've both got battering rams."

"I hope they try the knob first," I said. "The doors ain't locked."

Joe shot me a surprised look, and I shrugged. "What? I unlocked them after the demon fight before the angel got all explainy. We knew they'd get in if they wanted to, so why not make it to where they could get in without busting up everything? That's why the lid to the display case comes off, so you don't have to…" I was just about to say "break the glass to get the sword out" when I looked over and saw the broken shards littering the platform. "Yeah, never mind about that bit."

I heard a loud *CRUNCH* from the back of the sanctuary, letting me know that the intruders did not, in fact, check to see if the door was locked first, then it was on like neckbone. I stood up and pulled a sawed-off Mossberg 12 gauge out of my duffel. "Catch!" I yelled, and pitched it across the room to Joe.

Now most people react poorly to having loaded firearms thrown at them, especially when they're in a situation to have to use said firearms shortly after catching them. Joe, on the other hand, had seen all my moves before, so he just grabbed the shotgun out of the air, racked a shell into the chamber, and asked, "What's the load?"

"First three are beanbag rounds. Won't kill anybody unless you shoot them in the face. So try not to shoot them in the face. Unless they really, really need it."

I pulled a matching shotgun out of the duffel for me and turned to the pulpit area. "I'll cover the stage. You handle the back of the room."

"Got it." And he did. Joe was a man of the cloth, and one of the genuinely best people I knew, but he could also kick ass when needed. And tonight, an ass-kicker was needed. I'd worry about my soul in the morning.

A four-man team in tactical gear streamed through the door at the center of the back of the stage, fanning out and sweeping the room for threats. They were all big, tough-looking guys in their all-black gear with big tac vests and guns on slings and more pockets on their pants than I've got hairs on my ass. I chambered a round and let fly with a bean bag shell right into the forehead of the first dude who came through the door and moved left. I know, I told Joe specifically not to shoot anybody in the face unless he wanted to kill them, but that was before I was looking at dudes in helmets with face shields. They could handle a little more face-shooting than most folk.

My shot caught the dude square and knocked him flat on his ass. It looked like a cartoon, like somebody had yanked his legs right out from under him. He sat down hard, and stayed there, shaking his head and trying to make all those cute birdies stop circling around his noggin'. Hopefully he'd stay down long enough for me to take out his buddies, and then I could help Joe deal with the other ones.

I racked the slide and pivoted, taking the lead right-hand asshole in the side of his knee. All the armor in the world ain't worth a shit if you get shot where the armor ain't, and he went down hard, screaming and clutching a knee that was, at best, dislocated. At worst, well, he was going to know when it rained for pretty much the rest of his life.

I was moving by now, marching up the steps to the platform in a smooth stride, chambering a new round and taking aim on the second left-hand guy. He was squared up on me, an MP-5 in both hands, but I could tell by the look in his eyes that he'd never fired it at anything that could shoot back. Lucky for me he was scared out of his tighty-whities, because he definitely got the drop on me. He fired off a three-shot burst from the submachine gun, and one of the bullets came close enough to its target that I heard it go by my ear, sounding like a pissed-off hornet. He was facing me, standing full front, with all his body armor blocking almost anything I could shoot at and drop him fast.

Except one thing. I felt bad about it for a second, then remembered that this little shithead just tried to put three nine-millimeter slugs in my face, and my conscience was miraculously cleared. Then I shot him in the dick with my last bean bag round, and he went down clutching his jewels and trying to keep his eyes from popping out of his skull at the same time. He was definitely gonna need to see a doctor about that.

I spun, dropping to one knee as I did. Good thing, since the last asshole opened up in a full auto blast of lead that would have cut me in half if I'd still been standing. As it was, I heard the tinkle of shat-tering stained-glass windows behind me and hoped the church hadn't skimped on any of their other insurance to cover the sword. I ran the slide on my shotgun, took a deep breath, and yelled, "Drop the gun or I'm gonna shoot your ass!"

I watched him lower the barrel of the MP-5, sweeping it down to line up on my face, and I pulled the trigger. I'd loaded both shotguns the same way—the first three shots were non-lethal. The fourth, and the four after that, were double-ought buckshot. The kind of ammunition that could cut a man in half from the distance I was at. Times like that, it's like Sam Elliott said in *Roadhouse*, when a man points a gun at you, you can either die, or you can kill the motherfucker.

I pulled the trigger on that Mossberg, almost certain that I'd crossed a line I swore I'd never cross again—killing a human being.

9

This time was different from the last time I pulled the trigger on a human. That time, in the dark recesses of a museum in Florida, when I killed a nut job curator who'd summoned a demon because he was pissed about not getting Employee of the Month or some such shit, I didn't really know what was going on. I knew I'd just killed a person, and I knew it was bad, and was going to *be* bad for a long time to come, but I didn't know about the nightmares, the cold sweats, the moments I'd just freeze up walking through the liquor store and suddenly see that dead dude's face staring up at the ceiling, eyes wide open, his face more surprised than pained.

This time I knew all that was coming, and it almost earned me a bullet in the face, because I hesitated. I froze for a second as the DEMON agent brought his gun to bear on me, and in that little tiny sliver of a second, all kinds of things ran through my mind. It was like time just stopped to give me space to think about what was about to happen. I saw Amy, not in the wedding dress like I'd planned on her being in just a few months from now, but in black standing on the side of a Georgia mountain looking at a mound of dirt. I saw Skeeter, alone in his tech cave, pulling more and more away from the world without anything there to be his ugly tattooed anchor. It was like *It's a Wonderful Life*, only shittier. And I'm taller than Jimmy Stewart.

This time was worse because I knew everything it meant to take a life. I did it anyway because I wasn't ready to die yet, and I sure as shit wasn't ready to die in a church in North Carolina at the hands of some dipshit rogue government flunky. That was a little too *Modern Warfare* for me to stomach. The DEMON agent flew back, landed on his ass, then just hopped back up like nothing happened.

"What the fuck?" I asked, not really expecting a response.

"That wasn't silver shot, asshole," the agent replied before he put three 9mm rounds into the upper part of my chest. It felt a lot like getting hit in the chest with a ball peen hammer, three times in quick succession. It hurt like a son of a bitch, but since one of the things I kept in my "oh shit" bag in the back of the truck was a pair of Kevlar vests, it didn't do much more damage to me than I'd done to the lycanthrope assmunch currently taking his turn wearing a stupid look on his face.

I took care of the stupid look by standing up, taking three big steps forward, and slamming the butt of my shotgun into his jaw. That wasn't silver, either, but apparently head trauma somehow trumps being bulletproof. I didn't give a shit, as long as he wasn't going to be shooting me anymore. My chest hadn't hurt that bad since the time I decided that it would be funny to ride Old Man Perkins' mule across the middle of the football field during the Homecoming game back in high school. The mule didn't think it was nearly such a good idea and kicked the shit out of me when I tried to get on it. I couldn't really blame the critter, though. I was a big bastard even at sixteen, and I was in full pads at the time. Those pads are the only thing that kept me from getting my ribs stove in, but my coach didn't even let me sit out a single play. He just looked at me, shook his head, and said, "Well, when a dumbass tries to ride a jackass, sometimes the jackass wins."

I stood over the downed agent and looked at the others I'd shot. The one I shot in the forehead was still sitting up against the wall trying to get his eyes to focus. The one I shot in the knee was recovering better, still yelling all kinds of things that people really shouldn't say in church, but he had his hand on his pistol and was trying to draw it without making his leg scream too bad. I solved his dilemma by stepping forward and kicking him in the jaw. His head slammed back into the floor, and I felt bad about the concussion he was almost certainly going to wake up with. What's a little traumatic brain injury among friends, anyway?

The third guy, the one I shot in the dick, was probably the worst off out of all of them. He was writhing around on the floor with his hands cupped around his balls. "You shot me in the nuts, you son of a bitch!" he groaned as I walked up.

"You tried to kill me," I replied. Then I punched him in the side of the head. He forgot all about his almost certainly ruptured testicles as his eyes rolled back in his head and he slumped to the floor. My guys dealt with, I turned to see how Joe was doing. It had been a few seconds since I'd heard any gunshots, and I wasn't sure if that was good or bad.

It was bad. It was really, really bad.

The other four-man team had come through the back door of the sanctuary, and like me, Joe had dropped three of them with bean bag rounds from his shotgun. One of those guys was lying flat on his back in the center aisle, staring up at the ceiling but obviously out cold. Another lay right next to him curled up in a little ball gasping for breath. I judged he had at least another thirty seconds before he could get up and present a threat. All I saw of the third guy was a leg sticking out between two pews, so I don't know if he was unconscious or dead, but I assumed just knocked out.

The fourth guy was the problem. Joe knew exactly how many non-lethal rounds he had, and he knew the next shell was nowhere close to a bean bag. So while he had the DEMON agent dead to rights, he hadn't pulled the trigger. The agent had Joe cold, too, standing at the end of a pew with an MP-5 pointed at my friend's head. A classic standoff, and one that usually ended badly for both stander-offers.

"Put the gun down," I called.

"Kiss my ass," the agent yelled back. "If he was going to shoot me, he would have done it already."

"Same could be said for you," I replied. "Not for me. I've shot every asshole in my half of the building, and the way I see it, there's only one more chance to make a clean sweep. You're it."

"You won't shoot a human. We've heard about you. You like to pretend to be badasses, but you're really just a bunch of redneck fairies."

I'm pretty sure he didn't know just exactly how right he was about me being a faerie, and was trying to insult me by calling me gay. Not being in middle school for a few decades, some asshole making claims to my sexuality had long since ceased to be effective, and since I'd already shot one of these assholes who turned out to be a were, I decided to just cut this bullshit short and maybe get out of here before the local cops showed up. Even though we were working for the feds, and even though one of their own was *also* working with the same feds, there was probably still a picture of me hanging in the police station from the last time I spent any time in Charlotte. You leave a couple dozen pools of goo that used to be vampires in the middle of the town's swankiest theatre and they're pretty quick to revoke your key to the city. Plus, I *am* a faerie.

But if he was a lycanthrope, the lead shot in my twelve gauge wasn't going to do me any good. So I used the shotgun for its secondary purpose—a bludgeon. I shifted my grip on the gun and winged it right at the asshole's face. He ducked, and I drew Bertha, ejecting the magazine and slamming in one full of silver bullets. I learned a long time ago that it's important to know what kind of ammo you're loading, so I made it a point to keep my silver bullet magazines in one place, the magazines I called "Icy Hot" because they alternated cold iron and white phosphorous-tipped bullets in another, and one spare mag of normal ammo in my back right pocket to go with the one I kept loaded in the gun. That let me eject the regular mag and slam a silver home before the agent recovered.

He was turning to face me, his submachine gun swinging around, as I brought the pistol to bear on his chest. I squeezed off two shots, loud enough to hurt even as badly as my ears were ringing from all the shotgun fire, and watched as the first one slammed into his left shoulder. The impact picked the man up and slammed him into the wall behind him, but not before he got off a three-shot burst. I didn't feel anything, but when I turned to look at Joe, he wasn't standing where I'd last seen him.

"Joe!" I shouted, moving toward the groan I heard. He'd fallen between two pews and was struggling to get to his feet, despite one hand being covered in blood. "Stay down, pal. You're hit."

"Yeah, my arm. Hurts like a bitch, but I'm pretty sure he missed the major stuff." It looked like a bullet had grazed his upper arm, which sounds a lot less agonizing than it really is. I've had bullet wounds of pretty much every non-fatal type, and even a graze is still getting shot, which hurts like a mother.

I helped Joe up into the pew and looked around for something to bind his wound with. I settled for pulling out my pocketknife and cutting strips off his own shirt to try and get the bleeding stopped. Then I turned to deal with disarming the DEMON agents, only to find the one I'd shot standing right behind me with a wicked grin on his face.

"No lycanthrope mods for me, asshole," he said. Mods? What the hell was he talking about, mods? "I'm jacked up on faerie DNA. Silver doesn't do shit. Takes iron to put me down now." Then he stuck a stun gun in my chest and squeezed the trigger until the world went black. The last thing I thought as blackness overtook me was *what the hell did DEMON do to these guys?*

1 O

A   nd that's how I ended up blindfolded, gagged, and zip-tied
     to a chair in an abandoned warehouse with two truly giant
     Samoan-looking dudes and one nebbishy shithead with
crappy taste in pizza. As soon as I broke free of the chair, I pounced
on Nebbishy Guy, the one who'd been interrogating me. And by
"pounced" I mean "kinda half-stood up half fell forward onto the jerk
in front of me."

That probably saved me a lot of pain and twitching because the
two thugs I'd named Righty and Lefty based on where they stood
swung their stun batons at my body as soon as I exploded out of the
chair. Since I didn't do things the easy way and stand up like a normal
human being, their aim was off and I didn't get fifty thousand volts of
electricity jammed into each of my shoulders. Instead, I sprawled on
the floor on top of the red-faced douchebag who had just been
screaming questions at me.

While that wasn't comfortable, it didn't really hurt, and I was able
to roll off Screamy Guy and flex my legs enough to get the bottom of
the chair broken into manageable pieces. I was still zip-tied to it, but
now it was more like arm- and shin-guards than a chair. Righty
jabbed down at me with his stun baton, and I rolled to the left, putting

me right back on top of Screamy Guy. I heard the slap of shoe leather on the concrete next to me and knew that Lefty would be taking his shot, and I kept rolling left to avoid the other stun baton. I also managed to bring my knee up to grind Screamy Guy's nuts into the floor as I rolled off him.

Screamy's high-pitched wail of agony shifted into a pale whimper as Lefty nailed him in the side with the stunstick. I was all the way over onto my back by this point, and the big goon was overbalanced in his zest to shock the shit out of me, making it pretty simple to raise a big ol' foot and gently (okay, not really gently) shove him over into his pal, Righty. They went down in a massive tangle of shock batons, surplus black suits from the Big & Tall store, and profanity.

I struggled to my feet and looked at the carnage I had wreaked. Screamy was lying flat on his back, just twitching and grabbing his balls. Righty and Lefty were trying to get themselves untangled from one another so they could come at me again, and I still had pieces of furniture tied to my forearms and lower legs. I decided to take advantage of that and took a few steps forward, kicking Lefty in the ribs as he got up onto his hands and knees.

This bowled him over and squashed the breath out of Righty, who had been pushing himself up on one elbow. He splattered back to the concrete, and I dropped to one knee and buried my wood-armored forearm in Lefty's forehead. I heard a sickening *crack* and worried for a moment that I'd killed him. Then I remembered one of the unwritten rules of wrestling, which apparently translates into real life as well: never headbutt a Samoan. Lefty was out cold, but the crack wasn't from his skull breaking—it was from the wood strapped to my arm splitting right in half.

I grabbed a discarded stun baton and pressed it up under Righty's chin. "You've got about three seconds to tell me who's running this show and where they took my friend before I flash fry your brain, brother."

He opened his mouth like he was going to protest, then got a good look at the expression on my face and apparently thought better of it. "Look, we're just the muscle. We were just supposed to pick you up from these government weirdos and bring you here, then torture you until you told Theodore where some jewel is, or until your friends showed up to rescue you. If we find the jewel, that's cool, but if your friends get here and we can kill the wizard, that's worth an extra fifty large on top of the ten we were already getting. Theo didn't want to mess with that, on account of he don't like magic, but I figured we could deal with whatever happened."

"You dumbasses couldn't even deal with me, and I was strapped to a chair. Where's Joe?"

"He's in the janitor's closet over on the far wall. Theo figured if we couldn't beat the information out of you, we'd take turns zapping him in the taint and the eyeball to make you talk."

"You're a prick," I said.

"It's just a gig, man. All I want is to go home, put some ice on my bruises, and maybe get my cousin here a CT scan. You cracked his melon pretty good."

"That's all you want, huh?" I asked.

"Well, that and I know I don't want to get my face tased off."

"Yeah, well, I want Georgia to sell liquor in convenience stores, allow recreational weed, and abolish daylight savings time, but growing up is all about getting used to disappointment," I said, then I jammed the stun baton right into his junk and pulled the trigger. Hey, I didn't tase his face off. Asshole.

I shoved the stun stick through my belt and took a quick inventory. Bertha was gone, and so was my shoulder rig. The pair of silvered kukris I usually wore strapped to my belt were gone, along with my backup piece, a Judge revolver loaded with alternating silver shot and cold iron bullets. All I had on me were my truck keys, my wallet, and my pocketknife. My keys weren't gonna do me a damn bit of good, since I didn't know where I was, much less where I was in relation to my truck. Same for my wallet, since there was about twenty-six dollars in there alongside a bunch of credit cards that kinda laughed if you even looked at them like you wanted to charge something.

The ear thingy Pravesh had given me was gone, too, and I really hoped she didn't take that out of my check because it felt expensive. I was unarmed except for a stunstick, had no idea where I was, and I still had zip ties hanging off my wrists like a damn seventh grader with a shitload of Swatch watches running up their arms. Yeah, I'm old, gimme a break.

I stomped over to the door Righty had pointed to and gave the knob a yank. It wasn't locked, which surprised the hell out of me. What kind of two-bit operation were these idiots running, anyway? I mean, it's one thing for a highly trained monster hunter like me to outwit them and escape, but the least they coulda done was lock the door.

Joe was tied to a chair with his back up against the cinderblock exterior wall, and when I opened the door, he went nuts, thrashing side to side and trying to get loose of the zip ties they had him trussed up with. He was bound like I'd been, with the bad luck of his chair being metal, so there was no damn way he was getting loose.

"Joe, chill out. It's me," I said as I yanked the bag off his head. I pulled off his blindfold, and he looked down at the bright red ball gag stuck in his mouth. I plucked the hunk of plastic from between his teeth and tossed it aside. "We shall never again speak of the ball gag kidnapping. Agreed?"

He nodded. "Oh yeah. You wanna cut me loose?"

"I gotta poke around and see if I've got anything in here that will do the job. If those are like mine, there's a thin steel wire running through them meant to counteract my magical faerie powers."

"You don't have any magical faerie powers," Joe said.

"Somebody forgot to tell our kidnappers about that."

"Speaking of kidnappers…" Joe craned his neck trying to see around me.

"They're all rolling around in a lot of pain right now, but they'll be alright once their nuts stop throbbing."

"Throbbing testicles and ball gags, huh? This is not the kind of boys' night out I expected from you, Bubba."

"We have got to get you refrocked or whatever they call it," I said.

"Because I cannot deal with my priest friend having a dirtier mind than me."

"I've always had the mind, Bubba, just haven't said it out loud until they took my collar."

"I don't know if that makes it better or worse," I replied. "Here we go!" I rooted around in a small toolbox on the bottom shelf in the closet and found a pair of wire cutters. They were shitty, the kind you get in one of those twenty-dollar tool kits that your college girlfriend gets you because she thinks you'll like it, and you keep it in the trunk of your car and the handle breaks off the ratchet the first time you try to use it and then you're stuck moving this dumb plastic toolbox around until y'all break up and you can finally just throw the damn thing away and buy yourself a decent socket set. So yeah, it was a shitty set of wire cutters, but they were good enough to get the zip ties off my and Joe's wrists and ankles.

"Okay, what's the plan?" Joe asked as he rubbed his wrists and ankles, trying to get feeling back in his extremities.

"You're asking me? I thought I was the one who was never allowed to make plans?"

"You're never allowed to make the first plan," he replied. "Your first plans are pretty disastrous and usually end up with buildings on fire and a lot of explosions."

I thought about it for a second, then remembered the aftermath of most of my college-age Friday nights. "Okay, that's fair. What makes this any different?"

"This isn't the first plan. This isn't even Plan B. We don't trust you with those, either. This is Plan Z, the plan we go to after everything has already gone to shit and extreme violence and mayhem is almost certainly the best response to the situation we've found ourselves in."

"I don't know what's worse," I said. "The fact that you've thought about this, or the fact that we find ourselves looking for Plan Z as often as we do."

"Definitely the second," Joe said. "So what about it, Bubba? Now that the world is on fire, where do we go from here?"

I thought about it for a minute. "Well, the first thing we gotta do is figure out where we are. I'm guessing they took your phone, too?"

"Oh yeah. Phone, transceiver, and the little Ruger I had strapped to my ankle."

"You had a holdout gun? Damn, you really aren't a priest anymore," I said. I walked out of the closet back over to where Screamy and the Samoans (which isn't a bad name for a ska band) were starting to recover. I drew the stun baton from my belt and clicked the trigger a couple times to get their attention.

"Okay, here's the deal. I need your cell phones, car keys, and any cash you've got on you. I don't give a shit about your credit cards, but I'm totally stealing your car. Now cough it up." Three cell phones skittered across the concrete, along with two sets of keys.

"What about you, Chuckles?" I asked Lefty.

"I rode with Lloyd," he said.

"Lloyd? That's like the lamest bad guy name ever," I said.

"What, just because we're Samoan you think we're supposed to be called Afa and Sika? Racist redneck." He spat on the floor near my foot.

"No," I replied. "I just think Lloyd sounds more like an accountant than somebody who's supposed to be scary."

"I wanted to be an accountant," Righty, now Lloyd, said. "I flunked math. Like, a lot."

I grabbed up the cash, phones, and keys and headed for the door. "Joe! Let's roll," I called over my shoulder. "We gotta go see a woman about a sword." I was *not* looking forward to what Director Pravesh was going to say about the way my night had gone.

11

Y ou didn't think you should maybe *arrest* them?" Pravesh had this weird vocal tic where her "s" sounds got really slithery when she was pissed. And she was all kinds of pissed at me. "You know, that thing where you bring suspects into custody and interrogate them? You've heard of this, right?"

"I'm sorry," I said, not really even the least little bit sorry. "Did you miss the 'Monster Hunter' part of the name? I'm not Bubba the Asshole Arrester, or Bubba the Henchman Whisperer, or even Bubba the Douche Questioner. No, I'm Bubba the Friggin' Monster Hunter. I hunt down the stuff that goes bump in the night, and I put a shitload of bullets in it. That's the gig, lady. Not asking questions, not some kind of Nancy Drew detective shit, and *not* arresting people who tie me to chairs and use cattle prods on me!"

Director Pravesh just plunked her elbows on her desk and dropped her face into her hands. "Two of them. What in all my previous lives did I ever do to deserve *two* of them?" She cycled through a bunch of languages I didn't recognize, I'm guessing asking different deities what she'd done to piss them off so bad. Finally, after a full minute of prayer, or maybe concerted blasphemy, I couldn't really tell, she leaned back in her chair and looked at me.

"Fine. You didn't take the kidnappers into custody. Did you at least identify them? Take some ID? Anything that would help us locate who hired them?"

"I took their phones," I said, pulling them out of my pockets and depositing them onto her desk. "And your guys downstairs can search the Escalade in the parking garage. I took that off them, too. I'd expect there to be some guns stashed in there somewhere, and from the smell of the interior, probably some seriously dank weed stashed in the glove box, or maybe the center console."

"Is that what that smell was?" Joe asked.

I looked over at him to see if he was serious, and he had the same disingenuous look on his face he always had. "Man, sometimes I forget your college years involved a lot more praying about important shit and a lot less praying to pass a drug test than mine."

"Okay," Pravesh said. "Hand over their phones, and when your friends get back with the Star of the World, we'll at least have one of the precious artifacts you were tasked with keeping safe."

"I mean, I'm still here, so you've for sure got two of them, counting the sword. Wait, what do you mean 'when my friends get back?'" I asked. I'd been wondering why Amy hadn't at least shown up to bitch at me for getting myself kidnapped again, but since we were rushed straight into Pravesh's office as soon as we got back to the Homeland Security office, I figured it was a punishment postponed, not avoided. Now I hear that she's not even in the building? This didn't make me a happy Bubba.

"When you two vanished, I sent your fiancée and the mini-mercenary off to secure the Star of the World. By all accounts, it was in the possession of a demonic bar proprietor that we're familiar with. I sent enough cash and promises of favors along with them to hopefully persuade him to let us keep the stone safe until the immediate threat has passed."

"Wait a minute," I said. There was a *lot* to unpack in that statement. "I've got some questions. First, you have a demon bar in Charlotte?"

"Several. There is only one that is a Sanctuary, however, and the owner has been useful to us in the past."

"Two, the demon that owns that bar has a gem that is part of this spell, and you think he'll just give it to you?"

"No. I think he will rent it to me, at an exorbitant cost, in both mundane cash and favors of the mystical sort. Also, I promised that he wouldn't have to pay business or income taxes for the next ten years. That is assuming you get there before someone else shows up with cash in hand. Mort is not known to favor a bird in the bush over money in front of him."

"Demons pay taxes?" Joe asked. While not the most important thing in the conversation, it was kinda hanging me up, too.

"The Director of the Internal Revenue Service is an Archduke of Hell. Demons file early, and they never cheat on their withholding. Ever."

"And three," I interrupted. "There was a choice between sending me to a church and sending me to a bar, and you picked the *church?*"

"I may have just met you, Mr. Brabham, but I feel like I already know you, if by reputation alone. You have been responsible for the destruction of drinking establishments in several states and two different planes of existence, but you almost always leave the houses of worship standing. I chose the most budget-conscious choice. Not to mention the fact that Mort is more than capable of defending the Star of the World against most threats without any help from us. He is a powerful demon, a skilled magic user, and has some association with the Lords of Chaos."

"I'm guessing that's not a biker gang," I said.

"No, they are a primordial force of the universe."

"Could still be a biker gang."

"They are not a biker gang."

"Okay, if you're sure," I said. "Now lemme get this straight. Amy and Geri went off to this demon bar to meet the demon bar owner and rent a magical necklace from the demon who runs the demon bar before the agents of DEMON get there first. That's literally never getting old."

"Agree to disagree, but yes, that is where they are."

"How long ago was that?"

Now Pravesh started to look a little concerned. Just a tiny bit, because she did a crazy good job of keeping her emotions locked down, but I saw what I thought was a weird flicker in her eyes. "It's been about two hours now."

"I'm gonna guess by the look on your face that this bar isn't all that far away."

"About twenty minutes." I was starting to learn that in Charlotte, "twenty minutes" was code for "halfway across town." Atlanta has the same kind of code, except in Atlanta, "about an hour from here" means "five miles, two if it's rush hour on 285."

I was halfway to Pravesh's door when she called out to me. "I'll have someone drive you there!"

"No need," I called back. "I kept the keys to the Escalade. Come on, Joe. Let's go see Skeeter and grab some firepower. I got a feeling this is going to get messy."

Thirty minutes later I was behind the wheel of an appropriated Cadillac, with Nathaniel Rateliff and the Night Sweats blasting out of the impressive sounds system, heated leather seats wrapping my ass in butter-soft leather, and the wind whipping my beard sideways. I tucked it under the seat belt and turned to Joe. "This thing rides pretty good. Might think about getting one for my next ride."

"Bubba, these things cost around eighty grand. More if you get a bunch of options."

"I love my truck," I said. Since losing the safety net of having the federal government and the Catholic Church to pick up the tab on repairs, I'd gotten a lot more careful about putting my F-250 in the kind of situations that used to get it smashed on the regular. It's funny how money matters a lot more when it's *your* money.

"Where is your truck, anyway?" Joe asked.

"I assume it's still at the church, where we left it. I'm more concerned with Bertha's whereabouts. I ain't seen her since I got knocked out, and none of the guys that were trying to interrogate us had her." I'd gone to a lot of trouble to get that gun back from my psychotic little brother, and I didn't relish the thought of losing it. A good gun is like a good recliner—once you get it broke in good, you want to hang onto it pretty much forever. Same goes for underpants, too, something I haven't managed to make Amy understand yet. She keeps throwing out my favorite drawers just because they might have a little hole in the taint.

"Maybe after we pick up Amy and Geri we can swing over to the church and get your truck and look for your gun. And mine, for that matter. I just bought that little Ruger. I don't want to lose it this soon." I knew what Joe was doing, and I appreciated it. He was just trying to keep me talking so I didn't freak out. Skeeter hadn't been able to raise Amy or Geri on their comms, and their phones hadn't moved since they got to the demon bar a couple hours before. Either they were in trouble, or...well, there wasn't really an "or" that made any sense. They were in trouble, and that meant that whoever was trying to do them harm was in trouble, along with Pravesh for sending them off on their own, anybody that was helping the people that tried to hurt them, and pretty much anybody within a mile radius.

We pulled into the parking lot, and I saw the black Suburban that Pravesh told me to look for. I didn't need her telling me that, though. I've seen enough government vehicles to recognize one when it's sitting right in front of me, and this black Chevy might as well have had "FED" written on the doors in bright pink spray paint.

I pulled up right next to it in my SUV that screamed "rich-ass criminal" at least as loudly as the Suburban screamed "mid-level government agent" and got out. I drew the forty-caliber Smith & Wesson Pravesh lent me and pulled open the driver's door while Joe walked around to the passenger side. The normal person-sized pistol felt too small in my hands, and I was a little worried I wouldn't be able to get my big ol' sausage fingers out of the trigger guard if I needed to in a hurry, but there was nothing in the Suburban that I needed to worry about. There was a cell phone in a hot pink case sitting in the cup holder. Amy's phone was nowhere to be seen.

"I thought you said the phones were together, Skeeter," I said, pressing the earwig in my right ear.

"They're in the same general vicinity, Bubba. You understand that a GPS is a Global Positioning *Satellite*, right? Like from space? They're accurate to within maybe a hundred yards, not six inches. Yours still shows you on the far edge of the parking lot, but I'm guessing from what you're saying that you're right in front of the bar."

"Yeah, I'm in the front seat of Amy's SUV. Geri's phone is here, but I don't see Amy's."

"She probably took it with her into the bar. That's a good sign, Bubba. It means she's probably still in there." I could hear the lie in his voice. I can always hear the bullshit in Skeeter, but since it's almost always bullshit to help me, I usually let it slide. This was no different. He didn't want me to lose it, so he was helping me keep hoping. Hoping she was perfectly safe on the other side of that door, hoping that nothing else had gone sideways on this stupid trip, hoping that Pravesh hadn't sent her into the same kind of shitshow I'd just gotten out of. Because God help me, and now that I knew angels were real I was way more inclined to believe in God, if anything bad happened to that woman I would tear Charlotte down to the fucking foundations.

"Well, she ain't out here," I said. "So let's head into the demon bar looking for the DEMON agents." I didn't even snicker at my own joke. Maybe I was wrong and it could get old.

"You won't find any agents in there, Bubba. There was a... disagreement between some DEMON agents, the Charlotte police, and the bar patrons a few days ago. It didn't end well."

"Oh," I said. That explained the fresh coat of paint on the exterior. And the little splotches of red that weren't quite covered up all the way. Blood is really hard to paint over. It takes a couple coats of primer, at least. "Well, whatever. Let's go see what kind of shitshow is on the other side of that door."

"It'll be fine," Skeeter said. "This trip has been screwed up enough already. What else could go wrong?"

Sometimes I really hate when he asks stupid questions.

12

Mort's was quiet when we walked in, a decent-looking place with newish tables and chairs, a long bar running down one wall, and a few booths on the opposite side of the room, only one of them occupied. There was a smattering of beings around the room—a half-shifted werebear, a faerie with her wings on full display laughing at a couple of guys that looked human, a massive humanoid with greenish skin sitting at the bar that I would have called an orc if I believed in orcs. Then I checked myself and decided that the part-faerie redneck taking orders from a government agent and an angel didn't get to not believe in anything, and mentally reassigned that one as "orc."

The bartender looked human, but I just assumed she wasn't. She was dark-haired, medium build, maybe Mexican or Latin American heritage. She was pretending to wipe down the bar with her left hand, and I couldn't see her right, which I assumed was resting on the butt of a sawed-off shotgun. I'm sure somewhere there's a bar that doesn't have a sawed-off shotgun under the bar, I just don't think I've ever been in one. Those kinds of places require neckties and are way more dangerous than the ones where the bartenders are packing.

"Hey there," I said, sliding onto a barstool. Joe sat next to me while I bounced up and down a little to test the seat. These were good stools. You can tell a lot about a place by their barstools, and these were nicely padded, with the bar for your feet at just the right height. This was a place built around serious drinking. If the jukebox was decent, I could see myself spending some time in a place like this. If most of the clientele hadn't wanted to eat me, of course.

The bartender looked at me, her green eyes piercing as she pointed over her shoulder to a sign that said "Sanctuary." "Can you read, human?"

Well, that took care of any lingering question as to whether or not the bartender was a cryptid, or at least some flavor of supernatural being. "Yes, I can read. I heard this place was a Sanctuary. I'm not here to start trouble. I just need information."

"Yeah, that's how most of the worst fights in here start. Some dickhead human looking for information. You see the addendum?" She pointed back to the sign, and I noticed a little placard hanging under the "Sanctuary" sign. "Rules of Sanctuary Do Not Apply to the Following: Quincy Harker, Jack Watson, Rebecca Flynn, the fucking angel Glory, Keya Pravesh. And maybe not Faustus, but ask management first before you shoot him."

"That's a lot of exceptions," I said.

"I'm thinking of adding a note about anybody working for, with, or in the vicinity of those people. I've got my attorneys working on some language."

"Sounds like you're going to need a bigger sign."

"I'd be better off if asshole humans didn't come here trying to get my joint involved in crap I have no interest in and can make no profit from," she replied.

I cocked my head to the side. "You don't look like a Mort," I said.

She laughed. "Oh, you really *are* new in town! That's adorable. I'm a hitchhiker, sweetie. I look like whoever needed the last favor. I do things for humans, and I get to ride around in their meatsuits for an agreed-upon period of time in exchange. They get something they really, really want, and I get to see how the mortal half lives."

"People just let you hijack their bodies?" Joe asked. "That sounds...obscene."

"You think that's obscene?" the woman I now knew to be Mort asked. "You should see the kind of things humans have rattling around in their brains all on their own. Don't worry, it's not like I can just go on a killing spree in their bodies. They have veto power over anything I want to do. Although you'd be surprised how rare anyone uses it. I pretty much have free rein to do whatever I like until our rental agreement is over."

"And you have to give the body back at the end of the term?" I asked. "You can't just hop in there and possess the person?"

Mort laughed. "Nah, it's not worth the effort. I did the whole possession thing way back in Salem. That shit's hard. Now I just make deals, and I've got a waiting list of bodies to hop into. I haven't been without a willing chauffeur since 1865. Wouldn't have been stuck building my own meat suit then if I'd cast an understudy for that dipshit Booth."

"Wait a minute," I said. "You're telling me that you possessed John Wilkes Booth and shot Lincoln?"

"No way, pal. I borrowed John Wilkes Booth's body so he *could* shoot Lincoln. I made him strong enough and fast enough to jump out the balcony and get away, but he was too damn noble to let me keep running, so we went out in a blaze of glory in some shitty barn in Maryland. If it weren't for me, he would have been caught in Ford's theatre when he broke his leg. I kept him going. But like I said, the host has veto power, and he decided it was more noble to die for his cause and got himself shot. Dumbass."

"And you possessed the little girls in Salem that were hung for witchcraft?" Joe asked, a look of horror on his face.

"Nah, there were no witches in Salem, and only one demon. Yours truly," Mort said, a proud grin on her face. "That one was a legit possession. I hopped into this magistrate asshole Hathorne and stirred up a serious hornet's nest. Got him to convince people there were witches all around them, and then wormed his way into the tribunal that convicted all those innocent girls and women. I picked up some serious souls for the boss that way. All the other judges, all the people that named witches, all the people that lied to get those women hung—it was like an all-you-can-eat smorgasbord of asshole souls. But you didn't come here to talk about me, and your friend here is making some of my clientele nervous, so why don't you ask me what you want to ask me, then leave?"

I looked around the room as surreptitiously as I could, which is not very given that I'm enormous and I was one of two humans in the joint, so most eyes were on us already. Pretty much everyone was looking in our general direction, but they were focused on Joe. I guess they could see holy, even if the Church was too dumb to recognize it. "I'm looking for two women."

"Good for you, pal. Too bad I don't run that kind of business. Bye." Mort turned away, but I reached out and grabbed her wrist. She turned back very slowly and looked at me. "You want to be very careful with your next words and actions, mortal."

"I know you've got a gun in the other hand. I know you can cut me in half with that scattergun before I can bring my pistol above the bar. But my fiancée is missing, and her car is still outside. I need to know where the hot blonde and the annoying younger woman that came in here a couple hours ago are now. Because there's just the tiniest chance you aren't fast enough to kill me, and that would be real bad for you."

Mort stepped forward and put her other hand on the bar, showing me the twelve-gauge I expected to see. "Since you asked nicely, I'll tell you. Just remember, nothing is free."

"This is," I said, and this time when I met her eyes, I let her see how globally pissed off I was. "I've had a shitty night. I've been beat up, shot at, tased, kidnapped, tied up, tased some more, and then I find out my fiancée is missing. Now you have two options. You can tell me what I want to know and I can leave this place, never to return. Or you can screw with me some more and I can see how much damage that body can take, then I break the next one, and the next one, and the next. And I promise you'll run out of bodies before I run out of ass-kicking."

Mort rolled her eyes and looked to the floor. "Lucifer protect me from humans whose mouths write checks their asses can't cash." She turned back to me. "I'm going to help you. Not because I'm afraid of you actually hurting me, but because I've had a really shitty week, too, and I don't want to replace the furniture or walls again if our conversation goes sideways. Now take your goddamn hand off me before I get annoyed."

"I don't think it matters, Bubba," Joe said, poking me in the side. I turned to him, and he pointed at a squirrelly looking little dude who was sidling over toward the far wall of the bar, making a beeline for a red EXIT light over a nondescript metal door.

"Well, that's who I was going to tell you to talk to, because that's the guy I rented the Star of the World to, and he's the last guy your ladies were speaking to before they hauled ass out the door. I heard doors slamming right after they left, and tires squealing, but I didn't go out and look because, frankly, I didn't give a shit. There was no trouble inside my place, so for once I didn't have to replace the tables. Now you can talk to Gary if you can catch him before he makes it to the emergency exit, but if you throw a punch, then you've broken Sanctuary, and all bets are off."

Joe started after the little dude who was about halfway to the door, and I turned to follow. Mort grabbed my wrist, and I jerked to a stop. She might have been wearing a human body, but there was nothing normal about the power in that grip. I turned back to her. "I'm serious. You start anything in here, you better be prepared to finish it."

I gave her my best "trust me" grin and said, "Don't worry. I always am." She let go of my arm and shook her head, muttering "humans" under her breath as she put the shotgun back under the bar.

Joe and I caught up to the scrawny little guy about five feet from the door. I threw an arm around his shoulder and said, "Gary! Buddy, pal, old salt, how've you been? How's the wife? How're the kids? Where's my fiancée?" I shook him a little with each question, until on the last one I practically threw him to the floor.

"I don't know you, man. And this is a Sanctuary. You can't be starting something in here."

"That's not what Sanctuary means, Gary," I said with a grin. "Sanctuary just means that if I'm going to start something, I'd better be willing to back it up. And trust me, I'm willing."

"Yeah?" Gary asked. "You're willing to beat my ass, but what about everybody else in the place?" I looked around, and sure enough, every eye in the joint was on me.

I rolled my head from side to side, cracked my knuckles, and said, "If I kick your ass, I gotta fight every other asshole in this bar?"

Gary scrambled back to his feet and even found the balls to bow up at me a little. I would have been impressed if it wasn't quite as funny to watch. It was a little bit like watching Skeeter threaten to whoop somebody's ass—you knew what was about to happen wasn't going to be pretty, but you also knew it was gonna be entertaining as hell. "That's right. You want a piece of me, you gotta deal with all my friends, too."

"Joe, we're gonna have to fight a whole bar full of assholes to get to the one asshole we really want to punch. Is there a word for that where we come from?" I asked, making sure my voice was loud enough for every being in the bar to hear me.

"A word for beating up an entire bar full of cryptids and supernatural creatures?" Joe replied. "Yeah. We call that a typical Friday night."

I grabbed Gary around the throat, and it was on like Donkey Kong.

13

I punched Gary in the face, just the once. Not enough to cause any lasting damage, not even enough to break his nose. I just popped him hard enough to scramble his eggs a little and dropped him to the floor, where he sat on his ass with his eyes crossed.

"Don't move, asshole," I said. "We ain't done. I just need to handle this bullshit first." I looked over to Joe, who had a pistol in his hand and was drawing a bead on the werebear. I didn't know if he was loaded with silver, and I didn't have time to worry about it, since the orc had apparently just been hanging around looking for an excuse to break a human or two into toothpicks. He was on his feet before Gary even hit the ground, and barreling my way, sending chairs and tables flying out of the way.

Now I'm a big dude. But it's been a while since I played college ball, and I might have let my weight room routine slide a little. Or a lot. Either way, my days of benching four hundred pounds are long behind me, and it shows in the migration of a lot of mass from my arms and chest to my belly. I can still kick a lot of ass, but more often than not, I find myself outclassed in a purely physical matchup these days.

So it wasn't really that unusual for me to feel like I was punching above my weight class, but I hadn't felt *this* out of my league since I fought a dragon in Fairyland. Even if orcs aren't such a big deal in D&D, they're a lot more impressive in a bar fight. This dude was pushing seven feet tall. And well over three hundred pounds, without even the slightest hint of beer belly. I had just a second to think "this is how the hobbits felt" before he was on me, slamming his shoulder into my chest and knocking me flat on my back.

It looks a lot easier to fall flat on your back when the wrestlers on TV do it, but they also ain't doing it on a concrete floor most of the time. When you're slammed on your back by a giant green-skinned asshole who wants to stomp your head into paste, it hurts like a son of a bitch. What else it does is give you a couple seconds to draw your gun, which is exactly what I did while the orc stood over me grinning. I drew the Smith & Wesson Pravesh had provided for me and put a forty-caliber slug in the giggling bastard's left knee.

The orc screamed and dropped to the floor, and I rolled up to my feet and let out a sigh of relief. Apparently orcs aren't from Faerie, since I didn't need cold iron to hurt him, and that made life a *lot* easier. I carry a lot of different ammo for Bertha, and the same types for my backup Judge. All I had for this pistol was what Pravesh had in stock, which consisted of regular ammo and some kind of special hollow-points with silver nitrate tips. I was really hoping that's what Joe had loaded up with, since the werebear was headed his way and looked pretty pissed.

I looked down at the orc, who looked a lot less intimidating lying on the floor shrieking with both hands clutched to his bleeding knee. "That looks like it hurts," I said. Yes, I'm a dick. Usually only to monsters that want to rip my lungs out. Sometimes to my friends, too.

"You bastard!" I didn't know an orc's voice could get that high. He must have been really hurting.

"You good to lay there and bleed and cry?" I asked. I moved the pistol over and pointed it at his other leg. "Or do I need to give you a matching set?"

I don't speak Orcish, but since he didn't do anything except writhe and curse, I figured he was pretty much out of the fight. Joe had his pistol pressed up against the werebear's junkal region and looked like he was making threats about shooting off important parts, so I turned to the two guys who looked human that had been sitting with the faerie chick.

Spoiler alert: they weren't human. They were faeries. Glamoured to shit faeries who might have looked like human schmucks in a dive bar but were really faerie knights, complete with swords and honest-to-god armor. I ejected the magazine from my pistol, slammed a new one home, and shot the nearest faerie in the chest. He slammed to the floor, his armor making a sound like the Tin Man banging a tractor, and smiled up at me.

"That wasn't cold iron, human. It did no real damage," he said.

"I know, asshole," I replied. "That one was already in the chamber. The new mag is all iron-jacketed rounds, and the first one goes to your face. Or you can get up, put your little pigsticker back in its sheath, and go the hell home. It's your call."

He thought for a long moment, longer than I wanted him to, given that I was totally bluffing about the bullets being iron. Pravesh gave us each two magazines of normal ammo and one with the funky silver-tipped rounds. I didn't have shit that would hurt a faerie except my rapier wit. Lucky for me that today, and only today, it was enough. The faerie knight clanked to his feet, gave me one of those "If I ever see you again I'm going to ruin you" nods, and walked out the door. His buddy followed, and we were left with a bleeding orc, a really pretty faerie woman, a werebear with a gun at his balls, a hitchhiker demon, and whatever Gary was. An asshole, for sure, but I wasn't sure exactly what *species* of asshole. Shit, for all I knew, he was human.

Except when I turned around, there was no Gary. Just a patch of empty floor and a side door slowly swinging closed. "Well, shit," I said. I turned to Joe. "Either shoot his dick off or let him go. Our best lead is getting away."

He turned to look at me, and the werebear did what lycanthropes generally do at the first opportunity after you threaten their balls with a pistol. Yes, I have a large enough sample size to say that this is what usually happens when you get distracted while holding a gun to a were's junk. The bear drew back a massive paw and knocked the *shit* out of Joe. This wasn't just some "get that gun away from my pee-pee love tap," this was a "goddammit, next time you gotta buy my dinner first" swat. A paw the size of Joe's entire head slammed into the side of his melon, and I could have sworn that I saw his jaw and his skull move in opposite directions for about half a second.

Joe didn't go down. You can't really "go down" when you're doing a sideways cartwheel across a bar floor. The bear hit him, and Joe went flying ass over teakettle a good fifteen feet across the bar. He took out a table, three chairs, about seven empty beer bottles, and what looked like a plate of really suspect nachos before he sprawled on the floor, out cold.

The bear took a step toward him, claws out and mouth watering at the thought of getting some of that pretty holy man meat for lunch, and I shot him in the leg. It didn't do shit, because not only were my bullets not cold iron, I hadn't loaded up with the silver either. So all I really did was make the bear stop, turn to look at me with a confused expression that would have been really cute if it wasn't on the face of a monster that wanted to turn my friend's insides into his outsides, and make a little quizzical noise. Kinda like "*Hurr-urr?*"

I knew that shot to the knee wasn't going to do a damn thing, so I was already moving by the time the bear turned to focus on me. I took half a dozen big steps across the room, stepped up on a chair, then used that to hop up onto a table, and launched myself through the air at the werebear like a missile. A big redneck missile.

A big, *stupid*, redneck missile. I nailed him square. I hit that bear with the kind of flying tackle that would have gotten me on the first string if I'd been able to do it in college. And it didn't do a damn bit of good. Because while three hundred fifty pounds of hair, tattoos, and attitude will lay just about any human being flat out, and probably put them in traction for at least a couple weeks, it doesn't do shit to a thousand pounds of half-shifted werebear.

That big fuzzy sumbitch plucked me out of the air like I was a toddler, or a stuffed animal. He just caught me like Rey Mysterio trying to take down The Big Show. Only without the mask. And with a little more body hair. The bear held me up for a minute, then proved to me that we were in fact in Charlotte, North Carolina, one of the greatest cities in the history of professional wrestling, and spun me around into a perfect sidewalk slam worthy of the late great Big Bubba Rogers, crushing my back into a table and turning it into toothpicks and cheap varnish.

I laid there looking up at my fate, which was furry, seven feet tall, and had a lot of teeth on display. I tried to roll sideways to get to my hands and knees, but I couldn't move. I wasn't paralyzed, but I couldn't roll over because it felt like I had a couple broken ribs and if I moved wrong, I might pop a lung. Or one of the ribs might just decide "screw it" and burst out of my chest and run for the hills. Neither one felt like something I should let happen, so I just lay there trying to think of something. I felt on my hip for my gun, but I'd dropped it when I took flight. I tried to reach for the backup strapped to my ankle, but I couldn't get my foot high enough to reach it. I tried to sit straight up like The Undertaker, but that made something new grind in my chest and I flopped back down with a gasp of pain.

The bear looked at me, then looked at Joe, then looked back at me. He pointed down at me, and I swear he grinned. Then he picked up a chair in each hand and raised them high over his head. I could see how this was gonna play out. He was going to skewer my chest and gut with one chair and drive a leg of the other one right through my face. If Joe couldn't bail my ass out, this was about to be the end of the road for the Bubba show.

Then a sound like a thunderclap cut through the bar and the were-bear's right hand and the chair it was holding disappeared in a haze of blood, fur, and splinters. "Put the other chair down and you'll still be able to scratch your ass tomorrow," said a nasally voice that sounded more beautiful to me than a chorus of angels.

The pain in my chest lessened enough for me to roll up onto on elbow and see Skeeter standing in the side door with a smoking shotgun in his hand. He looked around the bar, then looked at me and Joe. "This isn't as bad as I thought it would look," he said.

"You got here in time to stop the worst of it," I replied, managing to only gasp a little with every word. My chest was feeling a lot better somehow, so I was able to push myself up onto hands and knees and stagger upright with only a couple of attempts. Maybe I hadn't been quite as stove up as I thought. "How'd you get here, anyway?" I asked.

Skeeter motioned with the barrel of the twelve-gauge for me to step aside, and I did, since I'm not usually one to argue with crazy armed gay men, even if they are my best friend. "When you found Geri's phone and no Geri, I knew everything had already gone to shit. That girl is a Millennial. There is no damn way she voluntarily left her cell phone in that car. I got one of Pravesh's goons to take me over to the church and I drove your truck over here."

"How'd you drive my truck?" I asked.

"That's what you want to ask me right now?"

"It's my truck." Of course that's what I wanted to ask him right then. I wanted to know how he was able to drive my truck. I don't let *anybody* drive my truck. Not even Amy, and I sleep with her. At least Skeeter was skinny enough that his narrow little butt wouldn't change the ass indentions in the driver's seat, but it was gonna take me forever to get my mirrors back right.

"I have a key," Skeeter said. "That's how I drove your truck."

"I never gave you a key to my truck." That goes along with nobody else ever driving my truck. Nobody else has a key to my truck, either. I patted my pocket, and yep, my keys were still there.

"You never gave me a key to your house, either. Not any of the times we replaced the doors. The truck was easier, though. I cloned your key fob. Cost me about sixty bucks and twenty minutes."

"Well, I'm glad you did," I said, not completely sure if I was telling the truth or not. "Now let's get Joe on his feet and go find the girls."

"Yes, *please* get the hell out of my bar," Mort said. I turned to see her with the Sanctuary sign down and a Sharpie in her hand. "Now, you're Bubba, and the good-looking one is Joe, and the little one is Skeeter, right?"

"Yeah," I said.

"Good." Mort put the cap back on the Sharpie and held up the sign, showing me that it now had three more names added to the list of people who were not protected by the rules of Sanctuary. Oh, well. I've been blacklisted by better places than a demon bar. Hell, I'm not allowed to set foot anywhere in the Historic District in Savannah after a disagreement with a bunch of dwarves about who could outdrink whom. I don't think we ever did find out the winner, but there were about six buildings that were definitely the losers.

"Okay," I said. "If we're ever back in Charlotte, we'll find someplace else to drink. And you can send the repair bills to Director Keya Pravesh at the local Homeland Security office. She probably won't pay 'em, but you can send 'em." I scooped Joe up, throwing one arm over my shoulder as his eyes rolled around in his noggin', and headed to the door, thinking that my ribs were really healing quicker than usual. Must be something in the North Carolina air.

14

Joe and I followed Skeeter out into the parking lot, where sure enough, my truck sat there gleaming in the sunlight. I felt a little tight in the chest when I first laid eyes on her, like at the end of *Rudy* or *Old Yeller*.

I did what men normally do when faced with unexpectedly emotional situations, like being reunited with our trucks after an absence. I changed the subject. "You really messed up that bear-dude, Skeet. He's gonna have a rough go of it without one paw."

"It'll grow back when he shifts," Skeeter said.

"Really?" I knew weres healed most injuries when they shifted, but I didn't know they could regrow entire limbs.

"I don't know, Bubba. I ain't the monster expert. I'm the tech dude. I saw some fuzzy asshole about to smoosh my best friend into paste, and I shot his ass. If his hand grows back, fine. If it don't, fine. He shouldn't have messed with my people." That pretty much summed up mine and Skeeter's relationship right there. Ever since we were barely teenagers, we've given each other shit, talked the kind of smack that would get you beat up or shot if you said that crap to anybody else, and generally been unmitigated assholes to one another.

But God help the dumb bastard who tried to mess with one of us.

Skeeter was *my* punching bag, as a couple of the receivers on the high school football team learned to their discomfort when we were in ninth grade. They were shoving Skeeter around in the parking lot, alternating between using racial slurs and homophobic ones, because it was Georgia in the nineties and that's how straight white dudes talked—like assholes. I walked up, didn't say a word to either of them, just smacked the taste out of one dude's mouth and then backhanded the other one to the ground.

For once I'm not exaggerating. I didn't make a fist, I didn't throw a punch, I didn't kick either one of them. I just laid slap after slap across their cheeks until they looked like lobsters that had just come out of a pot. I smacked one, and when he did like the Bible told him to and turned the other cheek, I slapped the piss out of that one, too. And he wasn't turning the other cheek out of humility, he was turning almost completely around from me knocking the bejesus out of him. Then I laid into the other one, and I beat those boys like swaybacked mules. I only stopped because after a few minutes of laying heavy leather like that, my hands started to hurt. When I was done, I yanked them both up by their collars and brought their faces close to mine.

"Skeeter is my friend, do you hear me?" I asked. "If I ever hear of either one of you saying shit like that anywhere in the same *town* as him, or I even think one of y'all might have laid a hand on my friend again, then next time I hit you, it won't be with an open hand. You got it?" They nodded, and me and Skeeter headed off to play video games.

"I got that," I said to Skeeter, my head jumping back to the present. "Now would be a good time for you to tell me that you've got some idea how to find that asshole Gary who snuck out before all the fun started."

"Skinny dude, looked like he was being chased by hellhounds?" Skeeter asked. I nodded. "I saw him. He looked scared as hell."

"He should be," I replied. "Did you see which way he went?"

"No. I tagged his car with a tracker before I came inside."

"How did you know which car was his?"

"I didn't," Skeeter said, looking at me like I was an idiot. "But it's the middle of the day. There were only six cars in the parking lot, and two of those are the ones you and Amy drove here. I just tagged all four of the others. Figured if one of them was important, we could just track the one that wasn't still here."

"Not bad, Skeet. Help me get Joe into the back seat. You can navigate."

"Good. I hate driving your truck, Bubba. It steers like a pregnant whale."

"Don't be talking bad about my truck, Skeet. I love my truck."

"Your truck is enormous. Have you ever even tried to parallel park this thing?"

"Are you on drugs, Skeeter? No, I do not parallel park the F-250. I park it at the end of the lot, because it takes two spaces or it hangs out in the aisle too much. Or I park it on top of bad guys." I had the back door open and was wrestling Joe into the seat. He was just awake enough to be more of a hindrance than a help, so I just kinda pushed him over and let him roll off into the floor. I folded his legs and shut the door.

"What the hell happened to him?" Skeeter asked.

"He got punched by a bear," I said.

"It says a lot about our life that I don't have any more questions after that answer," Skeeter said, then opened the passenger door and climbed inside.

I just nodded and walked around to the driver's door. When I opened it, an even more beautiful sight awaited me. Sitting perched in the console, her glorious barrel gleaming at me, was Bertha. My Judge was there, too, but I coulda replaced it. Bertha was one of a kind. There was only one Bertha. And now we were reunited. "You brought Bertha, too?" I asked.

"Yeah," Skeeter said. "Somehow the priest was in a hurry to get all the discarded firepower away from his church."

"And that's how you tell the difference between big-city Catholic Churches and the tent revival snake handlers we've got back home."

"Yeah," Skeeter agreed. "Those rednecks would have stole your guns and been halfway to the next town by now."

H alf an hour and about seven different roads named "Queens" something later, we pulled into an office park on the north side of the city. From what I could tell, most of the businesses in this little cul-de-sac were closed, but there was a Hyundai parked in front of one low-slung brown building. "That our boy, Skeeter?" I asked.

"Yeah, that's the car."

"Well, nobody else left the bar after the fighting started, so it must be my new friend Gary. Let's go say hello." I slid out of the driver's seat and reached back for Bertha. The assholes that kidnapped me had taken the shoulder rig off me and everything, so it took a little maneuvering to get everything situated right. Then I tucked the Judge at the small of my back and opened the back door.

Joe had managed to get himself up off the floor and was sitting all the way against the passenger door with his eyes closed tight. "I don't think I can help, Bubba. I'm sorry."

"We'll get you to the hospital as soon as I get the girls out of here. You just chill out and try not to move much. Concussions ain't nothing to screw around with." I wish somebody had told me that when I was playing Division I football. I got my bell rung so many times I felt like Notre Dame after some practices. I hate to think what the first-stringers went through. I worried sometimes about long-term brain damage from repeated head injuries, then realized that I was a lot more likely to suffer acute brain damage from some beastie ripping my damn head off one day. Either way, Joe didn't look like he could open his eyes without painting the inside of the truck, so he was out of this scrap.

I pulled open one of the cabinets under the back seat and grabbed a pair of silver-edged kukris on a leather belt. I wrapped it around my waist and buckled it on while Skeeter dug around for more different types of shotgun shells. I was a little worried about him and that gun, because if he got caught with the wrong load in the chamber, he could have a real problem. I didn't feel a whole lot better when he clipped a 9mm pistol to his belt, because while it's easier to swap out ammo in that Glock than in the Mossberg, Skeeter can't shoot worth a shit, so him having a pistol did not reduce my level of concern about this rescue attempt.

Well, maybe we'd get lucky and there wouldn't be anybody in there with Gary. That could happen, right?

Of course it couldn't, and we knew it hadn't happened as soon as we stepped through the front door. The sound of chanting came through the thin walls into the open front lobby area, a generic space with a half-circle reception desk and a pair of cheap wooden doors flanking it. The walls were covered in generic motivational posters with pictures of sunsets and eagles and that shit, and there was a trophy case along one wall full of hunks of clear glass. There was no kind of signage to tell you what the hell the company was, though, which was the kind of little detail that made a place scream "this is a front." And judging by the Gregorian soundtrack coming through the open right-hand door, the innocuous front masked a bunch of assholes trying to do some nasty magic. Probably all wearing stupid masks and robes, or some such shit.

"Skeeter, are there magical rituals that you have to get stoned to perform?" I asked, trying to keep my voice down and my breathing shallow. I did not want to catch a contact high when I might need to shoot up the place at a moment's notice, and with the amount of kind smoke wafting out of that door, it was a real possibility. Whatever they were chanting, I guess it was Cthuluian for "I wanna get hiiii-iiiiigh."

"Yeah, but they're usually done by indigenous cultures, and they usually use native plants and roots and stuff," Skeeter said. "I don't know of any magic rituals that involve smoking copious amounts of weed."

I pulled my shirt up over my nose and said, "Well, let's get moving. Maybe Gary will be so mellow he just gives us the girls and lets us waltz right out of here in a Grateful Dead singalong."

I motioned for Skeeter to follow me, and I crept across the front office as quietly as I could. Which was pretty quietly, given my size and the amount of hardware I was carrying. It didn't matter, though.

Just as I came up to the door, I either stepped on a trigger plate, or broke an infrared beam, or set off a motion detector, because a klaxon started to blare, the fire alarms started to strobe, and all the overhead lights came on a deep red.

"Hey Bubba," Skeeter said from behind me.

"Yeah?"

"I think they know we're here."

"Yeah," I agreed. "Time for Plan Z." He didn't have to ask. I used to say it was Plan B, but apparently by the time we got to my kind of plan, we'd run through the whole damn alphabet. Plan Z was the same as it always is—run into the room and beat the shit out of anything that moves. It's a lot like Plan A, but without the sneaking, or the actual "planning" parts.

I suck at Plan A. I wasn't built to sneak. But I'm real good at Plan Z, and I charged through the door with a kukri in my left hand and Bertha in my right, just looking for somebody to get medieval on.

15

It was almost like I'd seen this movie before. Or this Netflix original series. Or whatever these schmucks were trying to imitate. They had all the trappings—the big circle drawn on the floor, a shitload of candles around the room, half a dozen assholes in dark red hooded robes and goat masks, Gary's weaselly ass standing just outside the circle hopping back and forth from foot to foot in excitement, and an emaciated bald guy standing behind a table situated at the top point of the star. On the table was a bowl of what looked like blood, Pilate's sword, and a necklace. I assumed that the pendant was the Star of the World, the Earth anchor of the cryptid-killing spell. If that's what was going on here, then the blood in the bowl was drawn from all the beings DEMON had been experimenting on all around the country, and for all I knew, the world. With the blood to bind them, the spell would find every creature that shared even a strand of that creature's DNA and destroy them.

"Nice of you to join us," Skinny Asshole said. He grinned, and I felt my blood run cold. He was legit happy we'd found him, which means this whole mess had been a trap. "I was afraid that I wouldn't be able to destroy the fae as well, but Gary has managed to deliver not only the artifacts, but you as well, with a foot in both Courts and just enough magic in your blood to destroy them all. Well done, Gary. Your contribution to our cause has been great."

"So, uh, do I get my money now?" Gary asked. "And when can I take that necklace thingy back to Mort?"

I barely even saw Skinny Asshole move, but all of a sudden his right hand came out of the sleeve of his robe, and I saw a flash of silver as he stretched his arm out and cut Gary's throat so deep he almost decapitated the little shithead. His eyes bugged out as blood cascaded down his chest, and he died with a surprised look on his face. Well, that answered that. Gary was human. Had been, anyhow.

A shit-eating grin stretched across Skinny Asshole's angular face, almost all the way up to his gleaming bald head. He had a long scar running down the left side of his face, obviously affecting his eye, since that one was milky white. All in all, he was a creepy-looking mother. I don't like it when creepy guys smile at me. It usually means I'm getting hit really hard in the near future.

The boulder that slammed into my back let me know that I was right again. I hate being right. Fortunately now that I'm a man in a committed relationship, it doesn't happen often. I flew off my feet and hit the floor on my belly like I was trying to body surf the concrete. Pro tip—concrete does not body surf well. My breath went out in a *whoosh* and my weapons went flying. I scrabbled at the floor, trying to get up, flip over, get to my gun, or generally do anything to keep myself from getting stomped on by whatever had just knocked the ever-loving piss out of me.

I was up on my knees when Skeeter's shotgun barked twice, driving me flat again. A spike of adrenaline jolted me to my feet, and I turned to see a massive musclebound creature with gray skin and a pair of wicked-looking tusks jutting out of its lower jaw drop to its knees, a massive red bloom spreading across its breastplate. The creature, maybe an ogre, maybe a hobgoblin, toppled over like a bag of bloody potatoes and didn't move again.

"Got 'im," Skeeter said.

"That you did," I wheezed.

"Get them!" Skinny Asshole yelled. He looked a lot less confident now, which gave me hope that there wasn't another ogre lurking around the warehouse. It's not like there was a lot of place for one to hide, since the room we were in was just a big empty space, but I did see a couple of bathroom doors off on one wall, and maybe a storage closet next to them. The way this trip had gone, I didn't trust one not to come running out of the crapper pulling up its pants with toilet paper stuck to its foot en route to beat my ass without even stopping to wash its hands.

For now, though, all I had to contend with was six dorks in long robes and stupid masks. Make that five, since one of them tripped on his robe and fell face first on the concrete floor before he took three steps. The problem was, they all seemed to be human, so I couldn't shoot any of them. Not that I had Bertha, since she was lying on the concrete a good twenty feet in front of me.

"Don't shoot the humans, Skeeter," I said.

"Got it," he said, and tossed the shotgun aside. I almost laughed at the grim expression on his face until I watched my best friend pull an Asp baton from his belt and snap it open, then slip a pair of brass knuckles on his right hand. "What?" he asked, laughing at me. "Billy's been making me learn self-defense. He says if I'm going to work with you, I need to be able to handle myself in a fight."

"I like this guy more and more, Skeet," I said, grabbing an onrushing cultist by his robe and slinging him into the guy beside him, sending them both to the ground in a pile of tangled limbs, red robes, and stupid masks.

Two of the others slipped by out of my reach, and I hoped Skeeter had learned enough to keep him from getting his face turned to pulp as I focused on the last guy. This guy was the least stupid of the bunch, because he'd taken the time to pull his robe and mask off before he started walking toward me. He was big, with the kind of muscles that said he spent a lot of time in the gym training for strength not looks. His arms and shoulders were easily the size of mine, despite him giving up several inches and probably a hundred pounds to me.

"You know, if you just let me take a sample of your blood now, this will hurt a lot less," he said. He looked almost apologetic, like he didn't want to fight. That worried me a little. All the real badasses I knew hated violence. They knew how to be violent, and when push came to shove, they would end a debate with extreme prejudice, but they weren't the guys out at the bars on Saturday night taking that old Elton John song seriously.

"I've got a strict policy, bub," I said. "My blood stays on the inside. Now you can respect that policy, or I can lay you out. Your call."

"Okay," he said. "Hard way it is." He got close, but instead of throwing a punch, he flicked out his right foot and slammed it into my left thigh. The big muscle in my leg spasmed, and while I was trying to figure out where to start with the curse words, he did it again. Twice. Now I could barely stand as that leg knotted up, and as I tried to correct my balance, that's when he came in swinging. He threw quick left hook followed by an uppercut with his right, and if all had gone according to his plan, he would have turned out my lights with that one combination.

Problem was, I shit all over his plan. You see, I've spent a lot of years now fighting monsters that are stronger than me, faster than me, more resistant to pain than me, and in a lot of cases smarter than me. What I've yet to come across, however, is one that's more willing to do abjectly stupid crap to win a fight.

With my right leg jacked up, and this musclebound jerk throwing hands like he'd beat up a lot of fat rednecks in his time, I had to even the playing field a little. And the way I did that was the best way I knew how—I cheated. I pushed off with my left leg, driving forward so his uppercut glanced off my chest instead of snapping my head back, and I wrapped Muscles in a big old bear hug. Then I made like Magnum T.A. and put him in a belly-to-belly suplex that would have brought the crowd to their feet at an old NWA match. If you don't watch wrestling, I put my arms around him and picked him up, then spun around to slam into the ground on top of him. Kind of like that whole concrete body surfing thing again, except this time Muscles was my boogie board.

My spectacularly vascular boogie board let out a strangled noise that sounded like a chihuahua that's been discovered the hard way napping in its owner's recliner. Since I was on top of him, I smashed my forearm into his throat to help me get up and made sure to bury a knee in his gut before I got to my feet. I looked down at the crumpled ball of anabolic agony that thought he could get between me and my girl, and said, "We done? Or do you need a little more?"

He waved me off, then returned to clutching his junk, so I think that was his way of telling me that whatever Skinny Asshole was paying him, it wasn't enough. By now Heckle & Jeckle, the robed morons that I'd thrown into one another, were back on their feet, and now they had their masks off. They should have kept them on because they were at least two percent intimidating with them. Without the masks, they looked like a couple of interns at an accounting firm. I don't think either one of them topped a buck-fifty, and they looked to be in their early twenties and scared out of their minds.

"You should run away now," I said, pointing toward the door behind me. They looked at one another, then back at me, then they both nodded and sprinted for the exit. I gave a quick glance back to see that Skeeter was holding his own against one of his attackers, and the other one was laid out unconscious on the floor.

"Go! Kick that moron's ass and get the girls. I've got this," he called to me. This was a new Skeeter, a more confident Skeeter. It was pretty cool to see. I turned to the ritual area, where Skinny Asshole had apparently decided that he didn't need my blood to do whatever he was doing. He stood at the top of the circle chanting in a language I didn't recognize, and I watched him slash his own palm open with the curvy dagger and let the blood drip down over Pilate's sword and the necklace.

"Hey! Asshole!" I called, drawing the Judge from the small of my back. I knew the first round was silver-and-iron birdshot, and I was too far away for it to do any real damage, but he didn't know that, and maybe shooting him with some birdshot would mean I didn't have to shoot him with the .45 bullet I had in the next chamber. "Cut that shit out!"

He froze, as most people with any sense will do when there's a gun pointed at them. Then he grinned at me and said, "I can't get all of you abominations, but I can destroy these!" Then he shouted out more words in that crazy language, and the outline of the circle started to glow. I pulled the trigger on my pistol, but the shot stopped in midair at the edge of the circle and just fell to the ground, harmless. I squeezed the trigger again and had the same result with the bullet as with the shotgun shell. Holstering the Judge, I drew my other kukri and flung it overhand at the magician, hoping the silver plating would slice through. No such luck, as it bounced off to clatter to the floor.

As he kept chanting, the surface of the circle started to swirl with red and yellow energy, oozing across the magical barrier like oil on a puddle. The light grew brighter and brighter as he kept up his ritual, and then I was at the circle, pounding on it with my fists. It was like I was hitting a steel door, booming, thunderous blows that did nothing.

His chanting reached a crescendo, and he reached down and picked up the two artifacts, holding them high above his head. I saw through the hazy circle him take a deep breath, and I knew I was about to see the end of every earth-born species of cryptid. Then a blinding white light streaked past me, *through* the circle, which exploded in a miasma of red and yellow nastiness, and a pissed-off guardian angel stood in front of Skinny Asshole looking like she really wanted an excuse to kick somebody's ass.

"Shut up," she said, and slapped the magician so hard he spun completely around. The sword and necklace fell to the floor, and Skinny Asshole staggered back until his ass hit the table full of spell components. The bowl of blood toppled to the floor, shattering into a million gross pieces, and Skinny Asshole reached down and picked up the curvy knife, holding it up to the blond chick in gleaming golden armor with huge white wings.

"I was really hoping you'd do something stupid," Glory said, then she waved her hand and a blazing white sword appeared. I had the feeling that one magician was about to have a really bad night.

285

16

Glory grinned at the terrified magician and waved her white sword in the air in front of her. "Go ahead," she said. "Give it a shot. Maybe you'll get lucky. Maybe this is the first time in a few millennia that I'm too slow, or maybe, just maybe, the teeny tiny enchantments you've got on that letter opener are enough to hurt me. Or maybe you'll just give me an excuse."

Angels are kinda scary when they're pissed off. I looked for Skeeter, but he was nowhere to be seen, and I didn't blame him. Glory was acting a whole lot more like somebody whose moral compass just kinda spins around in a circle than somebody who was supposed to be on the side of the angels, literally.

Skinny Asshole dropped the knife and fell to his knees. "I surrender! I'm sorry! I'll never do magic again, I swear it! I was seduced by his power. I didn't know what I was doing! I didn't believe it would really work!" I couldn't even keep track of the excuses he spewed as he rapid-fire threw them at Glory to keep her from skewering him.

I wasn't worried. Sure she was pissed off, but she was an angel, right? They don't just randomly murder people, even if a pretty good case could be made for this guy deserving a little murder. I became a lot less sure of that when she laid the edge of her blade against his neck and the white flame started to lick across his skin. He screamed, but he didn't move. I think we both knew if he did, he'd either open up an artery, or Glory would. And right at that second, I wouldn't have put money on either side of that bet.

"I just watched a friend die, you scrawny prick," Glory said, and her voice was low and dangerous. The light around her grew brighter until I almost couldn't bear to look at her, and the squealing man on the floor pressed the palm of a hand to his eyes. "I watched someone I trusted murder one of the best people I know because of this stupid... whatever the fuck this is. I don't know if it's some kind of master plan, some kind of twisted vendetta, or just some kind of xenophobic assholery writ large. I just know that I watched a good woman's soul walk into the light just minutes ago, and the people I love are breaking in half right now. *And I'm here dealing with you.* Tell me again why I shouldn't just cut your goddamn head off and call it a day."

"Because we're the good guys, and that's not what we do," came a thready voice from behind me. I turned to see Skeeter holding Joe up over his shoulder. Joe looked like seven miles of bad road, but he was mostly clear-eyed, and he could hold enough of his own weight that Skeeter didn't go sprawling, which was an improvement.

Glory whirled around, her wings flashing open and bathing the room in even more brilliant white. "Says who?" she said, and her voice was low and steady. She wasn't screaming, and she hadn't raised her voice once. She just looked across the warehouse at Joe, and suddenly she was in front of him, holding him up with one hand by the front of his shirt. She plucked him out of Skeeter's grasp and lifted him until he was a couple inches off the ground, and repeated, "Says. Who?"

"Says me," Joe said. "Says Pravesh. Says Bubba. Says Skeeter. Says everybody you've ever saved. We protect, we rescue, we defend, and yes, sometimes we kill. But we don't murder."

"Maybe this one just deserves a little murder," she said, her face grim. This was touching on a philosophical conversation Joe and I had played with for something like twenty years, and I knew exactly where he stood on this.

"No one deserves murder. He gets his shot at redemption. He

probably won't take it, and some demon will end up ripping him apart inside of five years, but *we* don't get to take that away from him. You kill a man, you take away everything he's got, and everything he's ever gonna have. Good guys don't do that."

Joe was bringing out the heavy artillery early. In our debates, I'm usually six beers in before he starts quoting *Unforgiven*. Glory didn't seem swayed, but at his next words, her eyes snapped up to lock onto his.

"And you know what happens to you if you do this." No judgement, no condemnation, and no explanation. I looked at Skeeter, and he gave me a shrug that said not only did he not know what the hell Joe was talking about, he didn't know how Joe knew what the hell he was talking about.

"I don't care," Glory hissed, and the tips of her wings turned black. Wisps of white started to waft off her as the light around her dimmed, but it wasn't a "things are calming down" dimmed. This was definitely a "shit is getting way worse" dimmed.

"Would she want this?" Joe asked.

Glory lifted him higher, extending her arms so his feet dangled nearly a foot off the ground. "You don't talk about her! You didn't know her! You never heard her voice, saw her play with her granddaughter, or laughed when she made Harker put a dollar in the swear jar. You don't get to do that."

"If you do this, you won't either," Joe said, his voice kind. I knew that voice. I'd heard that voice on my porch after I had to kill my daddy and Joe stayed with me all night while I drank moonshine, punched inanimate objects, and cursed the universe, my brother, God, and anything else I could think of. That Joe was my anchor when life was too much. He was my compass, and I was really hoping he could guide one pissed-off angel home tonight.

"I don't give a shit," Glory said, but this time when she swore, it didn't have the same fire behind it. This was a good girl cussing, somebody who didn't really have the rhythm of it, wasn't comfortable with it. "I've seen how the Fallen live. It's not so bad. They can hang out here, screw with the humans, live forever, and do whatever they want without following the dictates of some absentee father and his gang of dickhead Archangels."

"It's not so bad?" Joe asked. "You know that Hell wasn't Lucifer's punishment. It was never seeing his Father or his family again unless it was in battle. It isn't the fire that burns, it's the cold. The absence of grace that seeps down into your core and destroys everything it touches. It wouldn't be not going back to Heaven, Glory. It would be abandoning everyone you love. Everyone who still needs you. Could you be that selfish?"

She blazed brighter, and I could almost *feel* the fury rolling off her, then in a blink, the light was gone. She dropped Joe to his feet and fell to her knees in front of him, her body wracked with huge, gasping sobs. "It hurts!" she wailed. "Why does it have to hurt so much?"

"Because that's how you know you love them," Joe said, kneeling beside her and taking the weeping angel into his arms. He brushed her hair off her face and kissed her on the forehead. Glory's eyes were closed, and Skeeter had gone to tie up Skinny Asshole when it started to look like Joe was going to talk her off the ledge, so I'm pretty sure I'm the only one who saw his eyes glow softly white as he said, "Well done, my good and faithful servant."

It took a long time to get ahold of Pravesh, and when she finally made the scene, we found out what had gone down across town. Glory still wasn't talking to anyone but Joe, and Pravesh wasn't much of one for chitchat either, but from what we were able to gather from Skinny Asshole, tonight was supposed to be Shaw's grand finale, when she was supposed to lead a huge monster rally where Harker got torn apart by a combo platter of cryptids, demons, cops, and DEMON agents while her pet magician was over here casting a spell that would destroy every divine, fae, or cryptid on this plane. Shaw never planned to *have* a demonic anchor. She just wanted to get rid of anything on Earth that could stand up to a demon so she and her buddies could have a perpetual buffet.

Amy and Geri were tied up in a storage closet, keeping to the theme of the night where I was scrambling around for wire cutters to free people zip-tied to chairs. I vowed to start carrying a Leatherman, then wondered where in the hell I had room on my belt for anything else. Whatever. That one was a problem for Future Bubba. Current Bubba was hugging his fiancée and clustering off to one side of the room while a bunch of DHS agents took everything including the artifacts and Skinny Asshole, whose name was Bert, into custody. For safekeeping, they said. I hoped Skinny Asshole liked Cuban cuisine. Actually, I didn't give a shit. He tried to kill everything, so I hoped he was allergic.

"So…what's going on with Joe and the hottie?" Geri asked. This kid could give me lessons in blunt, I swear. She never looked up from her phone, which she'd been typing on non-stop since Skeeter gave it back to her, fulfilling the stereotype to a T.

"She's an angel," I said. "Joe's…comforting her?"

That paused her thumbs for a couple seconds. "Joe is comforting an angel? Isn't it supposed to be the other way around?"

"Kid, you've been around for a couple months now," Skeeter said. "When are things *ever* the way they're supposed to be with this bunch?"

We all laughed, and it felt good. It also felt a little sacrilegious, given what we knew about Pravesh and Glory losing a friend just a couple hours earlier, but we needed something to break the tension. It had been a long night, and it wasn't quite over yet. The eastern sky was just starting to turn purple and lighten up, but I felt pretty confident that the universe could find some way to crap on my head again before dawn.

That way came in the form of Regional Director Keya Pravesh, who walked over with an envelope full of cash. Geri snatched it out of her hands and started counting hundreds. "Not that I don't trust you," she said, "but you work for the government, so I don't trust you."

"I shall attempt to remain only mildly offended," Pravesh said. She looked around the cluster of us. "Thank you. Your help here was invaluable."

"Glad to help," I said. I was being honest, too. Especially since if they managed to cast that spell, I'd probably be dead myself. I am not above some enlightened self-interest. Actually, it's kinda my thing. Well, maybe not the "enlightened" part.

"That's good to hear, because we have a…situation that I need your assistance with. One that my other team is too personally involved with." She wasn't looking any of us in the eye, and it's always been my experience that it's a bad sign when the government agent who is in charge of handing out the shit sandwiches walks up and holds out a lunchbox but won't meet your gaze.

"Same rate?" Geri asked.

"Yes, plus you will be deputized as temporary agents with the Department of Homeland Security."

"We're in," the little money grubber said.

"Hold on there, Greedo," I said. "What's the gig? If it's too personal for your other crew, what level of Defcon is this?"

"Oh, it is absolutely Defcon Fucked," Pravesh said, and if profanity had seemed out of place coming from an angel, it was downright *wrong* in the prim voice of Director Pravesh. "You heard what happened tonight? Lucas Card impaled Jack Watson, great-grandson of the legendary Dr. Watson, with a hammer after Watson inadvertently murdered Cassandra Harrison, one of the descendants of folk hero John Henry."

"Yeah, it sounded a lot like *League of Extraordinary Gentlemen* went sideways," I replied.

"Then you know who Mr. Card really is," she said.

"I know, but I want you to say it. Tell us the assignment, Pravesh. No government bullshit, just plain English. What's the gig?"

"Mr. Brabham, the Department of Homeland Security would like to hire you to…hunt down Lucas Card, also known as Vlad Tepes, also known as Count Dracula. Your primary objective is to bring him in alive, but if that is not possible, you are authorized to use lethal force."

You could have heard a pin drop as none of us took a breath for a long moment. Then I nodded. "Okay," I said. "You've got a team. We're gonna hunt down Count Dracula."

Nothing Like The End

IV

BLAZE OF GLORY

1

Who the fuck are you and what the fuck are you doing in my apartment?" The voice coming from behind me was low and gravelly, like somebody gargled with cheap bourbon every morning after breakfast, and it sounded *pissed*. I had to get the next few moments very right or I was going to have a bad day, maybe my last one ever.

"Technically it's your uncle's apartment, isn't it?" I asked, not turning around. I moved slowly, extending my arms from my sides so my empty hands were visible. I was pretty sure he wasn't going to blast an unarmed man in the back, but he'd had a hell of a week, so I wasn't taking any chances.

"I own the building, asshole. They're *all* my apartments. And you didn't answer my question."

"Which one? Who am I, or what am I doing here?"

"How about we start with who you are and who you're working for, and we'll decide if you live long enough to tell me what you're doing?"

"I'm gonna turn around now so we can talk face to face. That okay?"

"I don't give a shit if you stand on your head. If you don't start giving me some answers in the next three seconds, I'm going to turn you to ash and leave you for the goddamn Roomba to take care of."

I was pretty sure he wouldn't actually do that, but not a hundred percent. Like I said, he'd had a real shitty week, and he might be looking for somebody to take his frustrations out on. I'm an appealing target for that, since I'm so damn hard to miss. I turned around and got my first look at the famous, or infamous, Quincy Harker, Demon Hunter.

He was skinnier than I expected. I don't know why I thought he'd be bigger, but maybe I expected him to *look* more like a badass. He was tall-ish, a little over six feet, with kinda spiky brown hair, a couple days' worth of beard, and glowing purple eyes. Okay, *that* looked badass. I needed to see if Skeeter could rig up some contact lenses that would glow in the dark or something. He was dressed all in black—a long sleeve t-shirt, black jeans, and black Doc Martens. I approved of his footwear choice. I liked my motorcycle boots better for my line of work since the rubber soles were better for blood-soaked floors, but Docs were good, too.

"You look good for a guy your age," I said. "What's your secret?"

"I moisturize," he replied. "You're that guy from Georgia, right? The Hunter?" I raised an eyebrow and he continued. "Giant with a hick accent, ponytail halfway down his back, and a fuckton of tattoos shows up in a vampire's apartment and there are only a few options. And since Luke hasn't pissed off any biker gangs lately, you must be the Southern Regional Hunter."

"*Former* Southern Regional Hunter," I clarified. "I got fired. Rob Brabham. Call me Bubba."

"I'm gonna call you an ambulance if you don't tell me why you're snooping around my uncle's apartment in the middle of the night."

"Well, that's a step up from turning me into dust bunnies, so I'll call it progress," I said. "Your boss Pravesh hired me to find your uncle and bring him in before he kills somebody. Or a bunch of somebodies, if history serves as any example."

"Call her back and resign," Harker said, the glow in his eyes dimming a little, but not entirely. The spheres of purple light around his hands did fade into nothingness, though, so I felt like getting blasted through a wall was less imminent. Maybe I'd even have a chance to get a shot off before he blew me into next week.

"Can't do that," I replied. "My team needs the cash. Besides, hunting monsters is what I do. You think I'm gonna give up a chance to chase down *Dracula*? Hell no, son. I'll do my level best to bring him in without hurting him, but there's no way I'm passing on a chance to hunt down the most famous monster in the world."

"Pretty sure I can *make* you pass on it," the trim man said, and his eyes brightened again.

"You're welcome to give it a shot," I said, a grin twitching the corners of my mouth. I'd wanted to try myself against this dude since the first time I heard about him, and I could tell by the expression on his face that he wanted the same thing.

"Oh, Jesus Christ, will you two put them away and zip it up?" The voice from the door froze me as my hand was drifting over to yank Bertha from her shoulder rig and see how Mr. Magic Eyes felt about a fifty-caliber enema. I looked past Harker to the gorgeous blonde standing in the doorway of the apartment glaring at both of us. Next to her was an equally attractive Black woman who looked equally pissed off. It seemed that our better halves had shown up to talk us into our better senses.

I straightened up and dropped my hands back to my sides. Harker's glowy eye thing winked out like a switch was flipped, and he turned around to face the women at the door. "I'm guessing the blonde is yours?" he asked.

"I'm not stupid enough to use those words out loud, but yeah. Quincy Harker, meet Amy Hall, my fiancé and the newest employee of the Department of Homeland Security." It hadn't taken Amy more than a day of talking with Pravesh after we got our temporary agent status for her to convince the Regional Director that somebody needed to look after DHS's interests in Georgia, and that she was that somebody. I knew that "look after their interests" was code for "keep Bubba out of prison," but if it got us health benefits, I was good with it. Emergency room visits are expensive, and in our line of work, unavoidable.

Harker ducked his head when he realized how his words sounded to most people. Like, literally everyone. "Yeah, probably not the best way to phrase that one, but whenever I say something too sexist, I blame it on my Victorian upbringing. Bubba, this is Rebecca Gail Flynn, the second-newest employee of the Department of Homeland Security."

"Looks like Pravesh is collecting former cops and government agents like Pokémon," I said.

"I'm not sure I know what that is," Harker said.

"Shit, you *are* old," I replied. "If we ain't gonna fight, can we go drink a beer and talk this shit out? I don't know that many methods of conflict resolution, so since whooping your ass is off the table, and you don't look like you're much of one for arm wrestling, I reckon we oughta move right to the drinking part."

"Yeah, let's go," Harker said, moving toward the door. "But for the record, you kicking my ass was never *on* the table."

Five minutes later, the four of us were sitting on a pair of couches, beers in hand, looking at each other across a coffee table. Harker was leaned back with his feet up, so I resisted the urge. Besides, it was his coffee table, after all. I had to give him credit, it seemed awfully damned efficient having the whole team living under one roof. I might be willing to try it when we got back, but I was pretty sure now that Skeeter had a boyfriend and Joe had a girlfriend, neither one of them were interested in shacking up with me, Amy, and Geri. Hell, I only let Geri stay in the spare bedroom because I wasn't totally convinced she was over wanting to murder me, and I wanted to keep an eye on her.

"Now what's this bullshit about Pravesh hiring you to chase down Luke?" Harker asked, sipping on his beer.

"It's not bullshit, Q," Flynn said. She was sitting on the couch next to Harker, her shoes kicked off and her feet curled up under her. It was a pose calculated to look relaxed, but the line of her shoulders said different. Her body language screamed that she still wasn't sure we weren't going to start throwing each other through the furniture and was alert for any sign of trouble. I could see the bulge of an ankle holster within easy reach of her left hand and was determined not to be the one starting anything.

"Director Pravesh hired us to look for Mr. Card because your team has…had a rough couple of weeks," Amy said. My fiancée had a gift for understatement. In little more than a week, Harker had been part of a riot in a demon bar, a massacre in a chain restaurant in a mall, *another* riot, this one in a city park, at least one more bar fight, which barely made the list except it led to yet another riot, where they saw one of their friends betray them all and accidentally kill the mother of one of their team, who had secretly been in love with Dracula for years. And since the feeling was apparently mutual, they all got to see Lucas Card, their benevolent badass vampire pal/uncle revert to the behavior that earned him the nickname of "The Impaler" on the battlefields of Europe half a dozen centuries ago.

So yeah, they'd been through some shit lately. Made me fighting a demon, then fighting agents of DEMON, then getting kidnapped and tased to shit look like an ordinary Saturday night. It wasn't all that far off from an ordinary Saturday night, which said things about my life choices I wasn't ready to examine while we were supposed to be tracking down the most famous vampire in history.

"We're fine," Harker said, and I managed not to laugh in his face, mostly because I didn't feel like spraying beer all over the coffee table.

"Are you nuts?" I asked. "Look, man. I've been through some shit, too. You don't spend any time in this business without it. And I've done the whole thing where you shove your problems in a little box and deal with them when the time is right. Except the time ain't never right, and the lid always blows off the box at the worst possible moment, usually when it's got a good chance of getting you, or some-body else, or a *lot* of somebody elses, killed. Now y'all have been through as much shit in a week as we went through in a year, and we just got back from an eighteen-month trip to Fairyland. Why don't you sit back and let somebody else carry some of the load for a while?"

The skinny man in all black took his feet off the table and leaned forward, looking me straight in the eyes. His weren't glowing this time, which I took to mean that we were ever so slightly less likely to throw down than we had been fifteen minutes ago. He looked at me for a long time, longer than I was real comfortable with, but I wasn't going to break. There's something about looking deep into some-body's eyes that tells you a lot about them, especially if they're a magical sort, and there was shit in Quincy Harker's eyes that I could have gone my whole life without seeing. There was rage, and pain, and more rage, and suffering on a scale grander than I could imagine, and then more rage, and doubt, and regret, and ultimately, resignation.

"Because it's my load to bear," he said. He looked at me with a hundred years' worth of bad decisions hanging behind his eyes, and said, "I have to find him because he's my only family, and that makes him my responsibility."

"Not your only family, asshole," came a familiar voice from over my left shoulder. I turned to see another gorgeous blonde standing there, flanked by a Black woman who looked like she could kick the ass of every man in the room, Director Pravesh, and a sharply dressed…being with obsidian skin, slightly pointed ears, and yellow eyes. I only knew Pravesh and the woman who'd spoken. She was Glory, Harker's—I shit you not—guardian angel, and I hoped she was there to talk him out of trying to hunt down Dracula on his own.

Because from what I'd seen looking into his soul, Quincy Harker had already been through enough pain for half a dozen lifetimes, and I had some experience with family members going over to the dark side. If he went after Luke, the worst thing wouldn't be if Harker didn't find him. The worst thing would be if he did.

2

Amy stood up and walked over to the newcomers, shaking hands and introducing herself like a civilized human being. I sat on the couch and drank the rest of my beer like a giant hillbilly who just finished looking into the abyss of a wizard's soul. Assistant Director Flynn (if I was going to spend any time with these people, I was gonna *have* to come up with something better to call her) stood up and gestured to folks in turn.

"Bubba, this is Jo Henry, great-granddaughter of the legendary John Henry, and...Faustus, the demon. Yes, that Faustus. I believe you've met Director Pravesh and Glory," Flynn said.

I gave everybody a little wave, then turned my attention back to Flynn. "You said 'that Faustus' like that's supposed to mean something. It doesn't. Should it?"

The demon looked a little offended that I didn't know who he was, but he didn't start a fight, which was good. I was still a little sore from the whole kidnapping and being tased thing, so if I could go twenty-four hours without a supernatural fistfight, I was all in favor of that. The three women looked mildly amused, except for Glory, who looked very amused. "You've never heard of me?" the black-skinned demon asked. "The Tragedy of Doctor Faustus? Faustian bargain? Nothing?"

I just kept shaking my head. I'd heard of a Faustian bargain, but I didn't know it was named after anybody, and especially not a demon. That seemed weird to me, since most people didn't believe demons were real. I was about to say something when a big TV on the wall at the far end of the room came to life and Skeeter's face appeared. Except, this wasn't the Skeeter I was used to seeing. This was Skeeter as drawn by an animation company, and with a rainbow horn sticking out of the middle of his forehead.

"Um…Skeeter? What's on your head?" I asked.

At the same time, Harker looked to the screen and asked, "Who the fuck is *that*?"

I looked at him. "Dude, does literally every sentence with you include an f-bomb? I mean, I cuss a fair amount, but you've got some next-level shit going on."

"That's a dollar," Jo said, walking over to me with her hand out.

"Excuse me?"

"Every time you swear, a dollar goes in the swear jar. If you like, you can just put a hundred in every Sunday and consider yourself covered for the week. That's what Harker does."

"Where does this swear jar money go?" I asked, pulling out my wallet. I wasn't sure that I agreed with this policy, but this woman looked like a total badass, and I figured if I objected too strongly, one of us and a lot of furniture was gonna get broken. So I bought my way out of this fight with a twenty. I decided I could get by without dropping a Franklin in the jar. I also only had a couple hundred bucks in my wallet and didn't want to go broke before we got out of the starting blocks on this mission.

"My daughter's college fund. She's twelve."

"I'm pretty sure we've paid for her PhD by now," Harker said. "But you didn't answer my question. Who the fuck is that?"

I waved a hand at the screen. "That's Skeeter. He's my best friend and tech nerd. He's somewhere in the bowels of the building where Pravesh works setting up all his shit."

"Another dollar," Jo said. She was still standing by my elbow, glaring down at me.

I pointed at the twenty in her hand. "I don't expect I'll be here all week, but that oughta cover me for a day or two." Turning my attention back to Harker, I said, "We're gonna need access to traffic cameras, ATM cameras, Ring doorbells, and anything else hackable if we're going to have any chance to find your uncle, so Skeeter's gonna do what he does, and hopefully not piss off anybody with more jurisdiction than Homeland Security."

"But how did he get into my network?" Harker asked. "It's supposed to be hacker-proof."

"It probably was, a couple years ago," Skeeter said. "But tech doesn't stand still, and bleeding edge from three years ago is off the shelf at Best Buy today. Do they still have Best Buy stores? Like, ones you can walk into? Or are they like dinosaurs and Radio Shacks now?"

"No idea," Harker said. "You hacked me?"

"Kinda." Skeeter looked a little sheepish. Me, I woulda looked all kinds of embarrassed if I was a disembodied head on a TV screen with a rainbow unicorn horn in the middle of my noggin, but it was hard to make Skeeter blush. "There was a back door built into your network. It wasn't easy to find, and it wasn't easy to open, but I eventually got in. Can't figure out how to make it not put this damn horn on my avatar, though."

"What was the backdoor?" Flynn asked.

"There was a login prompt with the username 'Sparkles' pre-filled, and it had a password hint. It said, 'speak, friend, and enter.' So I did, and it let me in."

"I don't get it," I said.

"Oh, thank goodness," Faustus said, coming over and perching on the arm of the couch next to me. "I didn't either, but I was too embarrassed to admit it. At my age, people expect you to know everything and get so disappointed when you don't."

"Don't worry, Faustus," Jo said. "We don't expect you to know much of anything that doesn't involve skulking, sneaking, lying, cheating, stealing, or betrayal. Those things we expect you to be an expert in."

"That's fair," the demon said. I kinda liked this dude. I made myself a mental note to be careful. My dealings with demons so far had all been the kind where they tried to kill me, except for Mort, the demon bartender I met here in Charlotte, and he'd threatened, if not tried. Apparently there were a lot more different kinds of demons in North Carolina than just the "eat your soul while you watch" kind I'd met up to now.

"You just typed in friend and that was the password?" I asked. "Seems dumb."

"It would be, if that was the password," Skeeter said. "I typed 'mellon,' the Elvish word for 'friend.' *That* was the password, like in *Lord of the Rings*."

"Is that the one with all the dwarves, or the one with just the one dwarf and the bunch of hobbits?" I asked.

"That's the one with all the hobbits," Skeeter said. "The one with all the dwarves is called *The Hobbit*."

"That's confusing," I said.

"You are the worst nerd ever," Skeeter replied.

"That's 'cause I'm not a nerd, Skeet. No matter how many times you try to teach me to play *D&D*, I can never understand what dice does what, I can't remember which hobbit movie is which, I don't care if the Hulk is stronger than Superman, and I can't remember if *Star Trek* is the one with R2-D2 and *Star Wars* is the one with Spock, or if it's the other way around. But I know I like the little dude from *Shawn of the Dead* in whatever one of them spaceship movies he's in now."

"There is so much wrong with that sentence I cannot even begin to express it," Skeeter said, a note of utter despair in his voice.

"If we can quit worrying about who is or is not a nerd for a moment and perhaps focus a little bit of our attention on finding my uncle before this giant lummox hunts him down and shoots him, that would be great," Harker said, raising his voice to overpower me and Skeeter.

"Are they always like this?" I heard Flynn ask Amy.

"Nah, they're a lot worse when they're together in the same room. That's when Bubba usually ends up flinging beer cans at Skeeter's head."

"Empty beer cans?" Flynn asked.

"Most of the time."

"I only threw a full one at him once!" I protested.

"That was the time you hit me," Skeeter whined. "I had to get stitches."

"You tried to pick up the cute nurse at the emergency room," I reminded him.

"All I did was ask him if he wanted to come over and change my dressing later," Skeeter said.

"How do you ever accomplish anything?" Flynn asked Amy.

"Like this," she said, taking a step forward. "Can we focus before either me or Harker decides to start shooting people? I'm not sure what would happen if he threw enough magic into the network to fry you, Skeeter, but I don't think you want to try."

She waited a few seconds, looking back and forth between me and Skeeter, then said, "Okay. Skeeter, have you made any progress tracking Card's movements since he left the football field the other night?"

"Not much," he admitted. "There have been a few sightings mentioned on social media, but none of the photos were anything more than a blur. There has been some activity near a memorial park on the east side of town in the past few hours, but there aren't any cameras inside the cemetery, so I don't have anything more solid than that."

"That's enough," I said, standing up. "I'll swing over to the DHS office to pick up Geri and Joe, then we'll head for the cemetery. Amy, you stay here and keep searching the apartment and talking to his team for anything that would help us find him. If we're lucky, he'll be visiting old friends' graves tonight and be in a mellow mood, we can talk to him a little bit, and get him back here without a scrap."

"That doesn't work," Harker said. He stood and looked up at me across the coffee table. "I can't have you hunting my uncle. That's not gonna happen."

"Yeah," I said. "It really is." I took a deep breath and tried to put myself in his shoes. They were too tight, so I thought back to when my feet were in less comfortable shoes, then decided that the whole shoe metaphor wasn't working. "Look, I get it. He's family. I promise you, I will do everything in my power to bring him back without hurting him. But I've had to hunt down my own family, and it was the hardest thing I've ever had to do. So please, take it from somebody who's been there—if he's gone completely around the bend and has to be put down, you want somebody else to be the one to do it. And it looks like I'm elected."

Harker gave a little half-snort kind of laugh. "You think I'm afraid of you hurting him? This is *Dracula*, you moron. One of the original monsters. The O.G. vampire, the baddest of asses. You can no more take him down than you could do a cartwheel. If you go out there, even with your team of no doubt very qualified cryptid hunters, you'll be slaughtered. You are out of your league, and you can't even see it."

I took a deep breath, reminding myself that I was outnumbered, that I was in his house, and that Quincy Harker could basically shoot laser beams out of his hands, so backhanding the taste out of his uppity little mouth was probably a bad idea. I let that breath out slowly, then said, "Son, you don't have any idea what leagues I play in. I've taken down trolls, werewolves, shapeshifters, and just about every conceivable monster that's ever lurked in a closet or under a bed. I've beaten Bigfoot in unarmed combat, won a dance-off with a Faerie Knight, and killed a redcap in the middle of Queen Mab's castle. Who, by the way, is my friggin' grandmother. Then I broke out of Grandpa Oberon's dungeon and stormed the Shadow Realm of Fairyland where I slew a friggin' *dragon* before I kicked Puck's ass from here to Tuesday. Your uncle might whoop my ass. Hell, it wouldn't be the first time I've been beat in a fight.

"But here's one thing he won't do, and I guaran-damn-tee you this: Count Fucking Dracula will not, under any goddamn circumstances, hurt any humans in this city on my watch. If he does, I will find him, and I will take him the fuck down. And God Almighty help anybody who tries to stand in my way. Do you understand me?"

Harker gave me a level gaze, locking eyes with me once more. But this time, I wasn't the one going soul-diving. He stared at me for a long minute, then nodded. "Go find him. Bring him home. But hurt one hair on his head, and we're going to war."

"I won't do anything he don't make me do," I replied, then headed for the door. I stopped after a couple of steps because the formerly closed door was now standing wide open, and in it stood a dark-haired young woman in a leather jacket and jeans, twirling a silver stake between her fingers.

"You guys got that shit figured out?" she asked. Without waiting for a response, she walked over to me and stuck out her hand. "I'm your new right hand. I've hunted more vampires than literally any person on the planet. You might say it's in the blood."

"Oh, really?" I asked.

"Pretty much," she said with a nod. As I shook her hand, she said, "Name's Gabby. Gabriella Van Helsing, if we're gonna be all formal about it. Hunting Dracula's kinda just what my family does. Now it's my turn."

3

I stood there, looking down at this chick who just introduced herself as a Van Helsing and told me she was there to help me hunt down Dracula, and it wasn't even the weirdest thing that had happened to me in the past couple days. As I stood around looking stupid with my mouth hanging open, she walked past me and surveyed the room.

"Hey, Harker. Becks, Jo, Glory. Director Pravesh, thanks for the call." Then she walked over to the demon and pulled him down into a kiss that lasted a lot longer than I expected anyone to survive kissing a demon, but I was starting to understand that Faustus wasn't like other demons I'd met. After a long enough kiss to make the rest of us start that whole awkward looking around so we don't have to focus on the two people making out in front of us thing, she turned him loose and pulled back a little.

"Hi," she said.

"Hi yourself," the demon replied.

"No meat suit these days?"

"Depends. Not when I'm around friends. Kinda like taking your shoes off when you get home from work."

"Or your bra," Gabby replied. "Natural is a good look. The whole glossy black skin and bald thing is kinda hot, like a hairless goth Nightcrawler."

"Or perhaps Nightcrawler is based on me? He is, after all, German and obsessed with religion and devils."

"Could be," she said. "But unless you've got Chris Claremont on speed dial, that one will have to remain a mystery." She turned back to me. "When do we leave? And who's going on this little hunting party?"

Everybody started talking all at once, claiming their spots on the team, arguing with each other as to why they should stay behind, suggesting weapons, places to search, and dinner destinations (that last one was Faustus, who I think just wanted to screw with people). I let them go for a minute before I looked over at the screen and gave Skeeter a nod, then stuck my index fingers in my ears.

A couple seconds after Amy did the same, Skeeter blasted out a deafening horn from the television. The whole room fell silent, and just as the first couple of folks drew in a breath to start swearing at Skeeter, I said, "None of you get a vote in who goes on this hunt."

Every head whipped around to me, and Harker opened his mouth. I raised a hand, and remarkably, he didn't say a word. "This is my show, and there's only two people who get a vote in who goes on this hunt. That's me and the person picking up the tab. Director Pravesh, did you call Ms. Van Helsing in?"

She nodded. "I did. She has pursued many vampires, including Mr. Card, in the past. Her experience may prove useful."

"Okay, then," I said. "She comes along. Director Pravesh is paying the bills, so she gets an opinion. None of the rest of you do." I held up that hand again. "I know he's your friend. Family for some of you. And I know this is a real bad time for y'all. So you need to do what people do in times of tragedy. You need to gather together, eat too much fried chicken and green bean casserole, and be here for one another. I'll handle the hunting down the newly crazy lord of all the undead."

"I won't get in your way, but you can't stop me from looking for Luke," Harker said, his voice low and steady. I could tell he was holding himself back, and I appreciated the effort. I'd been where he was—with my only living relative (as far as I knew at the time) gone off the deep end and feeling like I was the only person who could help them. Didn't end well for me. I hoped I could do better by Harker and Dracula.

"I can't," I agreed. "You're right about that. But I won't help you, either, and I will strongly encourage you to stay here with the people who need you. These are your people, Harker, and running off after your uncle right now will hurt them more than you'll help him. I'll find him. That much I promise you. And if he can be brought back without harm, I promise you I'll do that, too."

"But you don't think you can," he said.

I thought for a second. I've been trying to do that a little more, the whole thinking before I speak thing. It's not the easiest thing in the world for me, but I'm getting better at it. "I don't know. I honestly don't. I wish I could tell you something better, but until I find him and see what kind of state he's in, I won't have any idea if he can be talked down off this ledge."

"And if he can't?" Glory's voice was kind, soft, but with a hint of steel in it. She was asking the question so Harker didn't have to. Still guarding him, even from himself.

"That's where I come in," Gabby said. My head whipped around, and she shrugged. "You might be the big bad Hunter, but I'm a Van Helsing. This is my legacy, my chance to do what my great-grandfather never could. I know Luke. We've talked about this, about what to do if he ever went completely dark, and he made me promise if he ever got so out of hand that he couldn't be pulled back from the edge, that I wouldn't make Harker deal with him." She looked around at her friends. "I know some of you will hate me if I do it, but I promised Luke if he lost it and went somewhere he couldn't come back from, that I'd put him down. And I intend to honor that promise. Now let's get out of here, big guy. There's a couple hours before sunset and we need to raid the Homeland weapons closet and pick up your friends before we hit the trail for tonight's hunt."

I didn't wait around for the fussin' to start up again; I just spun around and headed for the door. As I walked past her, Jo reached out and put a hand on my arm. I stopped and looked at her.

"Please," she said, her voice barely louder than a whisper. "If there's any way…"

"If there's the slightest chance he can find his way back, I'll bring him home," I said. "I promise." Then I was out the door and headed for the elevator with Amy and this new chick Gabby in tow.

"That was sweet," Gabby said. "Bullshit, but sweet." She reached out and pressed the button.

I grabbed her shoulder, spun her around, and slammed her up against the wall. "Look, lady," I growled. "I don't know you, and I don't really care to. I've got a job to do, and it's to locate and bring Lucas Card into custody. That's what I was hired to do, and as long as you're good with that, I'm good with you. But the second you make this into some kind of weirdo revenge fantasy or life quest to fulfill your great-grandpappy's legacy, you and me are going to have a problem."

"What then, big guy?" she asked, a smirk pulling one corner of her mouth up. "You gonna beat me up? Kick my ass? That's real tough, a giant like you beating the shit out of a little girl like me."

"He won't have to kick your ass," Amy said as I stepped back. "Because I'll kick it for him. Bubba has a thing about hitting women, in that he doesn't like to do it. I have no such qualms, so if you try to take Card out and I don't think it's the right play, I'll beat you like a swayback mule."

I was incredibly proud of her right then. I mean, she'd been a federal agent for a while, so I'm sure she'd threatened people for years. But that was a solid eight out of ten redneck threat, bringing in the old swayback mule bit, and I was certain that was not in her vocabulary before she met me. I was totally taking full credit for that part.

I held up both hands. "You know, I've always wanted to say this, but girls, you're both pretty. Now simmer down—" I have no idea what the rest of that sentence was going to be, because both Amy and Gabby extended their middle fingers in my direction, and the elevator arrived to give us an escape from a conversation I was uncomfortably sure we would revisit multiple times before this case was over.

F orty-five minutes later, we were loading gear into the back of one of Pravesh's Suburbans. Amy had commandeered it for our first case up here and never given it back, so I was interested to see if she was going to try to drive it home to Georgia when our business in Charlotte was done. Skeeter was set up in a windowless room deep in the heart of the Homeland Security Regional Office, with a mini-fridge full of Red Bull and a Sam's Club's worth of chips and cheese puffs. Every once in a while I thought about what was going to happen to that man if his metabolism ever slowed, and it was terrifying.

"Okay, I think that's everything," Joe said, loading a Pelican case into the SUV. "We've got three MP7 submachine guns, a Remington 700 rifle for me, a Mossberg 800 shotgun, and four Glock 17 pistols with spare magazines for everything."

"Who's on the shotgun?" I asked.

"That's yours, Bubba," Amy said. "Since you're going to insist on being the first one through the door, you've got two breaching rounds in the twelve gauge, then white phosphorus loads behind."

"That'll work," I said. "It'll get me through the doors, deter anyone from getting too close, and give me time to throw the shotgun at somebody's head and draw Bertha so I can get to work. You got your backup?"

Amy nodded and pulled up one leg of her pants to show me the little Ruger she wore strapped to an ankle. I've never understood ankle holsters. I've been in a lot of situations where I needed to shoot something, and in exactly none of those has it been convenient to either get my ankle up to my hand, or kneel down so my hand was by my ankle. I keep my backup in the waistband of my jeans, right around my butt crack. It occasionally leads to the holster smelling of chili farts, but I figure that makes the ammunition more lethal.

"What about you, kiddo?" I asked Geri. "You got any surprises in the back of that Suburban?"

She grinned up at me, and I drew in a sharp breath at the resemblance between her and her older sister. Sometimes she looked so much like Brittany that it hit me right in the gut. "If I told you, it wouldn't be a surprise, now would it? But I do have a new silver-edged katana I've been looking for an excuse to try out." And all resemblance to her dead sister were gone in an instant. Even with her plans to murder me on the shelf (for now), Geri was one bloodthirsty chick.

"I've got some party favors, too," Gabby said, holding up a short-barreled gun and grinning.

"Is that what I think it is?" I asked.

"That depends. What do you think it is?"

"I think that's an M320 40-millimeter grenade launcher."

"Then yep, it's exactly what you think it is." She tossed the grenade launcher into the back of the SUV along with a bandolier of shells.

"And exactly what in the blue hell do you think you're going to do with a grenade launcher?" I asked.

Gabriella Van Helsing looked at me like I was the stupidest human being she had ever laid eyes on and said, "Well, Bubba, I thought I'd use it to blow some shit up." Then she walked past me and got into the passenger seat of the Suburban. "We gonna do this thing, or what?"

"Or what indeed," I mumbled as Joe and I headed for my truck. "Or what in-flippin'-deed.

4

I ever tell y'all I hate cemeteries?" I asked as I closed the back door of my truck and walked over to the Suburban where the rest of the team was gathered. They were all geared up looking like the second coming of *Platoon,* while I looked pretty much normal. I think that says more about the fact that I usually look like I'm headed into a fight than about their dress for the day, but this was not the time to give deep consideration to my sartorial stylings, or lack thereof. Definitely lack thereof.

"Only every time we set foot in one," Amy said. "Which, given our line of work, is pretty often."

"Now that's not fair," I protested. "I didn't gripe about the cemetery where we fought the zombies in Fairyland."

"That's because we weren't in a cemetery, Bubba," Joe said. "We were in an abandoned town, then a church. We didn't set foot in the cemetery."

"Okay, there's that," I said. "Skeeter, you got any more specific idea where we should be looking for Dracula?"

"He prefers Luke these days," Gabby corrected me.

I looked down at her, which I do to everybody, on account of being six and a half feet tall. It's a life of talking to people's foreheads and bald spots, but at least I can reach things on the top of the fridge. "I ain't real interested in what he wants. I don't want anybody to forget, even for a second, that we're on the trail of one of the most dangerous monsters in history. We let our guard down because he likes his current nickname, and this hunt might be over before it starts."

The smaller woman shrugged. "Okay, whatever you say. You're the boss."

"Please God don't ever say those words again," Amy said with what I thought was an exaggerated sigh.

"Skeeter?" I asked the air, hoping to bring this hunt back on track.

My best friend's high-pitched voice came through the earwig Pravesh had grudgingly provided. The last bunch of tech she gave me didn't fare too well, and I hadn't yet found the heart to tell her that was just a thing she was going to have to get used to in her life. Having me and my friends on payroll had a fair number of, shall we say, ancillary expenses associated with it, not the least of which was the amount of our shit that got wrecked in an average hunt. And I really didn't want to bring up some of our bar tabs until she was more accustomed to our methods.

"There was an image of him entering this graveyard last night around three, and not leaving until just before dawn, so there's something here that's important to him. I ran the records of the people buried there, and I came up with three possible names that could matter to Card, or to Harker and his crew in general."

"We'll split up and check out those grave sites all at once," I said. "Amy, you and Gabby go to one. Joe, you take Geri to the second, and I'll take the third. Skeeter, where are we going?"

"I sent GPS coordinates to your phones," he replied. "Amy, you're going to the main building in the center of the cemetery. It's a combination mausoleum and office, so I don't know if Card was looking for records, visiting a friend, or retrieving something he had hidden inside one of the crypts. But he seemed to be heading in that direction when he went through the gates."

"We'll find out," Amy said. She gave me a kiss on the cheek and headed off through the gates toward the center of the memorial park.

"Joe, I've got you headed to a section of graves off in the northwest corner. There aren't very many plots used up there, so it might be a good place to hide gear or cash if he needs it," Skeeter continued.

"What is it about that area that makes you think Dracula may have gone there?" Geri asked. The kid had a good head on her shoulders. She'd make a hell of a Hunter someday, if she didn't get herself killed. Or sent to prison for smothering me in my sleep.

"There's a section of eight plots all purchased by a Lucille Westenra. That seemed like a solid clue."

"Why?" I asked.

Every head turned to me, and my entire team looked at me like I was the world's biggest idiot. I know for a fact that I'm not because I've met a lot of professional wrestlers in my day, and some of those guys make me look like a rocket scientist.

"Bubba, have you ever read the book *Dracula*?" Joe asked.

"No," I admitted. "I liked that move with Keanu Reeves and Gary Oldman looking like he had a butt on the top of his head, though."

"Lucy Westenra was Mina Murray's best friend," Geri said. "Dracula turned her, and that's what got the whole thing with Abraham Van Helsing started."

"Oh. She was friends with Harker's mama?" I asked.

"Yeah," Geri replied.

"And Drac turned her into a vampire?"

"Yep."

"And now we think that Drac bought a bunch of empty graves in her name?"

"Pretty much," Skeeter said.

"That makes sense. We should totally check that out."

Joe and Geri didn't say anything, just turned and walked off toward the corner of the massive graveyard. "Okay, Skeet," I said. "Where am I going?"

"I've got you heading to the place I think was most likely where Card went," he replied.

"Where's that?"

"The grave of his last Renfield."

While I walked through the graveyard in the last hours of sunlight, Skeeter filled me in on vampires, Renfields, their relationships, and the guy whose grave I was headed to. "Basically," he said. "Renfields do the stuff during the day that vampires can't do."

"Because of the whole burning up in sunlight thing."

"Yeah, that. Totally a thing. Sometimes they're living friends of the vampire before they were turned, sometimes descendants, sometimes groupies that think if they serve the vampire long enough, they'll be turned out of gratitude."

"How often does that happen?" I asked.

"The turning or the Renfield being a groupie who wants to be turned?"

"The turning."

"Nowhere near as often as the other," Skeeter said. "You'd be amazed how many people want to be vampires."

"No, I really wouldn't," I said. "Remember, my brother was into the whole 'evangelical monster' shtick. A lot of people spend a lot of their time scared, and some of them will do whatever it takes to feel like they can take care of themselves. From carrying a big-ass gun, to hurting somebody different from them, to trying to become a creature that can't die."

"Bubba, I am a gay Black man born and raised in Georgia. I am an expert on fear. Everything from police lights to a pair of White dudes walking behind me on the sidewalk scares the shit out of me. You don't have to explain the motivation of fear to me."

I felt myself blush a little bit. "I'm sorry, Skeet. I didn't think about that. You're gonna know a hell of a lot more about what it's like to be scared all the time than I will."

"Little bit," he agreed. "Now this Renfield, he wasn't any of those things. He was just a guy Card hired to work for him as a personal assistant. Apparently over the years they became close. According to my sources, he was almost like family."

"What happened to him?" I asked.

"He was murdered by a Cambion who infiltrated the Department of Homeland Security. That same half-demon murdered Mort's half-human daughter, Christy, which Mort blames Harker for. That explains some of the animosity between the two."

"How did you find all that out?"

"Pravesh has a three-inch thick file on Harker," Skeeter replied. "I read it the last few nights. Not recommended, by the way. There's some stuff in there that will definitely make you think twice about closing your eyes."

"You think Dracula's gonna be here visiting the grave of his butler?" I asked, looking around. "Not now, obviously, because of the whole daylight thing, but later?"

"No," Skeeter said. "I think he has already been here, and best-case scenario is you come up with some kind of clue to where he'll go next."

I could do that. I've seen enough cop shows on TV to know how to look for clues. Even though I'm a Hunter, it usually doesn't take a whole lot of detective work. Most of the time I can just wander around in the general area where somebody thinks there's a monster, and if there is one, it finds me. I'm like a walking, talking challenge to any critter worth their salt. This seemed like it was going to take a little more than my normal blundering into the bad guy. Dracula hadn't lived for five hundred years or whatever without picking up a trick or two. I just had to make sure none of those tricks got me killed.

After what felt like half a damn mile of walking, I got to the coordinates Skeeter gave me as the sun dipped below the horizon. If Dracula, or Luke, or Lucas Card, or whatever was going to show up, it would probably be soon. I know if I'm in the mood to visit dead people, I try to knock that out early in my day, so I can compartmentalize all my feelings before I try to get anything done. I assumed that a vampire would be the same way. I reached under the long-sleeved shirt hanging open over my Stone Cold Steve Austin t-shirt and unsnapped Bertha's holster. I wasn't any kind of quick draw artist, and there wasn't really such a thing as a quick draw on a Desert Eagle anyway, on account of it being too damn big and heavy, but if I was up against the O.G. vampire, every half a second was going to count.

I looked around until I spotted the correct headstone. It was nice. Nothing extravagant, just a nice, granite stone with a name and a pair of dates. "Sylvester Thomas Efor the Fourth," I said softly. "I can kinda see why you wouldn't mind being stuck with the name 'Renfield.' You started off with a pretentious pain in the ass of a name, Renfield might have been an improvement."

There was a misshapen hunk of metal perched on top of the marker, and as I picked it up, I recognized it for what it was. "Skeeter," I said to the air, keeping my voice low. "Why is there a spent hollow-point bullet on the top of this Renfield dude's grave?"

"No idea, Bubba," Skeeter said. "Does it look like it was fired on a range or like it came out of a breathing target?"

"Now how am I supposed to know that?" I asked, then took a closer look at the bullet. "Never mind. This totally came out of a body."

"There's blood on it?"

"Yeah," I replied. "Or something that dries to look enough like blood that it may as well be it. Is this the bullet that killed this guy?"

"He...wasn't shot," Skeeter said.

"How was he killed?"

"It's gross," he warned.

"Skeeter, I have fought almost every kind of monster in the book, seen the inside of way more living creatures than anybody who isn't a taxidermist should, and I lived in the dorms for a couple years of undergrad. I think I can handle gross."

"His heart was ripped out as part of a demonic summoning ritual."

"You were right," I said. "That's gross. So if this bullet didn't kill him, why is it here?"

Before Skeeter could answer, a twig snapped from off to my left and I turned to see a trio of figures walking up the hill in my direction. "Gotta go, Skeet," I said. "Looks like there's asses that are gonna need kicking in about twenty seconds."

5

Now, I don't view every single person or group of people I meet as potential subjects for an ass-whooping. I don't even think everybody I meet in a graveyard at dusk is going to necessarily require a beatdown. But when there's three of them moving in a spaced-out triangle with the kind of precision that comes from working together for a long time, and they're all wearing tactical pants, tight-fitting black hoodies, and combat boots, that tends to push the needle toward a scrap. But what really sold me on having to beat the shit out of the three people coming my way was the hardware they were carrying.

The lead guy had on a helmet with night vision goggles flipped up out of his way, and was carrying a submachine gun on a sling around his head and one shoulder. To his right was a tall woman with a shotgun held out in front of her, and to the left was a massive bear-looking dude that carried a machine gun big enough to give Bertha caliber envy. I couldn't tell exactly what the gun was, but it looked like it would be more comfortable mounted on the side of a helicopter than being toted by a man, but he didn't seem to be having much trouble with it.

There I was, alone in a cemetery looking for the world's most

JOHN G. HARTNESS

famous monster staring down the barrels of three guns carried by what looked like either mercenaries or bodybuilders, or both. I was pretty sure my life had been turned into one of those movies that Netflix is always importing from Korea, and that never ends well for the good guy. He usually survives, but he gets the ever-loving crap beat out of him first, and I was getting kinda tired of that.

"Y'all need to lower your weapons and head on back to whatever video game you popped out of," I said. "I'm a federal agent on official business, and that business don't include whatever y'all are."

"You haven't been a federal agent for a year, Brabham, and the only reason we're not pumping you full of lead and silver right now is because there's no paycheck in it," said the lead guy, stopping about ten yards in front of me but not lowering his gun at all. His teammates came even with him and spread out to each side, making it impossible for me to shoot all three of them before they cut me to ribbons. Not that I was taking it off the table, mind you.

I decided to try diplomacy first, since they hadn't technically threatened to kill me, and because I had managed to stick to my "no killing humans" rule so far on this trip. Although given the way he toted that machine gun, the big guy on the left was less human than me, so he might be fair game for shooting. "You know my name, now how about telling me who y'all are and what you're doing playing Capture the Flag in a graveyard on a weeknight. Don't you kids have school tomorrow?"

The woman snickered, and the guy in the center shot her a look. I knew his type: the insecure former high school football star who managed to make second string at a Division I school and spent the rest of his life trying to recapture the greatness that let him swim in his little senior high pond with so much swagger but didn't translate into shit-all outside of the two-stoplight town he was raised in. The kind of dude that keeps *Soldier of Fortune* in the shitter next to the *Sports Illustrated* Swimsuit Issue and has to think long and hard about which magazine to yank it to. He probably poured creatine powder into his Budweiser, for shit's sake.

"We're here for the vampire, Brabham, so if you don't want to end up on our shit list, you better get back into your redneck chariot and fuck right on off out of here." He at least lowered the gun a little, so when I stomped toward him, I wasn't walking *directly* into the barrel of his rifle.

"I don't know if it's a Charlotte thing or a proximity to Quincy Harker thing, which now that I think about it kinda counts as the same thing, but y'all use 'fuck' like a comma up here, don't y'all?" By now I was right in front of their peckerwood leader, so I reached up with my left hand and brushed his gun to the side. He didn't resist, just looked at me kinda confused, like a dog that had finally caught the car he'd been chasing forever.

"And it ain't nice to point guns at somebody just because you think you might need to be scared of them."

He tried to bring his submachine gun back around, but I wrapped a hand around the barrel and didn't let him. "Scared?" he spluttered. "The day I'm scared of some fat redneck is—"

I didn't get to hear what day that was going to be on account of that's about when my right palm connected with the side of his face in a slap that knocked him all the way down to one knee. I put everything I had into that slap, and the only thing holding him even remotely upright was the fact that I still had ahold of his gun. His eyes crossed and uncrossed a couple of times, and I bent over a little bit and hauled him back upright by his flak jacket.

"I'm guessing nobody ever taught you the benefit of shutting the hell up when faced with a vastly superior force, so here's a free lesson. When a man my size gets within arm's reach, you've got a few options. You can shoot him, you can stab him, you can step back to get some separation and do some kind of badass martial arts Jet Li shit, or you can shut the hell up. But insulting the giant standing a foot in front of your face is about the dumbest choice on the list. You grew up being the biggest, the baddest, and most likely even the toughest sumbitch you'd ever met. Then you went on to learn how to shoot stuff, stab stuff, and blow stuff up, so you *still* thought you were the baddest mother in the valley. But now you're swimming in deep waters, son, and I'm the shark right in damn front of you, so you need to listen to me, and listen good."

I jerked him close, so he had to get up on his tippy-toes to keep his feet from dangling in the air. "You're punching above your weight class, you little prick, and you need to go home, polish your pistol, and forget about hunting Dracula. This is some first-string shit, and you're a career benchwarmer. Now get out of here before you get hurt."

I didn't expect him to listen. I expected him to try something stupid, like maybe a knee to my balls or a headbutt to my mouth. I didn't expect him to smile at me with a look in his eyes that had "bat-shit crazy" written all over it.

"In all that education you got on ass-kicking, didn't anybody ever teach you not to underestimate a smaller opponent?" he asked, then slammed a fist into my gut with way more force behind it than he should have been able to muster.

All the air rushed out of my lungs, and only my iron constitution and many years of spectacular alcohol abuse kept the contents for my stomach from running for freedom too. I dropped the peckerwood and staggered back a couple feet, just far enough for him to level me with a spinning kick that came out of nowhere. There was the Jet Li shit I'd mentioned earlier, which is really effective against somebody my size. I'm not saying big guys can't be fast, because Kareem proved that wasn't true. But a fast big guy will always be slower than a fast little guy, or a fast medium-sized guy, and this normal-sized guy was even faster than he was supposed to be.

I spun around and kissed the grass between two headstones, thanking my lucky stars that I hadn't slammed face-first into a big hunk of granite, then got the wind knocked out of me again as a couple hundred pounds of hyper-masculine asshole dropped onto my back with both knees. The only reason I didn't hear important things in my torso snap, crackle, and pop like breakfast cereal was that I was wearing my own body armor, which didn't keep me from feeling the impact of him jumping on me, but it at least spread the blow out enough that he didn't break anything.

Now I've been pinned to the ground beneath all kinds of monsters that wanted to gut me, decapitate me, and more than a couple that wanted to pound my head into paste, not to mention the featured dancers at about a dozen of the South's least selective gentlemen's clubs. I know how to handle myself whilst prone, so to speak. And while my television preferences tend more toward the tights and pyrotechnics kind of wrestling, I had spent a good chunk of the last couple years studying Greco-Roman escapes and learning some Brazilian jiu-jitsu. In between interdimensional voyages and dragon battles, of course.

So I wasn't completely helpless when I found myself spread-eagled underneath my opponent, and I daresay I was in a lot better shape than he expected me to be, because the expression on his face when I twisted around, got my legs under me and flipped us both over was priceless. I didn't try to grapple him; I just shoved him off me and scooted backward on my butt until I had enough room to stand.

I didn't want to shoot him because even though he was stronger than a damn Clydesdale, there was still a chance he wasn't some kind of beastie. That ruled out my kukris, too, because chopping pieces off somebody is a long road from a less-lethal solution. And I'd left my caestae in the truck, figuring that if I got hand-to-hand with Dracula, they weren't going to do me any good. All I had was my wit, my charm, and my bare fists against this trio of well-armed dickheads, at least one of whom was definitely enhanced, if not straight up supernatural. Yeah, I was completely unarmed.

"If you leave now, I'll let you walk out of here," Peckerwood said. "But if you don't throw down your guns and stay the hell out of our way, you're gonna find out the hard way what DEMON's best geneticists can do for a body nowadays."

That was the second time in a couple of days that somebody in way too much black tactical gear said something about DEMON playing fast and loose with the gene pool, and I tucked that little tidbit away for further examination later. Right then, I had more pressing matters. "You're with DEMON?" I asked. "I thought Harker shut you assholes down."

"We *were* DEMON," the woman said. "Now we're free agents."

"And you're standing between us and a hell of a payday," the hairier of the two men said, and when I looked at him, I could definitely see something a little off about his features. His face was flattened a little, and his beard was short and coarse, more like a pelt than facial hair.

Great. Mercenaries. I hadn't dealt with them much, but I'd heard stories of some other Hunters running into guns for hire in other parts of the country, and the jury was still out on which type of asshole we liked fighting less: true believers or profiteers. I leaned more toward true believers being worse because if you can convince a merc that a fight ain't worth the payday, they'll usually leave you alone. So that's what I was gonna have to do—convince this particular trio of assholes that I was going to cost them more in doctor bills than they were going to make bringing in Dracula.

Some days I freaking love my job.

6

You do know I'm the guy mommy monsters tell their baby monsters bedtime stories about, right? The big bad Hunter that'll come take them away if they don't eat their monster vegetables and say their monster prayers? Do you really want to throw down with me? Especially when you're this damn outnumbered?" I took my time standing up, mostly on account of my everything hurting from being slammed to the ground and dry-humped by an asshole, but also hoping that the rest of my team would cut the shit and come to the rescue already. We were coming up on the part of the movie where Rohan damn well better answer or these three were gonna beat the crap out of my Gondor.

"Do you ever shut up?" Big Fuzzy said, raising the barrel of his machine gun.

I dove behind a headstone as he opened fire, chewing up trees, turf, granite markers, and anything else that happened to be in his path. The *BRRRRRRRR* of the minigun sounded like when I was a little kid and stuck a playing card in the spokes of my bike, only multiplied by a million. I stuck my head out from behind the tombstone and squeezed off three rounds with Bertha, catching the massive gunner in the leg with one of them. He went down screaming, so I guess whatever he was gene-swapping with hadn't made him totally immune to bullets. At least not silver ones. I mean, I *had* come to the cemetery hunting a vampire, so I loaded up on silver nitrate-tipped hollow points before I left the truck.

With the biggest threat out of the way, I felt like I could almost handle the other two. At least I did until the female merc snatched me up by the back of my Kevlar vest and flung me across two rows of graves. "There's no way he's gonna show up here now, Rick. We might as well call it for tonight."

"I'm not going to leave this idiot here to tell Homeland about us. Especially since you decided to use my name," Peckerwood said with a growl. It was full dark now, and we were far enough away from the road for it to be dark where we were. I had a moment's hope that I could use that to my advantage, but the bullet that ricocheted off the marker behind me let me know in no uncertain terms that Peckerwood's night vision goggles were working just fine.

Since I didn't have NVGs, and my quarter-faerie heritage didn't give me the ability to see in the dark, along with all the other magical powers it didn't give me, I was fighting almost blind. Fortunately, Amazonia the Giant Asskicker wasn't trying to hide her movements, so I was able to drop to the turf and not get cut in half by the shotgun blast that split the night.

"Goddammit!" I heard from off to my right. That meant the muzzle flash had blown out Peckerwood's night vision, so for the next few seconds, none of us could see worth a shit. That was as good as I was going to get, so I got up off the ground and hauled ass back to where the female merc had fired from.

She leapt up from behind a headstone and caught me in the ribs with the butt of her shotgun, then made to spin the gun around and blow my head off while I was laid out. Too bad for her my body armor was working overtime because I was still on my feet and together enough to snatch the shotgun out of her hands and slam the ass end of it right above her goggles. She dropped like a rock, and I spared about half a second to hope I hadn't killed her, then remembered the whole "trying to shoot me in the back with a twelve-gauge thing" and gave less of a shit. I fired the shotgun straight up into the air, squeezing my eyes shut as I did. I didn't know if Peckerwood was looking, but hopefully I'd bought myself a few more seconds of even footing while his eyes readjusted to the dark.

The quick *crack-crack-crack* of a submachine gun, followed by the sensation of someone slamming a hammer into my chest told me I had not, in fact, bought myself any seconds at all, and my opponent was very much capable not only of seeing me, but also of shooting my ass. The 9mm rounds didn't make it through my Kevlar, but it still hurt like a son of a bitch. I flopped to the turf, only exaggerating the pain a little bit, and groaned loudly.

"That's some good body armor you've got, Brabham," Peckerwood said from the dark. "Maybe you are back working for the government. Oh well. Too bad they didn't give you a helmet." I saw him step out from between two headstones and aim his rifle down at my face. I brought Bertha up at the same time, firing as I went. The first two went wide, but the next three smacked into Peckerwood like fifty caliber freight trains. He flew backward, and the bullets he meant to send into my skull ripped harmlessly through the dirt behind my head.

I stood up, ejected the empty magazine, and slammed home a fresh one. I stuck with silver ammo, assuming that DEMON had either pumped lycanthrope DNA into these idiots, or something else that had a problem with silver. My other options were cold iron or white phosphorous, and the prospect of having a flaming mercenary screaming out his last moments in front of me was something I decided to pass on.

Peckerwood was writhing on his back when I got to my feet, but it only took him a few seconds to recover enough to push himself up on one knee. "I am abso-fucking-lutely going to kill you for that, you asshole."

"Maybe," I said as I took two steps forward and planted my left foot. "But you ain't gonna do it tonight." Then I snapped my right leg straight and kicked him square in the face. He almost cut a flip before he slammed back into the turf, but this time he didn't pop right back

329

up. Apparently whatever genetic modifications they had, invulnerability wasn't something that came as an option.

Now I had an unconscious Peckerwood snoring into the turf in front of me, a heavily concussed Amazonia dreaming a few feet away, and a Big Fuzzy bleeding somewhere off to my right. I glanced around for him, but the string of profanities he was spewing from the moment I shot him in the leg had stopped, and after a few seconds, I pulled out my flashlight to better scan the area.

"Oh, come on, dude," I called. "Just come on out, I'll put handcuffs on you, we'll get your leg patched up, and then you can go off to Gitmo like a nice psychopath." I was pretty sure he wasn't going to end up in Gitmo with the normal humans, but standing in the middle of a cemetery shouting about the government's super-secret cryptid prisons was not how you kept them super-secret. I moved the flashlight across the ground where the pool of blood lay next to his discarded machine gun. I was right, that was totally a minigun, only modified all to hell so it could be carried by a person rather than mounted in the door of a freaking helicopter.

"Damn," I said as I took in the mods that had been done to this thing. There was a kind of frame that looked like it went over the shoulders with a mounting point for the gun in the front of the chest. A battery pack mounted underneath the gun, and a bizarre Doctor Octopus-looking contraption fed the ammo belts from a backpack-mounted ammo can. I reached down and gave it a tug, but the damn thing must have weighed a couple hundred pounds. And Fuzzy was wearing this thing like a teenager totes his book bag. Yeah, he was a long way from original factory parts.

A twig cracking behind me was the only thing that kept me from being intimately acquainted with how modified the big boy was, as that half-second's warning let me dive forward, leapfrogging over a tombstone before turning around to face my attacker. My attacker that was now almost seven feet of fur, teeth, and claws.

"Dammit, I shot your ass with silver!" I yelled at the werebear. "That's supposed to put you bastards down." I looked, but couldn't see any kind of wound on the transformed merc's leg, so either these genetically modified weres didn't have the same weakness to silver that normal ones had, or he'd managed to cut the bullet out of his leg before he shifted. I hoped it was the second part. I mean, anybody who can cut a bullet out of themselves is a massive badass, but a werebear that isn't afraid of silver bullets is five hundred pounds of fur and rage that I do not have any answer for.

Fuzzy dropped to all fours and came at me, a lot faster than I expected. If I was going to fight all these damn shapeshifters, I was seriously going to have to pay more attention to the National Geographic channel. I tried to dodge around headstones to slow him down, but apparently those things are not planted with the intention of standing up to a quarter-ton of rampaging lycanthrope because he knocked them flat like granite dominos.

I drew Bertha and yelled, "Stop!" That had all the effect anyone would expect it to have on a werebear who carries a two-hundred-pound machine gun in his *weaker* form. Which is none, of course. So I squeezed the trigger and emptied the magazine into the onrushing bear.

Or…I, at least, fired seven rounds at said onrushing bear. Because I sure as hell didn't hit him with enough bullets to stop his big ass. Look, it was dark, he was a *black* bear in the dark, and he was all hunched over on all fours. It's not like he was standing on his back feet in the middle of broad daylight with a big "Shoot Me Here" sign on his belly. Although that would have been damned helpful.

Fuzzy stumbled once, then recovered and kept right on coming. I ejected the magazine and slammed home a fresh one, this one my cold iron/phosphorous rounds. I vaulted a particularly tall monument and stopped, squaring my feet before emptying another magazine in the general vicinity of the bear. I know I hit him at least twice because after the second streaking ball of white fire slammed into him, Fuzzy let out a howl the likes of nothing I've ever heard. He shrieked like a horror movie scream queen and started rolling over in the grass. The smell of burnt fur filled the air, followed by the pork roast stench of burning flesh.

Turns out nobody likes being set on fire, not even magically enhanced werebears. Who knew? Fuzzy writhed in agony for almost a full minute, screaming the whole time, before he finally stopped pouring smoke from his bullet wounds and shifted back to human. The transformation healed his wounds, but Fuzzy was curled up into a ball on the grass twitching and sobbing from the pain he'd endured. Sometimes remembered pain is just as bad as the first time around. Although that's probably not the case with white phosphorous burns. That stuff looked like it hurt *a lot*. I almost felt bad for Fuzzy until I remembered that when I set his furry ass on fire, he'd been trying to rip my guts out with his claws. All sympathy vanished immediately.

"Bubba, are you okay?" Joe asked as he and the rest of my crew jogged up, weapons and flashlights in hand. "We heard screaming and thought you might be in trouble."

I looked around at the fallen mercenaries, two out cold and one twitching in agony on the grass, and marveled at their spectacular timing. "I'm fine," I said. "There were only three of them. They were totally outnumbered."

7

W here to now?" I asked as we headed back to the trucks. "I'm assuming y'all didn't see any more of Dracula than I did?"

"Not a fang," the new chick, Gabby, said.

"We've got an address of another place that was very important to Card during his early life here in Charlotte," Amy said, holding up her phone. "I'll text you the address."

"Good deal," I replied. I looked at Gabby. "You ride with me."

She looked surprised, as did the rest of the team. "Why?" she asked. "Am I getting called into the principal's office?"

"Any school that would hire my ass as principal is going to have some weird ideas on education," I said. "Nah, I just want to get to know you better, especially if you're gonna be walking around behind me with loaded guns."

"And live grenades. Don't forget the boom-boom." She had a glint in her eye that made me seriously reconsider letting her get in the truck with me, but then I remembered that keeping her out of the truck would mean putting her in the SUV with Amy, and that had a lot more potential for disaster. At least if she blew me up, there was a chance I could survive. A slim one, but a slim chance is better than nothing.

I called up the address on my phone and slipped it into the holder on my dash. I plugged in the aux cable and put the truck in gear. "Okay, what's your deal?" I asked.

"I told you," Gabby replied. "My great-grandfather was the first Van Helsing to hunt Dracula, and I'm going to be the last."

"You're that sure you're going to catch him?"

"No, but I'm an only child with no kids and no desire to have any, so unless a sibling magically appears in my mid-thirties, I'm it for the Van Helsing line."

I let out a short laugh. "Be careful what you wish for," I said. She raised an eyebrow and I continued. "A couple years ago my long-lost mother came back into my life and told me about a half-sister I never knew I had. Who is three-quarters faerie and at the time was banging Puck in Fairyland. There was a rescue mission, I met my maternal grandparents, realized that faeries are crazy enough to make rednecks look normal, and we fought a dragon. You might not want to get a miracle sibling, is all I'm saying."

She chuckled. "Okay, I can see that. But that's it. That's the whole deal. I'm a Van Helsing. We hunt vampires. Dracula in particular. He's my white whale, and when I finally found him, he turned out to not be a monster. Kinda screwed up my world view, ya know?"

"Darling, I'm a college-educated White dude from the mountains of Georgia in the twenty-first century. Almost every piece of what I grew up knowing to be true has been proven to be bullshit over the past thirty-odd years." I watched the lights of the city go by on my windshield for a couple minutes, then asked, "What are you going to do once this is finished?"

"What do you mean?" She didn't turn to look at me, and her voice had that guarded tone that told me she knew exactly what I meant, had thought about it, and didn't want to get into it with a stranger while she was on literally the hunt of her life.

I didn't give a shit what she wanted. She was heavily armed woman with an agenda, and before I went into a building that might hold one of the most dangerous supernatural beings in history, I wanted to know where her head was at. I figured I couldn't keep her away from the mission without convincing Pravesh to rendition her to some place that didn't officially exist, and the way she kissed the demon when she walked in the door told me there might be some resistance from my new business associates about that idea. But I could at least try to find out what was going on in that head of hers before I took her and her grenades into an enclosed space.

"I mean this is the end of a chapter, maybe even a book, for you. There's only a few ways this plays out. First, and worst for you, is we find Dracula and he kills you. Second, and thinking about it this might be worse for you than the option where you die, is we find him and you kill him."

"Why is that worse?"

"Seriously?"

"Okay, I get it. I kill Luke, I'm either going to have to kill Harker or die trying."

"Yeah, he doesn't seem like the type to let things go."

"Not so much."

"Okay," I said. "That brings us to Door Number Three, which is the one we really want to open, but we don't even know where the door is, much less the key. That's the one where we find Drac, convince him to stop being Bad Drac and come back to being Good Drac—"

"Let's agree on Less Bad Drac," Gabby interrupted. "Even with all the good he's done in the past century or two, he still has a lot to atone for. There's a lot of blood on those manicured hands."

"Okay, whatever. We talk him back from the edge and he comes back to Harker's team with us. That still leaves you without a mission. The thing you've built your whole life around is done. Then what?"

"Dude, I have no idea." We were at our destination, so I pulled the truck over to the curb and put it in park. Gabby was still looking out the window, making no move to get out, so I sat still. "I don't know what I'm going to do if I live through this. Shit, I don't know what I'm going to do if we find his ass. I *like* Luke. So did my great-grandfather. Later, you know, after the whole book thing. But I made a promise to my dad before he died. If you can't keep a promise to your family, what does that make you?" Now she looked at me, and I got a good look at the real conflict in her mind. I decided that she might not know what she was going to do when she found Dracula, but she at least wasn't a complete psychopath, so I could probably let her and her explosives be around my family.

"I don't have any idea," I said. "I killed my father and kid brother after they turned into evil werewolves, so I am not the best person to give advice about family stuff." With that, I opened the door and slid out, leaving her staring at me from the passenger's seat.

"Hey Bubba," Joe said as I walked up beside Amy. "Why are we at a hipster Irish pub?"

He nailed it. We were standing in front of The Hills of Eire, a faux Irish pub with all the dark wood and darker beer anyone could want in a bar, but absolutely not an ounce of authentic Irish anywhere about the place. I mean, the flag hanging out front was right, at least, but the music coming out the open door was Post Malone, not Flogging Molly, and there wasn't a lit cigarette anywhere in sight. I know you're not allowed to do that in bars anymore, but I figured a real Irish pub wouldn't care about the law.

"Can't say as I know, Padre," I said. "Amy, wanna enlighten us?"

"It might be an Irish pub now, but five years ago it was a house, one of the last surviving freestanding structures in this stretch of downtown, and it was home to one Mr. Lucas Card, his Renfield, and occasionally his nephew."

"Harker," I said.

"Quincy Harker, yes. This is also where Mr. Efor, that's the Renfield's real name, met his end at the hands of an Agent Smith of the Department of Homeland Security," Amy said.

"That's the half-demon asshole, right?" I asked.

"Not to put too fine a point on it, yes. Smith murdered Efor in a ritual designed to open a portal to bring Smith's demon uncle, Orobas, into this plane of existence."

"Now hold on a minute," I said. "I know I'm not the demon guy, that's Harker's shtick, but I didn't think summoning demons required a human sacrifice."

"Not always," Joe said, his voice grim. I looked over at him and involuntarily took a step back. He was *pissed*. "The rituals are always disgusting, and frequently involve blood and other bodily substances, but they don't have to have a human sacrifice as a component. The fact that Smith used one that did speaks to exactly what type of evil bastard he was."

"I mean, not for nothing, Joe, but I figured that from the whole 'half-demon' thing. Most of them aren't known for their sunny dispositions and caring ways," Geri chimed in. She was leaning on the grill of the Suburban behind us, waiting for the old people to stop yapping and point her in the direction of something to shoot. Between her nonexistent impulse control and Gabby's mission-oriented psychosis, there were a lot of people around who wanted to kill stuff more than I did, and that was not a circumstance I was accustomed to.

"Not all demons are bad," Gabby said, walking over to perch on the SUV's bumper next to Geri. I needed to do anything in my power to discourage them from becoming friends. I had a sneaking suspicion that batshit crazy was something that multiplied when it found a kindred spirit, and Geri was hard enough to handle already. "I mean, Faustus is okay."

"Just because you screwed him doesn't mean he's a good guy," Geri said, scorn heavy in her voice. Okay, maybe it wouldn't take much to keep them from becoming besties. Seems like sometimes like repels like. "He has a whole concept of dealing with the devil named after him, I don't think he's all about the rainbows and kittens."

"Oh, he's dangerous, don't get me wrong," Gabby agreed. "But he's bailed Harker out of some serious shit more than once, so on a scale of one to Lucifer, Fausty is a three. Four max."

"Whatever," I said. "Faustus isn't the topic of conversation. Neither is Agent Smith, or Orobas, or anybody else who's been dead for years. We're here looking for Luke. He's the most famous monster in history, except maybe Godzilla, and he's on the run from his federal agent nephew. Now you think he might just be in there bellied up to the bar?" I asked Amy.

"That's where I come in." Skeeter's voice came directly into my ear, something I've never gotten used to, despite nearly a decade of using those earwig things. Maybe if he didn't sound quite so much like Gilbert Gottfried with a lisp it wouldn't be so jarring, but I could tell from the look on everyone else's face that they had the same reaction. "I appropriated the bar's security feeds, along with the data from the ATM cameras all up and down the block, and Card definitely frequents this bar regularly. Like almost every night regularly."

"What the hell did we go to the graveyard first for?" I looked around, hoping somebody had a good answer for why we wasted all that time and I had to get almost eaten by a bear.

"Because if we could corral Card in a less public setting, there would be less potential for damage to property or innocent bystanders. It's hard to wreck a cemetery," Amy said.

"Have you met me?" I asked. "It would not be the first cemetery I have torn to utter shit."

"Okay, that's fair," she replied. "But the point stands that it had a lower potential for getting civilians killed. This is more risky."

"But this also has one serious upside," I said, yanking open the heavy wooden door.

"What's that?" Joe asked.

"There's booze here," I said, then the half-faerie monster hunter walked into a bar.

8

___

It was loud, bright, and full of twentysomethings looking for a fling. You know, all the things I hate most in a drinking establishment. There was hardly a shadowy corner to be found, much less any place quiet enough that I thought a vampire could tolerate with their enhanced hearing. "We need to split up," I said to the others as we stood just inside the door.

"I agree," Gabby said as she ran her eyes across the gorgeous brunette behind the bar. "I'll take the bar." She didn't wait for any kind of acknowledgement, just slipped through the press of people and over to the bar like a big cat stalking its prey.

I shrugged and looked at Joe. "Well, that's my first choice taken."

"I'll go upstairs and take a look around," he replied, pointing to a set of polished wooden stairs to our left. "Geri, why don't you come with me?" The girl didn't say anything, just fell in right behind Joe without any kind of smartassed comment. Sometimes I thought my old friend might have some kind of magical powers after all.

"I reckon that leaves us to check this floor?" I asked Amy. "Wanna try the bangers and mash?"

"Okay, first, you aren't allowed to eat sausage after sunset anymore. You fart too much and I have to sleep with you," she replied, holding up one finger. Another slender digit extended to join the first, and she said, "and you should check the basement. It's the most likely place for Card to be, if he's anywhere near this place, which I doubt." She pointed to my right at a set of stairs going down. They were "barred" with a velvet rope and a sign that said, "EMPLOYEES ONLY."

"That makes sense. You can keep an eye on Gabby while you check the rest of this floor." I stepped over the flimsy barricade, rationalizing to myself that I was currently an employee somewhere, just not an employee *there*.

"Be careful," Amy said, and when I turned around, there was real concern on her face.

"Hey, what's up?" I asked. "I'll be fine. I always am."

She shook her head a little. "I don't know. This feels different somehow, like it's...more *something* than usual. I don't know if it's more dangerous, more significant, or what. But it definitely feels like it's *more*. So be careful. I've just about got you housebroken; I don't want to have to paper train another fiancé." Then she leaned across the rope and gave me a kiss.

"I'll check this out, you keep Gabby from molesting the bartender, and in twenty minutes we're out of here and on the road to Door Number Three, wherever that is," I said.

"Okay," Amy replied, but she didn't look convinced.

I turned and headed downstairs, noting how quickly the place went from all hardwoods and faux antique lamps to bare concrete steps and cheap fluorescent lights. "Skeeter, is there even a chance this dude's here?" I asked.

"I don't know, Bubba. It makes as much sense as anything, I guess."

"You don't sound convinced."

"I'm not. Part of me feels like Harker and his people might be throwing us red herrings so we don't find Dracula, but they're not even the ones coming up with these locations. It's all stuff I'm finding in the official records, so it's pretty legit."

"Official records?" I asked. "It ain't like Dracula kept a blog."

"Well, kinda," he replied. I stopped, only about halfway down the steps. I had to hear this shit. Skeeter had been poking around in the O.G. vampire's diary? "Dracula is a member, founder, actually, of this secret group called the Shadow Council. He started it with, get this, Frankenstein's monster, back in Europe in the nineteenth century. Throughout history, all these folk heroes from all over the world have been members."

"Kinda like that League of Extraordinary whatchamacallits movie you made me watch," I said.

"Sorry about that. It was better than *Green Lantern*, but just barely."

"I liked Green Lantern!" I protested. This was an ongoing debate between us. Skeeter said that the Green Lantern movie was absolute trash that ruined the possibility of a whole outer space franchise of DC Comics movies. I said that it was stupid, but fun, and generally harmless. Yeah, it was a bad movie, but more bad in a *The Replacements* way than emotionally scarring and genre-crushing like *Cats*.

"Whatever," Skeeter replied. "But yes, the Shadow Council has had a lot of famous members throughout the last couple of centuries, including Dracula and Adam—that's Frankenstein's monster's name, by the way, not the one from the Garden of Eden."

"Okay." Given the circles we were traveling in lately, it was a distinction that needed making. "Anybody else?"

"Oh yeah. Dr. John Watson, John Henry, Aleister Crowley, and Sir Richard Francis Burton, to name a few. There are whole volumes of their adventures in the Council Archives, and all those books are digitized and online. But that's not what's important, at least not as it pertains to what we're doing here."

"I was really hoping you'd get around to that part. I could have already had this basement searched and be checking out the beer list by now."

"Hold your horses, Bubba. The important part as far as you're concerned, is that all while Dracula never kept a diary, all the Renfields *did*."

That rocked me. That was some pretty significant shit—an up close and personal view to everything Dracula had done for the last century and a half. "And you've got access to those diaries?"

"Yep. And the first thing they talk about once Dracula moves to Charlotte and establishes his Lucas Card identity is the basement of his house and how he sets it up to be completely light-tight, with an escape tunnel."

"You're thinking Card might use that escape tunnel to come and go from under his old stomping grounds with nobody being the wiser?"

"Makes sense, don't you think?"

I paused for a second, then drew Bertha and checked the magazine. I'd reloaded my spare mags at the truck and traded out my cold iron and phosphorous rounds for more silver-tipped bullets. Now I had one in the pistol, two in the shoulder holster tucked under my right arm, and one in each back pocket. Hopefully I didn't run into anything that needed more ammo than that. If I did, I'd only be able to handle it with the dead werebear's minigun, and I couldn't carry it. I tried.

"Just out of curiosity, what would you have done if one of the others had volunteered to check the basement?" I asked.

"I would have told all that to the entire team instead of just you," Skeeter said. "The rest of them are good, Bubba, and on any given day better than you at some things. But you're the Hunter. If there's one place more likely than another to have a monster in it, that's where I'm sending you."

"I'm blessed."

"Not the word I'd choose, but sure, let's go with it. Now are you gonna go look for a vampire in the basement, or stand there with your piece in your hand all night?"

I didn't answer, just proceeded down the stairs into the basement. One thing about a building getting blown up, I guess, is that when they rebuild the place, the basement gets rebuilt, too. Because this didn't look or feel like what I thought a vampire's basement should be like. It was dry, with normal-height ceilings, and I didn't see a rat or rat turd anywhere. It was basically an ordinary restaurant/bar basement, with more cheap fluorescent lights illuminating every corner and stacks of kegs and racks of spare glassware neatly arranged along the walls. In short, it was as much a lifeless hipster hellhole as the bar upstairs.

"Nothing here, Skeet," I reported.

"Check the freezer," he said in my ear.

"Oh hell no. I've seen that movie too many times. I set foot in that freezer, somebody's gonna come along and lock me in, my cell signal will shit the bed, and before I know it, they're serving Bubbasicles on the dessert menu upstairs."

"You could just stick a beer keg in the door to block it open," Skeeter replied. "Drama queen." That last part he muttered under his breath, loud enough to make sure I still heard it, but soft enough to give himself plausible deniability. He learned that trick in school when he would call our US History teacher, Mr. Nathan Bedford Forrest Smith, a racist under his breath. He was right, but what the hell did he expect? Saddled with a name like that, in Georgia no less, it was a miracle Mr. Smith didn't come to school every day wrapped in a white sheet, and I don't mean the Shroud of freakin' Turin.

I lugged a keg over to the freezer, opened the door, and stepped inside. I not only stuck a keg in the doorway, I also jammed a bunch of cloth napkins in the hole where the lock thingy goes into the doorjamb. Just to be sure. The freezer door stood wide open behind me, no kind of automatic closer on it, but like I said, I knew how this was going to go down if I wasn't vigilant.

It was a freezer. Not a terribly interesting freezer, but revealing enough that I knew I'd never order the fish and chips from this joint. Not if the giant boxes of frozen cod were any indication of quality, and they were. There were boxes of frozen fish, frozen French fries, and anything else you would cook in a fake-ass Irish pub that you'd order frozen because nobody who walked in there would be expecting fresh ingredients with their hookup spot.

"It's a freezer, Skeeter. Not even a very interesting freezer."

"Is there a door in one of the walls?"

"Yeah, the door I came in through."

"That ain't what I meant, and you know it." I did, but sometimes screwing with Skeeter over headset is the only fun I get to have on these missions. Up to this point my evening hadn't been all that enjoyable, so I was making sure to get my giggles in where I could.

I looked closer at the shelves, noticing scratch marks on the floor in front of one. "Hang on, Skeet. I think I've got something."

I grabbed the corner of the shelf and gave it a tug. Nothing. The shelf was loaded down with frozen food, and I couldn't budge it, not even with my strongest yanking. I cleared off one of the aluminum wire shelves until I could see the wall behind it, and sure enough, there was the outline of a door in the back wall of the freezer.

"There's a door here," I said. "It's behind a heavy-ass shelf, so I don't know how anybody could use this as a secret entrance."

"Maybe if they were super strong, like, I don't know…a vampire?"

"Point taken," I said. "Gimme a minute to get this thing cleared off." I set to it, yanking boxes and cardboard flats of boxes down off the shelf and stacking them semi-neatly on other shelves, until they got too full. Then I put shit on the floor. I felt a little bad about the poor schmuck who had to clean up after me, but not as bad as I feel for most of the people who have to clean up after me. At least there were no body parts in this mess. Well, no human ones, anyway.

A few minutes later, I had the shelf emptied and dragged out of the way, revealing a small rectangle cut into the freezer's wall. It looked like the door opened inward away from me, so I grabbed the recessed handle, gave it a twist, and shoved it wide. "Skeeter," I said.

"Yeah?"

"There's a tunnel."

"I'll call the team."

"No," I replied. "I'm going in alone. No point in all of us getting ripped apart by a vampire underneath the largest city in North Carolina. This is the biggest city, right?"

"Yes, it's the biggest city, and the point of having a team is to have them back you up. I'm calling them."

"Okay, fine, but tell them I'm not waiting." And I didn't. With a regretful glance at all the crappy frozen food on the floor of the freezer, and still half-expecting somebody to come along and lock me in to freeze to death, I entered the hidden tunnel under the streets of Charlotte looking for Dracula. You know, like any sane person would do.

9

It didn't take long for the smooth stone walls of the tunnel to turn rough and hacked from red clay. Most of Charlotte might be new construction, but whoever made this escape hatch was here long before Dracula set himself up as Lucas Card. At least, before he assumed that identity here. The air was clean, though, and I could feel a slight breeze tickling the hairs on the back of my neck, making me even more nervous. The only thing that kept it from being an absolute parody of a horror movie was the warm glow of the LED lights, which were apparently tied to motion sensors because they popped on as I walked forward, and as I looked back, I could see darkness behind me where the lights timed out. Somebody had upgraded this tunnel, and within the last few years.

I'd been walking for about five minutes, taking it slow, when I heard something behind me. The tunnel was mostly straight, but there were enough bends that I could only see twenty yards or so in either direction. I knelt and tucked myself as tight as I could to the wall, which isn't all that tight, but I hoped it would give me a half a second's drop on whoever was coming if they weren't my people. I was apparently still enough long enough that the motion sensor thought I'd moved on because after about a minute, my section of tunnel was plunged into blackness.

Good deal, I thought. Now anybody approaching would not only give themselves away by the lights following their progress, but they'd also have a lot harder time seeing me. A huge redneck on his knees in the dark is a lot less conspicuous than a huge redneck on his knees in a brightly lit tunnel. The lights flickered on at the last bend in the tunnel, then I saw Joe step into the light. I stood up and waved as the lights overhead snapped on.

"Glad y'all could catch up," I said. "I don't know where this leads, but if I was going to be a vampire living in Charlotte, a network of secret tunnels ain't the worst place I can think of to live."

Amy closed the distance between us and hugged me as best she could in the cramped quarters. Everyone else could stand up straight, but I was hunched over like my best Quasimodo cosplay. "Glad you're okay, Bubba."

"You okay?" I asked. "You look a little rattled." She didn't look rattled, she looked *pissed*. But I didn't want to say that because if I said she looked pissed, and she wasn't pissed, then she'd *be* pissed, and at me, instead of whatever different flavor of upset she was that I'd mistaken for pissed in the first place. It's a weird kind of self-fulfilling prophecy that I've always had with women—if I think they're pissed at me about something, invariably within a minute and a half of me opening my mouth they end up actually being pissed at me, whether they were when we started or not. What can I say? I'm gifted.

"There was a drunk asshole in the bar," she said. "He got a little handsy and I put his face in a wall."

"Aw, damn," I said, thinking that this was a time to be sympathetic for the way she was treated and not simply proud that she beat the guy's ass. "I'm sorry, babe. Dudes suck."

"Yeah, he was bad enough," Amy said. "But when the bouncer started giving me shit like it was my fault this drunk banker-bro couldn't handle his mojitos and put his hands on the wrong blonde…"

"Let's say that I was the voice of reason, and that tells you how close to Armageddon-level shitstorm we were," Geri said. "He's lucky it was you he grabbed. If he'd smacked me on the ass like that, I would have shoved that hand down his throat. Without it being attached to his wrist anymore."

"I'm trying to keep my dismemberments down to a couple a month," Amy replied, giving the younger woman a smile. The relationship between the kid sister of my dead college girlfriend and my current fiancée was something shrinks could pay for their vacation home with. If I went to a shrink. And if I had any money. Hell, if I had any money, I could probably benefit from therapy, but I don't know if I want to inflict my past traumas on anybody, even a therapist. I made a mental note to ask Harker about it if we lived through the week. He seemed a little more enlightened than me, and that dude had to be carrying around more baggage than Samsonite. If there was a shrink that could handle his shit, my issues would be a breeze.

"But you're okay?" I asked. "Nobody got seriously injured and there are no new warrants out for us?"

"No," Geri said. "I smoothed things over with the bouncer and bought a round for the douchebag's buddies. That settled them right down."

"When in doubt, buy a round," I said. "Good philosophy."

"Glad you approve because you owe me a hundred bucks."

"What?!? What the hell did you buy them, Johnny Walker Blue?"

"We're at a hipster bar downtown in a city, Bubba. We aren't buying shine out of the back of a pickup truck down at the crossroads by the farmer's market," she replied. "I gave the bouncer fifty bucks to not call the cops, and it was another fifty to buy four drinks for the assholes. Well, forty, but I tipped ten bucks."

"That was nice of you," I said. I was still grouchy about being out a hundred bucks for booze I didn't drink, but at least she tipped.

"That was more for me than anything," Gabby said. "But it was worth it." She held up a bar napkin with a phone number on it and high-fived Geri. Great. My fiancée was getting in bar fights and my team was hooking up with the bartender while I was slinging fried cod around to break into an underground passage.

I looked at Joe. "You got any exploits you'd like to share?"

"Nope," he said. "I talked to the manager. He didn't recognize Card from the photo, although I suppose he could be hypnotized to forget."

"That never has made sense to me," I said as a thought hit me. "How come Harker had a picture of Dracula on his phone? I thought vampires couldn't have their picture taken."

"They couldn't for a long time," Gabby said. Every head turned to her. "Family business, remember? If there's one thing I know, it's vampires. Well, vampires and hot bartenders. But anyway, it's the silver."

I turned that over in my mind for a couple seconds, then shook my head. "Nope. Need a little more."

Gabby smiled the smile of the patient talking to the stupid and said, "Silver Chloride is used in developing photographs, and vampires don't react well to silver, so their image can't be captured by any film that has to be developed using that specific chemical. Same reason vampires didn't have reflections in old mirrors—they used silver backing. New mirrors don't use silver, so vampires show up in them. And there are no chemicals in digital photography, which means nothing for the vampire's mystical nature to interact with."

"Man, I would hate to be the first vampire sneaking up on somebody standing in front of one of the new, non-silver mirrors and I suddenly realize I'm not near as invisible as I thought I was," I said, laughing.

"Yeah, that would suck," Geri agreed.

"It wasn't my best night," came a deep baritone from the darkened tunnel ahead of us. We all froze, then broke into a flurry of drawn guns and blades as a well-dressed man who looked about fifty appeared in a pool of light that had been dark a second before. "I am Lucas Card. I believe you are looking for me. Can we talk first, or must we dive straight into the fighting?"

Well, shit. The big bad Hunter just got ambushed by Dracula while he's yukking it up with his friends. Card held his hands out at his sides and gave us a wry smile. "I am, as you can see, unarmed."

There was none of the Lugosi accent in his voice. He sounded like a cultured American, if his speech pattern was a little antiquated. He wore a nice suit, neatly pressed, and his dark hair was just long enough to curl a little at the collar. He looked more like an older Christian Bale than Gary Oldman with a butt on top of his head, but I held no illusions that he was any less dangerous for not having a weapon.

Even so, I holstered Bertha and motioned for the others to put their guns away, too. As we did, I noticed for the first time that Gabby's pistol was still holstered on her hip. I raised an eyebrow at her and said, "What's the deal? I figured you'd be the quickest on the draw out of all of us."

"If he was coming for a fight, I would have been. But I know enough about Luke to recognize that he's not going to take on five heavily armed humans in a dirty tunnel wearing a two-thousand-dollar suit."

Card smiled at her. "It is good to see you again, Gabriella. You are correct, I would not knowingly enter into combat wearing this suit. But you are wrong about one thing."

"What's that?" she asked.

"They are two-thousand-dollar shoes," he replied. "The suit cost six."

"Apparently it pays better to be a monster than to hunt them," I said.

He didn't seem the least bit offended at me calling him a monster, which I took as a good sign. Six-thousand-dollar suit or not, I was pretty sure if I pissed him off, Dracula wouldn't hesitate to throw down, no matter how dirty the floor. "It has better life expectancy, too, Mr. Brabham. Now, please, let's sit down and have a reasonable discussion. I have no desire to kill any of you, regardless of your intentions toward me." That last was directed at Gabby, who shrugged but somehow manage to look not the least bit ashamed of her plans.

"Sorry, Luke. But you know the deal. If you've gone around the bend, I'm going to put you down," she said.

Card looked at her, and for the first time, I got a glimpse of the monster behind the mask of gentility, and the cold look in his eyes scared the absolute bejesus out of me. "No, Gabriella," he said, his voice slow and even and without a hint of anger. There might have been a hint regret in his eyes, and somehow that was even scarier. "You will try."

1 0

"I assume this is somewhat different from how you expected our initial encounter to go, Mr. Brabham," Dracula said from the overstuffed armchair.

"You could say that," I replied. "So far there's been a whole lot less punching and shooting than I expected. I guess that's a good thing."

"Almost always," he said. "I do apologize for the lack of seating. I did not anticipate hosting social gatherings when I outfitted this particular safe house. Or safe hole, rather." He gestured around the room, which was a long way from anything I'd call a "hole."

We were in a large room underneath the city, with thick steel doors in two walls. Each door had a massive metal bar across it, holding it shut from anything short of a nuke or a really determined rhinoceros. And if you got a rhino into the sewers of a major metropolitan area, you were the kind of person that wasn't going to be stopped by a door, no matter how solid. The room was about twenty feet to a side, with a pair of comfy-looking chairs, a few floor lamps, a small writing desk with a wooden chair that looked like it would turn into toothpicks if I looked at it wrong, and a nice round rug. The walls were lined with shelves, and every shelf was stuffed with books. All kinds of books—classic novels, trashy romances, popcorn thrillers, history books, biographies, essay collections—you name it, Dracula's library had it.

"Any time I'm on the run, having company isn't at the top of my list of priorities. Ammo and beer take up the top couple of spots on my list. Looks like books are your number one through about thirty-seven," I said.

"When you have put together as many of these small refuges as I have through the years, you learn what you absolutely need, and what you can survive without," Luke said, one perfectly polished loafer crossed over his knee.

"Well I sure as hell couldn't survive down here," Geri chimed in. "There's no Wi-Fi. Like *none*. I can't even get cell signal."

"We're underground, kiddo," Joe said with a smile.

"I know that, but does underground have to be so damned primitive?"

"Now that you have found me, what do you intend to do with me?" Dracula asked.

I wasn't sure how much of the finding we actually did, and how much of it was Drac finding us, but I decided against pressing the issue. "Well, I thought we'd talk for a little while, kinda see how you're feeling about the world, figure out if you're gonna go full-on psychopath and try to kill the entire city, and then either go back and tell Harker that you're cool, just working through some shit, or we'd throw down and do our best to kill you. Depending on how the initial conversation about how you're feeling goes. Make sense?"

He smiled, and I could see where the idea that he could hypnotize people with his eyes came from. He was a good-looking dude, and I'm betting that more than one woman, and probably more than one man, had to explain why they ended up in bed with him, and hypnosis was a way better excuse than "he's real pretty." Then I started to wonder if he was hypnotizing me to think I wasn't hypnotized, and that sent my brain down all kinds of weird rabbit holes, and after a few seconds, I noticed that Card was sitting there staring at me with a kinda concerned look on his face. I gave myself a little mental shake and brought my attention back to the issue at hand, namely the vampire in front of me.

"Are you all right, Mr. Brabham?" Dracula asked, and I almost believed that he gave a shit.

"I'm okay," I said. "Just a little mental gymnastics going on. So, back to the main topic. Are you going to murder the whole city?"

"Of course not," he said, looking like it was the stupidest idea he'd ever heard. I decided if he thought *that* was the stupidest thing he'd ever heard, then he obviously hadn't met me. "Not only would that expose my existence to the greater world, but it would deprive me of my primary source of sustenance."

"Yeah, I guess if you make filet mignon out of your only cow, you ain't getting much milk for breakfast," I said.

"Exactly. So no, I do not intend to go on a murder spree across the city. You can easily disabuse my nephew of that notion."

"Okay, then," I said, clapping my hands together. I reached down beside me and patted Amy's shoulder where she sat in the armchair across from Dracula, and said, "Let's go report back and get something to eat. I saw a diner I want to check out."

"That is not to say that I am not killing to feed," Card said, and Amy froze halfway out of her chair. Everyone turned their full attention to the vampire, who hadn't moved, just sat there with his legs crossed in the comfy chair, the warm yellow glow of a torchiere lamp cascading down off the ceiling onto his head and shoulders.

"Would you care to elaborate on that, Mr. Card?" Amy said as she fully got to her feet.

"I am killing criminals for my meals," Dracula said. "This country is far too lenient on its criminals, so whenever I get hungry, I find someone who deserves to die, and I make that happen. Death, I mean."

"We get your meaning," Gabby said, her fingertips drumming across the butt of the pistol on her hip. I could almost hear the gears turning in her head as she tried to decide if this was bad enough for her to try to claim Drac's scalp or not.

Since I really wanted that answer to be "not," I gave Joe a look and nodded at Gabby. I hoped he took that look to mean "make sure she doesn't get us all killed," and not "I like this girl, can we keep her?" But sometimes mine and Joe's nonverbal communication wasn't exactly perfect.

"Now you can go back and report to Quincy that I am perfectly safe, and within my right mind, and that I have no interest in returning home at this time. I will contact him when I am ready to return." He looked perfectly calm, placid even, but there was the slightest tension in his shoulders and jaw that told me this dude was half a second from flying out of that chair and opening a Costco-sized can of whoop-ass on us.

Unfortunately, we hadn't been hired for a wellness check. "Sorry, Drac, no can do," I said, sincerely sorry for the rest of this conversation. Mostly because I figured it was going to be painful as hell. Physically, not emotionally. "We weren't hired to find you and make sure you were feeling okay. We were hired to bring you back to Director Pravesh so she can make that determination on her own."

The vampire stood, a slow smile creeping across his face. "And the possibility of going toe-to-toe with the most famous monster in the world didn't play into your decision to accept the assignment at all, did it?"

Geri cut me off before I could say anything. "Okay, dude, first off the fact that we're broke as hell had a lot more to do with taking this job than anything else. I like ramen as much as the next girl, but after a week of the stuff, I kinda want something to eat that either grew in the dirt or used to have a face. Preferably some of both. And secondly, you think *you're* the most famous monster in the world? Jesus, you're not even a Kardashian. *Piers Morgan* is a more famous monster than you, dude."

Dracula looked taken aback at this fiery young woman doing everything but snapping her fingers in his face. "I do not know who that is," he said.

"Duh. How can you claim to be famous when you don't even know who PewDiePie is?" Geri fired back.

Now, if I'm being honest, the only reason I knew PewDiePie was a human being was context because I barely know any more about pop culture than the seven-hundred-year-old vampire standing in front of me. But a distraction is a distraction, and I took advantage of this one to reach into my front pocket and pull out a little present Amy picked up for me when she went rummaging through the Homeland Security armory. There were a lot of downsides to working for the government, not the least of which is that it's a lot harder to lie on your taxes if the people you're paying the taxes to are also the people who write your paychecks *and* approve your expense reports.

But one nice thing is that they keep cool toys lying around on shelves, like silver-plated brass knuckles with mystical runes engraved into them I slipped one of these onto my right hand while Geri had Drac distracted, and when he opened his mouth to reply to her, I stepped forward and laid him out with a massive right cross.

At least that was the plan. Like most of my plans, it went sideways at the moment of execution. Because apparently when you're the oldest vampire in the world, you're also the fastest vampire in the world. He was sure as hell the fastest vampire I'd ever seen. Or not seen, if I'm being accurate, because I barely saw a blur as he was standing in front of me arguing with Geri one second, and before I could pull my hand out of my pocket and take a single step, he was across the room standing by the door glaring at me.

"That wasn't very nice, Mr. Brabham," Card said, and I felt a shiver of fear run down my spine. Right on its heels was a tingle of excitement because, let's face it, there was nothing I wanted more than to throw down with this guy and see if I could kick Dracula's ass.

"Well, they don't call me Bubba the Monster Befriender," I said. "Like they say in one of my favorite video games, if you'da been paying attention, you wouldn't be disappointed."

"I'm not disappointed," he replied. "Just resigned. You aren't going to stop trying to bring me back to Pravesh until either I go with you or one of us is dead."

"Pretty much," I said.

"And I am not ready to see her right now." He did look regretful, which I guess is about all you can ask for from a monster that's about to kill you. Except for asking them not to kill you, I guess. But that was probably off the table from the moment I tried to sucker punch Dracula.

"She needs you." My head whipped to the left as Gabby spoke, and I was amazed to see that she didn't have a gun or a knife in her hand. But judging from the look on Card's face, the picture she had showing on her phone hit a lot harder than a bullet. "Remember this? We were all in Atlanta, trying to save the world, and Cassie was back here in Charlotte taking care of her granddaughter. We'd beaten the demon, Glory got her wings cut off, and Harker got blasted out of his socks. You went out for wings at Taco Mac with me, Jo, and Watson while Flynn and Adam stayed back at the hotel to watch over the wounded."

"I remember," Card said, staring at the photo. I couldn't see the picture, but I could see the emotions warring across his face. There was regret, and pain, and rage, and longing, and all the things we feel when somebody we love dies and when somebody we love does something unforgivable. I've been there, and I've been there when both of those things happen at the same time, like when my werewolf father murdered my girlfriend, Geri's big sister. It's a hell of a conflict, and sometimes you just need something to focus on.

Gabby wasn't here to kill Dracula. She was here to give him something to focus on, something to bring him out of the haze of pain and guilt and grief and back to himself, back to his family. We were just her escorts. "Jo needs you, Luke. She's lost everybody who's ever been anybody in her life except you, Harker, and Ginny. Harker's more twisted up inside than any six people I know, and Ginny's twelve. That leaves you to help her get through this shit, and instead of standing with her and doing what you know goddamned well Cassie would want you to do, you're down here feeling sorry for yourself and drinking felon smoothies for breakfast! Now are you going to get your head out of your ass and go help the closest thing to a daughter you'll ever have deal with her mother's death, or are you really the monster Great-Granddaddy Abraham wrote about? Are you the monster he hunted? Or are you the friend he loved?"

Card opened his mouth to respond, but whatever he was going to say was lost in an explosion of light and sound as the world turned to nothing but noise and pain as grenades rolled in both doors and blew us all right to hell.

11

I woke up on a concrete floor feeling like I'd been run over by a truck. It wasn't the first time I'd felt it, but it was the first time in a long while, and also the first time there hadn't been copious amounts of alcohol, and almost always a brawl about SEC football, involved. I lay there for a few seconds, flexing my fingers and toes and silently counting all my parts to make sure they seemed to be still in working order, then I opened my eyes.

Only to see more concrete right in front of my face. I rolled over so that my face wasn't pressed up against a wall and looked around the room. I was in a big room along with Amy, Gabby, and Geri, who were all unconscious in the middle of the room. That left two notable players missing from our party, and as I sat up to take stock of my surroundings, I reached up to tap the comm in my ear, only to stick my finger in my ear instead.

"Shit," I said. "Comms are gone." I patted myself down, confirming what I was already pretty sure I'd find—all my weapons and my phone were gone, too. I still had my wallet, the fourteen dollars in cash, and the little flashlight I keep in my left front pocket. Bertha was gone, as was my Judge revolver, my kukri, my silver knuckle duster, and my pocketknife. They left me Bertha's shoulder rig and the paddle holster in the small of my back, but took the spare magazines out of my back pockets and the ones from the shoulder holster, too. They were thorough, whoever these assholes were.

"Ohhhh," Geri groaned and started to stir. "I feel like I gotta puke."

"Yeah, don't do that," I said. "There's no good receptacle for that, and I don't even have a stick of gum for after."

She nodded and took a few deep breaths, then sat up and opened her eyes. "Where are we?"

"No idea," I replied.

"Joe and Luke?"

"Also no idea."

"Any idea how we're getting out of here?"

"Three for three," I said. "I woke up about two minutes ago, so I haven't had a chance to take a good inventory yet."

"Not that there's anything to inventory," she said. She was right, too. We were in a good-sized room, about twelve by fifteen, but there wasn't a damn thing in the room but us. No bed, no toilet, no window —this was not intended to be a long-term storage solution for people. That was good and bad. Good because the door might not be reinforced. Bad because it said our captors didn't plan on us being around long enough to escape.

"See if you can wake the others," I said. "I'll try the door." I mean, I'm sure there's a situation where a whole group of people get kidnapped and dropped off in an empty room and the door just opens out into a Baskin-Robbins, right? That's totally a thing that happens.

Not this time. The door was locked up tight, and at least at first glance, it was solid. Felt like thick steel, no rattle in the frame, no wiggle in the knob, none of those things that would give a person held captive on a particular side of the door hope for ever seeing what was on the other side of said door. And I very much wanted to not just see what was on the other side, I wanted to *be* on the other side of that door. So I yanked on the knob a few times, with no effect whatsoever.

"Ow, shit," Gabby groaned from the floor. "Tequila again?"

"Nope." Amy's voice sounded like I felt, like she'd been dragged butt-nekkid down a gravel road. "DEMON."

"Demons or the agency DEMON? I always get confused," Gabby asked.

"Yeah, me too," I agreed. "It was decent branding, but a little too on the nose, if you ask me. Which nobody did."

"Pretty sure it was the black tactical gear DEMON, not the wings and forked tail demons," Amy said. "The last thing I remember is people in all black with gas masks coming into Luke's hideout. I'm guessing after they tossed flash-bangs into the room, they followed up with some kind of knockout gas."

"Seems right," I said. "I don't remember anything after the whole world went boom."

"They took you down before they even threw in the gas, Bubba," Geri said. "My vision cleared enough for me to see some dude nail you in the back with a stunstick and then smack you in the back of the head. I was afraid they'd killed you."

"Nah, they just hit my head," I said. "Ain't like they hurt anything I use. Anybody remember what happened to Luke or Joe?"

"No idea," Gabby said, and the others nodded their agreement.

"Okay, what's the plan?" Amy asked, looking to me.

"Haven't we established, like a whole bunch of times, that I am not the plan guy?" I protested.

"This seems like anything we do is going to involve a lot of destruction, and those are the plans we usually let you handle," Amy replied. "Or we point you in the direction of where we need chaos sown and let you just kinda…happen."

Gabby laughed. "Sounds like he and Harker have more in common than either one of them would ever admit."

"Okay, does anybody have anything even resembling a weapon?" I asked. "They stripped me clean, and there ain't shit in this room."

"I've got my ID and a debit card, but they took everything else," Gabby said.

"They even took my IDs," Geri said.

"What do you care?" I asked. "All your IDs are fake." It was true, too. This chick had about eight different driver's licenses, passports, and birth certificates, spread out around four different countries of origin and six states where she purported to live. I'd asked a few times how she got all that stuff, and why, but she just muttered something about the stuff she'd done before meeting up with me and never gave me a real answer.

"Yeah, but they're *good* fakes. And those are expensive. Plus I had a lock pick set stashed in one of the passports."

I wondered about that for a second, then filed it away. This was not the time to explore the more James Bond aspects of Geri's nature. "What about you, babe?" I asked Amy.

"They got almost everything," she said, pulling off her belt. "But not quite." She did some kind of twisty hand thing with her belt buckle and the whole thing came apart, revealing a small compartment full of what looked like modeling clay.

"Babe," I said, taking a step back. "Why is your belt buckle full of plastic explosive?"

"Don't be silly," Amy said. "Plastic explosive is way too inert to do us any good. This is a specialized blasting putty that ignites way more easily."

"Doesn't answer the question about why you have it," I pointed out.

"We spent a lot of our time in Fairyland in various dungeons," Amy reminded me. "I decided after the first time that I don't like dungeons. So when we got home, I had Skeeter find me something I could have with me at all times to make sure I was a lot harder to lock up." She ran her thumb across the end of her belt, then pulled at what looked like a strand of the leather but turned out to be a long, thick thread that must have doubled up three or four times in the belt, because she pulled a good eight feet of string out of that leather strap.

Amy knelt by the door and used her finger to scoop up the goop from her secret belt buckle compartment and smear it into the keyhole of the doorknob. Then she stuck the thread into the hole and played out the fuse until it was fully extended. She grabbed her belt buckle and held it in her left hand next to the fuse, and gripped the other piece, which had been what I thought was a decorative belt buckle but was really the lid to some Inspector Gadget Boom-Boom-Belt, in her right.

"Y'all probably don't want to stand next to the door," she said. "If this works, it's going to get loud over there."

"And if it doesn't work?" Gabby asked.

"Then I ruined my belt for nothing and Skeeter and I will have to have a conversation with the guy who sold us this setup. If we don't all die here, of course."

"Of course," Gabby said, moving to the far wall. It was only ten feet or so, but it was better than nothing. "Hey, are you trying to light a spark to ignite the fuse?"

Amy looked at her. "That was the plan."

"Then use this," Gabby said, tossing her a small plastic lighter of a sort found in a million convenience stores all around the world.

"Why didn't they take your lighter when they were taking everything else useful?" Geri asked.

"Dunno," Gabby replied. She pulled a small Altoids tin out of a pocket and help it up, along with a small purple aluminum cylinder. "But they left my stash and my one-hitter, too, so maybe they were hoping we'd get high and be more docile when they came to murder us."

"Or maybe they were being merciful?" Geri asked.

"Nah, hoping we'd be easier to handle if at least one of us was stoned was probably more like it," I said.

"Their mistake," Amy said, flicking her Bic and lighting the fuse. She turned her back to the door and clapped her hands over her ears, and the rest of us followed suit. A few seconds later, there was a muffled metallic *bang*, like applause from C3-PO, and I turned around to see the results.

"Well, shit," Amy said. The knob was still in the door, although looking very much the worse for wear. "I was hoping the whole thing would swing wide open."

"We don't have that kind of luck," I said. "But maybe you softened it up a little." I stepped up to the door, raised a big boot, and slammed my heel into the knob, doing my level best to shove the goddamn thing right through the door. That didn't happen, but I did feel the locking cylinder give under my foot. I kicked it again, then a third time, and with a fourth kick and a massive grunt, the innards of the doorknob sprang out the other side, and the whole assembly fell apart with a clatter.

"Well, the good news is we can get out of here now," I said, grinning at the trio of women.

"The bad news is we have no idea where our friends are, no idea where *we* are, and you just made enough racket to let everyone north of Columbia know exactly where we are and that we've decided to leave our cell," Gabby said.

"Okay, that's all true," I said. "But when you say it like that, it sounds bad for us."

On the other side of the door, an alarm started to blare and the sound of slamming doors and running feet reached my ears. "That all sounds bad for us, too," Amy said. "Let's get the hell out of here and find something to fight with."

"You mean you don't think we can survive on my good looks and charm?" I asked.

"Not for a second, pal," Geri said, pushing past me and yanking the door open. "Now let's get the hell out of here." With that, she ducked through the door and was gone.

"Everybody's a critic," I grumbled.

"Don't worry, babe," Amy said, reaching up to pat my cheek. "I think you're adorable. Now let's go get our friends back."

"And blow some more shit up," Gabby said, a psychotic glint in her eye. She followed Geri, leaving me and Amy alone in the room.

"That one scares me a little," I said.

"Your fiancée just pulled explosives out of her belt, and *Gabby* is scary?" Amy raised an eyebrow.

"She's nuts," I replied. "An exploding belt buckle? That's hot as hell." I grabbed her hand and pulled her along with me as we charged into a secret government agency's hideout to rescue a defrocked priest and Count Dracula.

Yeah, that was weird, even for me.

1 2

We emerged into roughly the center of a narrow hallway with a door at each end. To the left, a metal door with a crash bar and a red EXIT sign glowing over it. To the right, what looked like a wooden interior door with a knob, but no deadbolt. "Okay," I said. "Amy, you take Geri and go get help. Me and Gabby will go find our boys, bust them out of wherever they're being held, and meet you outside in ten minutes."

"I'm not leaving you," Amy said. "Without me and Skeeter, there's no way you get out of this in one piece."

"You know I did actually hunt monsters before we met, right?"

"How many did you hunt before you and Skeeter met?"

"We met when we were kids!"

"Irrelevant."

"I'm not going, either. Send her," Geri said, pointing at Gabby.

"Okay, one, I can't send her anywhere. She doesn't work for me," I said.

"Wasn't going to bring that up unless it became an issue, but yeah," Gabby said.

"And two, I am not going to sit in a funeral home with your parents and look at another daughter of theirs in a casket. Doing that shit once was too many times. We all know there's a good chance you're gonna get yourself killed in this job, but when your ticket gets punched, it will *not* be because of anything I can prevent. Now get your ass out that door, find a pay phone, and get us some backup."

Geri looked up at me with an unreadable expression on her face. We'd never talked much about my relationship with her sister, or about the events that led to her getting murdered by my psychotic werewolf father, and I had no intention of ever changing that, but by the look in her eyes, she could see all she needed to know written all over my face. She didn't say a word, just turned around and started off down the hall.

I let out a sigh of relief. Watching Brittany die at my father's hand had been the worst thing I ever lived through, and that includes killing my own father, getting stabbed with a sword by my little brother, and then killing that same brother a few months later. The look on Brit's mother's face when she saw me walk into the funeral home was the kind of thing that leaves scars. The pain, the loss, the hatred for me...all that shit still weighed on me decades later. I didn't ever need anybody to look at me like that again. So when Geri stopped after a few steps and turned around, my blood froze, thinking she was going to refuse to leave and end up getting her damn self killed.

But she held up an index finger and asked, "Ummm, just one thing. What's a pay phone?"

I showed her that she was number one in my heart with an extended finger of my own, and she laughed and ran out, hopefully to return in mere seconds with the cavalry. I turned to the others and said, "Alright, let's go save our guys."

I took the lead as we walked down the hall toward the door. It all seemed almost eerily mundane, if you ignored the blaring siren going off like a pissed off fire alarm. I got to the door and looked at Amy. "Got any more MacGyver shit you wanna tell me about? Like an X-Ray machine so I can see what I'm walking into?"

"Nope, exploding belt buckle is all I had," she said.

"Oh, well," I replied. "Guess we do this the hard way." Then I flung open the door, which fortunately opened away from us, and charged through. And right into a solid wall with nothing but a thin layer of sheetrock between my head and the cinderblocks that made up the exterior of the building. I learned this fact the hard way, as I slammed into the wall and stopped cold. I reeled off to one side, looking around to see if anyone threatening was nearby, but all I saw was my fiancée and Gabby, both trying in vain to stifle their laughter.

"So, looks like the hall opens into another hall," Amy said, masking her laughter with coughs.

I leaned my back against the unyielding wall and poked at my face, trying to see if I'd broken anything. I didn't feel or taste blood, so I was fairly certain I didn't have a broken nose, and a cursory examination of my cheekbones didn't show any damage there. My forehead hurt a little, but my vision wasn't blurry, so I figured it wasn't a big deal. "I'm fine," I said. "Thanks for asking."

"We could see you're fine," Gabby said, stepping around Amy and starting up the hall. We were now in what looked more like an office area, with drop ceilings and linoleum floors instead of the open rafters and bare concrete we'd just left. The hall ran past two doors with "Men" and "Women" signs on the doors, which to no one's surprise held small one-seater restrooms.

Gabby walked to the door at the end of the hall past the men's room entrance and put her hand on the knob. The second she touched it, the alarm fell silent. "That's odd," she said, taking a step back from the door.

I walked up to her, moving as softly as I could with my boots squeaking on the tile. I slipped up beside Gabby, pressed my ear to the door, and motioned for the others to be quiet. There were voices coming from the other side, but they were indistinct, like they were on the other side of a large room. I put my hand on the knob and heard an unmistakable sound come from the other side of the hollow-core door.

"Get down!" I hissed, and dropped to the ground. I reached out for both women, trying to drag them to the floor with me, but they were already on their way down. A thunderous *BOOM* came from the room beyond the door, and wood exploded into the hall, driven by what I could only assume was double-ought buckshot. I sprang to my feet and looked through the hole in the door at the room beyond.

A man dressed in black tactical gear was racking the slide on a pump-action shotgun, so I decided to skip niceties, like opening the door, and just ran through it. It was already kinda busted, and when I put a shoulder to it, I finished its transformation into nothing but kindling and failed aspirations of privacy. I slammed into the shotgun guy, wrapped my arms around him, and spun around, slamming him to the ground in a spine buster worthy of Arn Anderson himself. I got up, snatching the shotgun from his hands, and looked around the room.

The room was your basic office setup, with a few desks and cubicles in the center of the room, fluorescent lights, and cheap motivational posters on the walls. There was even a water cooler for the cube drones to hang out around, if there had been any employees, which there weren't. I wasn't sure if the whole place was a fake office, or if they'd all gotten the hell out of Dodge when the alarm went off. I didn't care, as long as there were fewer civilians to get hurt in the crossfire.

There was one door set in the far wall, with a pair of guards holding submachine guns flanking it. They were dressed in all black, complete with helmets and tactical vests like they were going to take down a drug kingpin or something. So far I hadn't seen any insignia on any of the guards, so either these guys weren't DEMON, or after the mess with Harker and the football field, maybe there *wasn't* a DEMON anymore. But even if they weren't DEMON, they were sure as hell armed, and I dove forward to take cover behind a desk as they raised their guns in my direction.

One three-round burst ripped through the cubicle walls, and I heard a voice say, "Cut that shit out! We're supposed to keep destruction to a minimum, remember?"

"What about Keith blowing away the door?"

"That's Keith's problem. Now go secure the big idiot for the boss. I'll guard the door."

"Why don't you go get him while I guard the door?"

"Because your gun's pointed at the ground and mine's pointed at your face."

While Tweedledee and Tweedledumbass were arguing over who was going to hunt me down and kill me in a cubicle farm, which would literally be the worst death I've ever imagined for myself, I looked back at the doorway and motioned Amy toward the unconscious guard I'd squished into the carpet. She ran in, crouched down to stay below the line of sight of the others, and started searching the pancaked guard for a sidearm or a backup piece or something she could use as a weapon.

I slunk forward into the cube farm, which was pretty big, forty feet across and thirty feet to the door. I thought if I kept my head down, I had a good chance to get the drop on Tweedledumbass, and if I could take him out, then we'd have plenty of guns for Gabby, Amy, and me to take down one guard without any fuss. I kept my ears peeled, listening for anything that would give me an idea of the guard's location, but he was either perfectly still or moving silently.

I couldn't say the same for myself, as I bumped into a desk chair and sent it rolling forward into a file cabinet, making a horrendous racket. The only thing that saved me was instinct because I dropped flat an instant before bullets ripped through the fabric-covered dividers.

"I said not to tear everything up!" Tweedledee called from the door.

"If you want to come do this, then do it. Otherwise shut the hell up!" Tweedledumbass replied in a whisper that could have been heard across a busy intersection at rush hour. That exchange gave me all I needed to know right where Tweedledumbass was, so I stood up, jumped onto a desk, and launched myself over the cubicle walls like the world's biggest redneck stage dive.

I am not nearly as spry in reality as I am in the movie in my head, so this attack did not go exactly as planned. Or even a little bit as planned. I caught the toe of one boot on the wall as I leapt over, "leapt" being an exceptionally generous way to refer to the kind of hopping flop that I did, and when my toe caught, all my forward motion was immediately halted. Well, sort of. I mean, I definitely stopped flying through the air, and slammed down on the desk in the next cube. But the cube wall came with me. And since they're all interconnected, *all* the cube walls kinda came with me.

I smacked into the surface of the desk as sections of cubicle wall collapsed like demented dominoes all over the room, with metal clips flying into the air as they gave up any pretense of being able to hold that shit together after an impact of over three hundred pounds of flying redneck. I skidded across the surface of the desk, wiping out a monitor, a small flowering cactus, a couple of family photos, and a desk lamp as I body-surfed the desk blotter across the cheap laminated surface. I skipped across the desk like a stone on a lake, then bellyflopped onto the cheap gray indoor/outdoor carpet at the feet of a stunned Tweedledumbass, who looked down at me like it was Christmas morning and somebody had given him the pony he always wanted.

"Found him!" he yelled over to the guard by the door.

"Then kill him!" Tweedledee yelled back.

Tweedledumbass swung his eyes back to me just in time for them to go wide as he saw the butt of the twelve-gauge I took off the first guard swing up and slam straight into his balls. His face went pure white, then green as he doubled over, then his eyes rolled back in his head as I slammed the shotgun into the side of his skull and left him lying in the wreckage of the cube farm, out cold.

Then there was one. I stood up and chunked the cactus, which had attached itself to my leg by way of a *lot* of pointy sticker thingies, across the room to explode against the wall in a shower of clay pot and dirt. Tweedledee spun toward the wall, and I ran straight at him. My plan was to slam into him, pick him up, and use his ass as a battering ram to go through the door he was guarding, turning him into a human shield on the other side, since I had no idea what I was barreling into.

The flat *crack-crack-crack* of three rounds from a pistol had me pinwheeling my arms as I tried not to run into the line of fire and turned Tweedledee into Tweedledead. His face basically disappeared, and he collapsed in pile of nonfunctional person parts on the carpet, a rapidly growing dark red stain under his head. I spun around to see Gabby holding a small pistol in both hands with a little wisp of smoke coming from the barrel.

She looked over at Amy, who was staring open-mouthed at her, another pistol in her hand. "Hey, Bubba?" Gabby asked. "I got him."

13

W hat the hell are you doing?" I yelled at the smirking psychopath. "We don't kill humans!"

She cocked an eyebrow at me with more disdain than The Rock ever managed in his whole career, and said, "Okay, one —*I'm* not part of your *we*. I'm part of me, and me definitely kills humans if they're armed assholes who would as soon kill me as look at me. And two—you're welcome."

I was speechless. Skeeter can attest to the exact number of times that's happened to me since middle school, and you can count them on one hand and still be able to flip the bird. I sputtered for a second, then finally managed to get out, "What the absolute hell am I supposed to be thanking you for?"

"For not using the grenade I took off the first guy you took down."

"That was not your decision," Amy said, glaring at Gabby.

"Okay, that's fair," the dark-haired nut bar said. "You should totally thank your girl here. She kept you from getting all kinds of blown up. But look on the bright side."

"What exactly is the bright side?" I asked.

"I've still got a grenade for the next room," she replied with a completely psychotic smile on her face. Harker had mentioned she was a lot to handle, but he never mentioned that she was auditioning to play The Joker in the next Batman movie. Or in real life, for that matter. This chick made Harley Quinn look well-adjusted.

I gave Amy a "keep an eye on her" look and crossed the last third of the room, stepping over Tweedledead on the way to press my ear to the door. I could hear chanting coming from the other side, and what sounded like the crackle of electricity and the hum of machinery. I didn't recognize the language, which is never a good sign.

See, there are two things to keep in mind when dealing with magical crap. First, if the bad guys are talking in Latin, you're almost certainly in trouble, but you can probably get out of it. That's because Latin is a real language, spoken by humans, and you can disrupt their concentration, and usually their spell, with a big enough distraction. Since I had an insane woman with a grenade at my disposal, distraction was something I had in spades.

But I know what Latin sounds like. Not only have I been to see Joe at work a few times and heard it spoken, but I've dealt with enough spell-slinging dickholes in my life to recognize it when I hear it. This wasn't Latin. That was bad. Because most of the time if the bad guys aren't chanting in Latin, they aren't chanting in any earthly language. Now I'm sure there are non-earthly languages that aren't Enochian, but the people I get called on to beat the shit out of are not usually fluent in Klingon. So if it's an unrecognizable language, it's a way safer bet that it's an ancient demonic tongue than, say, some *Lord of the Rings* fanboys speaking in Elvish. Also, Enochian sounds kinda like if you spoke German backward through a drive-thru speaker while chewing on charcoal briquets, and that's exactly what I was hearing coming through the doors.

"They're doing some kind of demon magic shit in there," I said.

"Then you probably can't stop them by throwing a cactus at 'em," Amy replied. She joined me at the door and pressed a pistol and two spare magazines into my hand. "I took this stuff off one of the guards. We've each got a nine millimeter and three magazines. Gabby has the only grenade."

"Does that sound like a good idea to you?" I asked.

"No, but she got to it first," Amy said. "And I have a new policy, enacted this very morning. I do not wrestle with people holding grenades. If she wants a grenade, I am not the chick to take it away from her."

"You always were the brains of this operation. Got an idea better than me flinging the door open and trying to ruin whatever ritual they're casting?"

"Nope," Amy said.

"You got any ideas that don't involve shooting people?" I asked Gabby.

"Yeah, but they involve blowing people up, so I'm guessing you aren't going to like them either," she replied.

I shook my head, then checked the magazine on the pistol, chambered a round, and yanked the door open. I stepped through into a scene out of some kind of high-tech *Dungeons & Dragons* game. Skeeter would probably know some game that really is a high-tech *D&D*, but I'm not that flavor of nerd, so I didn't know what to call whatever I was looking at, other than scary as hell.

The room was big, close to forty feet on a side, and the drop ceiling had been taken out to gain a couple extra feet of height. There was a big-ass circle drawn on the floor, at least twenty feet across, and whatever magic was powering it was damned potent because white flames ran all along the outer edge. There was a row of glowing rune-type stuff written just inside the circle and another flaming ring inside those. Whatever they were summoning, they wanted to make damn sure it couldn't get out.

Or maybe all that protection was designed to keep the pissed-off vampire they had tied to a chair trapped inside while they performed their ritual. And it was definitely a ritual. There were more than half a dozen dudes in robes with weird animal masks and the whole deal. There was a shitload of candles around the outside of the circle, an altar, and...a battery. Like a *big* battery, sitting beside the altar, with lines of that same white fire running along the floor from the perimeter of the circle to the battery, which sat there pulsing in time with the chanting. Something told me whatever they were planning on powering up was not just a backup for their computer in case of a blackout.

The room was crowded, but my focus was immediately drawn to the two men strapped to chairs back-to-back inside the circle. I kinda figured whatever we found, Luke would be in the middle of it, but my stomach did a weird flip flop when I saw Joe trussed up right next to him. They were sitting in wooden chairs with arms, and I could see what looked like silver chains twined around their handcuffs and leg irons. That explained why Luke didn't just sneeze and snap his bindings—the silver was screwing with his juice. Luke and Joe were each surrounded with some type of aura: Luke's a dark, roiling black mass like smoke swirling around him, and Joe's a bright white glow that pulsed in opposition to the chants.

"What the hell?" Amy asked as she stepped in next to me.

"Do not let them interrupt the ritual!" a skinny bald White guy with glasses yelled from where he stood at a stack of technology. I guessed he was in charge because at his command, four of the seven chanters broke off and started moving in our direction. I took one step forward before an explosion almost took off my left ear.

That's what it felt like anyway. It was really just Gabby stepping up next to me and firing off three quick shots at the oncoming cultists, for lack of a better word. I definitely suffered more from the gunfire than the bad guys did because the guy she shot didn't even break stride.

"That's a problem," she said. "Well, Bubba, you don't have to feel bad about shooting these assholes, because they aren't human."

"I noticed," I replied. "Problem is, that means it won't do any good for me to shoot them, either."

"Is he always so glass half empty?" Gabby asked.

"Only when faced with imminent doom," Amy said.

"Less talking, more punching," I said, and charged the oncoming assholes. I slammed into the lead dude: a tall, thin man in a dark red robe with a mask that looked like some kind of stylized gargoyle. If there's anything I've learned from watching the bad guys in lucha libre, it's to screw with the mask every chance you get. So instead of my usual tactics of punching people until they stop doing whatever it is I don't want them to be doing, this time I reached out and yanked the guy's mask sideways. His eyes disappeared from behind the little peepholes, and he immediately started flailing around. I shoved him straight backward, and he tumbled into the guy behind them, taking them both down in a heap.

I reached for the next guy, but he'd seen what was up and yanked his mask off. I almost promised to not screw with his vision if he'd put it back on, that's how ugly this dude was. He looked like if Ryan Reynolds in *Deadpool* got poison ivy on top of a patch of really bad acne, and then got dragged on his face behind a motorcycle over broken glass for about a mile. This dude was *jacked up*.

He was also strong as hell, which I learned when he grabbed my arm and yanked me forward, stepping to the side and slamming his other forearm into my throat in a clothesline. I went down, sputtering for air and clutching my Adam's apple, and barely had the presence of mind to roll over so the stomp he laid down on my midsection hit me in the back instead of my gut. I'm pretty sure he would have ruptured something important if I hadn't because even through the muscles of my back, I felt my kidney scream in protest.

I writhed on the ground trying to decide which hurt worse, my neck or my back, and Amy threw herself at the stompy prick and took him down. I looked up for the fourth guy, hoping I wasn't about to get a foot in my other kidney, but he was squared off against Gabby, and she had a knife flashing through the air between them. I briefly wondered what else she took off the guards in the first room, then turned my attention to the pair of douchebags who were untangling themselves from each other and getting to their feet right in front of me.

I grabbed the lead dude's ankle and yanked it straight up as I stood, upending the skinny prick and dropping him on his head with a sound like a cantaloupe being tossed off a dormitory roof into a parking lot. I realize that's all kinds of specific, but I had a very specific set of college experiences, so go with me. He didn't move, so I figured he was either concussed or dead, but either way he was out of the fight.

That left one guy, who had peeled off not just his mask, but his robe, too, revealing a twenty-something guy with an athletic build, close-cropped red hair, and a scar running along one jawline. He had full sleeves of tattoos on his arms, horror-show images of demons and people being tortured. I can appreciate good ink, having a lot of tattoos myself, but this was some demented shit. He had on jeans and a shirt that looked at least a size too small, so I knew he wasn't just a gym rat, he was a vain gym rat.

He was also a *fast* vain gym rat because he came at me with a series of kicks that looked like something out of a Bruce Lee movie. I barely got out of the way, and he shot past me, only to spin on his heel and come back with more flick-footy crap. I dodged and weaved as best I could, and blocked one or two kicks, but several of them got through, and he was as strong as he was fast. I needed to end this fight quick, or his buddy was going to recover, or one of the others was going to take down Amy or Gabby, and then we'd be seriously in the soup.

So the next time he landed a kick to my side, I wrapped my arm around his calf and yanked him forward. Then I turned into his leg and drove my opposite elbow straight down on his knee, bending his leg backward like a grasshopper. He screamed, a high-pitched shriek that was cut off by me grabbing him around the throat, picking him up, and slamming him down on top of his buddy, who was trying to rise.

They went down in a tangle of pain and profanity, and I took the opportunity to punt the first jerk in the head. His eyes rolled so far back in their sockets nothing but white was showing, and I left him laying. I still didn't know what these guys were, but I figured a head injury that serious and a shattered knee would keep those two out of my hair long enough for me to help Amy and Gabby out.

At some point I had apparently forgotten that Gabby was a psychopathic vampire hunter and that my fiancée was a self-rescuing princess because they needed my help about like I need more beer in my diet. As soon as I turned around, I saw Gabby step back from the guy she was fighting and yell, "Bubba, throw this asshole somewhere, fast!"

She planted a side kick in his gut, and I stepped forward to do as I was told. The cultist was another skinny White dude, so it wasn't much of a stretch to fling him across the room in the general direction of the tower of technology and the guy I took to be their boss. The flying douchebag slammed into all the equipment and took it and the bossman down in a heap.

"Now duck!" Gabby yelled, diving to knock Amy to the floor just as a thunderous explosion ripped through the room. Equipment and body parts flew everywhere, and I felt something wet slither down the back of my shirt. I was pretty sure it was a piece of bad guy and decided that this was definitely going to be a two-shower night.

The room was dead silent, all chanting having ceased in the wake of the explosion. The only sounds were the ringing in my ears, groans and screams from bad guys hit by shrapnel, and a high-pitched giggle from my right. I looked over and saw Gabby up on her knees, grinning like a kid at Christmas at the carnage where a couple bad guys and a whole lot of computer shit used to be.

"What the hell did you do?" I asked.

"I told you I still had a grenade," she said, then fell into more giggles.

14

---

on't stop the ritual!" Skinny dude croaked from the floor. I had to hand it to him, he was a tenacious prick, if nothing else. He was struggling to pull himself out from under a bunch of toppled computers and monitors, and I saw a thick leather-bound book lying on the ground a few feet from him. I didn't know the bad guys still used spellbooks these days, but apparently so, because Skinny was struggling to get to that one with everything he had. Problem was, there was blood leaking from a lot of little holes where Gabby's grenade had sliced him up like a Cuisinart. I felt like we had better than even odds he'd faint or bleed out before he could reach it.

I turned my attention to the circle that had Joe and Luke trapped within it, and the couple of chanting assholes keeping it upright. The circle was partially visible now, thanks to the spray of blood and viscera from Gabby's grenade. It looked kinda like a half-sphere sticking up out of the floor with one side coated in raspberry jam. I tried not to think too much about what the white parts in the jam used to be as I hauled ass over to the nearest cultist and tackled him from behind.

I'm not some great wizard, and I don't really know that much

379

about how magic works. But I know that casting and summoning circles, if enough juice is poured into them, can become almost impenetrable. This one had already repelled shrapnel and guts flying at it, so I kinda figured it would keep assholes out, too. So when I tackled the asshole I was aiming at, I hit him in the back around the kidneys with my right shoulder and drove him face-first into the space in the air where the circle was supposed to be.

Spoiler—it worked. And apparently magical circles have zero give in their surface, because this Aleister Crowley cosplayer hit a blank spot in the air with a sickening *splat*, and I saw blood erupt from the general vicinity of what used to be his nose. The cracking sound didn't come from the magical boundary, so I guessed he probably had a busted orbital socket to go along with his pulped snoot. He slipped down the circle like some cartoon creature hitting a wall, and lay on the floor, out cold. Whatever type of cryptid or beastie he was under his human suit, it didn't respond well to massive head trauma. That excluded lycanthropes and Alabama fans, because both of those species have skulls way too thick to ever damage.

That should have left two robe-wearing twits to continue the spell, but since one had been on the side facing the explosion, he was currently lying on the floor in a pool of greenish blood, sliced to ribbons from the grenade and resulting shrapnel. With him out of the fight, I went around the circle to the left and walked calmly up to the last guy, who was struggling to keep any sort of rhythm to his chanting. It was kinda like if you put on a record of Gregorian chants, but your record player was on the back of a mechanical bull, so the needle just kept bouncing. I mean, I think that's what it sounded like. I've never owned a record of Gregorian chants, not even in the early nineties when it was cool for about twelve minutes.

I leaned on the surface of the circle, feeling a kind of static electricity-type tingle through me as I made contact with the magic. I had a fleeting thought that I shouldn't touch the giant technomagical sphere with my bare hand, but by that point I was already leaning on it and to snatch my hand back because of a little shock or any semblance of discretion or self-preservation would make me look like a wuss, so I left it there. "So," I said to the cultist, who was staring into the circle and very deliberately not meeting my eyes. "How's it going?"

He stopped chanting for a moment but kept his eyes on the glowing runes in the circle and kept making funky symbol thingies in the air with his fingers. "Um...okay," he said. I could still hear chanting, so I guessed that his finger-waving bullshit was keeping that part of the spell going. I briefly considered chopping off his hands, but the jerks had taken all my knives away when they kidnapped me, so no dice.

"Whatcha doin'?" I asked, hoping I could get him into a good monologue and then lay him out before Skinny over there recovered enough to get to the spellbook.

"We're draining the demonic essence from the vampire and the divine essence from the God-touched one and storing it for our Master's use against the blasphemer Quincy Harker." Now I'd just met Harker the one time, but judging by that meeting and everything I'd ever heard *anyone* say about the man, "blasphemer" was one of the nicest things anybody had ever called him. But it seemed like a bad thing to this dude.

As a lot, these cultists hadn't been an imposing bunch so far, but this dude made Skeeter look buff, and that was before his new boyfriend started him on weight training and self-defense classes. He was mid-forties, with a little bit of gray stubble poking out from under his golden goat mask, and even though all I could see of his physique were the hands and wrists sticking out of his robe as he held his arms out to the circle, I could tell that this dude didn't have to wear skinny jeans because anything he put on his body was skinny by default.

"That sounds like it's pretty painful for, what did you call them? The vampire and the 'God-touched one,'" I said. I kept my voice casual and was working on keeping things as chill as possible in a room where a literal grenade had just gone off because this nerd was the only thing keeping the spell going, and I vaguely remembered hearing something about magical backlash if spells were interrupted. I didn't know what magical backlash was, but it sounded like it sucked. And

I've been in rooms that suffered multiple explosions before. The rooms don't usually survive. I wanted to keep him talking as long as I could, hoping I wasn't doing too much damage to Luke and Joe in the process. If I could figure out some way to power the spell down without bashing this dude's head in, it would be better for everyone.

"It will probably kill them both, but they would have to be destroyed anyway. They aren't pure enough for the Master's new world order," skinny asshole replied. There was a bead of sweat running down the side of his face, and his hands shook a little, like the effort of keeping the spell going all on his own was getting to be too much for him.

But that wasn't the most worrying thing. It was the words he used. I've heard shit like "not pure enough" my whole life. It's the kind of thing that gets thrown around a bit in the woods of North Georgia, usually in the direction of people with more melanin in their skin than me. And since my best friend is a gay Black man, I've heard a lot of the shit that gets thrown his way. And "purity" is a big component in that shit.

Now that I knew I was part faerie, "impure" came to have an additional meaning, since I wasn't even close to pure human. And since Joe and I had just shut down a spell intended to destroy all supernatural creatures in this plane of existence, I was pretty sure that the kind of purity these assholes were talking about was slightly different from the kind the chickenshits in white robes talked about back home. But it was the same trash at its root—hatred, fear, and stupidity. It didn't matter if these dudes wanted to kill me because I wasn't human or Skeeter because he wasn't White, I was going to stop them regardless.

"What happens if you stop chanting for too long?" I asked.

"As long as I maintain my concentration, I can stop my incantation. It just helps me focus. If my concentration breaks, the spell ends, and that could have…unpleasant consequences."

I looked inside the circle, and the auras around Joe and Luke were fainter, but they both also looked like they were fading fast, too. Joe sagged in his chair, only held up by the straps around his forehead and chest. Luke looked better by comparison, but since he started off having been dead for a few centuries, he still kinda looked like death warmed over. I tried to keep the nerd talking while I thought of a plan, or more realistically, Amy thought of a plan, but I was running out of conversation and he was ramping up the speed of his finger waving, which was increasing both the speed and the volume of the chanting, so I gave up on talking him down and moved to Plan...I dunno, D. Whatever. I moved on to the plan where I hit things.

"I'm gonna need you to shut up now," I said. I stepped forward and punched him in the jaw, and it felt like punching a brick wall. Which I've done. It sucks, and I don't recommend it. This asshole didn't even flinch when I slugged him, so I pulled out my borrowed pistol and shot him in the knee. Except I didn't. I pulled the trigger, but the bullet smacked into something just before it hit his thigh and dropped harmlessly to the ground.

"Well, shit," I muttered. "I guess we do this the hard way." I stepped forward and wrapped my arms around his waist, immediately stepping back as fire coursed up both arms. "Goddammit!"

"You cannot stop the will of the Master," the last cultist standing said.

"Look around, asshole," I replied. "We've stopped every one of your friends. What makes you think you're any different?"

"Because they were human, or at least mortal. I am the Mighty Ferondicus, Demon of the Ninth Circle, and your puny human weapons cannot stop me!"

"Yeah?" I asked. "What about my partly faerie foot up your ass?" Then I kicked him straight in the butt as hard as I could. Nothing. He didn't even flinch. Just kept waving his hands through the air faster and faster as the chanting grew louder and louder.

"You can't stop me, human," he said, a nasty grin spreading across his face. "Once we drain the essence of these two, Skyffrax will be reborn to the earth and our Master will reign supreme for a thousand years!"

As hard as I tried, I couldn't help thinking that maybe he was right. This might be the fight I couldn't win.

15

I couldn't win that fight, not with my fists. But having friends meant I never had to win on my own. And yet again, the woman I love showed me why I'm a lucky son of a bitch because she saved the day and probably a good portion of the world in the next couple minutes.

"Bubba!" Amy called. "Leave that asshole and come help me!" I looked over to her, then ran to where she was standing at the pile of tech. There was a rolling cart with an overturned pair of big monitors, a couple of CPUs, and a wheeled rack of other equipment. Amy was rooting around between the pile of wrecked shit and the wall, and Gabby was choking out Skinny Dude, who had given up on crawling to his spell book and had turned toward Amy.

"Help me with this!" Amy said over her shoulder.

"Help you with what?" All I could see was her kneeling by the wall.

"This!" She scooted over, and I saw a pair of thick black cables running to an electrical box on the wall. It looked like whatever had been powering all the computer shit was hardwired into the wall.

"What do we care about this crap?" I asked. "We need to get that circle down!"

"The wires run into the circle," Amy said. "If we can break their connection, we should be able to collapse the barrier and get them out." She had her hands wrapped around the wires and was pulling for all she was worth, but they were in there tight.

Chanting asshole got even louder, and I looked over my shoulder to see the runes in the circle glowing brighter and brighter as the auras around Luke and Joe grew fainter. "Get out of the way," I said.

Amy scooted to the right, and I emptied the rest of my magazine into the electrical box. Sparks flew, and the smell of charred electrical gear filled the air. I tossed the pistol aside and reached down for the cables. They came loose with a firm yank, and the hum and crackle of computer equipment fell silent. "Did that do it?" I asked.

"Yes," Amy said. "Shit. Shoot him!" she yelled, pointing behind me. I spun around and saw Chanting Asshole, also known as Demon Douche Ferondicus, running into the circle with a knife raised his over his head. He made it to within two steps of Luke before half a dozen gunshots rang out and he collapsed in a pool of blood.

I looked over to see Gabby standing there with her stolen pistol and a look of something like regret on her face. "Not how you thought the night would end, huh?"

"Saving Dracula isn't supposed to be the family legacy, but I guess it's more of what Great-Grandpa Abe actually did. Let's get them out of here."

I ran to Joe and cut him loose as Gabby worked on freeing Luke. Amy started emptying the pockets of Skinny Dude and Chanting Asshole, along with their other buddies. "I've got this dickhead's little magic diary. Maybe there's something in his phone that could lead us to their so-called Master," she said.

"Good call. I'll help as soon as Luke is able to move under his own power," Gabby said.

Joe looked like shit. He was pale, with dark circles under his eyes, like he'd been tortured for weeks instead of the few hours it had been since I'd last seen him. I knelt by his side and started cutting through the zip ties that bound him to the chair. "I'm here, pal," I said. "You're gonna be okay now. Just let me cut all this shit and we'll get you to a doctor."

"They hurt me bad, Bubba," Joe said. "They cut into my soul." He reached up and pulled his shirt up, showing me the runes that had been carved into his chest. I vowed right then that Skinny Dude would never see the inside of a jail cell, and this "Master," whoever the hell he was, was going to answer for this shit.

"You're gonna be fine, man," I said, my voice low and calm like I was talking to a frightened animal. "You're okay now. Your soul is fine. Better than fine. Your soul is better than any soul I know." I was talking nonsense, but soothing nonsense, to keep him from freaking out. They'd cut him up good, and whatever magic they used did a real number on Joe, so I needed him to stay calm. Finally the last of his bonds were cut and he sagged forward, almost collapsing to the floor before I could grab him.

"It's gonna be okay, brother," I said. "Let's get you out of here."

"I don't know about that okay thing, Bubba," Gabby said from behind me. I turned, and she had Luke cut loose, but she was looking past me, and her face was whiter than the vampire's.

I turned to see what had her spooked, and I saw the battery on the floor. It was a massive cell, easily the size of a dozen or more car batteries, and the cables running into it were matched on the other side by the cables Amy and I had yanked out of the wall. Somehow, these guys had been using the battery in their ritual, and now the ritual was over, and the magical backlash had only one place to go—into the battery. A high-pitched whine filled the room, and the battery began to glow brighter and brighter. Sparks flew out of it, and it started to shake from side to side.

"Get out of here!" I shouted. "That thing's gonna blow!" I grabbed Joe and put one arm over my shoulders, trying to help him walk. It was useless; he was completely out.

"I can't move him!" Gabby cried. I looked over to her, and Luke was as limp as Joe, only thicker-set and bigger.

"Get Joe! Amy, get those doors open!" I shouted, pointing toward a set of double doors in the far wall. Even from where I was, I could see the chain hanging between them.

"I got it!" Amy yelled, and sprinted for the doors, stolen pistol in her hand. I saw her fire the first shots at the lock before she even got close, then I shifted over and picked Luke up in a fireman's carry over my shoulders. He was a solidly built man, a soldier from a time when war was waged by men with swords and the power to swing it. In other words, he was a heavy sumbitch. But I got him up and saw Gabby wrestle Joe to his feet and start half-running/half-dragging him across the room toward the doors.

Amy got the lock busted open, just before I reached the exit, and she and I jostled a little as we pushed them open and maneuvered Luke through.

I busted through the door and hauled ass across the expansive parking lot. The sky was still dark, dawn barely starting to lighten up in the east. I carried Luke toward a dark sedan and spun around when I heard Amy shout out.

"Shit!" I heard her say. "I dropped the spell book."

"Leave it!" I shouted.

"Keep going!" Gabby yelled through the open doorway where she and Joe were ten feet from safety. "I'll get it!" She bent over to pick something up off the floor, then straightened up as the world exploded in a flash of red and orange fire.

"NO!" I screamed and ran for the building, which was swiftly turning into an inferno. I made it halfway there before I tripped over something on the ground and went sprawling. It was Amy, knocked cold by the explosion but breathing. I looked between her and the blaze, then dragged her and Luke to relative safety behind a nearby burgundy Ford sedan.

Then I turned back to the burning building, a huge industrial warehouse that took up most of a city block. Its cinderblock walls had been white once, and its now rusted and demolished tin roof had probably gleamed in the sun. Now it didn't even reflect the pillars of flame reaching up through the holes blasted in the walls. Smoke poured from the doors, pushing me back before I got within five feet, and I dropped to one knee, coughing, my eyes streaming. I heard a weak cough that wasn't my own and could just barely see enough to make out a figure struggling through the doorway.

The smoke cleared enough for me to make out the figure in the door, and my heart sank as I realized it was too short, too slight to be Joe. I ran to her anyway, and Gabby dropped to her knees before I could get there. She held a thick, singed book tight to her body, and I could see the glint of a cell phone screen in one hand.

"We got it," she said. "We got his spell book. You should be able to track his Master from it. And this." She held out the phone but kept the book clutched to her midsection. I took the phone, and she fell to her side on the asphalt. "Joe...he shoved me at the door. He's stronger than he looks. I kinda flew, I think."

I knelt there, staring at the door, willing another body to walk out through the smoke. I tried to stand up, but a hand on my shoulder kept me kneeling. I looked up to see Amy standing there, tears rolling down both cheeks. "Don't," she said, as much a whisper as a word. "You can't go back in there."

She was right. I knew she was right, but I still wanted nothing more than to jump up and go charging back into the burning building, looking for my friend. But I couldn't. The flames were too high, too hot, and the acrid smoke billowing out of every window and door made my eyes water even from ten yards away. I couldn't go back in because there was nothing to go back in for.

A rattling gasp drew my eyes back to Gabby, who pulled the spell book away from her midsection and held it up to me. That's when I saw the blood pouring down over the waistband of her jeans, and the chunk of rebar sticking out of her chest. "We got the book," she said. "But Bubba...I don't feel so good."

And she was gone.

EPILOGUE

I don't know how long I stayed like that, on my knees in a parking lot in front of a burning building with a dead woman on my lap. I don't know how long I sat there staring, tears running down my face waiting for Joe to stagger out of that inferno, charred but grinning that lopsided grin and making some smartassed crack about trying not to get set on fire on our next trip. I don't know how long I sat there, smoke and soot and blood in my hair, watching for a sign of life I knew wouldn't come.

I just watched. I watched the building burn. I watched firefighters run past me with hoses and airpacks. I watched EMTs load Gabby's body onto a stretcher, pull a white sheet over her face, and wheel her away. I watched a pair of local cops walk up to me, moving slowly with their weapons drawn, and I watched Amy intercept them with her bigger badge and move them away. I sat there on my knees, leaning back on my heels, and I watched. Because I couldn't do a goddamn thing else.

Some time later, I felt a hand on my shoulder. No one had touched me in an hour, a week, a minute, a year, however long it had been since I knew he was gone. I looked up, and Amy was there. She didn't try to hug me, didn't tell me to get up and get my shit together, didn't tell me we still had a job to do because the Master, whoever the fuck he was, was still out there. She said the words I'd been dreading since I realized Joe wasn't walking out of that building.

"Skeeter's here."

I stood up then. I stood up because I couldn't sit there wallowing in my own shit anymore. I stood up and took everything I was feeling, folded it up real tight, and shoved it way down inside, in a box that I knew I'd open again and again in the middle of the night when Amy was sleeping and the house was quiet. But that was for later. Because right then my best friend needed me, and I finally had a reason to get up off my knees.

Skeeter stood there in front of me, not saying anything, just looking up at me with hollow eyes, asking me without words to explain why his uncle was dead. To tell him what happened, why I was standing there when Joe wasn't. I didn't have an answer. There wasn't one. Just the two words I hate the most, that I've said so many times for so many stupid reasons and hardly ever meant them more.

"I'm sorry," I said.

"It's not on you," Skeeter replied, his voice thready and brittle, like he would shatter if somebody hit the wrong frequency.

"I know. Don't matter," I said.

"No, it don't."

"All the bad guys dead?"

"All the ones in there," I replied. "There's some 'Master' asshole still out there."

"Good," Skeeter said. I looked in his eyes, and I recognized the look I saw there. I recognized it because I'd seen it in my own face, and in Harker, and in Luke. "Because when you find that son of a bitch, I'm gonna put a bullet in his head my damn self."

"I'll help," Amy said, putting a hand on Skeeter's shoulder. He turned to her, and she wrapped him up in her arms, and that's when he broke. He could stay mad with me because hitting bad guys and blowing shit up was how we rolled, but when Amy reminded him there was love in the world, too, he felt everything again and he fell into her arms sobbing from the bottom of his shattered heart.

I turned away. Not because I didn't want to see Skeeter like that. We'd each seen the other at our absolutely worst over the years and made it through with a little bit more scar tissue and a couple of new gray hairs. No, I turned away because I wasn't ready to not be mad. I wasn't ready to not want to tear everything to the ground and salt the earth. I wasn't ready to let myself hurt anymore. I was up off my knees, and the only thing that was going to hold me up was rage.

There was a slender form standing by a black Suburban ten yards away. I walked over to him. "Luke get somewhere safe before the sun came up?" I asked.

"He made it to his apartment. Thanks." Harker didn't look me in the eyes, this time because he didn't want to see what was in my soul, not the other way around. He just kept flipping through the battered grimoire that Gabby and Joe died to rescue.

"Anything in there gonna lead us to this Master asshole?" I asked.

"Eventually. Not going to be easy. This is some heavy magical shit, and it's going to take me some time to figure out where it came from. Plus my German is a little rusty."

"German?"

"Yeah, this whole thing's written in German. Seems our 'Master' was one of the führer's admirers, or maybe one of his people. Wizards are a long-lived bunch. If he got out of Europe, it's entirely possible this guy was a real Nazi back in the day."

"Good. No gray areas that way."

"No," Harker said. "Never any gray areas with Nazis. No debate, and no fucking quarter." He looked over my shoulder. "How's your friend?"

"Fucked up. How are you? Gabby was one of yours."

"I start the day fucked up, and it usually goes downhill from there. I think her death is hitting Luke harder than the rest of us, though. He was close with her great-grandfather. Very close. And she's the last of them, so he feels like a piece of his past died with her."

"No more Van Helsings, huh?"

"Not that we know of."

"What's next?"

"Go home," Harker said, and before I could tell him to kiss my country ass, he raised a hand. "I'm not screwing with you. It's going to take me weeks to decipher this book. It's not just the German, these are spells I've never seen before. I've got to research this, find out where this guy learned magic, and try to figure out his next move. There's nothing for you to do here. Go home. Bury your friend. Mourn him. Get drunk. Blow up a car, whatever rednecks do when people die."

"Usually it's more green bean casseroles than explosions," I said.

"That sounds horrible," Harker replied.

I laughed, and immediately cut it off guiltily, looking around like I'd farted in church. Then I glanced at Harker, who was smirking at me. "You're an asshole."

"I know. It's one of my most consistent qualities. But one of you has to keep your shit together. I'm gonna guess that's usually not your strong suit, but you've got to step up now. Your family needs you. Go home and take care of them. When I have something on the Master, I'll call you. I promise. You'll get your shot at this prick. But we might all have to get in line behind Luke."

"I don't mind shooting his dick off while Luke's got him hoisted up on a pike," I said.

"That's…specific."

"I'm not the one who invites Vlad the Impaler to my family reunions," I replied.

"Fair."

I held out a hand, and this time he looked in my eyes. "I'm sorry," Harker said, and I could see my loss and pain reflected in his eyes. It didn't take mine away at all, not even a little, but it made it just the tiniest bit easier to carry, knowing I wasn't alone.

I walked over to where Amy and Skeeter were sniffling. Geri had joined the group hug, and I stood there for a moment with my arms wrapped around the remnants of my family. I tried to pour every ounce of love and strength I had into that embrace, and after a minute that might have been an hour or a week, I reluctantly pulled away and looked Skeeter in the eye.

"Come on," I said. "Let's take him home."

THE END

ABOUT THE AUTHOR

John G. Hartness is a teller of tales, a righter of wrong, defender of ladies' virtues, and some people call him Maurice, for he speaks of the pompatus of love. He is also the best-selling author of EPIC-Award-winning series *The Black Knight Chronicles* from Bell Bridge Books, a comedic urban fantasy series that answers the eternal question "Why aren't there more fat vampires?" In July of 2016. John was honored with the Manly Wade Wellman Award by the NC Speculative Fiction Foundation for Best Novel by a North Carolina writer in 2015 for the first Quincy Harker novella, *Raising Hell.*

In 2016, John teamed up with a pair of other publishing industry ne'er-do-wells and founded Falstaff Books, a publishing company dedicated to pushing the boundaries of literature and entertainment.

In his copious free time John enjoys long walks on the beach, rescuing kittens from trees and getting caught in the rain. An avid *Magic: the Gathering* player, John is strong in his nerd-fu and has sometimes been referred to as "the Kevin Smith of Charlotte, NC." And not just for his girth.

Find out more about John online
www.johnhartness.com

STAY IN TOUCH!

If you enjoyed this book, please leave a review on Amazon, Goodreads, or wherever you like.

If you'd like to hear more about or from the author, please join my mailing list at https://www.subscribepage.com/g8d0a9.

You can get some free short stories just for signing up, and whenever a book gets 50 reviews, the author gets a unicorn. I need another unicorn. The ones I have are getting lonely. So please leave a review and get me another unicorn!

ALSO BY JOHN G. HARTNESS

THE BLACK KNIGHT CHRONICLES

The Black Knight Chronicles - Omnibus Edition

The Black Knight Chronicles Continues - Omnibus #2

All Knight Long - Black Knight Chronicles #7

BUBBA THE MONSTER HUNTER

Scattered, Smothered, & Chunked - Bubba the Monster Hunter Season One

Grits, Guns, & Glory - Bubba Season Two

Wine, Women, & Song - Bubba Season Three

Monsters, Magic, & Mayhem - Bubba Season Four

Born to Be Wild

Swamp Music

Houses of the Holy

Shinepunk: A Beauregard the Monster Hunter Collection

QUINCY HARKER, DEMON HUNTER

Year One: A Quincy Harker, Demon Hunter Collection

The Cambion Cycle - Quincy Harker, Year Two

Damnation - Quincy Harker Year Three

Salvation - Quincy Harker Year Four

Carl Perkins' Cadillac - A Quincy Harker, Demon Hunter Novel

Inflection Point

Conspiracy Theory

Histories: A Quincy Harker, Demon Hunter Collection

SHINGLES

OTHER WORK

FRIENDS OF FALSTAFF

Thank You to All our Falstaff Books Patrons, who get extra digital content each month! To be featured here and see what other great rewards we offer, go to www.patreon.com/falstaffbooks.

PATRONS

Dino Hicks
John Hooks
John Kilgallon
Larissa Lichty
Travis & Casey Schilling
Staci-Leigh Santore
Sheryl R. Hayes
Scott Norris
Samuel Montgomery-Blinn
Junkle

Made in the USA
Middletown, DE
10 July 2021